Praise for Harry Bingham

'Exceptional . . . particularly the absorbing protagonist . . . Fiona's narrative sears the page'   *Kirkus Reviews*

'A copper who rivals Lisbeth Salander in guts and determination'   *USA Today*

'With Detective Constable Fiona "Fi" Griffiths, Harry Bingham finds a sweet spot in crime fiction – a female protagonist with stunted emotions, a passion for protecting women . . . think Stieg Larsson's Lisbeth Salander . . . Denise Mina's Paddy Meehan or Lee Child's Jack Reacher'   *Boston Globe*

'What really matters in this novel is the sweet, strange complexities of Fiona's mind . . . A dark delight'   *Washington Post*

'A most intriguing detective'   *New York Times*

'In Bingham's hands she [Fiona Griffiths] comes exuberantly to life . . . Richly enjoyable'   *Daily Telegraph*

'A quite brilliant novel and Griffiths is a superb protagonist'   *Crime Fiction Lover*

'This compelling crime novel amply proves the freshness and flair that Bingham has brought to the police procedural'   *Daily Mail*

'Fiona Griffiths will haunt you long after you finish this book, and send you scurrying to find what else Bingham has written'   *York Press*

Harry Bingham is a successful crime thriller author and the creator of one of the most critically-acclaimed and engaging female protagonists in crime fiction in DC Fiona Griffiths. He also runs The Writers' Workshop, an editorial consultancy for first-time writers, and Agent Hunter, a service which helps connect writers with literary agents. When he isn't working, he's probably looking after not one but two sets of twins, but can still just about remember a time when he found time for rock-climbing and wild-swimming. He is married and lives in Oxfordshire.

Also by Harry Bingham

Libraries and Information

- 4 JAN 2023

This book should be returned by the last date stamped above.
You may renew the loan personally, by post or telephone for a
further period if the book is not required by another reader.

www.wakefield.gov.uk

wakefieldcouncil
working for you

An Orion paperback

First published in Great Britain in 2016
by Orion
This paperback edition published in 2017
by Orion Books,
an imprint of The Orion Publishing Group Ltd,
Carmelite House, 50 Victoria Embankment
London EC4Y 0DZ

An Hachette UK company

1 3 5 7 9 10 8 6 4 2

A CIP catalogue record for this book
is available from the British Library.

ISBN 978 1 4091 5276 7

Typeset by Input Data Services Ltd, Bridgwater, Somerset

Printed and bound by CPI Group (UK) Ltd, Croydon, CR0 4YY

MIX
Paper from
responsible sources
FSC® C104740
FSC
www.fsc.org

www.orionbooks.co.uk

To N., as ever

Jupiter shall emerge, be patient, watch again
another night, the Pleiades shall emerge,
They are immortal

Walt Whitman
From 'On the Beach at Night' (1856)

1

October 2014

'Well?'

Bev runs her hands down her hips and gives me a wiggle.

'*Well?*'

I say, 'Great. Really nice.' I'm not sure what to say.

'My jeans. They're new.'

'Oh.'

Now I know where my attention's meant to be, I know how to focus. The jeans are a kind of washed-out indigo. Skinny-cut. Low-waisted, but not ridiculous. Slim dark leather belt, discreet scarlet buckle. The jeans are close-fitting enough that Bev's phone makes a hard, flat shape in her back pocket. When I did a spell in Traffic, during my first two years in the police, and I was just a regular uniformed copper like everyone else, I remember an accident victim with very tight jeans, who suffered multiple fractures to both femurs. We had to cut her out of those jeans to get at the wounds. One of the paramedics did it with a scalpel, handling the blade delicately enough that it made only the finest pink graze down the girl's thighs. Two parallel tracks pricked out in dots of blood.

'New jeans,' I say. 'They look *great!* Where did you get them?'

'It's not about where I got them,' she chides me mildly. 'I've dropped a whole size. These are a ten.'

She gyrates again, and now I know what to say, I say it

1

with enough enthusiasm and repetition that Bev is satisfied. We finish getting changed and troop through to the chirpily upbeat café, where we get fruit smoothies and pasta salads.

'I mean these are Gap,' she tells me, 'And Gap does a fat size ten. My last ones were Next and they do a really thin size twelve, so in a way I haven't gone down as much as you think, except that the Next ones were my target jeans – I bought them before I could really get into them – so I think I have actually. Gone down a size, I mean.'

We go round again. The same little tour of girly chat.

Bev and I have been swimming together now for more than a year. Once a week, pretty much without fail. She's got thinner: her main ambition in all this. Me, I don't think I've particularly changed shape, though Bev swears I have, but I've been running and doing weights too, and I'm now fitter and stronger than I've ever been, which isn't saying a lot, but it's still nice. I don't even hate exercise the way I always assumed I would. I like it, actually.

We finish our salads. Bev asks me if I'll 'help' her with a low-fat granola. I say yes and she goes to get one.

As she returns, two men heave themselves over towards our table. Their gait has that post-gym male slowness. A slowness designed to exhibit how much they've knackered their muscles, how buff they must be underneath their clothes.

I set my face into its default mode for these encounters: mostly blank, but garnished with random, pre-emptive hostility.

The men get close. One of the two – T-shirt tight over his pecs and biceps, gelled hair, a prowling smile – says, 'Well? And how are the two prettiest girls in CID?'

I say nothing.

Bev – surprised, pleased, flustered – gives some kind of answer. Stays standing, I think because she wants to show off her newly resized legs. She introduces the men to me: Ellis

Morgan and Hemi Godfrey. Both coppers. Both uniforms. Morgan in Traffic. Godfrey in some other division, I don't know what.

Everyone sits.

I try, vaguely, to make nice, because I think Bev wants me to, but I'm already wondering how fast I can leave. Very fast, my normal answer.

But then Godfrey says, 'You want to go somewhere we can get a proper drink?'

I'm thinking, 'No, absolutely, definitely not,' but Bev is saying, 'Yes, that would be lovely, wouldn't it, Fi?' and throws me her female-solidarity look hard enough that it's probably sticking out between my shoulder-blades.

I say something. Not sure what, but more *yes* than *no*.

There's a discussion about arrangements. I don't participate, but it's agreed, I don't know why, that we head for The Grape and Grain, a wine bar north of here which has some weird associations for me.

We drive there in separate cars. Bev rides with me.

'That's Hemi *God*-frey,' she says. '*You* remember,' and starts telling me things that I mostly don't remember. But it's clear enough that Bev is excited by the prospect of this not-quite-date date. Clear too that she wants me as her chaperone. The figleaf which allows us all to pretend that this isn't a full-on mating dance.

We drive over the estuary, where the Taff flows into Cardiff Bay. The last light of evening, a troubled orangey-grey, is dying behind us. Bev uses the vanity mirror in the passenger sun visor to reapply her make-up and scolds me mildly to drive smoothly.

I drive as smooth as a gusting wind permits. Her lips darken and the light dies and car headlamps thread a shining necklace over the turbulent grey.

We get to the bar.

Go inside.

The first time I came here, I was wet through. Boots with holes in and a second-hand coat that wasn't man enough for the weather. I arrived dripping, in the entrance, half-expecting one of the waiters to clear me away, the way you'd remove a drowned mouse or a dead pigeon.

I think I'm standing like that now. Remembering.

'Fi, are you OK?'

The words are nice, but there's a steel in Bev's voice which isn't normally present. The steel is there to remind me that this is payback time. That Bev's patient acceptance of my various faults – my forgetfulness, my ill-temper, my general weirdness – isn't unconditional. My support of her whole diet-'n'-fitness thing has certainly ticked one box, but there are other conditions too and one of those, in the handsome shape of Hemi Godfrey, is even now coming over from the bar to greet us.

I polish up one of my better smiles and give it to Bev. 'I'm fine. I'm really fine. This'll be fun.'

We greet each other with kisses this time, which we hadn't done earlier, as though the movement from gym to bar has nudged us over some invisible but important social boundary.

Godfrey waves a twenty-pound note at the bar. 'What can I get you?'

He wants to go large. Get a bottle of fizz, something like that. But I don't drink, Bev's hardly a boozer, and even Morgan doesn't want much, so we each go our own way. A glass of red for Morgan. White wine spritzer for Bev. Orange juice for me. Beer for Godfrey, which seems more natural to him than champagne would have done. As he guides us to our table, bleached wood under a swag of dried hops, he tries out his 'two prettiest girls in CID' line again, but it doesn't work so well this time. Perhaps because we're not the prettiest: Jane Alexander is definitely better looking than either of us, though she is, admittedly, a few years older. Or maybe because the

4

paucity of real competition means that the compliment was always walking with a limp.

A moment of doubt flickers round the table. The sudden tick of anxiety.

I jump in. Do my bit. Be the friend that Bev wants me to be.

'Ellis, be a love, and get us some crisps or something. I'm starving. Hemi, you look like you've had a proper workout. Weights, was it? We mostly stick to swimming, me and Bev.'

Morgan jumps up to get snacks. Godfrey jumps on the male-friendly conversational leads I've tossed him. Bev dives in after. Morgan comes back with a bowl of nuts and a plate of vaguely Italian-looking nibbles.

I tear up a piece of salami and ask Morgan to tell me what's new in the world of Traffic.

He laughs. Glances sideways at the others. Leans forward and, in a confidential whisper, says, 'How long before those two actually start snogging? And do you think we have to stay until they do?'

I laugh.

Conversation flows. It is mostly the Bev and Hemi show, but Morgan and I do enough that the necessary figleaf remains in place, no matter that it has a tattered, end-of-season curl to it.

I hated my time in Traffic. Hated it, even though I love corpses and love driving, and Traffic supplied both things with far greater frequency than my current berth in Major Crimes ever does.

But Morgan, it turns out, is not an idiot. Nor does he, any longer, spend his time scraping cars and corpses from these city streets. Instead, he's attached to a small liaison unit that works with the University Hospital, the city's highways department, the ambulance service and – inevitably – some computer types working on strategies to drive down the frequency and severity of accidents. Morgan doesn't boast about it, but it sounds like he's in charge of things and that his team is doing good, intelligent, valuable work.

At one point, he asks, 'Sorry, I didn't get your name properly. It's Fiona . . .?'

'Griffiths. Fiona or just Fi, whichever.'

He nods, as though docketing the information in a file already partially filled. He doesn't tell me what's already in the file.

Bev is now playing with her necklace and laughing at almost everything Godfrey is saying. Godfrey's face is shining and pink. His energy is up, a cocker spaniel scenting pheasant.

I'm thinking I've done enough, it's OK to leave now, and I guess Morgan is thinking the same. Then his phone goes.

A work call. He goes outside to take it.

I play with an olive and pretend to be interested in whatever Bev and Godfrey are talking about now.

Morgan returns, but doesn't sit. He's got that important-work-thing face that people get.

Godfrey says, 'Are you OK, mate?'

'Yes. Big bloody problem outside Brecon, though. Chemical tanker overturned. Spilled its load. The car behind smacked into it. Whole damn thing ignited.'

'Brecon? But that wouldn't be in Cardiff, now, would it?'

Godfrey glances at Bev, hoping to get another harvest of necklace-twisting laughter, but Morgan's face is too serious for that.

He looks at me.

'My car's in Penarth. I can get a squad car, or . . .'

I roll my eyes.

'You haven't had a drink, have you?' he adds.

'No.'

'Do you mind?'

'No.'

He looks at Bev and Godfrey, his mind already elsewhere. He tells them to have a good evening, but I already have my coat on and in less than a minute we're in my car and heading north.

Morgan's on the phone again. Talking to the officers on the scene. Then making other calls, commandeering resources from Cardiff and Bridgend.

As we cross the M4, and between calls, he says to me, 'Wind's pushing the smoke over Brecon. They're starting to evacuate.'

He doesn't add, because he doesn't need to, that Dyfed-Powys's tiny rural force will be overwhelmed by the sudden demand on resources. We're not the only ones now flying north to help.

I say, because Morgan is an inspector and senior to me, 'Permission to speed?'

He says yes, and I start driving the way I always want to. Racing over the black tarmac. Swerving past the cars ahead, when the road permits. Pushing the car up to ninety-five on the straights, braking hard just before we hit the bends.

Nantgarw.

Pontypridd.

Cilfynydd.

On a roundabout outside Abercynon, I misjudge my speeds a bit and we skid a few yards before my little Alfa-Romeo collects her nerve and agrees to head for the road ahead of us, not the thickly wooded bank rising to the side.

Morgan smiles. Says, 'Steady.' But I keep my speed up and my foot down.

Merthyr.

Aberfan.

Pentrebach.

Morgan says, 'I'll find someone to run me back later. No need to stay.'

I nod. But my face is with the road and the road is heading up into the mountains. We pass the Llwyn-on Reservoir doing more than seventy. The wind here is both strong and gusty and I drive by feel as much as sight.

Morgan says, 'You're the Fiona who's Roy Williams's friend, right?'

Roy Williams: a former colleague of mine. I'm not his friend, not really. But I once helped extricate him from a situation that was blackly menacing to us both, and he's remained a steadfastly loyal ally ever since.

'Roy? Yes.'

Morgan nods, satisfied. 'He told me you were mental.'

Cantref.

The high pass over the Beacons. Pen-y-fan inkily dark against a purple horizon.

Then the swoop down towards Brecon and the A40. An empty landscape.

Sheep, trees, wind, grass.

The distance ahead of us burns with light. Not the tanker fire any longer – that will have long since been extinguished – but the bright white of emergency incident lighting, shot through with the flash of blue lights, the sombre amber of recovery vehicles.

Morgan gets on the phone again. Confirms our location. Tells me where he wants to be set down.

We drive on in silence.

The windows are closed but the air coming in through the vents has an acrid, burned metal scent to it.

I say, 'Do they know what spilled?'

'Isocyanates.'

I don't know what to say to that, so say nothing. It doesn't sound good, though.

As we get close to the makeshift evacuation HQ – a couple of vans and a white tent thrown up on the A40 on the

Sennybridge side of Brecon – Morgan says, 'Thanks for the ride. And for not quite killing me.'

He meets up with whoever's commanding the Dyfed-Powys operation. Disappears into the tent. Disappears, I expect, from my life, unless by some appalling mischance the gods of policing ever send me to work in his Traffic Incident Harm Reduction Unit.

Someone from Dyfed-Powys approaches me, offering a cotton facemask and a mug of tea.

How you know you're in Britain: at the scene of every major emergency, someone's thought to bring along a tea urn.

I don't normally drink caffeinated tea, but I don't particularly want to head home just yet, so I take both gifts, the face mask and the tea. Don't wear the former or drink the latter. Lean against the flank of my gently panting car, feeling the coltish mountain air compete with the burned-brown scent that returns whenever the wind drops.

People – some in hazchem suits, mostly just in anoraks and woolly hats – pass me by with little more than a look. A yellow generator powers two banks of floodlights. The grass at the tent entrance is already being trodden into mud. Vehicles come and go.

I drink some tea.

Someone asks me where he can find Jim Jones. I point at the tent, not because I know if there's a Jim Jones there but because it's easier than saying something.

Drink a bit more tea. Pour the rest away.

A scrap of moonlight plates our little world with silver.

I put the face mask on to see if it makes a difference to the smell. I don't think it does, but I'm not sure.

Then another person, a uniform, Dyfed-Powys not one of ours, approaches.

'South Wales CID? You're the one who brought Inspector Morgan?'

'Yes.'

'Listen. We've had a crime reported. The country above Pen-y-cae. We've got no officers spare. Crime report came in on a mobile and—' He shakes his head. When you get an emergency like this, every damn fool in the area gets on their mobile and the network collapses under the burden.

He stares, wanting a response.

The guy is older than me, bigger than me. I can't tell if he's senior or not, because his coat covers his rank insignia. Either way, he can't really order me around. Out here, I'm a long way off my patch and I'm under no obligation to take orders from other forces.

I'm about to be obstreperous, for no particular reason except that I like to exhibit consistency in all that I do, but then decide I don't care anyway. A long mountain drive beneath this racing moon? What have I got that's better than that?

So I say yes. Meekly nod, take details. Suddenly wish I'd drunk the tea I've thrown away, but don't make a fuss even about that.

Climb back into my car and return to the hills. The wild country above Pen-y-cae.

2

I don't, this time, drive like I have seven devils on my tail. Don't drive like the lunatic I mostly am.

I lack an excuse now, with no Major Emergency to bend the rules for me. But my mood's changed too. The racing journey to Brecon was good, but I drive back over the mountains with almost legal quietness.

Not to Pen-y-cae itself. The report came from one of the little valleys creasing the hills down into Cray and I make my way there, first to Cray and then into the winding lanes beyond.

Hedges, of hawthorn and hazel, press close, their tops rising much higher than the car.

Through the gaps, the gates and farm openings, I get scattered glimpses of fields, low barns, the slope of mountain.

Deep Wales. Real Wales.

This is the Wales that pre-existed the Romans, that will outlast our foolish time on earth, our crawl across the face of this dark planet.

My attention is divided between the narrow road ahead of me and the blue glow of my phone sat-nav.

The phone hasn't travelled these parts before and the poor dear looks nervously uncertain. But she proves a trusty guide all the same.

We fetch up at a small village. Two or three dozen houses. A stone church, a tiny pub.

Ystradfflur. The valley of flowers.

I park. Take cuffs, latex gloves and evidence bags from my glovebox. Get a torch out of the boot, but I've hardly flicked it on before a dark shape arrives beside me.

'Police?'

'Yes. Detective Sergeant Fiona Griffiths. I understand there's a—'

But the truth is, I understand nothing and my mostly invisible interlocutor seems to know that.

'It's up here. Brace yourself.'

Into the churchyard. A black metal gate swinging unlatched. The moan of a yew tree sifting the wind. Torches whose beams probe the darkness in the far corner of the graveyard.

The church itself is unlit, except for a dim lamp shining in a room to the side.

We walk towards the torches. On a tarmac path at first, then step off. The brush of long grass wet around my ankles.

An outbuilding of some sort. Two men – the ones holding the torches – outside it.

They peel away from it and towards us. Words exchanged through the darkness.

They're words I don't hear, or don't respond to, because by now I've seen in through the little building's doorway.

Candles. Ten or twelve of them, sputtering but alight. Perhaps the same number again which have been blown out by the travelling wind.

A wooden table. A table-top laid over trestles. Nothing fancy. The sort of thing you'd see at a village fete or agricultural show.

And a young woman.

Dead. I know she's dead before I even step towards her.

Know she's dead from the stillness in her chest. The fall of her hands. The cast of her skin.

Know it from the supreme peacefulness of this little *mise en scène*, the way the weather quiets itself in her presence.

She's dressed in white. Knee-length dress. Summery. Cottony pintucks and broderie anglaise.

No shoes. No coat. No cardigan even, as this wild October howls outside.

No sign of injury. No cut, no bruise, no stain of red.

Her right hand has fallen off the table. A slim hand points to the floor as though begging for early burial.

Her left hand is folded over her belly, but doesn't touch it. A black book lies between her hand and her stomach. Leather cover, gold edging.

The woman has long blonde hair that flows over the end of the table. She's attractive. Tallish. Hard to tell her height exactly because she's lying down, but a good few inches taller than me. Nice skin. Brown eyes. Pretty face.

I spend a moment taking in the scene, its loveliness, its sweet perfection. Then – a good girl, a detective sergeant trying hard not to foul up everything she touches in the first ten minutes of getting involved – I snap into police mode.

Pull my gloves on.

Check the woman's lips for the faintest ghost of breath. Check for a pulse, in her wrist but also her neck.

She is glassily still, glassily cold.

Blood has started to pool on the underside of her calves, her fallen arm.

'Who is she? Do you have an ID?'

'Never seen her before. She's not from round by here.'

All three men, the same answer. Shaking heads and looks of mystification.

'OK, now I need everyone back. Onto the path, then out of the churchyard. Have any of you touched her? Has anything been moved? I'm going to need your names and contact details. On the path there, please stay on the tarmac. What's your name, sorry? Huw? OK, Huw, I'm going to ask

13

you to guard the gateway here. No one allowed in except emergency services. No exceptions, no excuses. Got that? And you, Gavin, what's the other side of that little building there? A field, is it? OK, same thing for you if you don't mind. Take the gate. No one in or out. If you see anyone where you think they shouldn't be, you shout like hell. Now, Dafydd, tell me, is there by any chance a doctor in the village? No? Cray, anywhere local? No, OK. Have any of you called the police on a phone that actually works? Like a landline, you remember those?'

And yes, they'd tried obviously. But the winds have brought down a phone line somewhere. And the mobile signal, never good, seems completely absent, either because of the overload or, more likely, because the local mast has lost power.

And right now, there are two detective sergeants who stand here in this darkness that's lanced through with our torchbeams.

One detective sergeant is a good officer. She recognises that it makes sense to secure the scene as fast as possible, which means summoning resources from South Wales. Neath and Merthyr lie no more than half an hour away. It would take longer than that to assemble all the resources we truly need – the divisional surgeon, SOCOs, whoever the nearest duty officer is, and enough uniformed support to secure the crime scene and start securing statements – but all those things are going to arrive far quicker from our side of the Beacons than if we try to get them from the overburdened Dyfed-Powys force.

The bad detective sergeant knows all that. Knows that every Dyfed-Powys officer within fifty miles will be fully occupied with the chaos down on the Brecon-Sennybridge road. And before the good detective sergeant has even cleared her throat, the bad one is issuing her instructions.

'OK, Dafydd, I'm going to ask you to take a message through to Brecon. There's been a bad accident on the A40,

14

and you'll find a makeshift command centre . . .'

I give him the necessary details. Who to ask for, what to say. Scribble a note to minimise the possibility of error. The note says, 'Dead white female 20s found Ystradfflur. No signs of violence. Onset of lividity. Scene secured. Forensic examination will need to cover churchyard & field. Request divisional surgeon, SOCOs, uniformed resources when available. Will remain on site until relieved.'

Dafydd has a car, a Land Rover, parked no distance from mine. He roars off into the night with a backsplatter of mud and a sense of mission.

'Drive slowly, Dafydd,' I murmur.

I check that Gavin and Huw both know what they're doing. They do.

I re-park my car, lights flashing, outside the entrance to the church. I'm blocking the entire lane, but that's intentional. Whoever put the dead body in the little outbuilding either carried her from somewhere very close by – improbable, since none of the local men recognise her – or, more likely, brought her by car. If they brought her by car, they'd have parked as close to the church as possible, to make their journey shorter and easier. I've no idea whether there'll be any forensically significant evidence present, but I don't want the passage of some tractor to wreck anything that we do have. I tell Huw to stay in my car with the windows wound down, so that he can't himself compromise anything further.

I re-enter the churchyard.

Hesitate. I want to return to the saintly beauty of my corpse, but I should do my job too.

Head for the dimly lit room beside the church. The vestry, I assume.

Try the door. It opens.

Not much there. No corpses. No blood. No signs of struggle.

15

A small table, a couple of chairs. A small brown teapot. Two mugs, a kettle.

A forgotten scarf.

A brown pottery bowl holding a wooden acorn and about thirty pence in small change.

An old wooden cupboard, full-height, warped by age and damp. One door hanging a little open. Inside: no bodies, no obvious murder weapons. Just the kind of stuff that I assume most churches have. Spare hymn books. Candles. A couple of shrink-wrapped packs of communion wafers. Wine. Some clerical robes. Spare tea bags. An order of service that says, 'The Church of St David at Ystradfflur'.

A musty smell.

I try the door into the church proper. It's locked. No obvious keys.

Try the church's main door, the west door. Also locked.

I stand outside in the wind. Feeling its pull at my coat, trousers, hair.

I'm not thinking anything at all. I suddenly find myself not in space, not in time. There is nothing more of me than the momentary now: a flapping wind and a stone church rising into blackness. Nothing distinguishes me from them, or me from anything.

I don't know how long I'm there. With the flapping wind. The towered stone.

Then it changes. Alters back to how it was: a small detective alone in a churchyard that holds one dead person too many.

I return to the outhouse.

Its occupant is, I know already, my best-ever corpse. Quite likely the best one I'll ever have. Better even than the time I lifted Mary Langton's head, black and dripping, from a bucket of oil.

I have an urge, a very strong one, to get a joint from my car and perfect the moment, but I know that I'd never manage to keep the scene forensically clear of ash, not in this wind and this darkness. And in any case, this corpse is so good, she's beyond improvement.

I use my phone to take photos of the scene from every angle. Interior. Exterior. Close up. Wide view.

That photography will be need to done again, and properly, as soon as the SOCOs arrive, but it's still better to have a record from as early as possible.

There's not much more I can do but wait, and wait is what I long to do. To plunge into the moment. Without noisy interruption. Just me and my dead friend, alone in this stormy night.

I smell her hair. It's new washed. Pale blonde and well cared for. Thick, high- and low-lights, glossy. The smell is of shampoo, but there's an aroma of something else as well. Middle eastern, exotic.

Feel her fallen hand.

Soft skin. Becoming translucent in death. Clean fingernails, no polish and kept short. Cut back, maybe, not filed, though I'm hardly an expert.

No make-up. Neat eyebrows. A tiny prickle of leg hair. Not much, but more than most girls would allow to grow.

'Who are you, love? And why are you here?'

She doesn't tell me, bless her, but she's a bit too dead to speak. I decide that she needs a name, so I give her one: Carlotta.

I don't know why I choose that.

I tell her, 'Don't worry, Carlotta, we'll find out. We'll make it all OK. We'll make everything OK.'

Everything, that is, except for making her not-dead: a legitimate enough quibble if she chose to raise it, but she keeps her silence.

I spend time stroking her hair with my latex-covered hand. I want to trace the curves of her beautiful face, her lifeless body, but I'm painfully aware of the minute forensic exploration which will shortly follow and I limit myself as much as I can bear.

Limit myself and listen out for the blast of sirens which will signal the end of this little paradise.

No sound, no sirens, beyond the blowing wind.

And my note, of course, was designed to delay the inevitable for as long as possible. 'Onset of lividity': something that happens only hours after death, thereby signalling that there's no great need to rush a doctor up here, because the fact of death is already well-established. 'No signs of violence': which is true, but which implies that what we have here is a natural death, not a murder, though the entire set-up here strongly suggests some kind of foul play. 'Scene secured': so don't rush. 'Forensic examination will need to cover churchyard & field': so even if you get here tonight, you'll be unable to achieve anything useful until dawn.

'Will remain on site until relieved': don't worry, folks, South Wales CID is here, you just take care of your road accident and we'll sort things out in the morning.

Time passes.

The candles flicker, but stay alight. The yews in the churchyard try and fail to catch the wind.

I stand for a while, stroking Carlotta's hair, then go out to check that Gavin and Huw are doing their stuff.

They are. I apologise for how long it's taking to get people up here, 'but there's a hell of a mess in Brecon. It could take a bit of time.'

Gavin and Huw are either farmers or farm-workers. They're used to night-time lambing, milking cattle in the grey hours before dawn. Guarding this blowing churchyard is no great hardship. Gavin sits by the field gate as though part of it.

I return to Carlotta. Stroke those dead lips, just once, then sit on the floor, holding her dead hand and listening to the wind.

The candles burn. The wind blows. The night passes.

At half-past two, my phone signal returns. A sadness, but I've already had longer here alone than I could have hoped.

I call Brecon. Ask, with undisguised impatience, just how long it's going to take them to get up here.

Get a muzzily exhausted response. I think my little outpost has been all but forgotten in the mayhem.

'Are you saying you need resources *now*?' asks the operator.

'I'm saying I have a corpse, a ton of suspicious circumstances, and I've been waiting God knows how long for any support whatsoever.'

We snipe at each other a bit until the operator decides she doesn't care. 'We'll get on to it,' she says.

I made the call from outside in the churchyard. Partly so I could do it in Gavin's hearing. Partly because the signal was better in the open air.

When I re-enter Carlotta's little funeral chamber, I tell her we don't have long left. 'It's going to get quite busy, I'm afraid.'

She hears me out, but doesn't answer.

I feel her lips again.

Because she is lying on her back, the blood has drained from the soft tissues of her face and is pooling at the back of her skull and neck. Lips normally get thinner under those circumstances, lose some of that youthful fullness, but Carlotta's mouth looks quite pert still. She's not plump, not by any stretch, but her body has a softness to it, an almost old-fashioned fullness.

I don't touch her dress, but I do smell it. It smells clean, looks clean. Some corpses excrete or urinate post-mortem, but Carlotta has kept things tidy. She's that kind of girl.

I smell the hair, the candles, the hair again.

The vestry was musty. The hair smells different from that.

Carlotta and I keep vigil together. She on her side of that dark line, me on mine. Our little ship riding the night.

Then – too soon, too soon – I become aware of blue lights outside. Torch beams.

I press Carlotta's hand to my lips. Not a farewell, really, just a farewell to this phase.

The introductions are over. The investigation is about to begin.

3

Dawn.

Alun Burnett, a heavy-set DI from Carmarthen, sits in the vestry opposite me. The mugs, teapot, kettle, and some other bits have been removed in evidence bags, but Gavin-the-Gate's wife has produced tea and bacon butties from her non-crime-scene-relevant kitchen, and Burnett and I are alone with our treasure.

Burnett says, 'Cardiff? CID?'

I nod. 'Major Crime. Under Dennis Jackson.'

Burnett stares at me from eyes so deep he must spend his whole life walking through shadows.

Burnett's force is a tiny one. Just over a thousand officers, of whom a full nine hundred are lowly constables. That force is spread out over the largest police region in England and Wales. The largest and one of the safest. Burnett has, quite possibly, never encountered a murder or, if he has, he's probably never encountered a good one, the sort that actually requires complex investigation.

'I'm not just handing this over,' he says.

I shrug. I'm not asking him to and it wouldn't be my decision anyway.

'But I'm not saying we mightn't need some assistance.'

I take a bite of my bacon butty. It's got butter and some of the fat from frying, and the bacon inside is still warm. It's like the food-equivalent of a hot water bottle except, presumably, more fattening.

Burnett looks like a man who'd know what to do with a bacon butty, but he's holding it away from him like someone who's found an unexploded mortar shell in their garden.

I say, 'Jackson isn't into land grab just for the sake of it. I mean, if this investigation is being properly conducted, why give himself more work?'

Burnett nods.

'Manpower shouldn't be a problem,' he says.

'Or womanpower,' I say, for no reason, except to be annoying.

'Or womanpower,' he echoes, but in a way that doesn't really tell me if he's annoyed or not.

I take another bite of my butty. He starts in on his and, once he's had the first mouthful, he realises how good it is and starts to snarf it down.

'Theoretically,' I say, with my mouth still full, 'if this investigation was taking place in Cardiff?'

That isn't, I know, a complete sentence, and I did that annoying teenage thing of letting my voice rise towards the end. A High Rising Terminal, it's called in the lingo.

Burnett says, 'Yes?'

'OK, we've already covered a lot of the basics. Divisional surgeon has confirmed death. Corpse secured and removed. Scene's been secured. Photographs taken. Movable evidence removed. I know there were some delays in doing all that – ' Burnett and I have already yapped about whose fault it was that they arrived so late – 'but no real harm done.'

Burnett nods. Chews and nods.

'Now it's daylight, we'd be looking at a fingertip search of the churchyard and the field the other side. Every damn officer you can get. SOCOs to supervise. Exhibits officer on hand the whole time.'

Burnett nods.

'And any CCTV at all. Vehicle movements from the ANPR system. Given where we are, we'd be incredibly lucky to get anything useful, but we have to do it anyway. There were plenty of police vehicles on the A40, so we'll have a very full record of any movements there.'

Burnett nods.

'We'd need to interview everyone in the village. What their movements were. If they saw anything out of the ordinary. Any vehicle they didn't recognise or which looked too clean or out of place. These small villages, people know each other. You can ask questions which wouldn't make sense in town.'

Burnett nods. He knows that, of course.

'Missing Persons. Check the Bureau website, obviously, but you need to call as well.' I give him the names of some people at the NCA he should talk to. 'Get one of their analysts on it and stay right on top of whatever they're doing. That's where an ID is most likely going to come from.'

Another nod. But now Burnett is taking notes as well, his fingers still agleam with bacon fat.

'The pathologist,' I say. 'I assume you'll be working with the University Hospital?' Cardiff, in other words, not Carmarthen.

Burnett nods. 'Yes. We wouldn't have the experience . . .'

'Good, then you'll be working with a pathologist who knows what he's doing. First thing to get is a cause of death, of course. But I think you'll want to be a bit more specific in your briefing.'

'Go on.'

'OK, the deceased was a young, attractive woman. Her hair was clean. Washed sufficiently recently that it still smelled of shampoo. But I think her nails were cut, not filed, and they were cut quite close too. That hair on her legs. I think maybe she hadn't shaved them for a week or more. I mean, plenty of women don't, but ones who look like Carlotta? They shave their legs.'

'Carlotta?' Burnett is doing raised eyebrows at me. He's laughing at me, I think. '*Carlotta?*'

'She needs a name. I always give 'em one anyway.' I shrug and continue. 'We need whatever a pathologist can give us there. Were the nails cut or filed? How much hair growth was there on the legs? Other things too. She has highlights and lowlights in her hair. When do we think those were last done? Can we identify any products used? Her lips. Did you notice those? Look, it's hard to tell without professional examination, but her lips didn't lose fullness the way I'd have expected. I think there might be fillers there. Collagen or whatever. If that's correct, and if we can identify anything about the kind of filler used, we might be able to get a list of the clinics that use that type of filler, then show them photos, see if we can get an ID. If there's evidence of other cosmetic procedures, that would be potentially helpful in the same way.'

I continue. The black leather book was a Bible, of course. We suspect that it and the candles were both taken from the vestry, but that conjecture still needs to be verified. Carlotta was also wearing a dress that was totally unsuited to the weather. Any forensic data regarding her dress or her underwear could be critical. I run through a handful of other points, including the boring technicalities which matter a lot. How to run an incident room. The importance of getting a really good indexer. That, and a top-quality action manager. 'Those two roles are the most important, really. I mean, apart from the SIO, obviously.'

I shut up.

My face moves involuntarily, I don't know why or what it signifies.

Burnett looks at me.

'You done?'

'Yes. I mean, for now.'

'We're not total newbies, you know. We do get incidents like this.' He mentions a death in Rhayader last year. A dead man in a burned-out van. Something the year before. A dead girl, Nia Lewis, found dead in a tangle of nettles in a wet field edge by Tregaron.

I say, 'Yes.'

I don't say that I had something to do with both incidents. That the first occupant of that unholy van was me.

Maybe my face indicates something, maybe it doesn't. In any case, Burnett stares at me a couple of moments, then clicks his biro to the off position. Jabs its now-blunted end at the vestry door, and the church and outhouse beyond.

'Weird, though. Why here? I mean, of all the places to choose.'

I say something to that. Yes, Ystradfflur is small, but then if you want to deposit your corpse somewhere remote . . .

Get halfway through that interesting and investigatively useful soliloquy before realising that I've misunderstood. Burnett signals my misunderstanding with broad shakes of his head.

'No, I get that. This village, I mean. But that building out there. I mean, how many churches still have them? One in a hundred? Probably not even that.'

I'm muddy with lack of sleep, but his words wake me.

I don't know what my face does or says, but he says, 'You don't know what it is, do you? That place you spent the night?'

No. No, I don't. But all of a sudden I feel the touch of something even stranger than the various varieties of strange I've already encountered these past few hours. The cold fingers of premonition, an icy *déjà vu*, tingle on the back of my neck.

Burnett says, 'A beer house. They used to be quite common, but . . .'

I don't understand.

'Beer house? Beer as in pub?'

He laughs. '*Bier*, as in funeral bier. It was a Victorian thing. Back in the day, if your granny died, you just laid her out in your front room till it was time to bury her. Nowhere else to put her, nowhere respectful. Of course, a lot of families didn't even *have* a front room. They just had a common living area below, a sleeping area above. So the corpse was laid out right in the middle of the family accommodation, sometimes for days at a time. The Victorians didn't like all that – unhygienic, you know – and built these bier houses. So your granny could lie out, under shelter and on consecrated ground, until it was her time to go below.'

I shiver a little at that. A shiver of delight, really, at the perfection of it all. Carlotta was only the last of the many corpses to have lain out there. Perhaps vigils were common too. Perhaps my long night's watch was once commonplace too. Carlotta and I, the unknowing inheritors of a much-longer tradition.

Burnett chuckles at me wanting to see if I'm creeped out, but he's chuckling at the wrong girl, and I think he sees it.

Disappointed, he checks his tea – cold, but still worth swigging down – and butty: crusts only, nothing worth salvaging. He stands up.

'They're not mostly called bier houses, though. Too formal, I suppose. I don't know what they call theirs in Ystradfflur, but we had one in the village where I grew up and everyone just called it the dead house.' He grins at me, summoning energy for the long day ahead. 'A corpse in a dead house? It's only natural.'

And with that, we exit that gloomy vestry into an Ystradfllur October dawn.

An eastern light, the colour of floodwater, fills the valley. Damp rags of early morning mist hang, unmoving, between the yew trees. The same mist exhales from the fields beyond, dewy and silver, standing no more than a foot or two high, but thick, almost solid. Fifty yards away, a bullock stares at us. Its feet are invisible and the big animal appears to float. A magic trick, no strings.

Hills rise to either side.

Who are you, Carlotta? And what brought you here?

Poor, dead Carlotta doesn't have an answer, but answers aren't her job. They're mine.

4

Midday, or a little after. I'm eating an apple and one of the sandwiches that arrived with one of the vanloads of uniforms from Carmarthen. I'm sitting on a stone wall and turn my face up to gather any warmth being offered by an unconfident sun.

Yawn.

Burnett, passing, sees me.

'Tired?'

'I'm fine.'

'You didn't get any sleep though. When did you start yesterday?'

'Eight-thirty. In the morning, I mean. I wasn't on duty last night.'

'Twenty-seven hours, twenty-*eight*? OK. Bugger off. Go home. Sleep. Call me tomorrow.'

I nod. Technically, I'd say Burnett is within his rights to tell me to bugger off, but is exceeding his authority in telling me to go home. When I cross back over the Beacons, I'm off his patch and can go anywhere I like.

I don't say that, though. Just hold up my sandwich, meaning, 'I'll go after this.'

In the churchyard, twenty-five officers in hi-vis jackets comb the ground. Any scrap of fallen tissue, every thread of agricultural twine is being meticulously photographed, collected, bagged and logged. Same thing in the field, except

28

it's bigger and there are, so far, only ten officers, fanning out from the entrance gate.

By now, Burnett's guys have knocked on every door in Ystradfflur. Not just the little village centre, but the cottages and farms up in the surrounding hills too.

Have you lost a twenty-something woman, last seen wearing a pretty little cotton sundress? Thing is we've found one. She's basically fine – I mean, yes, a bit dead, admittedly – but apart from that, really fine.

Nothing.

Nothing but puzzlement. A bit of surprise too, maybe, but nothing as strong even as shock. I don't think that's a sign of some collective guilt, just the rhythm of these country parts is different. Less labile. More accepting of what comes. Storms and sunshine. Birth and death. Dead girls in village churchyards.

Burnett says, 'Thanks for your help. It's made a big difference.'

I shrug. All part of the service.

And the investigation *does* feel tidy now. Well organised. Resources have been moving north from Cardiff and Bridgend all morning, but they'll go home reporting on an efficiently managed scene, a properly conducted inquiry.

I finish my sandwich.

Burnett's face says, 'Bugger off.' It might even say, 'Bugger off, right now, no excuses.'

So I do.

I don't want to go home yet, but I don't feel like going back to Cathays, to the office.

So to start with, I just drive. Anywhere my car feels like going. We choose our road according to how the light gleams from the asphalt and whether the hedges are full of wild clematis and the tilt of brown-flanked hills above.

I don't drive fast. Don't drive slow. Leave the radio on silent and ignore my phone.

Drive without plan, except that when the Beacons' four peaks – Corn Du, Pen y Fan, Cribyn, Fan y Big – gather on the horizon, steel shapes clustered against the sky, I'm not surprised.

I drive the last part of the way with only one hand on the wheel, the other groping emptily inside my jacket, the pocket on the car door. It's a gun I'm looking for, I realise, but I don't have one. Not here. Haven't so much as touched one since the last time I was here.

The road rises abruptly. A dirt track curves off to the left.

I take the track.

A farmhouse. Cleaned up, but scorch marks still visible on the grey stone.

A barn converted into offices once. Nicely done. Fancy fittings. Expensive.

The place is a mess now. Ruined walls, blackened rafters. Old black-and-yellow caution tape flaps from an empty doorway. The interior still crunches with cinders and fallen masonry.

A couple of years back, I was meant to have died in that barn. Me and a handful of others, no longer wanted by the gangsters who employed us. I escaped, obviously, but the whole situation descended into mayhem, only partly of my making.

I sit on the barn steps, wanting a cigarette. I don't have one, but the craving is strong enough that I go to my car and get a joint from the little stash I keep with the tyre irons and my emergency chocolate.

Smoke.

Grey smoke, grey sky.

If I wanted to die one windy October day, I probably wouldn't choose a little broderie sundress to do it in.

If I was going to the trouble of washing my hair, all ready for my death-day, I'd probably file my nails and shave my legs at the same time.

But if I wanted to lie out, dead, one stormy October night, I don't think I could have chosen a better place to do it. Carlotta, it seems to me, is a woman of style, taste and tact. I'll enjoy getting to know her.

I finish my joint.

Lean back against the wall.

Let the pale sun watch me as I snooze.

5

The next day.

Jackson wears glasses now. I don't know if he always did, or if he really needs them even. I half-suspect they're just a sort of stage prop. A way of lending an academic touch to his natural jowly toughness.

He reads, or sort of reads, from an email on-screen.

'Blah, blah. Death being treated as suspicious. Blah. Limited resources. Blah. Dyfed-Powys Force confident of managing the operation effectively blah.' He looks over and interprets for me, 'Basically, don't think we're thick-as-pigshit country coppers.'

'Sheepshit,' I say. 'It's not really pig country, is it?'

'No, but "sheepshit" doesn't sound right.'

'And pigs are intelligent. They're meant to be cleverer than dogs.'

'That's not saying much. *My* dog's an idiot.'

There's a pause while we wonder whether we've got off track and whose job it is to get us back again.

Jackson's, it turns out. He returns to his email. He still skips chunks, but the *blah*s have gone. '"Various specific resource requests . . . In particular, maintain current level of forensics support . . . data analysts as needed . . . supply a constable or similar with strong experience as an indexer in an MIR," and, what about this?, "supply a DS with good experience in Major Crimes to support DI Burnett in a variety of roles."'

I keep my face flat.

'Mervyn Rogers,' says Jackson, 'He's got a ton of experience. Or Jane Alexander.'

My face stays motionless.

Jackson's glasses come off. Tap the screen.

'Did you actually dictate that email?' he asks me. 'Did you say, "Dear Alun, I really, really want to be part of your murder investigation, and I'll make myself really, really useful in the early stages without telling you anything about what a pain in the arse I actually am, and, if you want, I'll draft the email to Jackson, so you get the resources you need and I get the posting I want."?'

I look at him wondering whether that's a real question.

I decide that it is.

'No, sir. I mean, I know that's the sort of thing I might have done, but on this occasion I didn't.'

'But you do want the posting?'

That's a stupid question, in all truth, and Jackson isn't stupid. I just say, 'When was the last time we had anything as good as this? You'd probably have to go back to Mary Langton, and even then . . .'

How do I tell him? How do I even express this thing?

To have spent the night with a dead woman, quite likely murdered, and to have spent it alone, in a dead house, in a blowing country churchyard – some things are beyond improvement. I couldn't imagine a sweeter start to an inquiry. I'm already more than half in love with this case, this corpse.

Jackson stares.

'You do remember that you are full time on Operation April? An investigation which you personally convinced us to initiate?'

'Yes.'

Operation April: an investigation into a possible criminal conspiracy amongst some of South Wales's most prominent entrepreneurs and businessmen. It was me that persuaded senior command to take the possibility seriously. It was me who christened the investigation. April, after April Mancini, a six-year-old murder victim and my first proper corpse.

'And you do realise that we have other detective sergeants with – what did he say? – "good experience in Major Crimes" and ones who are a damn sight senior to you? Damn sight more reliable at that.'

'Yes.'

'Yes,' Jackson echoes. He taps around on his screen, looking at I don't know what. Current officer assignments, I'm guessing.

I say nothing.

Look down at my feet. I got a new pair of boots recently. Black leather. Knee height. More of a heel than I normally go for, but quite comfortable. My sister helped me buy them and said, 'Fab' when I did.

I try to figure out why they're fabber than my old ones, but don't succeed.

Jackson looks at me again.

'OK. Mervyn Rogers doesn't have much on at the moment. He certainly doesn't have a full-time assignment on a major operation. He gets first dibs on this. If he says he doesn't want it, I'll let you assist, but I'm not letting this turn into a Fiona Griffiths marathon. If Rogers says no, I'll give you a couple of weeks with Burnett. Help him get organised. Then that's it. You come back here and do your work.'

I give him all the *yes, sir, no, sirs* he needs to keep him happy, then get up and start to leave. I'm wondering what I can say to Rogers to persuade him to pass this up, but Jackson knows me too well.

As I start wrestling with the door, whose self-closing mechanism always seems determined to trap me in its maw, Jackson says, 'And don't start messing around with Rogers.

You don't so much as talk to him till I do. If he tells me you've spoken to him, you're off the damn case no matter what.'

A thick finger jabs the air for emphasis. Dark hairs line the finger in question. Jackson is bigger, older, heavier, more senior, growlier than I think I can ever be. The solidity of his presence sometimes makes me feel that, next to him, I'm no more than a dandelion seed tiptoeing on the air.

I nod. Say, 'Yes, sir.' An almost proper one that time.

Then tiptoe out of the door and float away down the corridor.

6

Rogers, bless the man, stands back. Why he does it, I can't imagine, unless it's an act of kindness to me, in which case I owe him big time. He claims it's because he doesn't like 'these bloody country things. You just tramp around in mud, knocking on doors till you find whichever lonely nutter chose this particular moment to go round the twist'. But the office chatter is all of headcount reductions and budget restrictions and no serious DS would pass up a proper murder inquiry just because they didn't like a bit of Breconshire mud.

I'll settle with Rogers when I can – a gift of beer? a bottle of whisky? – but for now, I'm on a roll.

Carlotta's sweetly beautiful corpse is delivered to the mortuary. Burnett and I watch together as the pathologist, Dr Pryce, swabs and bags, slices and dices.

It's a process I love, that I love every time. The dark rituals of our profession. The rites that precede burial.

Pryce is always meticulous, which is another way of saying slow. The surface examinations alone take ninety minutes. But then the bone saw comes out. The quick red flick of blood, darkened with a smell of burning.

The chest cavity opens. Is wrenched open with a cracking of bone, kept that way with a body brick. And before too long, Pryce's deftly moving scalpel reaches the heart.

Pryce extracts the organ. Places it on a set of scales so he can record the weight. Then exhales, irritated, through his cotton mask. To the hanging mike, he says, 'Marked hypertrophy of the right ventricle.'

He palpates the heart. I resent that on Carlotta's behalf. It's one thing to be dead. It's quite another to have some pissy little pathologist poking at your most sacred organ and puffing with annoyance as he does so.

He sees what he needs and says, half to us and half to the microphone, 'Yes, really quite marked. The pulmonary blood vessels?'

He bends to examine them. When he opens his mouth he does so with a slight tap of the tongue against his upper palate, and when he changes his position he tends to breathe out heavily through his nose, so that even when he's not actually saying anything he seems to give off a series of tuts and puffs of annoyance.

This is my fourth proper PM with the good doctor Pryce and I like him less each time I meet him. But he's skilled at what he does. He checks his blood vessels and says, 'Yes. Fibrosis. Quite advanced. More than sufficient to account for the hypertrophy. Cause of death, impossible to be certain as yet, but the chances are we're talking about right ventricular failure.'

Burnett glances at me for help, but I'm not a medical dictionary and I keep my mouth shut.

He gives up on me and says to Pryce, 'You mean she died of a heart attack?'

'"Heart attack" isn't a medical term, Inspector. If you mean acute myocardial infarction, then no. She did not die of an infarction but, most likely, of a failure of the right ventricle. And, most likely, that failure arose because of strain placed on the heart by the build up of fibrosis in the pulmonary blood vessels.'

Pryce only smiles when he's been really annoying, but I bet he's got a big one hidden under that cotton mask of his.

I wonder how many of Pryce's teeth Burnett could break with a single blow of his fist. I'm guessing plenty.

Burnett says, 'And the fibrosis, in your view, arose as a natural organic process? An illness, basically?'

'Organic? No, not necessarily.' Pryce runs through some of the causes of pulmonary fibrosis. 'Inhalation of tobacco smoke would create or exacerbate the condition. Certain diseases of the connective tissue can produce fibrosis as a by-product. A variety of medications can aggravate an existing condition. And there are a number of trades and occupations notably prone to the condition,' and he starts telling us about coal miners and sand blasters and shipworkers and structural steel workers. 'Idiopathic fibrosis is also commonplace, that is a fibrosis arising where no cause can be identified. In those cases, I think you could say the problem was likely to be "organic" as you put it.'

Burnett throws me another glance, one that I interpret as meaning roughly, 'Is this guy always like this?'

I come right back at him with a look that says, 'You're on your own here, buddy.'

Burnett wonders whether to continue our game of glance-tennis, but concedes the match by saying to Pryce, 'OK, I think the deceased probably wasn't into heavy welding and I doubt if she spent much time down the mines or handling sand-blasting equipment. But you're saying that she could simply have had this problem with her tubing for no known reason at all – maybe something genetic, maybe something else, we don't know – and anyway, her heart starts to suffer. Everything gets a little bit worse. Then one day, this young woman just keels over dead. That would be consistent with what you've seen so far?'

'Correct.'

'And would she have known she had the problem? I mean, presumably she wasn't completely symptom-free, then – bang

– heart failure. Presumably there would have been something to indicate a problem beforehand?'

'Probably, yes, but not definitely. She'd almost certainly have suffered from shortness of breath, but she might or might not have thought to see a doctor. And diagnosis of the condition is complex. Ideally, a physician would order a lung biopsy, which would likely require a general anaesthetic. Because the procedure is invasive, some physicians tend to avoid it in favour of various spirometric procedures, even though those procedures are known to deliver some quite unreliable results.'

Pryce continues, but the picture is growing clearer for all his obfuscations.

Burnett interrupts. 'So. I recognise you have more work to do, and that you can't be one hundred per cent sure even when you've done it, but one plausible theory – one *highly* plausible theory – would be that she had a few symptoms. Shortage of breath, that kind of thing. Maybe she seeks medical help, maybe she doesn't. Either way, she doesn't end up getting the one diagnostic test that would definitely have revealed the issue. And one day, her right heart ventricle simply fails and she dies. All that could have happened without any external intervention. That is, we're looking at an ordinary, but natural, human tragedy. No murder, no manslaughter, nothing like that.'

Pryce says, with that slightly camp edge to his irritation, 'I *haven't* completed my work and you are asking me to *speculate*, but yes, what you are saying is highly consistent with the evidence I have so far located.'

'OK, good.'

Burnett throws me another glance and this one is easy to read. It says, 'Let's fuck off out of here.' My return lob says simply, 'You bet.'

We reconvene in the hospital café.

White ceiling tiles. Low-energy bulbs in cylindrical down-lighters. Walls and chairs in Hospital Yellow. A colour so blatantly designed to soothe those in medical distress that it makes me want to bubble blood from the corners of my mouth, just to show it who's boss.

'I hate hospitals,' says Burnett, coming to the table with his coffee and my juice.

'I hate them more.'

'That guy, Pryce. Jesus.'

'You had him on a good day. That was him trying to help.'

'But no murder.'

'No.'

'Just something very weird.'

'Yes.'

Burnett looks at me with those heavily shadowed eyes. 'I mean, maybe in South Wales you like to drag corpses into ecclesiastical buildings, surround them with candles and Bibles, then bugger off again, but in Dyfed-Powys we don't go in for that so much.'

I shake my head. Same here. It's not a big thing in Glamorgan either.

And the MisPer register has come up blank. A couple of possible matches based on visual ID only, but it only took us a couple of calls to rule those out.

We haven't yet been able to check DNA against the national database – it'll be a day or two before we get the results back – but DNA matching only works when we have the individual, or close family members, on file already. Carlotta doesn't seem like that sort of girl to me, though she could yet prove me wrong.

We might yet get something interesting from Pryce's various scrapings and swabbings – blood or skin caught under a fingernail, any indication of sexual assault – but his monotone comment to the waiting microphone was only, 'Fingernails, right hand. Very clean appearance. No visible foreign matter . . . Fingernails, left hand. Also very clean . . . Vagina. No visual evidence of assault. No foreign matter visible. No visual evidence of recent intercourse.'

Burnett's team has already reached most households in Ystradfflur and the surrounding valley, seeking an identification. No joy. No hint of joy even.

Pryce *did* find some evidence of cosmetic surgery. He wasn't, in fact, certain about the lips, but agreed it was worth researching. ('Sample removed for microscopy. Query possible presence of hyaluronic acid of non-human origin.') On the other hand, because we asked him to look for any history of past cosmetic surgery, he did detect, under magnification, a possible rhinoplasty scar under the tip of the nose. Also – an easy win – cheek implants on both cheekbones. ('Malar implants of expanded polytetrafluoroethylene located over both zygomatic bones.')

The human in me was disappointed. Carlotta was lovely enough already not to need surgical help. The implants weren't even all that large, in Pryce's opinion, suggesting that Carlotta was trying to perfect the already-good, not correct something problematically wrong. In my old-fashioned view of things, that smacks of vanity and I can't help feeling cross with her. It's my first quibble with Carlotta. Our first minor tiff.

The detective, on the other hand, was pleased. Because Pryce was plainly out of his depth in assessing the rhinoplasty, Burnett asked him to reserve final examination of the nose, lips and cheeks for a time when one of the hospital's consultant plastic surgeons was on hand to advise. It may be a few days before we get full details.

Burnett is thinking along the same lines as me.

'How many plastic surgeons are there in the country? There can't be that many.'

'About three hundred,' I say. 'I've already checked.'

Burnett does the same maths as me. Three hundred surgeons means it wouldn't be beyond our resources to approach each one.

'Helpful. That's helpful.'

'Assuming she had the surgery in the UK.'

'Yes, but . . .'

Burnett shrugs, meaning that most Brits don't go abroad for their surgery. Which is, presumably, true, except that most surgically enhanced Brits also don't wind up on a tabletop in the Dead House of Yrstradfflur surrounded by candles and the mountain wind. Which means that we're dealing with a somewhat specialist subset of such people. Which in turn means that we can't be sure Carlotta's own surgical habits follow the rules applicable to everyone else.

Also, of course, we don't know that Carlotta is British.

I wonder a bit why I chose to call her Carlotta. It's a Spanish name, I suppose, but that blonde hair doesn't exactly shout Spanish.

Burnett's thoughts are running on similar lines. He says, 'She doesn't look Welsh, does she?'

'Not really,' I say, which is true – but then what's Welsh? Not everyone looks like what they are.

Burnett sighs. Drains his coffee. Wonders about getting another.

'I'm not even sure we've got a crime here,' he says.

'No.'

There are various offences connected with disposal of a corpse, but the most obvious one, though rarely prosecuted, is prevention of a lawful and decent burial. Say what you like about the way we found Carlotta, there was nothing indecent about it, nor was there anything to prevent a lawful burial taking place in due course. If her heart failure took place under circumstances where medical help could and should have been sought, then someone might possibly have been guilty of manslaughter, though it would be very hard to make the charge stick.

Burnett thinks the same. 'We don't have to decide, though,' he says. 'We package it all up. Give it to a coroner. Let him decide.'

'Or her,' I say, just because I hate hospitals and I'm feeling pissy.

'Or her,' he says.

He's staring at my juice, which I've barely touched. He wears that male expression which tosses a light veil of politeness over a strong underlying message of get-a-bloody-move-on-woman.

I say, 'Her legs. Why didn't she shave her legs?'

Burnett doesn't quite roll his eyes at me, but gets close.

I say, 'Look, her hair was nice. Highlights, lowlights. Well looked after. She cares enough about these things to go out and get a nose job. Get cheek implants. Maybe lip-fillers. That kind of girl doesn't just stop shaving her legs for no reason.'

Burnett takes the opposite position, not necessarily because it's his, but because it's a good way to test out the hypothesis.

'She's feeling poorly. Short of breath. Bit under the weather. She just thinks, what the hell, I'll leave it a few days.'

I say, 'OK. She's feeling ill. Not rush-to-hospital ill. Maybe not even see-a-doctor ill. But let's say she's feeling ill enough that she wants a few days kicking around the house, wearing a dressing gown, eating yogurt and watching daytime TV.'

'OK, yes.'

'Well, that's when you shave your legs. I mean, that's when I'd shave my legs and I'm hardly the get-a-nose-job type.'

'No.' He stares at my nose, then looks sharply away when he sees me noticing. 'No, quite. So, we present our coroner with the Mystery of the Unshaved Legs.'

'And the Mystery of the Cotton Sundress,' I add.

The dress came from Monsoon. It's a 2014 style, and was selling for £59 during the summer, but was knocked down to as little as £22.50 in the autumn sales. The firm tells us that they shifted a few thousand of the dresses over the course of the year. They have stores in Hereford, Bristol, Cardiff and Bridgend, but also a mail order service that could send the dress just about anywhere.

We have no idea why an October corpse was dressed in a July-only dress.

'And the Mystery of the Unknown Body,' says Burnett, ticking off our puzzles. 'And the Mystery of Why The Bloody Hell Anyone Wants to Dump Her in the Dead House of Ystradfflur.'

He's right about that. Let's just say that you had Carlotta with you for some reason – a reason you wouldn't want to share with the wider world. Carlotta complains a bit about being short of breath, but she doesn't think it's a huge deal and nor do you. Unfortunately for you both, however, her right ventricle is about to collapse and promptly does so, leaving you with the annoying problem of where to leave her.

You presumably don't want to leave her wherever you happen to be at the time: too great a risk that whatever it is you've been up to gets exposed to police scrutiny. So you pop your sadly deceased girl into the back of a van or car, drive around till you find somewhere reasonably far from wherever you started and remote enough that the corpse won't instantly be detected. Ystradfflur clearly ticks the remoteness box, all right.

But that's where the puzzles really start. If you've been up to something wicked, wouldn't you simply tip your girl over a bridge somewhere? Tie a couple of bricks round her and topple her into the glass-blue bowels of a deep Welsh lake?

And instead, she appeared to have been cleaned and given a clean dress to wear. No injury. No sign of rough handling.

No graze of an arm against a wall, no scraped skin where her hand dragged.

And then the setting itself. Reverential, you have to say. A gesture of respect to the departed . . . but a respect that showed only in death. In life, anyone wanting to be nice to Carlotta would surely have given her access to a razor. I mean, yes, I know that Denial of Cosmetic Materials is not yet an offence. Isn't even a particularly big deal. But most people are nicer to living people than to dead ones. Carlotta, even if just in a small way, seemed to have had things the other way round.

I don't mention it again now, but Pryce did confirm that Carlotta's nails had been cut with scissors, not trimmed by file.

I take a sip of juice. I've drunk down about an inch. There are three and a half inches still to go.

Burnett looks at me, my juice, then casts a flickering glance down at his watch.

I say, 'Faeces.'

'Faeces?'

'We won't get anything from stomach contents, because the corpse was dead too long. Everything's been digested basically.'

Burnett nods. He knows that. It's the sort of thing which I know anyway, but Pryce said so explicitly during the PM.

'But you often get only partially digested food matter coming through in the faeces. Bits of sweetcorn. Tomato skins. I don't know, nuts.'

'You want to identify the corpse from nuts? She's not a bloody squirrel.'

Burnett likes that comment. He's about to repeat it, but then decides not to and tucks it away for use back in Carmarthen, where it's probably funnier.

'I'm just saying,' I just say.

'Are you ever going to drink that?' he asks. 'Or can we bugger off?'

I try to focus on the Juice Issue. Try to figure out if I'd be happier if I drank the juice or happier if I didn't. Then wonder if happiness is even the appropriate metric. I mean, maybe with drinks all that really matters is hydration.

Burnett stares. He wants a response.

I can't make a good decision under that kind of pressure, so end up saying, 'No.'

Then realise that's not a clear answer, because his questions weren't helpfully phrased, so I clarify. 'I mean, no to the first question, yes to the second.'

We leave.

Hospitals normally weird me out, but Burnett's presence grounds me and we get out without me doing anything embarrassing like walking into a glass wall or getting lost somewhere between Phlebotomy and Haematology.

Burnett, who's good at walking without crashing into things, has been studying his phone. When we get to the car park, he waves it at me.

'Churchyard search completed. Nothing obviously useful. A few bits of litter, wind-blown quite likely. Field search still on-going. But . . .' He shakes his head.

Traffic noise from Eastern Avenue rolls over the warm car park. It's the last day of October and unseasonably warm. A south wind ruffles our clothes. Pushes dead leaves up against the hospital walls, its doors and windows. A brown and yellow army, begging admittance.

'I'll chase Bridgend,' I say.

Bridgend: the forensics lab which is trying to get any data from the dress.

'Yes.' Burnett squints into the wind, making his eyes almost disappear. 'But no murder,' he says again. 'We've lost our murder.'

When he said that before, he was thinking like a detective. Implications for the investigation, lines of enquiry. That kind of thing. When he says it now, he's thinking like a politician. Murder cases bring promotion. Deaths from natural causes don't.

I say, 'You haven't had the write-up. From Pryce, I mean.'

'So?'

'So we don't have to tell anyone about the heart failure. If you tell Bridgend that the dress belongs to someone who died from a heart attack, they'll put it in a Jiffy bag and send it back.'

And Jackson will cut his support.

And I'll be off the case.

'How long before Pryce reports?'

I wrinkle my face. 'He's quick usually.'

Burnett's hands flutter round his jacket pocket before falling back. An ex-smoker, I'd guess, not quite free of the habit.

'We might get an ID,' he says. 'You never know, we might even get a MisPer call. It's about time.'

I say, 'Yes' but think 'No'. There are plenty of people – the old, the lonely, the homeless, the mad – who aren't quickly missed, whose names arrive at the Missing Persons Bureau either slowly or not at all. But pretty Carlotta, with her Gore-Tex cheek implants? Those people are missed. Those people generate calls. And if Carlotta's disappearance didn't generate calls, there must have been a reason why.

And unless that reason is approaching some kind of expiration date, I think the weird silence is likely to continue.

I suspect Burnett thinks the same.

'Get what you can on the dress,' he says.

'Yes, sir.'

He raises a hand. Gets into his car. Drives away.

I lean against my car. It's odd the weather being so unseasonably warm. Like something in the machinery of the

47

world has slipped and no one has yet noticed or figured out a fix.

The Mystery of the Unshaved Legs.

The Mystery of the Cotton Sundress.

The Mystery of the Unknown Body.

The Mystery of Why The Bloody Hell Anyone Wants to Dump Her in the Dead House of Ystradfflur.

A sweet little collection. A proper case, even if Burnett doesn't have his murder.

I call Bridgend. Ask them to bag up the dress and have it couriered to the LGC laboratory in Culham, Oxfordshire.

The person I'm speaking to, a lab assistant, says tensely, 'Do you mind holding a moment? My boss wants a – hold on a sec.'

There's a muttered conversation which I can't hear.

Then a male voice – strong, dominant, but also phoney – comes on the line. 'This is Dr Jenkins. We've been looking after the dress and we've already commenced our review—'

'Oh, yes, thank you. It's just we really needed the results fast – I mean I know you guys are really tied up.'

'We're not "tied up", no. There's just a process.'

We go to and fro.

I'm nice, but persistent and I keep mentioning Culham, which is the UK's largest private sector lab and, effectively, a death threat to any police-owned and operated lab.

Eventually Jenkins says, 'Look, it's *fine*. We'll have most of the data ready for you tonight, and the rest of it Tuesday, Wednesday at the latest.'

'Well, that's the thing you see. The inquiry is going to be active all the weekend and—'

By the time we finish speaking, Jenkins has promised me one data-dump tonight, a second tomorrow, and fast-track on all those things where the science just takes more time.

I thank him and hang up.

I'd never have got budget authority to go to Culham anyway.

The warm wind still blows. It's not long after four, but light leaks from the hospital windows. On Eastern Avenue, the cars drive with sidelights.

I wait a while for no reason, then climb into my car and drive slowly round the corner to Roath Park.

The big lake. Lights over water. Geese honking close to the waterline.

And my father's house, my mother's clucking welcome.

7

My father's house.

My beloved, complicated, dangerous father.

He's at home tonight, which he isn't always. He greets me as he always does. A crushing bear hug. Then standing me at arm's length, so he can properly look at me. And all the while, a shouting download of whatever is on his mind. 'Fi, love, brilliant to see you! Kath, sweetheart, Fi's here, would you believe it? You've got brilliant timing and all, we've got Mal and his missus coming round in a bit. You remember Mal, don't you, love? Ant! Where's Ant? That girl never takes her nose out of her phone these days. Ant, your sister's here. Staying for dinner, are you? It's sausages. Those ones with the herbs in. Them with mashed potato – lovely!'

My father and I have, I think, a very good relationship, but it's not always been straightforward. The first challenge came when I was ill in my teens. Dad was a roaring, anxious, supportive presence through that illness and its long aftershadow. He and I, always close, became even closer. Battle buddies. Resistance fighters. It became so that when I was actually ready for some independence – studying at Cambridge, entering my first relationships – I actually had to fight for the space in which to do it.

We handled all that well enough, I think, but then I chose to enter the police service. Given my father's record – his multiple prosecutions, the various further crimes of which he was suspected but never charged – my desire to work in the CID appalled him. It felt traitorous. A betrayal.

Was it that? Maybe, but I'm not him. Don't have his past, his allegiances, his friends. In any case, I joined the police and have never, not once, regretted my decision. I can't imagine any other career, any other calling. My relationship with my father settled down after those first few bad months – or at least, it appears to have done. My father is a silky enough liar, as indeed I also am, that I wouldn't necessarily know if he still harboured a grievance.

Anyway.

Mam fusses in and out of the kitchen, pleased to see me, but also anxious about whether her mashed potato is lumpy. Mal Edwards and his wife do come round for a drink that, inevitably, morphs into dinner too. Mal was one of Dad's tightest buddies from those early days. When I was five or six, Mal was one of those men who appeared most often at our dinner table, our parties, our family events. One of those smiling leather-jacketed men who would come knocking at our door, late in the evening, full of polite and solicitous friendliness towards my mother, but with eyes only for my father, and jingling a set of car keys that summoned my dad out to some important but unnameable night-time assignment.

That was then. This is now. Mal's in his sixties. With the profits he earned from those old, discarded games, Mal built up a little chain of holiday rentals in Majorca. Lives out there eight or nine months of the year and comes back, baked the colour and texture of beef jerky, emanating that slightly superior air of puzzlement at our decision to live here in the winds and rain when we could be sharing his pool and sun-umbrella life in the south.

At one point, I corner Mal and his wife, Dorrie, on their own.

'Mal, can I beg a favour?'

I explain that I'm putting together a photo album-cum-scrapbook to cover the early years of my parents' marriage. That it's going to be a big surprise Christmas present for them both. 'Dad wasn't big on cameras back then. Didn't want things recorded. But that means they don't really have much of a record of things until Kay was born, or even later. I know they'd love any photos you have of that time. Family stuff. Christenings. Whatever you have. I'll get them copied.'

Mal and Dorrie are both enthusiastic at the idea. Keen to help. Invite me round to their place on the Bay. ('Just a small place now, love. We think of Majorca as home, don't we, Dorrie?') They promise to say nothing to Dad till after Christmas.

Mal asks if I'm talking to any of the others in the old crew – he means Emrys Thomas, Gwion Cadwaladr, Howie Jones, a couple of others – and I say yes, all of them. Collecting up records of those weddings and picnics. Days at the racetrack or on boats out on the Bay. One by one, I'm going through their albums, finding pics of my ma and pa. Of me as a small girl. Of Kay as a newborn.

'Brilliant idea, love,' says Mal. 'Brilliant.'

And he's right. More right than he realises since – because this is me, because my stated motive is not always the same as my actual one, because my truth is formed in layers and the part which is most truthful lies most deeply buried – I have a secondary mission too.

Because my father is not my father. My mother not my mother.

In terms of love, yes, of course. In terms of loyalty, affection, history, shared relationships and much else – then yes, yes and yes.

But the biology speaks otherwise. It took me a long time

to realise this, but my parents adopted me when I was small. They simply came out of chapel one day to find me – aged perhaps two-and-a-half – sitting in the back of my father's open-top Jag. Mam and Dad had long wanted kids. Had failed to conceive any in the normal way of things. Were only too happy to accept this little penny dropped from heaven, and did all the things necessary to regularise my adoption.

As it turned out, Mam and Dad did go on to conceive two children – my sisters, Ant and Kay – but the mystery of my past remained deeply buried. Mam says she has no idea where I sprang from, and I believe her. Dad says the same, but I think he lies. His own past is too tangled, too murky for any deep truth to spring free and clear.

So I think my father knows more than he's telling me.

More than that: I think those first two missing years of my life have something to teach me about the illness that afflicted me in my teens. Two horrific years in which I lost my sanity. In which I was in hospital at least as long as I was ever out of it. Two years in which I believed myself, in the most literal way possible, to be dead.

I'm in recovery now. Not exactly sane, but still a thousand times saner than I was.

And yet, I'm also aware that my present sort-of sanity is a fragile, precarious thing. A soap bubble dancing over rock. A butterfly trembling on the storm.

I don't know whether learning the truth about my past will help my head heal itself. I don't know how far my head will ever truly heal. But I do know that I have to find out. That I have to try.

The simplest course of action, obviously, would be simply to ask my father and the men who knew him best. The simplest and the stupidest. If my father knew I was investigating him, those faint traces I'm seeking, almost obliterated by time and memory, would vanish for ever.

So my investigation moves crabwise, silent, out of sight. Deals with traces and half-traces and mere sniffs of suggestion.

These photos are part of the search. I'm trying to knit together who knew who. What my father's circle really was. Trying to gather enough material that I might yet find a diamond shining in the loam.

And yes, on Sunday, I do go down to the Bay to see Mal and Dorrie. They give me tea and cake and we sit in a litter of photos and other mementoes. I study them all, pick the ones I like, and they let me take them away to get them copied. No diamonds visible yet, but you don't always know what you have until you look at it in the right way.

A good weekend. Productive. Rich and busy in other ways too – a trip to the gym, a cinema date with Bev, a lunch with Ed Saunders – yet I feel unsettled nevertheless.

I can't get Carlotta out of my head. I check constantly for any data from Bridgend, any breakthrough from the MisPer people.

Nothing.

On Sunday lunchtime, I call Burnett on his mobile to see if he's heard anything. He's with his family. Half-puzzled at my call, half-irritated at being disturbed.

In any case, he has no news. Says we'll talk first thing Monday. Tells me to come over to Carmarthen for a case review.

I want to drive up to Ystradfflur again, just so I can spend more time in the dead house, recover something of those happy hours with Carlotta. Would do it too, except that Burnett will still have his SOCOs scratching around, and I don't want to share my private, night-time, wind-blown Carlotta with their big boots and stoic, official indifference.

Go to bed that evening. Restless, scratchy, wanting more.

And then, Monday – glory be – a crack.

A chink, a gap, a fissure, an opening.

I'm in Carmarthen with Burnett: in their 'Major Incident Room', a repurposed conference suite with a view south over the river. The room has some of the feel of an MIR. The whiteboards. The HOLMES terminal. The files, the papers, the felt-tipped List of Actions.

But already – and far too early – there are those signs of an inquiry in decay. The smiley faces on the whiteboard. The sidetable with coffee thermoses which already has more unwashed crockery than clean. No one manning the HOLMES terminal.

Those things betoken no lack of diligence. Rather they're testament to a lack of leads and, worse, the lack of any clear crime. Pryce hasn't yet submitted his written report, but he has confirmed, orally, that the presumed cause of death was simple heart failure. Neither Burnett nor I have felt compelled to communicate that news to Bridgend, but Burnett would have had to come clean with his boss, DCI Jim Pritchard. And, given that any significant crime in Dyfed-Powys means that resources have to be siphoned off from somewhere else, it's pretty clear that Pritchard has promptly siphoned most of them back again.

I open the mail.

Nothing much, but one gem nevertheless. A padded envelope from Pryce. A short note and an evidence bag. Our smallest size, about two inches square.

The bag contains one single seed. A blunt oval. Seamed down the middle. Three or four millimetres long.

It takes me a second or two to realise what this is, then toss the bag at Burnett.

'From Pryce,' I tell him.

'The faeces?'

I nod.

Burnett pokes the bag. 'So. Not a squirrel then.'

I read the note. It doesn't tell us much, but what it does communicate, I pass on.

'It's barley,' I say. 'Not wheat.'

'Barley?'

'Barley.'

We turn to Google.

Google and Wikipedia.

Research separately for a minute or two without speaking.

Then Burnett pushes back from his desk and, sighing, quotes from the screen in front of him.

'"Barley is the second most widely grown arable crop in the UK with around 1.1 million hectares under cultivation. Each year the UK produces around 6.5 million tonnes of barley." Blah, blah. "Although it is grown through most of the country, it is often the dominant arable crop in the north and west of Britain."'

'Because the weather's rubbish,' I say. 'Wheat doesn't like it too wet. Barley doesn't care.'

'Right. But that means we're talking about one of the most common crops in Wales. Maybe even the most common in these parts.'

I shake my head. I think Burnett is missing the point.

'Look, it's *barley*. Who eats that? I mean, who eats that in the form of a whole seed? Most barley is turned into animal-feed, or turned into beer, or exported to wherever they feed animals or make beer.'

Burnett pokes at the seed more thoughtfully now. 'There's *pearl* barley,' he says.

But pearl barley has had its hull and bran removed, and this seed is the whole damn thing. We click around online and get up a picture of bread made with barley. It's almost flat. Unrisen. A heavy, chewy, rustic eat.

'Some kind of health food place, maybe. A farmer's market . . .'

That's what Burnett says, but he hasn't read Bridgend's analysis of the dress in the same detail I have.

I call his attention to a section on the seventh page of their report: 'Lower right inseam, 53 mm above hem. (Picture). Dried barley awn or spike. Length approx. 2.5 mm. Positioning consistent with natural deposition.'

The 'natural deposition' bit just means that if you wear dresses anywhere with long grasses, you're quite likely to get an accumulation of seeds and grass spikes breaking off wherever the fabric is a little rougher, such as the inseam.

Burnett reads the section a couple of times, and says, 'OK, so barley again. But the report lists about twenty other deposits. None of them uncommon.'

'Yes, but not farmers' market-y either. And look, it's almost certain that Carlotta wasn't wearing this dress when she died. Somebody changed her into it.'

Burnett's with me now, following my logic.

He nods slowly. 'OK. Here's your hypothesis. In the day or so before she died, our victim, "Carlotta", eats some barley bread, or something like that. Something quite heavy and rustic anyway. Rustic enough that eating whole seeds of barley is part of the experience.'

'Yes.'

'Then she dies. Her heart just blows a gasket. Quite likely she was going to drop down dead, no matter where she was, no matter what she was doing.'

'Yes.'

'Then someone, or more likely two or more people, decide to change the woman into a white summer dress that's totally unsuitable for the season.'

'Yes.'

'That dress had been in a field of barley. These depositions here might have survived one wash in a washing machine, but probably not more, and maybe not even that, so quite likely, someone wore or handled that dress in a rural, barley-growing location, then folded it up, put it on a shelf, and didn't take it out again until it was used to re-clothe the victim.'

'You don't fold dresses. You hang them. But yes, exactly.'

'But the fact that the dress had been in barley fields and there were barley seeds in the stomach suggest another possibility. I mean, a possibility apart from the farmers' market idea.'

I say, 'Yes. We've got both ends of the barley-bread production process involved here. What about some artisanal bakery that uses its own grain in its products? Or a farm-shop?'

Burnett and I turn to the computer to seek out farm-shops in the very rough area of Ystradfflur. We find a couple, plus a bakery which makes a lot of its food purity. ('All our grains from local growers. Working with nature.') We widen our radius, start to find more targets.

And as we're doing this – good coppers, working the case as we're trained to do – a uniformed constable, Ceri Somebody, I think, comes to stand behind us. He breathes heavily through a gingery moustache.

'There's those monks,' he says. 'The ones with a brewing licence. They're up in the Beacons somewhere. Up the valley from that caving place.'

The caving place: Pen-y-cae.

The same broad area in which Carlotta was found.

We fool around on Google.

Ceri Somebody is right.

The St David Monastery in Llanglydwen. Only eight miles by road from Ystradfflur. Less than that as the crow flies, as the buzzard glides.

Burnett and I look at each other. He's thinking what I'm thinking.

The bible under Carlotta's hand.

The churchyard and the candles.

All that, plus monks who brew beer.

Beer, made from malt. Malt, made from barley.

Two minutes later, we're out of Carmarthen, heading east.

8

The Monastery of St David at Llanglydwen occupies three sides of a cobbled courtyard.

The main building looks like any other farmhouse of the area. Grey stone, slate roof. A little paved forecourt with neat black railings and some terracotta pots which might, at other times of the year, hold flowers.

To our left, a row of stone barns with wooden doors, painted black. At the end, the low wall and earthy smell of pigsties. To our right, a modern block. Oak boards, weathered grey. An external staircase and a wooden balcony that runs the length of the upper floor. Ten windows. Ten doors. And the balcony means that every door can be accessed directly from outside.

And at the end of the modern block, backing up to it, is a little church. Only the stubby little tower, the little belfry with its iron bell, and an arched east window, gives any clue that the building has an ecclesiastical purpose. Mostly it, like the surrounding buildings, simply merges into the landscape beyond. Grey stones. Grey clouds. The creep of moss.

There's no one here.

Burnett and I get out of his car, a pale-green Mondeo. No sign to indicate where we should go. None of the buildings appear to be lit. So, for a moment or two, we just stand there blinking in the wide, silvery light.

Then, from one of the barns, a man emerges. Brown robe.

Black leather sandals, worn with socks. A well-used yard-brush in his hand.

He sees us, leans the brush against the wall and comes over to us, smiling.

'Good morning, sir,' says Burnett. I'm Detective Inspector Alun Burnett and this is my colleague, DS Fiona Griffiths.'

He puts out a hand.

The monk, smiling again, exposes his hands to our view. They're the hands of a farm-worker. Mud. Muck. Dirt in the creases of his palms, the rim of his nails.

Apologising for the non-handshake, the monk offers a tiny bow instead, which Burnett – sort of – replicates.

The monk raises a hand to his lips indicating, I think, that he's of a silent order, or at least currently non-speaking, but he waves us towards the main farmhouse and escorts us there.

He swings open the front door for us – it's not locked – and takes us through an internal door into a handsome living room. A good-sized fireplace, not currently in use. Two big sofas. A grandfather clock. Panelled walls. Some religious pictures that don't mean much to me.

The monk hovers at an oak sideboard. Indicates a decanter of water. Glasses. And a wooden board containing some apples and, under a muslin cloth, bread and cheese.

The monk opens his hands over the food. Points to the clock.

It's just a couple of minutes before twelve. The bell in the little belfry is tolling. The monk smiles again. Bows. Rushes off. There's a sound of water running, then we see the monk running, wet-handed, to the little chapel. Other monks are arriving too.

'Matins,' I say. 'Lauds, terce, sext, then I'm not sure. None, I think. Vespers. Compline.'

Burnett stares at me, as though he too has been bitten by the silence-fly.

I say, 'The monastic offices. It's something like that. I know there are seven of them. I think this one is sext, or maybe terce. No, actually, it must be sext, mustn't it? Six hours after dawn.'

'Seven church services a *day*?' says Burnett. 'Bloody hell. I used to think Sunday morning chapel was bad enough.'

We inspect the bread. It's rustic enough to satisfy any belly, but it looks wheaty and though there are seeds on top, they're not the little ovoid bullets of barley.

Burnett eats a bit of cheese. 'Oh, now that's good. That's really good.' He hands me a bit on the tip of the knife, but I don't take it.

I sit in the window and watch the yard.

Burnett tries to talk to me, but I don't make it easy. Then he tries to check phone messages, but the signal in these parts doesn't make that easy. Burnett kicks around the room, as though looking for a pile of old magazines to read, much as he would if this were an upmarket doctor's surgery.

I say, 'We could look for the kitchen.'

'OK. Yes.'

It's not hidden. We find it at the back of the house, down a stone-flagged hall. A biggish room originally, but extended to make it even larger. On a stove, quietly bubbling, is a big pan of soup. Bowls, under a cloth, warming beside it.

In the extension area, we find more ovens. Catering-sized, these ones. Bread trays. Sacks of flour. And seeds. Barley. Wheat. Flaked oats. Poppy seeds. Stored in big glass jars, ten-kilo things.

Burnett holds our little evidence bag up against the jar of barley.

The seed in our bag and the seeds in the big jar look pretty much the same, except that our seed has a certain polish coming, I assume, from having passed clean through the digestive system of a fibrotic young woman who died before the seed's journey was done.

We bustle back through to our living room.

At twelve thirty-five, the church door opens and half a dozen monks exit. Four of them head for our farmhouse, two others for the barns.

The party coming towards us is headed by a tall man. Grey hair, closely cut. Must be in his fifties, but a brisk walker. When he sees us looking from the windows, he raises a hand and breaks into a semi-trot.

We meet him by the front door.

'Detective Inspector,' he says. 'I do apologise for your wait. Brother Gregory looked after you.'

He makes the last sentence somewhere between a statement and a question and looks at me as though challenging me to deny it.

I say, 'Fiona Griffiths. I'm a detective sergeant.'

He smiles. 'And you're here on business, I take it? Something I can help with? I'm Father Cyril, the head of our little house.'

Burnett is good. It's easy to play things loose with people who are accommodating and who aren't in any sense suspects. But tight is almost always better and Burnett stays tight as a drum.

He says, 'In the course of an important investigation, we found a barley seed. It's possible that seed originated here. If it did, that's fine. We just need to know.'

He holds up our little evidence bag. The ovoid bullet. The burnished seed.

But he doesn't let Cyril look at it, not really. Producing the bag, then not letting someone see it: another good move. Classic police. Those tiny little signals of control. Of threat.

'You want to know if we grow barley? We do.'

'And where does it go, once you've harvested it?'

If Burnett is good at his game, Cyril is good at his. He says, eyes creasing in smile, '"Therefore God give thee of the dew of heaven, and the fatness of the earth, and plenty of corn and wine." Not so much wine in Wales, but our barley gives us bread and beer and feed for our animals. It sustains us.'

'Do you sell any of those products outside the monastery?'

'Yes. We sell almost all our beer. We brew around ten thousand barrels a year and consume only thirty or forty ourselves. That beer provides most of our income. Pays for all those things we can't make or grow ourselves.'

'And the bread?'

'Yes, we sell our surplus. The village shop. The markets in Sennybridge and Brecon. But not much. Maybe five hundred loaves a week in total.'

'And would any of those loaves have had barley seeds on top?'

Cyril laughs. 'Brother Nicholas is the great artist of our bakery. You'd need to talk to him about his exact recipes, but yes: Brother Nicholas does like his barley seed.'

Weirdly, we're all still standing. That doesn't sound like a big deal, but it is. People stand only if there's no available seating or if there's something provisional about the gathering.

And that's only part of it. Burnett does the police thing well. Heavily present. Feet set apart. Mouth and eyes and face not doing those little dances of mutual social pleasing which we normally do with newly met strangers. He's not directly threatening, not in the slightest, but there's a lack of giving which causes most people to feel an edge of alarm. To over-cooperate.

But Cyril seems immune. He's taller than Burnett, lighter on his feet, and his blue eyes are almost constantly a-smile, as though laughing at some secret joke. A mirth that moves behind us, above us, out of sight.

Burnett asks to see – the loaves or the bakery, I'm not sure which – and Cyril says yes. Leads us back to the kitchen, from

64

which the soup has gone, the soup and the bowls. From a room next door, there is the sound of spoons moving on crockery. The sound of a man's voice talking. I try to hear what he's saying, but can't make it out.

Cyril takes us back to the bakery area. Shows us the catering-sized ovens, the bread trays, the kneading machine, the proving area. He talks the way a father might talk about his daughter's ballet things. Just about knowing what's what and where to find it, but the edge of unapologised-for ignorance is never far away.

We see some bread too. The bread made with ordinary wheat flour rises high and soft. The barley-only bread is low and heavy.

I say, 'May I?' but I've cracked the loaf open before Cyril gives permission. There are seeds baked into the bread too, not only on top, and the bread smells dense and malty and brown. I break a wheat loaf open too. It's not seeded. Not inside, not on top.

'These are clues?' asks Cyril.

Burnett ignores the question. Says, 'Do people ever come *here* to buy bread? Do you have any passing trade?'

'Ever? Ever is a long time. Perhaps very occasionally, I wouldn't necessarily know. But no, not really. Anyone local can get these loaves from the village shop.'

Burnett considers his next move. His hand moves a stainless steel bread tray around the countertop as he ponders.

The baking area is lit by cool white fluorescent lamps. Long cylinders of light that nudge blues into something bluer, that pushes clear whites into something shot through with duck-egg. Burnett produces a photo of Carlotta, a photo that doesn't quite tell you how dead she is. A photo that feels a tiny bit off, maybe, but in a way that would be hard to identify unless you knew.

I feel a sudden pang. Want to take the photo from Burnett,

65

angry that other eyes should be looking at the corpse I knew. Jealous of the intimacy we shared.

'Do you know this woman? Have you seen her before?'

I'm expecting – Burnett is too – that Cyril will say 'No,' but he doesn't. He says, 'Um.'

He says, 'Could be. Maybe. You'll have to excuse me, I don't always know . . .'

Burnett catches my eye, but all I have to offer him is a 'Me too, boss,' look of surprise.

Burnett: 'You think you *might* know her?'

'Yes, well, we are a small community, but welcoming. We offer a place of refuge. Sanctuary.'

Burnett: 'You'll have to excuse me—' Burnett stops where the word 'Father' would logically be, as though he can't quite bear to hear himself talking churchy. He reverses a yard or two and goes at the sentence again with a bit more vroom. 'You'll have to excuse me, this talk of refuge? In plain English, you take – what? – immigrants? Asylum-seekers?'

Cryil laughs. A pealing laugh, this one. Nothing secret.

'Immigrants? Yes. Exactly. We take refugees from the world. Those seeking sanctuary. If you, Inspector, felt yourself to be in some kind of trouble – spiritual trouble, I mean, an affliction of the soul – you might want to come and spend time with us.'

'And you do what? You offer *therapy*?'

'We offer prayer. We offer silence. The chance to participate in our community. Maybe only for a day or two. Maybe for the rest of your life.'

Burnett tries to get his head round that. 'So – what? – people just up sticks and come?'

'Yes.' Cyril hesitates, wondering whether to continue, I think. But he decides in favour. 'There are people who might look happy and successful to you. Perhaps, I don't know, they have money, jobs, boy- or girlfriends, whatever they want.

But they have lost their connection to God. And without that, what are they? Souls in trouble. People who need our help. Sometimes they know that. Sometimes they half-know it. Sometimes they have to learn it, or re-learn it. We are here for them all.'

Cyril smiles and darts a glance at his watch. 'Do you mind?' he asks, waving us back to the reception room where we waited earlier.

There are three bowls of soup there now. Bread. Butter. Water. Salt.

'It's one of the things about the monastic life. We're so regular in our timings that when we reach the midday dismissal, our bellies start to rumble.'

We eat the soup. It's good, I think, but I don't know. I don't really taste it. I keep thinking of the photo of Carlotta that Burnett carries in his pocket. I don't want him to have it. I want to take it off him.

Cyril tells us that the monastery gets a trickle of spiritual solace-seekers throughout the year. 'In summer, yes, especially, because the life here is a little easier. Some of our visitors are very regular. Some people might, for example, spend two weeks with us every year. The same two weeks very often. And others? Well, we don't judge. We don't ask.'

I say, 'So someone might pitch up, I don't know, for a day or two, a single night only? There would be nothing to prevent that?'

'No. We wouldn't wish to prevent it.'

'Do you have to book? Is there a booking system?'

The monk smiles. 'We ask people to let us know if they're planning a visit. It makes things easier. But sometimes, the people who need us most don't know in advance that they need help. We take no payment. We demand no notice. Our doors have no locks.'

I exchange a look with Burnett. This is a new world to both

of us. Give us some sex-workers in Cardiff or, I don't know, a shotgun-wielding drunk in Tregaron, and we'd know what to do, how to proceed. But here, we're like a blind man at a busy intersection. Tip-tip-tapping with our white stick. Trying to figure out what's pavement and what's on-rushing truck.

Burnett: 'So, theoretically, our girl here,' he brandishes the photo, 'she might be, for example, a Londoner. She might encounter some kind of crisis in her life. She decides she needs to get away. She could just hop in a car, come down here. Then what? She checks in with someone? Signs in at all?'

'Ideally, yes, she'd let us know she was here. But she wouldn't have to. Those rooms are all open.' The abbot indicates the little modern block outside our windows. 'There is clean linen. Water. Food is always available in the kitchen. We expect people will come here wishing to share our life. Our services, our work, our meals. And, to be frank with you, those are the visitors we most welcome, most take to our hearts. But other people have other needs. If people want a space for quiet contemplation on their own, apart from our little community, then we are happy to give them that space.'

If Carlotta had attended church services and the rest, presumably her face would be familiar to the abbot and his fellows?

'Maybe, yes, mostly. But women are asked to cover their heads while in church. At mealtimes, we do not talk. We don't socialise with our guests the way you might expect. And then, we're not a silent order. Except during the weeks of Lent, speech is permitted. But we place a high value on silence, an inner retreat. I myself have just finished four weeks in which I spoke not a word. During that time, my attention was inward. I'm afraid elephants might have walked through that courtyard without me noticing.'

But at least we've got something to work with now.

Burnett says, 'How many of you are there?'

Six monks, including Cyril.

'And you're not aware of any recent deaths in this area? Sudden, unexplained?'

'No.'

'Do you have regular members of the congregation? Locals, I mean. People who might come here rather than the ordinary village church?'

'No, not really. St Cledwyn's is better for weddings and funerals and the regular Sunday morning services. But, of course, we offer something a little different. There are a few people who like what we offer. Perhaps they come to some services or a moment's prayer. And our annual carol service is standing room only.'

Burnett asks to interview each of the monks, one by one. While that's organised, I go, with the abbot's permission, to see the guest accommodation block.

It's as he said. Each room spotlessly clean. Very bare: a bed, a chair, a chest of drawers, a hook for any hanging clothes. A Bible. A wooden cross. A small en-suite shower room.

Each room the same.

On each door, a laminated *Guide to Visitors*. The guide is consistent with what the abbot's already said. Visitors are encouraged to come to services and meals, but there are instructions about where to find food if someone doesn't want to attend the communal dining. There's a list of times: services and mealtimes. Some comments on how to deal with muddy work-boots or clothes wet from the fields.

There's no blood. No corpses. No pretty white summer dresses from Monsoon.

No forgotten suitcases or abandoned clothes.

No crucial heart-medication left behind to lethal effect.

I go back to Burnett. Tell him what I've seen and what I haven't.

He's just done with his second monk, about to start on

number three. Tells me, 'They think yes, she was here. Just a day or two. Didn't come to meals. Didn't help with the farmwork. Just sat in the back at most services. Then left.'

'They *think*?'

He laughs. 'Unbelievable, isn't it? You get a pretty girl coming here. OK, so she keeps herself to herself. Maybe dresses modestly and all that. But even so . . .' He shakes his head, ridding himself of an image. 'I did a spell in the Navy when I was just out of school. I mean, if a woman like that had come on board our ship, every guy there would have been—'

'Yes,' I say, not particularly needing Burnett to complete that beautiful thought.

Suddenly awkward, we scuttle back to safer territory.

Burnett: 'I suppose we should do the forensics. It doesn't have to be every last inch.'

I nod. Walk outside into the courtyard where my phone signal is better. Call Carmarthen. Ask for a couple of SOCOs.

It shouldn't be a hard job. Carlotta's hair was nicely washed, well looked after. And long. Long enough that breaks are almost inevitable. You can clean a room very carefully – carefully enough that it looks spotless to the ordinary eye – but still leave easily enough material for a forensics team to find. Broken hairs. Flakes of skin. The little clumps of skin cells that gather at the root.

The call doesn't take long. I glance inside. See Burnett interviewing Brother Gregory, who seems to have shed his silence for the time being.

I ought to go in and help, really. Partly that's just the role of any junior officer: take the notes, fetch the tea, say, 'Yes, sir,' on demand. But also, these monks might theoretically be witnesses. Might, very theoretically, one day stand in a courtroom. In which case, I should be there co-interviewing with Burnett, in order to preserve the evidential integrity of what's being said.

70

But I don't.

A grey pigeon flies with heavy wing beats across the yard. It sits on the low wall bounding the pig-sties and tries to remember what it came for.

I glance inside the farmhouse. Burnett is still interviewing and I bet he's doing just fine.

Wander over to the chapel. Go in.

It's a small room. Seating for maybe fifty or sixty people, tops. Up by the altar, two rows of wooden seats facing each other. Where the monks sit, I assume.

The remaining pews, arranged the normal way, take up most of the remaining space.

There are candles by the altar and the monks' seating. Some natural light from the windows that line one wall. But I can see that if you're a prayerful monk looking out at a row of similarly prayerful monks opposite you, you would actually have to strain round to see anyone seated at the back, and even then that person's head and face would be mostly in shadow. Add a hat or headscarf and any woman would be more than half-concealed, whether or not she was actively trying to hide.

Because I don't want to get back to Burnett too soon, I continue to tootle round the little church trying to think what this life must be like. Seven services a day. Forty-nine in a week. Two and a half thousand in a year. Fifty thousand in a generation. A whole heap of prayers, readings, chants, psalms, hymns. Heaped up, and for what? For who?

I don't know.

Down one wall of the church, the one where there aren't windows, there's a series of icons. Little gold-framed paintings of saints. There's a symbolism there – baskets, tombs, doves – which I don't know how to interpret. Under each painting, a little piece of darkened glass and a candle – lit – set into the wall.

Shrines, I think, *shrines*.

That word isn't one we encounter often in the police service and, when we do, it crops up in sentences like, 'Friends of the murder victim/accident victim/missing person are already bringing flowers to create a roadside shrine in her/his memory.'

Flowers. Football scarves. Cuddly toys.

Greetings cards inked with sincerely meant condolences.

Those are shrines that last a couple of hard rain-showers. Last just long enough to acquire a dark sprinkle of car exhaust, before they're discreetly tidied away by the municipal cleaning teams, working in the half-light of early dawn.

These shrines aren't like that. The meanings of these stretch back so far into the past that I can feel the medieval starting to crumble into the ancient.

St Anthony. The only icon that has a name underneath it. An old guy with a beard, and a halo, and a domed head, and those delicately posed fingers that are maybe intended to convey some specific religious meaning, but could equally well be signalling the prelude to some ordinary human action, like scratching an itch or picking a nose.

I stare at Anthony, who stares right back. He's a tough bugger, I think. Like one of those seen-it-all, done-it-all DIs that you get in Cardiff, or London, or any of the big cities.

The main difference: a DI wouldn't get away with that beard. Or that halo.

The two of us look at each other a while, but say nothing.

'So long, Tony,' I tell him, then walk back outside.

Away from the prayers and into the light.

9

We do the forensics and, yes, in one of the guest bedrooms, the middle room on the upper floor, the forensics team found six blonde hairs trapped in the gap between the mattress and the wall. A scrap of tissue stuck to the sink's porcelain upstand. A white cotton thread caught under a leg of the bed.

The hairs looked a good visual match for Carlotta's and analysis proved them identical. DNA was captured from both the tissue and the thread. The DNA matched Carlotta's.

So she *was* there: in the monastery, sheltering from the world. I pushed, of course, for a more thorough examination of her room. Pushed hard enough that I dragged an ill-tempered forensics guy from Carmarthen to pull apart the U-bend beneath the shower, looking for more traces of hair and any flakes of skin. No results back yet, though as Burnett said with some irritation, 'If she was in the room, she was in the room. We don't have to track every last flake of skin.'

For the same reason, we didn't examine the chapel, though we presume that Carlotta had indeed been there, sitting at the back, hair covered from the sight of the Lord, her face in shadow, as Anthony feasted his saintly eye on her Gore-Tex cheekbones.

As for Burnett's monkish interviews, they turned out to be frustratingly uncertain. Though the monks couldn't quite agree amongst themselves, it seems that Carlotta was present in the monastery for just two or three days, leaving either late on the Sunday night or early on the Monday morning, perhaps thirty hours or so before her death. The monks were, however, unanimous in saying that she didn't join them for mealtimes. They were unsure about how she arrived and left, though two of them mentioned that they thought they had seen a small blue car in the parking area at the back of the guest block.

Burnett didn't think the lack of clarity was suspicious in any way. 'Truth is, most people *don't* remember that well, especially if whatever we're asking about didn't particularly matter to them at the time. This girl breezes in for a weekend. Attends some services, but otherwise doesn't integrate much. The monks are just so used to those kind of visitors, they've stopped noticing them. They basically just didn't care.'

The monks. My bosses. And Burnett's too.

Pryce has now confirmed in writing his hypothesis of death from natural causes.

We have no Missing Person to match against our corpse.

So we have no crime. No crime, no grieving family, no confected outrage in the press.

We have nothing of criminal interest except the world's most perfectly presented corpse and that, alas, is not enough in our fallen world to justify continuing investigation. So we're told to finish, to wrap up, move on.

I have a kind of farewell lunch with Burnett in Carmarthen. A greasy spoon café just up behind the police station. The sort of place where the laminated menus stick slightly to the tables. Where lasagne represents the most adventurous meal choice.

Burnett opts for the roast chicken lunch. Me, for beans on toast.

'Pity,' he says. 'The case started out so promising.'

Pryce's chicken is an unhealthy-looking grey, the way my

74

sister looked when she had glandular fever. He examines it gloomily.

'We'll get the coroner to give us an open verdict,' he says. 'At some point, someone will have to report our girl missing, then we can pick up from where we left off.'

I say, 'Yes', but mean, 'No'.

No, I don't think anyone will report this girl missing.

I eat some beans.

Do that, and say, 'She didn't leave on Sunday night.'

'Oh?'

'Pryce didn't find any kind of gut problem. Let's say she left at six p.m. on Sunday, died sometime Tuesday afternoon. That's getting on for forty-eight hours. Normal gut transit time is less than twenty-four.'

'Or she took some bread for the road.'

'She had cheek implants. And lip-fillers.'

'What? So she can't take some bread?'

'Not *that* bread. That barley loaf is the kind of thing you eat if you're, I don't know, some kind of hippy, vegan, cycle-to-work eco-person.'

'Or if you want to eat healthy.'

'*I* eat healthily,' I say, somewhat primly, given the rather more hit-and-miss truth of my dietary habits. 'But I wouldn't eat that. I mean, yes, if you put it on my plate. But no, given an ordinary nice-looking wheat loaf or that barley thing, I'd take the first not the second.'

Burnett shrugs. 'It takes all sorts.'

The kind of remark that annoys me. *Yes*, it takes all sorts. There's the sort that wants to rack up fifty thousand services of prayer in the company of the good Saint Anthony. And there's the sort that want to pump animal collagen into their already perfectly adequate lips. But if the latter type of folk suddenly starts eating barley loaves just for the fun of it, something odd is going on.

I don't say that.

Don't say anything much.

We say our goodbyes in a windy car park by a grassy bank. Positioned up here, on a little mound overlooking the River Towy, the police building has the feel of a hill fort. A garrison outpost in hostile territory. Civilisation's furthest frontier and the first line of her defence.

Back to Cardiff.

The whole thing, soup to nuts, has taken less than the two weeks Jackson first granted me, and I've not even been on it full time. For once in my life, I've completed something without getting Jackson pissed off at me. Rather the reverse. He's pleased to have me back.

I tootle around my regular desk for a bit. Chat with Bev until my time-wasting starts to annoy her. Find Mervyn Rogers. Let him know that his generosity in letting me keep the Carlotta case hasn't, in fact, cost him much. That the inquiry is fading out to nothing.

He says, 'These country things. They never amount to much. Anyway, I don't care, I've got a GBH to get stuck into.'

'A GBH?' I say, with just a touch of longing. 'A section 20 or . . .?'

'Nope. Section 18, with intent. Nice bloody great stomach wound too. Witnesses. Forensics. All coming in lovely.'

Rogers grins at me. He's trying to make me feel bad, and I try to look like he's succeeding, but I'd still rather have a corpse without a crime than a crime without a corpse.

I get some peppermint tea and tootle upstairs.

Top floor. Conference suite on the Bute Park side.

Outside the door I want, a couple of paint-splattered buckets, a stepladder, and an old dustsheet. Lights not working in the ceiling. Some carpet tiles pulled up and not replaced. No wi-fi signal.

The idea is to make this part of the building look derelict. Unused. But there are some clues which say otherwise. Clues such as a biometric entrance security system, that requires both a fingerprint and a six-digit code that changes each week. Clues such as a digital CCTV camera which photographs everyone on entry and exit.

Even the absence of any wi-fi signal is telling. Inside the room, data is kept so secure that it's virtually in lockdown. There's no wireless signal: all devices have to be physically wired to the server, to ensure that no data can be intercepted by a receiver placed outside the room. Password systems are onerous and double-action.

There's no sign on the door.

No entry in the annual budget.

The name of our inquiry – Operation April – is never mentioned on any list of current operations.

Yet for all that it's the biggest damn deal in this building. Indeed, give or take the occasional investigation into terrorist activity, it's quite likely the biggest damn criminal investigation in the country.

We have four crimes, four actual known-about, well-investigated crimes to work with. Those four are: (1) A nasty people-trafficking ring, as nasty and brutish as they come. (2) A weapons export game which our beloved Westminster politicians decided to define as a non-crime, though it was a non-crime that claimed the life of at least one person and really more like two or three. (3) A payroll fraud, which sounds dull but which killed people just the same. And (4) A wire-fraud, a description which makes it sound really old-fashioned, all trilby hats and Burberry macs, but which was lethal, ambitious and, by only the narrowest of margins, a failure.

The progenitor of the first of those crimes is dead.

The progenitor of the second is known to us – Idris Prothero, of Marine Parade, Penarth – but we can't touch him, because his weapons export suddenly became legal and we were never able to connect him to the various people who kept dying around him.

Crimes three and four: good news and bad.

The good news: we got one of the principals behind the wire-fraud. Galton Evans: arrested, prosecuted, convicted, sentenced. He's doing a life sentence now, minimum tariff of forty years and the poor bastard is fifty-six now.

The bad news is that we failed to get the major criminal behind the payroll fraud and I don't actually believe that Galton Evans was even the senior operator behind the wire-fraud. Indeed, we now believe – me, Jackson, DI Rhiannon Watkins and Adrian Brattenbury of the National Crime Agency – that all four crimes are the product of a loose network of local rich guys. Men who have made some real money in straightforward, legitimate ways, but whose real interest is in originating and investing in criminal enterprises – enterprises which, in at least two cases, stood to make profits of well over a hundred million pounds a year.

We can't yet be certain that any conspiracy even exists. We have nothing approaching proof. But we do have a mounting scatter of data – pebbles rolling in the stream, straws tumbled on the breeze – that suggests we're more right than not.

I blip myself into the suite.

Enter unannounced. See it with fresh eyes. The way it really is.

A fucking smiley face on the whiteboard. Coffee things in a mess. Two DCs, not knowing I was coming, fooling around at the window, throwing a ball at the glass and catching it on the return. A coloured ball, a child's toy.

I'm furious, yes, and the ball vanishes as soon as the DCs turn and see me. The coffee things are tidied soon after. And, to be fair, this isn't how the room normally looks. If I'm there, or Watkins, or Adrian Brattenbury, the whole place has a polished, quiet functionality to it. A murmur of data gathered, work done.

But maybe this is the reality. Maybe that stupid coloured ball reveals the truth that Watkins's rigorous management normally obscures.

That this inquiry is failing. Going nowhere. Driving so far into the sand that our turning tyres only plough themselves deeper into the dust.

I ask where Watkins is. One of the DCs – Essylt Jones – points to the big conference room at the end of the suite. 'In there, with everybody. There are a couple of German guys.'

That last bit said with that High Rising Terminal. There are *guys*? And they're *German*? And they're in our *conference room*? That kind of inflection.

I scowl my opinion, but hurry to the room.

Watkins, my direct boss.

Dennis Jackson, her boss and my über-boss.

Adrian Brattenbury from the National Crime Agency, dark-blue herringbone suit, white shirt, and that look of quietly unfussy fitness. Physical fitness, yes, but mental alertness too.

Also, two men I've not met before. Grey suits. Close-cropped blond hair. That precisely defined German accent which somehow reproves the rest of us for speaking messily.

I blunder in, trying to remember if I'm late, if I was even told about this meeting, or if I'd been invited, if I was.

Jackson, introducing me because I don't, says, 'Fiona Griffiths, one of our detective sergeants.'

Everyone else has papers in front of them. A look of busy competence. I get a pen out of my pocket. Wonder if I've got any business cards on me. Don't. Smile brightly instead.

The German guys do have business cards. Markus Hauke and Moritz Windfeder. Both from the Bundeskriminalamt or BKA, the equivalent, roughly, of the American FBI.

Jackson says, 'Fiona, we're discussing Lake Geneva and all that.'

Lake Geneva: one of our targets, Owain Owen, recently paid €2,200 for a weekend conference at some luxury hotel on Lake Geneva, and he never turned up. We sent a guy out there ourselves – a big deal on our police budgets – and he spent the whole weekend looking for Owen, asking other delegates if they'd seen him.

Nada. Nothing. Nix.

Three of our other targets – Ben Rossiter, David Marr-Philips, and Nick Davison – were also travelling that weekend. Rossiter and Davison were on 'business' in Copenhagen. Marr-Philips on a long weekend in Amsterdam.

Jackson says, 'We know Rossiter and Davison were in Copenhagen. They were on the flight. They paid for their hotel room. Their mobile phones were there. But the phones apparently never left. Our Danish friends and colleagues have let us take a look at exactly which cell, which mobile phone mast, those phones were connected to. And basically, give or take the trip to the airport, the phones were in the same place the whole time.'

Windfeder says, 'Right. In a hotel bedroom.'

'Exactly.'

Windfeder: 'So they come in to Denmark. Everything is correct, everything is above the line. Then they leave their phones here in this hotel bedroom, they're paying cash for everything, use taxis or public transport. And – pfft – *verschwunden*.'

His colleague, Hauke, says, 'Disappeared. Gone.'

Jackson: 'Marr-Philips, the same thing, more or less.' He tosses some papers across to the German pair who scan them briefly. 'And it's not the first time. This is the third occasion that we've been able to track. Three times in a single year.'

Windfeder, the senior of the two, turns his pale eyes back to Jackson and Brattenbury. Those two, equally.

Brattenbury, who deals with the BKA far more frequently than we provincial coppers, says, 'We're looking for an interception warrant. Basically, we think these men, perhaps others too, are involved in a wide-ranging, dangerous and entrepreneurial conspiracy, or set of conspiracies even. We think they fly to locations around Germany, in order to convene somewhere within your borders. They do that, because they need to meet face to face at certain times and they think the risk of interception here in the United Kingdom is too high—'

Windfeder shrugs and says, 'And also because we are German.'

Brattenbury nods. A quiet, regretful nod. 'Yes. And also because you are German.'

What Windfeder means is that Germany possesses what are probably the world's strictest privacy laws. The national experience, not only of *die Hitlerzeit* but of the all-intrusive East German Stasi, means that the legal bar for interception has been set very high indeed.

Windfeder trims the papers in front of him into a neat pile, square-edged.

He says, 'Listen. From what you have told me, I agree. I understand your reasons. I would share also your beliefs about this maybe-conspiracy. I would want to listen to what these people are saying to each other. So. So.' The German pronunciation of that word, more definite sounding than ours. 'We present this material to our legal department. If there is the basis for a warrant, we will be happy – really happy – to do the rest.'

Jackson says, 'We're aware some of this material – ' he means all of it – 'is circumstantial, but we think it's very strong.'

Windfeder says, 'We will read with an open mind.' He does a gesture, a kind of windscreen-wiper movement in front of his face, to show us just how open his guys will be.

Hauke, encouraging: 'This material? *Ja*, it has certainly the smell of *Verschwörung*, conspiracy.'

Politely, positively, the meeting breaks up. The grown-ups are going out somewhere, then off to Bridgend for a pow-wow with the Chief Constable.

No such things for the likes of me. No pow. No wow.

On my desk: a fat report from a team of forensic accountants who've been looking at Owain Owen's finances. Sample excerpt: 'While there is certainly no "smoking gun", we note a succession of balance transfers, in amounts and on dates that might well support the theory that . . .'

Fuckery.

Expensive, necessary, well-directed fuckery.

I think, if Owain Owen was in this room now, he'd laugh. Far from being frightened by our meticulousness, he'd be comforted to see that our entire year of effort has so far produced nothing more injurious than that 'might well support the theory . . .'

I think we're not even close with the BKA. I think we're not going to get that warrant.

I kill the face on the whiteboard. Check that the DCs are busy on their appointed tasks.

And I have my tasks too. My List of Actions, agreed with Watkins and Brattenbury, actions which are still tardily incomplete because of the time I've been spending with Burnett in the wilds of Powys and Carmarthenshire.

I look at my List of Actions.

It stares back at me.

I make a little papery nest and lay my List of Actions inside it, to see if the list will mysteriously complete itself.

I'm guessing not.

Call up a photo of Carlotta's face, her beautifully dead face, on the system.

Phone down to the print room. Ask for a colour copy.

Tomasz Kowalczyk, king of the print room and all things papery, tells me '*Dzień dobry*,' and asks if I want the normal size. 'Six times four, yes?'

I say yes, then amend my answer. 'No actually, Tomasz. I want a fuck-off big print. What's the biggest you can do?'

It turns out that 'fuck-off big' isn't a standard paper-size, but Tomasz tells me he can do full-colour in A2, or monochrome in A1. I take the colour option. Two copies.

'*Tak*, Fiona. Forty minute.'

Barley seeds and flakes of skin.

I stand there, doing nothing, seeing nothing, for I don't know how long. Then something changes and I look up. See Esyllt, one of the DCs.

'Esyllt?'

She comes over and I show her Carlotta's face on screen. A few different views. 'That's six or seven thousand pounds' worth of nose,' I tell her. 'Maybe about the same for the cheeks. But they're nice, aren't they? I mean, that's a nice nose, isn't it?'

'Fiona, that person. Is she *dead*?'

I tell her what I want. All the plastic surgeons in the country. Not just emails, but phone calls.

'Starting with London. Then London outskirts. Then everywhere else.'

Esyllt looks at me. 'Fi, this is on the Action List, is it? It's just—'

She tells me something to do with other people having told her to do other things. I don't hear, really. It's just words.

I wait till her mouth has stopped moving and say, 'Yes, definitely. This takes priority. Keep me in touch with progress.'

Then Essylt says yes, or words to that effect, and goes.

Time gurgles and passes.

Tomasz emails: 'Ready.'

I fetch my photos. Big ones. Ones that feel substantial in the hand. One for the office, one for home.

Beyond our windows, in Bute Park, a cherry tree burns with late autumnal fire. Yellow leaves flaring against wet black branches. The leaves win all the attention, but you already know how this particular story ends.

I pin one of my Carlotta photos so her dead face fills my little cubicle. The view settles me and I click around till I get to the PNC database.

A blinking cursor asks: *Location?*

I tell it Llanglydwen.

Radius of search?

Twenty miles.

Crimes/Incidents (select from list).

Violent Offences (all). Violent Deaths (all). Missing Persons.

Search from date.

I hesitate. I've run this search before. So has Burnett. But we were looking for anything recent. Any pattern of crime that could make sense of our nice fresh corpse. But what if the pattern had lain buried for years? What if we were looking at only the most recent manifestation of something far older?

The PNC lets me search from as far back as the early eighties, though the further you go back, the ropier the data becomes.

I enter the earliest date offered.

The machine blinks and considers.

Violent incidents: two. In 1992, in a village twelve miles from Llanglydwen, a local farmer got drunk and walked half a mile to threaten a local haulier with a shotgun following a dispute over money. In 1998, the same farmer hanged himself from a tie-beam in his barn.

Missing Persons: one. Date: 2006. On a farm just three windy miles from Llanglydwen, a teenager, Bethan Williams,

84

went missing. No personal difficulties reported, beyond the normal teenage-girl stuff. No body was ever found, but investigators at the time concluded that she had most likely been abducted, raped, then killed. A local man was suspected – arrested and intensively questioned – but no meaningful evidence was ever found and no charges were ever brought.

In the summer of 2006, a crime without a corpse.

In the late autumn of 2014, a corpse without a crime.

And a case which was already strange dips its hands into the peat-brown waters of the past and comes out stranger still.

10

Watkins isn't happy with me.

'This thing with Essylt. You can't just reassign people. She had a set of specific, time-critical tasks to complete.'

'I know. Sorry, ma'am. I don't always . . .'

I trail off.

'Don't always *what*?'

'Think. I mean, I do, obviously. Too much. But when I'm on a train of thought, I . . .'

Watkins isn't fake pissed off with me. She's only a hair-trigger pull away from firing lasers from her eyes, spitting nails from her mouth. But, on a sudden, her mood changes. Swivels. 'Well, perhaps it doesn't matter.'

'Ma'am?'

'Operation April. There are . . . developments.'

'*Ma'am*?'

She talks. I hardly hear her. Or rather do – hear words, see strings of sentences, watch those softly pacifying euphemisms floating out into space.

The gist: Hauke and Windfeder continue to be helpful, positive, encouraging. But they've made it clear that they believe our warrant application has no plausible chance of success. They are only facilitating the whole process as a way to introduce the case into their system, to acquaint some of the decision-makers with the material. For them, this is a first step, not a final one.

I say, 'Well, we didn't think . . . we never thought we'd get there on our very first approach.'

'I know. But, Fiona, there are realities—'

'*Realities?*'

'Our budgets are shrinking. If we invest a lot of resource, we're expected to produce something. We've been on this a year.'

'*Produce* something?'

I'm aware that my conversational range appears unnaturally limited just at the moment, but fuck's sake. We've built, piece by piece, an astonishingly detailed, if, yes, circumstantial case against our targets. We've started to uncover what might just be the most sophisticated and ambitious criminal gang in British history. And some fucking senior policeman, whose copper's brain has been surgically exchanged for an accountant's pea-sized cerebellum, has decided to give up at the very first setback.

Watkins says, 'We're not closing the operation. This isn't over.'

Watkins is trying to gentle the blow, but I'm not gentled.

Our targets haven't crumbled in a full year of the most urgent surveillance we can muster. Their defences will hardly fail if we withdraw most of our troops.

And it's defences, plural. Always multiple safeguards, layer upon layer. Like one of those megalomaniac Indian castles, where intruders faced one moat that was swimming with crocodiles, then a dry moat patrolled by elephants, then a third one aswarm with tigers. Then walls, and more walls, and higher walls, and more archers, until you realise the purpose wasn't to create something unconquerable – that point had long since been passed – but to create a statement of Ozymandian magnificence. *Look on my works, ye mighty, and despair.*

Watkins says more things.

I don't hear her, not really. Don't respond. Just think, *we're giving up. After one year of effort. One solitary year and we're giving up.*

Watkins says something, something that might have had a question in it.

I don't hear her. Don't hear the question.

Say nothing. Do nothing.

She sighs.

'Look, I think maybe it would be good for you to be attached to a more . . .' She hesitates, looking for the right word. 'A more *traditional* inquiry.'

Lord help me, I think, she's being diplomatic. Trying to spare my feelings. And when has Watkins *ever* done that? I can only nod.

She's aware that my little adventure in Dyfed-Powys appears to be petering out. She starts telling me about an assault with intent in Twyn-yr-odyn. Says, 'We have the perpetrator but it's one of those where we need an experienced pair of hands packaging the case for the CPS.'

She says some other things too, but I'm not listening.

Fuck Twyn-yr-odyn.

Fuck senior policemen with accountants' brains.

I interrupt. Say, 'I'm not finished in Carmarthen, ma'am.' I tell her about my search on the PNC. Tell her about Bethan Williams, the missing teenager.

That pauses her. Rocks her back on her springs.

'And your corpse?' she asks. 'The one you found?'

'That's not Williams, no.'

I give Watkins two slim files, one on each of the two women. Photos. Dental records. Heights and weights.

Unless Bethan Williams grew four inches, changed her eye colour, and found a way to replace an amalgam-filled rear molar with a new and flawless tooth, the two girls are different.

Watkins looks at me. Says, 'OK, so there's something here.'

Yes! She thinks so too. I say, 'Yes, ma'am.'

'Worth investigating.'

'Yes, ma'am.'

'And anything you do will be under DI Burnett's supervision, of course . . .'

She continues. I scatter yes ma'ams whenever there's a gap. She says (tersely, uncomfortably) that Essylt can continue to work through the plastic surgery stuff I gave her, but I'm not to issue any further instructions without her, Watkins's, express consent. ('Yes, m'am. Thank you.')

And then, the best bit of all, the only good part, in truth. Watkins says, 'The plastic surgery, OK. That's covered. What else?'

What else: my favourite question.

11

Neil Williams sits at table under the light.

The room smells of dog and cat and mud and maybe sheep. An oil-fired range cooker. Lino that's unsticking itself from the floor beneath. Boots drying on a few sheets of newspaper. A flat cap, tweed, shiny with wear. A collie that barked twice at me when I entered, then jumped back onto the collapsing springs of an old armchair, where it's been quietly licking itself ever since.

'Bethan? I still think she might come back one day,' Williams says. 'I mean, I know that's not what . . . I know that. But you know, it could happen. She was sixteen when she went, so she'd be coming up twenty-five now. Her whole life still ahead of her.'

The right answer to that – the right police-ish answer – would combine sympathy with firmness. A little splash of, 'If you say so, sir,' with a good, thick spread of, 'Unfortunately, in these cases, the data tells us . . .'

I don't take that option. Say, to my own surprise and certainly to his, '*I* vanished once. I mean, I was tiny. Only two. I remember nothing about it. But . . .' And I tell him the story. The true story of my murky appearance in this world, when I simply appeared – from nowhere, unannounced and unspeaking – in the back of my father's Jag. 'My adoptive father, that is. I've never met my biological parents.'

Williams stares at me in surprise.

I say, 'So yes, it can happen. I'm trying to track down my original parents now. Maybe somewhere there's a father, like you, wanting to know what happened to his little girl. Believing that that little girl might yet walk through the door. And of course it's unlikely. These things are. But *could* it happen? Yes. Yes, I hope so.'

Williams – weathered face, brown hands, misting blue eyes – wants to reach out, to pat my hand, I think, or arm. He pulls back from that gesture, but taps a pile of papers on the table instead. Bills. A seed catalogue. Something to do with farm machinery.

'Just a minute, love,' he tells me.

Leaves the room.

The collie watches him go, but doesn't move.

I offer the dog my hand and he, somewhat grudgingly, licks it.

I get up. Open the fridge, which is mostly empty. A paper bag with tomatoes. A loaf of bread. A half-eaten tin of beans. A smeary packet of butter. Milk, within its sell-by date. Bacon.

I find the kettle, put it on. The handle is sticky with something, I don't know what. The counter too.

There's a plant on the window sill which has dried up completely. Is now only sticks and barren compost. I find a bin and throw it away. By the bin, a little curl of dead leaves, chestnut and sycamore, from the trees outside. Tramped in here or wind blown. I throw those away too.

Williams has come back into the room at some point during this. Is looking at it with my eyes.

Says, 'It wasn't like this. Not then.'

'I know.'

And I do. Back in 2006, Neil Williams was married. Wife's name was Joanne. When their only child vanished and their lives descended into the crapper, there were any number of

91

police inquiries, Social Services reports and the rest. Neil's farm isn't much – two hundred acres of upland grass that would be marginal at best – but he has, or had, a side-business as a straw and hay merchant that earned the family decent-enough money. No doubt this farmhouse always had an earthy agricultural quality, but no more so than plenty of the houses in the surrounding valley. Certainly none of those intrusive inquiries found anything remiss with the basic quality of love, care and hygiene surrounding the young Bethan.

'Joanne's gone?' I ask.

'After Bethan . . .' he begins, then starts again. 'Well, I suppose we were arguing a bit even before she went. Nothing so big. Not really. Just that Bethan wasn't sure about life up here on the farm and Joanne had started to take her side. So, I don't know, we were snappy and Bethan in the middle of all that. It was a bad few months, maybe, but you know, all families have their spats.'

He looks at me, wanting me to tell him that, yes, all families have their rough patches, and I duly give him the assurance he needs.

I ask, 'Your arguments. Did you ever get violent? Did you ever raise your hand in anger?'

He says no and I believe him, but there's enough in what he does and doesn't tell me to hint that those arguments were bad, even without overt violence.

'And after Bethan went, that was it really. Me and Joanne were both upset. Different ways of expressing our grief, if you catch my meaning. Hers was – well, she spent more and more time with her sister in Brixham. Torbay area, you know. England. And when she was here, it wasn't the same. We were always at each other. Stupid things. And, in time, she stopped coming.'

'You divorced?'

92

'No. It's still odd though. Getting letters to Mr and Mrs Williams. I throw 'em away, often enough.'

He waves the papers at me that he'd left the room to collect.

The stack is cold and damp: the temperature and humidity of the house beyond this kitchen.

Photos. School reports. Postcards. Letters. Drawings and paintings.

Bethan's life pre-abduction. There's not much there. Not in terms of evidence, for sure, and these things would have been carefully evaluated by police at the time. But there's not physically that much either. Just not much documentary record of a vanished life.

I turn pages. Look at Bethan's four-year-old depiction of her home and family. A fat dad with a big red body, stick arms and legs, a smiley blue face on top. The mum the same, except smaller, and there's some vague effort at a green dress. Little Bethan, with an orange body and holding a bright-yellow balloon, stands between the two.

'I loved that,' says her father. 'That happiness. But music was more her thing. Singing. Piano. I often think, if we hadn't lived here but, I don't know, Brecon, Carmarthen, St David, everything could have been different. A place like this? Well, it's paradise for a little girl. For a teenager, like Bethan . . .' He shakes his head.

The kettle's boiled now and Williams make tea. Builders' sludge for him. Peppermint from my own stash for me. While he's doing it, I run some searches on my phone: 'cleaning companies Carmarthen'. Tap through to any firms that look worthwhile.

'What happened?' I ask. 'What's your guess, this many years on?'

'You're her age, aren't you? Sorry, I know I'm not meant to ask.'

'I turned thirty this year. I know I look younger.'

'Oh.' Williams has some of the mannerisms of a much older man, though he is, I know, only fifty-four. He looks at me trying to fit his mis-appraisal of my age into whatever set of thoughts he had about Bethan. Then gives up. Says, 'Well, you'll know from the police reports, love. There's this . . . man. Len Roberts. Used to do some contracting work. Driving combines. Getting the silage in. That kind of thing. Very seasonal. Work like a devil for four months of the year, sit on your arse the rest.'

'And?'

'And he got close to Bethan. Or Bethan close to him. I don't know. I didn't like it. Neither did Joanne. But that's how it was. She used to go over to his cottage, that old place of his. They used to talk, I don't know what. It was like that maybe two months. Bethan swore the two of them weren't, you know, weren't . . .'

'They were just friends. They weren't sleeping together.'

'Exactly. And we believed her. She was a sensible girl. Head screwed on. Not giddy. Then . . .'

'Your girl vanishes. Everyone fingers this guy, Len Roberts, as the villain. His place is turned over. There's any amount of evidence that Bethan had been there, including on his bed, but no trace of violence, no trace of sexual assault, and no trace of Bethan.'

'Exactly.'

Beyond our windows, the air thickens. A low mist is beginning to form, water droplets swirling the other side of the glass. It darkens too. It's mid-November now, and the night gathers early, even more so up here, among these purpling hills. There are no curtains on the windows. No streetlamps lighting the yard beyond. Somewhere, in the darkness, a fox screams. Twice, maybe three times repeated. Not a mating cry, I don't think, but one of those warning shrieks that's almost like a groan of disappointment. The noise has an almost asthmatic quality, but also something darker, wilder, vulpine. We wait until the noise has gone.

I say, 'You should get this place tidied. Tidied and cleaned. It's not good for you living like this.'

He says the kind of things I expect him to say. That I'm right. That he ought to. That he makes the effort now and again, but . . .

I interrupt. 'I've got some numbers.' Wave my phone at him. 'They'll come out. Bring all their own equipment. Three or four cleaners. One solid morning's work.'

He stares at me.

I say, 'It'll be a couple of hundred quid. Do you have that? Is that OK?'

He nods. 'Yes. I suppose.'

He looks perplexed. Perhaps he didn't know that the South Wales Police, unlike their Dyfed-Powys cousins, arranged house cleans for crime-stricken men of a certain age.

I'm not sure my bosses know that either, but I make the necessary calls all the same.

I walk into the part of the house I've not yet seen.

Heaps of stuff. Way too much. Not quite hoarder levels, but definitely not-quite-coping levels.

'I'm going to get a skip too. I'm going to tell the cleaning people to throw away anything you don't definitely need. Nothing to do with Bethan. That stuff is sacred. But other things.'

I point to a stack of dead newspapers where the paper on top is dated 2012. A plastic crate full of dead oil filters and old cam belts. A cardboard box, full of something, I can't see what, but its sides are soft and outward sloping in the damp.

The collie's on my side now and wags his slow approval.

Williams nods.

I make the calls. It'll be more like five hundred quid when

it's all said and done, but five hundred quid well spent.

'Then get someone in here. Once a week. Once a fortnight. OK?'

He nods.

'Say, "Yes, officer, I promise to do that." And I'm going to check on you, mind.'

He doesn't say what I told him to say, but what he does say is close enough.

'A promise is a promise, Mr Williams,' I tell him sternly. 'And if one day, I do find my biological father, I wouldn't want to walk through the door and find him living in a pig-sty. I'd want to see a family home, ready and waiting for my return.'

Something has collapsed in his face now. His right hand is down with his collie. Massaging its neck, its ears. Getting those swift, long dog-licks in return. And Williams's eyes are more than just misty now. They're watery. Ready to overflow.

Some collapses are good, I think. Collapses that precede change.

He takes me to the door. Wants to hug me, I think, except he can't find a way to do it and I probably don't help him much.

'Thank you,' he says, 'thank you.'

'You didn't answer my question. About what you think happened.'

He's resting a shoulder on the door frame, leaning forwards into the night. An outdoors man, happier out than in.

'I used to hate that man. Used to think about driving down the hill and killing him.' A glance indoors into the kitchen catches the old pine dresser in its sweep. Where he keeps his shotgun, I'd guess. 'Two, three years, I used to think about that every day. Kept me going in a funny way.'

'And now?'

'And now? I don't know. If Roberts did hurt my Bethan, I would kill him. I would do it, not that I should say so to you. But if he didn't, and he always said he didn't . . .'

I finish for him.

'Then he's suffered as much as you. Another life fucked up.'

'Yes. Something like that. He's local. Lived here all his life. A wild one, yes, him and Geraint, his brother. But if he didn't do no harm to my Bethan, I don't wish him harm in return.'

'Have you ever spoken to him? Since then, I mean.'

'No.' His voice says he wouldn't do it either. One of those rural feuds which will dissipate around the time that glaciers return to these hills.

I step out into the night.

I parked my car in daylight two dozen yards from the house, but the darkness here is so complete that I only find my way by pressing my blipper and waiting for the car to light up. When it does so, I see the mist has been thickening invisibly all this time. There's twenty yards of visibility, no more. The car's amber lights are haloed and softened, beckoning me across the mud and granite chippings of the farmyard.

At the car, I call back, 'Thank you, Mr Williams. Good night.'

He says the same, more than once. Then the door closes. I can see him moving around in his kitchen. Watch for a while. The blue light of that interior world. The soft grey vapour of mine. The side of my car is cold and wet against my hand.

I would wait awhile longer but, behind me, that fox barks again and a sudden streak of animal, black and white, races past me so close I can feel the spatter from its moving legs, the hotness of its moving body.

Williams's collie out to combat the fox. Or find prey. Or otherwise navigate the dark paths of this nocturnal animal world.

A world without police.

I'm suddenly, inexplicably, reminded of my father. All those years he spent building his criminal empire. His night-time prowls. Those invisible pursuits.

The risk of capture and the hot, feral scent of success.

I'm doing what I can to understand those times, of course. Trying to uncover his past and mine. So far, I've got nothing useful from all the photos I've collected, from Mal, from Emrys Thomas, Gwion Cadwaladr, and the others, but I also know that sometimes you can have a clue in your hands and not recognise the message it flashes up at you.

More work is the answer. It always is.

I get into my car, let in the clutch and glide downhill.

Drive on to the place where my records and my sat-nav tell me Len Roberts has his cottage.

I find the place all right. Sign on the drive. Letters carved on slate. The cottage too, in the shine of my headlamps, looks much as it did in the photos put together back in 2006. A holly tree is grown bigger now. There's more moss on the roof. Clumps of grass digging themselves into the cracks between the house walls and the front terrace. A gutter drips.

It's the same place all right, but no lights. No car.

I get out. Fetch a torch from my boot.

Approach the front door. Knock.

Nothing. No answer and even the sound of the knock fails too quickly in this muffled air.

I try the latch and the door sticks a bit, but opens.

I'm not surprised, not really. Out in these parts, where the nearest neighbour is usually half a hillside away or more, locks aren't all that useful. Burglaries are rare, because most houses have little to offer thieves and, in any case, if someone really wants to gain entry, they'll just walk round the back and break a window.

I grope for a light switch. Find it, but there's no power.

My torchbeam finds a dark kitchen. Flagstone floor. An old scrubbed wooden table that doesn't rest quite flat. A couple of rush-bottomed chairs. Not a lot else. A few pots and pans, some mugs, but not the clutter there was in Williams's kitchen. A fridge, yes, but not powered up and the only things left in there have long passed the interesting-coloured mould stage and are squishing down into a rubbery black and brown namelessness.

I look further. Find a boot room: a few old shoes, men's sizes. A yard or two of black neoprene, or something like that. A plastic box with some electrical junk, rat-traps, hacksaw blades, rawl plugs. Some wire traps. Also a downstairs loo. Overhead cistern, old-fashioned pullchain. The water level in the bowl is well down from its correct level, and when I pull the chain, no water descends from above.

The walls, the floor, the cistern, everything has a kind of dampness. Water droplets gleaming in the torchlight. Houses, even Welsh cottages, don't accumulate this kind of chilly damp from a few nights left unattended. There's a density to the cold here which tells me this house hasn't been heated or dried for weeks at least, maybe longer.

The living room: a carpet, a sofa, a couple of chairs. Some photos. Not much.

I don't go upstairs.

When Neil Williams spoke of Roberts's place, he said, '*his cottage, that old place of his.*' I'd understood that as meaning the cottage itself was old, but I think now I got that wrong. Think he meant '*the place he used to have*'.

But if Roberts had sold up, this place would be occupied, surely? And if Roberts is still living here in this valley, somewhere down the hill from Williams, then why isn't he living here, in the house he owns?

I don't know. Don't have an answer, but am happy to get outside, to this freely moving air, this animal-tunnelled night.

I poke my torch around aimlessly, as though expecting it to find Len Roberts, Bethan Williams, the secret of my poor, dead Carlotta, but find nothing but mist.

I get in my car and drive slowly home.

12

Time evaporates.

It vanishes and passes in ghost-showers of rain, in morning mists that hang low over these city streets, clinging to the damp trunks of Bute Park and straying over the Taff's black waters like something undecided. When we have sunshine, and we do, I can't quite understand it. I'm puzzled the way I would be if I found camels grazing on the Hayes, or monkeys screaming in Alexandra Gardens. It's not a bad thing, just strange.

Essylt, under my supervision, and with the support of Aaron Howells, contacts every plastic surgeon in the country. Every one.

Do you know this woman? Is that rhinoplasty yours? Did your hands fix those Gore-Tex shields to her cheekbones? Did your hands cut through her cheek, from the inside, from the back of the mouth, to slip those carefully sculpted implants into place?

No, no, no and no. In different versions, the answers we've had three hundred and some times over.

Do you forget a patient? Would you ever simply start to forget the long chain of women – pretty, unpretty, medium-pretty – who came to you seeking help?

I don't think so. Apart from anything else, these surgeons have assistants, they have records, they have their before and after pics. And then too, they are specialists in the human face. Professional students of our female contours.

So we do our work, and compile our responses. Letters, statements, emails, denials. The whole stack of them amounting to a big round zero.

Watkins, brusquely, redirects Essylt to some other assignment. Gives me enough work, including that boringboringboring Twyn-yr-odyn assault, that my own Carlotta time is severely reduced.

I feel the vibration of Watkins's disapproval. Her half-sense that I pulled a fast one.

There hasn't yet been any formal decision about what to do with Operation April – that will only come when we hear back from the BKA – but the vibe is bad, and everyone knows it. Leads aren't followed. Reports go uncompleted. The project is dying.

One morning, I come in early, four a.m. early, and throw away all the coloured balls, the toys, the stupid smiley-faced distractions that accumulate in any well-lived in office. I leave anything that is directly work-related, or anything which is immediately personal – framed photos, tubes of hand cream – but everything else goes into a black bin-liner which ends up stashed in the waste collection area down in the loading bay.

The work stuff, I smarten up. File documents. Order files. Put loose paperwork onto the appropriate person's desk, on top of their keyboard, so they have to deal with it. Two of the DCs have solitaire-type programs on their desktops, which they open when Watkins is away and things are quiet. I turn on the computers and delete the programs.

By about ten to eight, I'm all done and I blip myself out before anyone enters it. I spend forty minutes in the canteen pretending to eat breakfast, then re-enter the suite once it's semi-populated and share the general bemusement and outrage at the pixies who have been busy overnight.

Watkins, I think, has guessed the identity of the pixie in

question, but she says nothing. Secretly, I suspect, I think she approves.

Meantime, work.

Some boring boring boring paperwork on stupid boring stupid Twyn-yr-odyn.

Some tidying-up bits and pieces on Operation April. A police-bureaucracy version of last rites.

But in whatever little gaps and peeps of time are left over, Burnett lets me pursue my enquiries amongst the British plastic surgery community. I'm not on his payroll, so he doesn't much care how I spend my time and evinces no great interest in what I have to say about my results. But I'm, at least in part, allowed to do as I want. And praise be for that.

Then, one evening, one of my swimming pool Thursdays with Bev, I get a text. Cesca Evans. Asking me if I'm around over the weekend. **'Maybe meet up? Cxx'**.

Cesca Evans is the daughter of a rich guy – a rich, bad, murdering guy – who I helped to put away for a beautifully well-deserved life sentence. You'd think that the man's daughter wouldn't become a friend of mine, but she has, or sort of has, I can't quite tell.

In any case, some time after we first met, she invited me to an exhibition where she had some silkscreen prints on display. The email was a round-robin thing, it wasn't personalised in any way, but I still thought that she probably wouldn't have included me on the guest list unless she actually wanted to see me. So I went. Put on a dark dress and silver jewellery, the sort of thing I thought I was meant to wear, and turned up.

The gallery was in Clerkenwell, London. Achingly hip. An old brick warehouse made over to look twenty-first century stylish. Lots of people. Young, metropolitan, confident, cool.

I got the clothes thing wrong. I was way too formal. Too by-the-book. The guys were in dark jeans and linen jackets. One man was there in a long-sleeved black T-shirt with a violently frayed collar, a hobo-type woollen scarf and an oversized felt fedora with a floppy brim.

The women were either carefully dressed-down, exquisitely selected street-grunge, or boldly dressed in the kind of clothes no high street store ever sells. Things that looked newly collected, hand-stitched, from some new local twenty-something designer. The sort of jewellery you'd talk about by starting your sentences, 'Oh, this piece?'

Not long after I entered, Cesca saw me and waved, but looked nervous. Didn't approach. Then, forty minutes later, when I stepped outside for a joint, she joined me, leaning over an iron guardrail and puffing smoke into the night.

We spoke stiltedly for a few minutes – she thanked me for coming, I told her I thought her prints were great – then, abruptly, she invited me to some kind of after-party.

I went. Didn't do much, but didn't disgrace myself. Left at two in the morning, got a hug and a kiss as I went.

Since then we've met up twice more. Once in London, once in Cardiff. I think I'm not a friend exactly, but somebody she's collected. A person stored up for possible future use, or perhaps just as a curiosity she likes to get out and examine now and again. In any case, she calls me her 'Strange Detective' or 'Strange Police Person' and begins her texts to me, 'Hi Strange, . . .' or, more often now, just 'Hi S, . . .'

Anyway. I say yes to meeting up. Don't hear back, but I suspect I was only ever just one option on a menu of choices.

The next day, however, I get a slightly peremptory text asking for my address. **'See you 5ish. Cxx'**.

Leave work a bit early. Pick some food up on the way home. I'm not sure what people like Cesca eat, so buy some upmarket nibbles – Italian salamis, grilled artichokes, ciabatta – in case they're needed. Feel like I'm making the same mistake: the dark dress and silver jewellery one. But since I don't know what the right foodstuff-provisioning methodology is, I stick with the one I've got.

Cesca arrives forty minutes late in a new silver BMW 1-series. Dark, patterned trousers worn below a black jumper, silvery-grey cardigan. Nice shoes.

She picks at my salami with long fingers. Wants to explore my house and does. She's disappointed, I think, at how normal it is. Stupid patch of grass at the back. Boring kitchen, bland living room. Nothing much upstairs.

On the back of the door, a child's dress. Pink with a white bow. Suitable for an age two to three, something like that.

Cesca fingers it.

She doesn't ask the obvious question, but her curiosity is obvious, so I tell her, briefly, the story of my strange arrival in the world.

'They just found you in the back of a car?'

'Yes.'

'How old were you?'

I point to the dress. 'That age. Maybe two or three, something like that.'

'Didn't they ask where you'd come from?'

'Of course they did. I didn't say anything. Didn't talk at all for eighteen months. And then, by the time I did, I'd presumably forgotten everything that went before.'

'Bloody hell, Ess.'

I nod.

'Do you think . . . I mean, do you ever think . . .?'

Cesca knows I'm not totally right in the head. The first time I met her, I kept losing my shoes, admitted that I'd burgled her flat, then made myself a joint from her own stash.

I know what her question is and say, 'Do I ever think there's a connection? Between my craziness and those missing years? Yes. I do. There has to be.'

She stares at me. There's something unusually blunt in her

105

gaze at times. Not rude exactly – you sense she'd be equally OK if you were the one asking the questions – but on the outer edge of blunt.

I don't know if her gaze is expecting a response, but it doesn't get one. I say nothing and she appears to dismiss the conversation. Loses interest. Goes into my bedroom. Opens cupboards so she can see my wardrobe. Picks around in it, the way I pick at people's bookshelves.

She's getting bored. Wondering if she made a bad choice coming here.

I don't know what I'm meant to be or do to keep hold of her. Don't know that I really *want* to keep hold of her. For what reason? She gave me something I prized – the piece of evidence that launched Operation April – but what does she have to offer now? Perhaps this whole friendship thing was a mistake from the start.

Back downstairs, we stand in my kitchen and eat my nibbles. Not properly eat, not even. Pick salami straight from the packet. Tear off bits of bread without warming it. The whole thing feels provisional. Temporary. When Cesca gets a text, she reads and answers it without apology.

When she looks up, she says absently, 'So, what are you working on?'

I don't answer her. Not straightaway. I just stand staring. The two of us alone in my kitchen, silent, staring, openmouthed.

It's one of those moments which seems vibratory somehow. One of those moments where a right turn, for once, means something decisively different from left.

I say, 'Do you want to see?'

'See?'

'This case I'm working on.'

She has a pause of her own then. A decision to make. Something in her face twitches, but she says, 'Yes, OK.'

'Do you have a bag with you? Overnight stuff?'

'Yes.'

'Good.'

I go upstairs. Pack a few basics for myself. Nothing much. Within four or five minutes we're out of the house. She slings a bag from her BMW into my Alfa Romeo, and we're off. Out of Cardiff, heading north and west.

Pontypridd. Treharris. Aberfan.

Cesca is a Welsh girl, in theory. Her father is born and bred Welsh, and her mother, though English, still keeps a large country house here. But Cesca's mental geography is different from mine. To me, there's Cardiff, there are the coastal towns to either side, the valleys above us, the sea below, and a whole wide world which spreads outwards from there.

For Cesca, I think, the globe is mostly dark. Its various bright points – London, New York, Paris, Gstaad – are connected by rushing trains and speeding aircraft. Though Welsh-blooded, she sees the darkling world beyond my car windows the way a tourist might.

When we drive through Aberfan, she says, 'Aberfan, isn't that where—?'

'Yes.'

In October 1966, a colliery spoil tip became unstable. Laid on weak sandstone riven by numerous underground springs, a vast agglomeration of rock and shale started to move. A hundred and fifty thousand tonnes of sodden debris moving so fast that the mass started to liquify. A literal wave of rock.

That wave demolished a farm. Overran a line of terraced homes. Killed some adults, a couple of dozen.

Crushed, buried, suffocated, drowned.

And that wasn't the worst of it, not nearly. Because the kids at Pantglas Junior School had just returned to their classrooms and those classrooms stood directly in the path of the deluge.

They heard the rock coming. Some thought it was a jet,

107

diving to crash. One teacher ordered his children to hide beneath their desks.

Acts of bravery. Defiance of the coming dark.

The rock struck the school. Buried it. Left a silence so profound that not a bird, not a child could be heard. Just the low tinkle of settling rock. A hundred and sixteen children died that day.

A hundred and sixteen.

It later emerged that the National Coal Board had been warned, and warned repeatedly, about their spoil storage, the obvious dangers. Did nothing.

When the coroner began the sad business of recording deaths, he read out the name of one child, reporting the cause of death as asphyxia and multiple injuries. The father interrupted and said, 'No, sir, buried alive by the National Coal Board.' The coroner, gently, kindly, suggested the man might not be thinking straight, but the father repeated, his voice faltering only a little, 'I want it recorded – "Buried alive by the National Coal Board". That is what I want to see on the record. That is the feeling of those present. Those are the words we want to go on the certificate.'

I tell Cesca these things and she stares out of the window, trying to read the savagery in these dark hills, the lines of heartbreak.

She says, 'You seem angry.'

'Not angry, no.'

'You are, though.'

Am I? I don't always know my own feelings well. Have more problems finding them than Cesca does reading tragedy from the landscape.

We drive on.

At Merthyr, we cross the Heads of the Valleys road. Leave the mining towns behind us, drive onwards into the Beacons. I feel the relief I usually feel when I make this trip. Leaving the neon behind. Entering the high hills and the indigo darkness.

I drive a few more miles. Say, 'Sorry.'

Cesca doesn't say, 'For what?' and I don't know that I'd have had an answer if she did.

Instead, she says, 'This case of yours. What is it?'

'We found a corpse. A girl a bit older than you, a bit younger than me. No rape. No violence.'

I tell her the rest too. Public information only, for the most part. Say where I found her. How I spent that first night. How she was dressed. Her heart condition.

'So she wasn't killed?'

'No. I mean, something was wrong, but not that.'

'Where are you taking me?'

I don't answer. Her fingers play with the radio, looking for something. She doesn't find it, whatever it might have been.

We come off the main road. Start slowing down as we get close. Hazel hedges and moonlight. A thin, unconfident mist.

Once, we encounter sheep in the road and I have to slow right down, nose them ahead of me until a mud track allows them scamper away into the night. We get to the little hump-backed bridge above the village. A stone arch, a glimpse of rushing water beneath. Then the village itself.

'Where are we going?'

'The place she was last seen. In here.'

A few hundred yards outside the main part of the village, I make the turn into the monastery. Park not in the courtyard this time, but the gravelled area behind the guest house. We park next to the monastery's tatty blue van, the one it uses to sell its bread. As far as I've seen, it's the only vehicle the monks have.

I get my bag. Cesca, seeing me, gets hers.

'This is a hotel?' Spoken with that High Rising Terminal.

'A monastery.'

Cesca's face changes quickly, fluidly. Settles on some

expression I can't quite read under the dim glow of the only external light here. At first I can't read her, then think maybe I can. Cesca was disappointed by her Strange Police Person's house, but this – this whole excursion, the crime at its root – is exactly what she wanted from me. A tourist attraction that finally delivers.

As we come round the corner of the guest block, a lone bell starts to toll. Compline. The last service of the day.

I suddenly remember: I haven't brought a hat. Tell Cesca the thing about women having their hair covered. From the back of my car, I get a hat, a cable-knit thing that keeps my ears warm and no doubt protects my modesty too.

Get back to Cesca, who is adjusting a pashmina round her head and neck. Some dark jewel-coloured thing that somehow completes what had already seemed a perfectly nice-looking outfit. We leave our bags at the foot of the stairs and go over to the chapel door.

Cyril intercepts us. Starts talking – welcoming us, in that graceful, but just too impersonal way of his – when he recognises me.

'Ah, detective! You're not here on business again, I hope? No? A short retreat for you both. *Please*. You will be most welcome.'

He tells us, briefly, about the rules. 'Between the end of compline and the start of matins, we keep the Great Silence. No word is spoken and please, not even between the two of you, not even in private. No food either. Water may be taken, but that's all.'

He pauses, smiling, but wants to hear that, yes, we've got it.

The man is polite, attentive, but I notice that Cesca gets full-beam monkishness. I just get the overspill. I'm not sure why. Perhaps the guy knows I'm not the spiritual-retreat type. Perhaps he thinks I've already heard his shtick.

110

In any case, Cesca, I see, responds. Speaks in a low, reverential voice, and keeps plucking at the folds of her pashmina to make sure it's balanced right.

To either side of us, monks sidle past with little more than a 'good evening' or 'welcome', but the tolling bell slows to one beat on, one beat off, indicating the service is about to begin.

We go into the chapel. There's one other civilian there, a pale-faced, beardy guy about ten years older than me. Grey tweed jacket. Intense-looking. We exchange nods.

Cesca doesn't take the back pew, the way Carlotta was said to have done. She goes up to the front. Not into the monks' stalls, but the first pew back. Genuflects. Crosses herself. Steps into the pew and kneels in prayer.

I can't quite handle genuflecting, but I can sit down and shut up, so I do that instead.

The service is longer than I'd expected. Three psalms, spoken not sung. The Gloria. The Nicene Creed. A canticle of some sort, then a chanted hymn to Mary. We tell her that she is 'more honourable than the cherubim, and beyond compare more glorious than the seraphim', though since I've never met her, nor seen those beasts besides which she is more honourable and glorious, I feel my statements lack a certain dependability. Then a couple of chanted prayers. Then a *kyrie eleison* which is short enough, Lord help us, except that we repeat it forty times. Then another prayer. Then another one. Then another one. And then we're cooked. One of the monks is blessing us and we're all forgiving each other.

Cesca has been surprisingly intent all this time, making her chants and responses with absorbed conviction. And now, as the service ends, it's as though she bobs up from whatever place she's been, looking around her, re-gathering her bearings.

Before we file out, though, one last rite.

The monks gather by the icon nearest the altar and murmur a prayer in Greek, I think, crossing themselves when they're

111

finished. Then the same with the next icon. And so on down the length of the south wall. Four icons in total.

Intense Guy in Tweed hangs back in silent prayer. Cesca and I drift bamboozled, so we just follow the monkish herd and say *amen* whenever it seems like a good idea.

We troop outside.

The air is chilling down to frost. The courtyard cobbles carry an extra glitter. Above us, a few dozen stars exchange private confidences, while those monks who hadn't already greeted us before the service do so now, in silence. Folded hands and smiling eyes.

Beyond us, one of the pigs becomes suddenly excited, moving around its pen, scratching its bulk against the low wooden door. Then we hear it grunt in piggy satisfaction as it lies back down.

We smile and go our separate ways. I take Carlotta's old room, of course. Cesca is next to me. Intense Tweed Guy goes off towards the village somewhere, a local man. He reminds me, just a little, of a man I once arrested for a firearms possession offence. The same intensity of demeanour. The same darkly flashing eyes.

In my room, I dig a toothbrush from my bag and brush my teeth.

Sit on my bed.

Why am I here? Don't know.

Why did I bring Cesca? Don't know.

I hadn't really expected her to get all holy, but then I had no great expectations either way. After all, I barely know the woman.

The walls here are nothing much. Paper thin, in the serviceable old cliché. I hear Cesca moving around next door. Running the shower, getting ready for bed.

I'm not tired.

Didn't bring anything to read.

There's a Bible by the bed, but I'm all bibled up for now.

I wish I had a gun with me. Not to fire, especially. Not for protection even. Just to have. I used to like sleeping with it. The gun just a hand-snatch distant from my pillow and my dreams all cushiony soft for its presence.

I open the door and sit on the bed, just to see what that feels like.

Much the same, it turns out, but colder.

I leave the door open.

Moonlight and frost talk together in hushed whispers. Their own Great Silence.

Aberfan: when the queen visited the village the autumn after the disaster – paying her respects, honouring the dead – a three-year-old girl presented her with a posy. The attached card read, 'From the remaining children of Aberfan', and the queen almost broke down in tears.

I try to feel Carlotta's presence in this room of mine, but can't. Which doesn't mean much. I'm not psychic.

At some stage, well after midnight, I sleep. My version of sleep, that is.

Jumpy. Alert. Undergunned.

13

The next day.

In the darkness of pre-dawn: matins. Only a faint pewter cast on the horizon even hints that night might be ending. A hint so tossed about by the rise of the intervening mountains that you have to look twice to be sure it's there.

After matins, breakfast. Brother Thomas reads from the Bible as we eat. Crusty bread. Fresh butter. Eggs. Jam in big jars that will, I'm sure, have been made in the kitchen behind us. Cesca, I notice, chooses the softer, risen wheat bread, not the heavy barley alternative.

Then chapel again. Lauds. A hymn. A psalm. A canticle. A psalm. A reading. The Benedictus. Some prayers – intercessions, are they called? – then the Lord's Prayer. Then one more prayer, just for the heck of it. A blessing. A dismissal. Then that thing with the icons.

We go outside.

A couple of monks go round the church to a low stone lean-to, running the length of the little building's south side. A wood store, or something like it. They come back with two barrow-loads of logs, their breath frosting in the cold air.

I say to Cesca, 'How are you doing?'

I don't say it, but I'm feeling pretty prayered up. Thickly buttered enough that any passing angels would see the glow.

Cesca says, 'Maybe spend the day here? Go back this evening?'

That takes me aback. Really? Inside this pretty, rich art student there is a spiritual seeker, a pious quester after truth?

I think I do a double-take, but say, 'Yes, great. A girl can't have too many canticles, right?'

And we do it. The whole damn thing.

Every service. Every meal.

Between services, we work on the farm, mostly in the company of Brother Gregory and Brother Anselm. Gregory has a slightly detached quality. The air of a man who is already half in heaven. We help him mix lime mortar for a repair job on one of the outhouse walls, but leave the stone-work to him

Anselm is better. He's got that smiley, crinkly-eyed, welcome-welcome monky thing all right. But there's humour too. Good, ordinary, earthy humour. When we muck out the pigs, he scratches their backs and asks them how they are. When we give them their food – food which includes a three-quarter loaf of that heavy, dark barley-bread – he buries the loaf under some potato peelings and says, 'Don't want Brother Nicholas to get upset. He thinks we all love this stuff.' And when, as we're shovelling dirty straw into a barrow, he encounters a particularly loose piece of pig muck, he smears it out with the blade of his shovel and shows me that the thing is rich in barley seeds, polished by the gastric tract just the way that Carlotta's seed had been. I laugh, and he starts laughing, and Cesca, not quite sure why we're laughing, joins in, until the three of us are leaning on our spades and laughing till our sides hurt.

Anselm tells us that the monastery is mostly vegetarian. 'Bread and herbs during Lent. At other times, we really only eat meat on major feast-days. These pigs have it easy.'

He says that, and scratches their backs again.

Later, in the apple store with Cesca, checking the late-autumn harvest on their slatted racks, discarding any fruits that are turning bad, I show her pictures of Carlotta.

'This is her? The dead girl?'

'Yes.'

She looks at a few of them. Comments, 'She's nice-looking.'

'Yes. She had a nose job. Also cheek implants and lip-fillers.'

'Really?' Cesca raises her eyebrows and looks intently again at the pictures. Does a half-shrug. 'Well, she looks nice. Not overdone. Not all plasticky.' Then nods, dismissing the subject, I think, but also giving her approval.

I realise Cesca is somehow treating the dead woman as one of her own. Her class, her wealth.

That's not, per se, because of the surgery. There are any number of Welsh girls who get their orange sunbed tans, pumped-up boob jobs and fish-pout lips. These days, money doesn't define who has access to surgery, but Cesca's reaction tells me that there are more subtle indicators at work. Things that separate the right sort of surgery from the wrong sort and she clearly thinks Carlotta had the right sort. The sort you get if you have enough cash.

Pryce, the pathologist, had indeed got a consultant plastic surgeon to look at Carlotta, but the guy was strictly reconstructive only: fixing up burns and crash victims. On the aesthetic stuff, he was out of his depth and never pretended otherwise.

I laugh at myself silently, reminding myself once again that sometimes the most important clues lie right under your nose. Or, to be more precise, in the all-but-invisible white scar line under Carlotta's columella. Those things you don't always know how to interpret unless you find the right kind of expert guide.

'Thanks, Cesca,' I tell her. 'Thank you.'

Before compline that evening, we tell Father Cyril that we'll be leaving afterwards.

Cesca says, 'It's been *amazing*, Father.' Starts asking him about whether they 'do retreats'. Cyril laughs and says they *are* a retreat. Invites her to come any time. The two of them start discussing whether a week is enough or if two would be better. Whether a full-on silent fortnight would be too much, too fast. (Cyril says yes.)

We say goodbye to the other monks, who give us that two-handed clerical shake and more crinkle-eyed smiles. We blast through our last psalms and canticles and, on this occasion, I kyrie my eleisons with the very best of them.

Weirdly, I do feel more peaceful, I realise. Something about the repetitions of the day, the tolling bell, the simple, arduous farm-work. I don't really get on with all that praising the Lord business and even my mother, a committed chapel-goer, would, I think, be taken aback by quite how much psalming is involved in this monastic life, yet there's undeniably something in the recipe which works. Which breeds peace.

We drive back to Cardiff, in silence at first, but once we're back on the A470, I glance over at Cesca and say, 'Well?'

She smiles. 'That was fab.'

'Are you religious? I somehow didn't imagine—'

'Not really. No. But I've been thinking I should meditate more. I mean, I'm a creative person . . .'

She starts telling me about how she thinks her art and fashion work would be 'more authentic' if she was 'more centred. Mindful, you know.' She makes it sound like a splash of monasticism would be a good career move. A little shimmy round the back, a cunning dodge on the fast-track to success.

And it's a helpful insight actually. There was something glossy about Carlotta, something well-groomed. The perfect hair, the careful surgery. I couldn't quite get my head round her being there, in that monastery. The place seemed too remote, too rustic for a girl like her.

But maybe that was wrong. The more privileged a young woman's life, the harder it becomes to find those real highs. Any Cardiff girl of my acquaintance in childhood would have been thrilled at the idea that, one day, she might backpack round Thailand for two weeks, could fund a trip to Australia with temporary bar jobs. But what of the Cescas and – perhaps – the Carlottas? The girls for whom Thailand lies just a first-class flight and a luxury hotel away? For whom those things are already stale? The monastery at Llanglydwen offers something that a platinum bank card can't buy: a place that even Condé Nast has yet to find.

As we get closer to town, she puts the overhead light on. Re-ties her hair. Uses a small nail file to pick any pig-muck from her fingernails, smooth off any rough edges.

Back at Cardiff, I offer her a bed for the night, but she doesn't want it. Wants to drive on to her mother's house outside Llantwit. Resume her Condé Nast life.

We say goodbye. I do so almost tentatively. I still don't really know what our relationship is. But there's nothing tentative in her hug, her double-cheek kiss.

'That was fab, Ess. You're the best.'

Ess: meaning S, meaning Strange. An odd sort of compliment, but I'll take whatever's going.

She drives off telling me that she hopes 'you catch your bad guy'.

I go inside.

Drop my bag. Open the fridge door. Commune with the contents, but eat nothing. Put the kettle on. Try turning the living-room lights on, but that doesn't suit my mood, so I turn them off again.

Peppermint tea.

iPad.

Call up pictures of Carlotta's nose. As many angles as I can find.

Read a *Daily Mail* piece on noses which tells me that an American actress called Scarlett Johansson boasts the world's most-perfect specimen. Either her or someone called

Kate Beckinsale. I look at images of those people's noses, then compare them with Carlotta's and, because I'm being thorough, mine.

Go nose-blind. Go to bed.

14

Monday morning. The Operation April suite.

I'm not pixieing today, but I'm still the first person in. A pale-lemon light struggles in from the east, but we're on the dark side of this brooding cliff, and a deep trough of shadow divides us from the sunlight fidgeting in Bute Park.

I make tea.

Peppermint.

Green steam, fragrant and hot.

Stand at the window, searching through my bundle of emails. Find the one I'm looking for:

Dear Essylt,

No, this patient isn't one of mine, I'm so sorry to tell you. That rhinoplasty is absolutely spot on, a really fine job, I must say. The cheek implants are also outstanding. My congratulations to the surgeon when you find him!

With kindest wishes,

Anil Aggarwal

I check him out. The guy's a leading plastic surgeon at a big London teaching hospital, but spends two days a week on Harley Street earning crazy money for purely elective cosmetic work.

I call his office. His PA tells me he's consulting this evening from six to nine. I ask if I can have half an hour with him

120

immediately afterwards. She needs to check, but calls back, says yes.

Good. That's good. But what next?

At the far end of the room, we have photos of our Operation April targets. Our A-list:

IDRIS PROTHERO.

DAVID MARR-PHILIPS.

OWAIN OWEN.

NICK DAVISON.

GALTON EVANS – in jail.

BRENDAN RATTIGAN – dead.

We have a B-list too. Ben Rossiter, Trevor Yergin, a half-dozen others. And it's a B-list only because we have less data on them, less focus. The truth is, all fourteen men could be part of our conspiracy.

Standing at twenty-feet distance, I plant my feet a shoulder's-width apart, left foot a little forward. Right hand in the shape of a gun. Left hand supporting my wrist.

Fire off six imaginary bullets at Owain Owen. Six each for the other A-listers too.

Thirty-six bullets, thirty-six confirmed hits.

That end of the room is awash with imaginary blood and the groans of the dying. It's also suddenly full of DI Rhiannon Watkins who watches me complete my silent massacre.

'All done?' she asks as I drop my hands.

'Yes, ma'am.' I waggle my still-gunlike right hand at her. 'Magazine's empty.'

She doesn't smile exactly – smiles are anatomically difficult for her – but she does twist up her mouth in a way that causes the corners of her lips to rise and widen. Then asks about my weekend. I can't tell her about the monastery, so I tell her about Aggarwal instead. The meeting I've arranged for this evening.

She narrows her eyes, but I jump in before she can come over all budget-restrictiony with me.

'My time, ma'am. My petrol. I know it's a long shot.'

'OK. OK, Fiona, good.' She attempts her version of a smile again and again escapes without injury.

'And look, we've heard from the BKA. It's a no. I'm so sorry.'

I shake my head. I don't want her sorry. Even knowing that this was coming, it feels like a body blow.

'We'll be making an announcement later this week.'

I nod.

She inspects me a moment longer. Doesn't tell me what she finds. Just gives me, from her desk, a bulldog-clipped bunch of paper.

'Take a look at this. You might find it interesting.'

It's an intelligence briefing on the Bethan Williams inquiry. The senior investigating officer's private not-for-wider-circulation conclusions.

'They're sure it was this guy, Len Roberts,' she tells me. 'A straightforward sex crime. But no corpse, no evidence, no prosecution.'

'It would be nice to speak to him, though, ma'am. Maybe if I can find a free afternoon this week to go up there . . .?'

Watkins opens her mouth. She's about to say something about my other commitments. My Actions not completed, my tasks not done. But she drops it. Says, 'Fine. Just tell Burnett. Keep him in the loop. And . . . just . . .'

'Ma'am?'

'If we're packing up, let's pack it tidy.'

I nod. Do as she wants. Spend all that day putting our files into proper order. Writing summaries where work has been completed. Where things are still in progress, I write the kind of guidance notes that will make it easier to re-activate things down the line.

It's work I hate doing – burial work, grave-digging – but I do it all the same. Mess nothing up. Piss no one off. Say 'ma'am' or 'sir' at the appropriate times. Don't swear. Commit no more invisible massacres.

All that till five-thirty, then home.

Eat some tinned fish. A carrot. An apple.

In the violet darkness of my bedroom, in front of the mirror, I shoot another cluster of bullets at my own forehead. Six rounds, all on target.

That bulldog-clipped pile that Watkins gave me. It all rings true but all rings hollow too. It sounded like a truthful record of what the SIO had been thinking, of the intelligence and suspicions that can never be quite tidied up the way evidence can. But there was, somehow, a phoney quality to it. Phoney the way people are if you point a video camera at them and tell them to behave naturally.

And one other thing. Something that niggles.

It turns out that Burnett was one of the officers working on that inquiry. No surprise there: every detective in Carmarthen would have been involved. But why didn't he mention the case? The monastery is just three miles from Neil Williams's farmhouse. A mile and a bit from Len Roberts's place. Any normal copper would have commented on those coincidences, but Burnett didn't. Why not?

I fire six more rounds into the darkening mirror.

Squeeze the trigger, don't pull it.

Left foot slightly forward.

Soft hands.

Six more rounds, six more kills.

Then get in my car.

The M4 a grey highway through the dark. Then London. A city gathering itself in slowly intensifying rings. A beast imagining itself into being.

Northolt. Perivale. Uxbridge.

White City. Marylebone.

Arrive at Harley Street, glossy with high-end German cars. Park behind the discreet silver curves of an Aston Martin.

I find Aggarwal's office and give my name to a mouse-voiced receptionist, who sends me to sit in a high-ceilinged waiting room. Pale-green walls. Architectural prints.

I wait like a good girl. Shoot no one, break nothing.

At nine-forty, Aggarwal is ready for me.

He's tired, but affable. Says, 'So. Our beautiful rhinoplasty.'

I show him photographs. Hard copy, but also on my iPad. Give him the hard copy of the report we got from the plastic surgeon in Cardiff, but say, 'This guy's fairly old school. He doesn't do any aesthetic work.'

Aggarwal flips the report. Skimming it, not reading it. Says, 'This gentleman is probably a very fine reconstructive surgeon . . .'

I finish his sentence. 'But he knows bugger all about aesthetic rhinoplasty.'

Aggarwal laughs like I've said something funny. '*You* can say that,' he tells me, wagging a finger. 'I can only say that his experience lies in a different field.'

He continues to chuckle, but gets a plastic face from a shelf behind him. Pinky-brown plastic, the colour of a child's doll.

'OK, rhinoplasty for beginners, right?' He starts to talk me through the art and science of the nose job. He says, 'We look at the patient's face and try to calculate what is looking right for this face. What we can do within surgical limits. So, our modern approach is very patient-centred, very personalised, yes?, but we also have in mind our ideals of beauty. And these ideals, we can be measuring them very precisely.'

Using his plastic face to elaborate, he starts giving me a mass of data.

The ideal nasolabial angle. The perfect nasofacial angle. Length of the nose to height of face. Nasal width divided by facial width. Nasal tip to nasal length projections. All this and more. The desired 'profile view of the columella', what a good dorsum should and should not be getting up to.

These things, he tells me, are backed by data. Science, not art.

He tells me that most of Carlotta's angles and ratios are near to perfect and, where they aren't, why they work better for the rest of her face.

'For example, you have this problem that her face is a little wide maybe. A little round, a little full. She is a pretty lady, most definitely, but not perfect. So whoever designed this surgery made the nose just a little stronger, just a little fuller, than what is most ideally perfect, so it looks spot on for this face.' He tells me that the cheek implants would have been inserted, maybe at the same time as the rhinoplasty itself, in order to add structure to a slightly under-structured face. Talks about some specific technical challenges to this operation.

Concludes: 'This surgery is absolute A-grade. Top class, really.'

I say, 'It wasn't done in Britain.'

'No? I thought maybe one of my dear colleagues . . .' Aggarwal waves an arm in a way that encompasses Harley Street, the little cluster of doctored-up streets around it.

'Not unless they're actively lying to a police inquiry.'

'I don't think so. Me, I would be putting my hand up. Look here, this is my rhinoplasty.'

He's joking, but also serious. Top London doctors aren't going to mess up their businesses by refusing to co-operate with the police.

'And if not London . . .?'

'Oh, this is Hollywood grade, absolutely.'

'You mean *actual* Hollywood?'

Aggarwal backtracks a bit. He tells me that London is one of the world's leading centres for plastic surgery. Also, surprisingly, or suprisingly to me anyway, Rio de Janeiro and Buenos Aires. Apart from that – 'If you are looking for the best? If you don't mind top-dollar price, and I do mean *really* top dollar? – Hollywood and New York, of course.'

Carlotta doesn't quite look British but, despite the name I gave her, she doesn't look Hispanic either. Her blonde roundness doesn't suggest Spanish, Brazilian, Argentinian blood.

Aggarwal thinks the same.

He rubs his face. His tiredness surfacing as mine does.

'Look, I'll get you names. Doctors in New York and LA, the top ones. Don't forget to pass on my congratulations.'

Driving home, the motorway is long and empty and extends infinitely into night.

15

On Wednesday there's a cake-and-fizz thing, a farewell to
Operation April. Everyone is careful to say this isn't the end,
but it looks pretty fucking ended to me.

This is meant to be a party, but it feels like a wake.

I leave early, intending to drive home and smoke myself
stupid in the garden, but as I drive angrily up Pen-y-Lan Road,
trying to avoid the traffic on Eastern Avenue, stupidly pissed
off by the fact that other people have cars and are allowed to
drive them, I think, *Fuck it, I do have one live inquiry, don't I?*
A live inquiry with some actual, proper investigative work still
to be done.

I've turned the car round before I know it. Drive up, away
from the coast, into the hills. The hills around Llanglydwen.

Roberts's house.

This time, I arrive in the light. A fading late November day,
yes, and the mountains to the east roll upwards into heavy
cloud, but still: no need for torches. And in daylight I see
something I hadn't noticed last time. A wooden board nailed
to a gatepost. Crude red letters that say, 'house for sale' then
a mobile number. The number was painted too big to start
with, so the last few digits are squashed and hard to read. I try
what I think is the number, but get an unobtainable signal.

The cottage is as I saw it before. No car. No light. No heat.
No human presence.

I stand in the doorway, looking out. Quiet pastures

steepening to a little fringe of wood, the bare hills above. I don't know what a physicist would say, but time doesn't flow in these valleys the way it moves elsewhere. There's something so changeless here, something so little altered since the retreat of the glaciers, that I feel myself in a kind of permanent present. One that knits the modern, the medieval, the Roman, the pre-Roman.

The tremble of those many pasts is with me here. A faint turbulence that plucks at my skin, the hem of my coat.

From where I stand, I can see the hillside where Neil Williams has his farmhouse. Down the valley, I can just about see the monastery's squat tower, the scatter of houses that forms Llanglydwen. Aside from that, nothing. Green fields, gluey with mud around the gates and feeding places. Sheep. Hedges, mostly bare now, but holding a few last flares of field maple, the dark bronze of haw berries.

And a shack. A thing of old timber and tattered corrugated iron. A farm shed you'd say. A place to store straw or shelter animals. Except that those things don't need fire and this place has a thin plume of ascending smoke.

I change my shoes for the heavy walking boots I keep in the back of my car. Walk through a couple of fields towards the smoke. Sheep cluster around, hoping for food.

Black muzzles, white coats. Those disconcerting alien eyes. 'Hello?' I call as I approach. 'Hello?'

No answer.

The shack has a door. Corrugated iron over a clumsy wooden frame. There's a latch of bailing twine, but the door rests on the ground anyway. I rap on the metal, say 'Hello' again and enter.

A strange darkness within.

The orange glow of a wood fire. An earth-scented dampness. The place in shadow mostly – no light, no electric light – but cut about with scraps of illumination from outside wherever

128

the iron is rusting away or a join was poorly made.

By the stove, there's a man, doing something with a knife. He looks at me. Says nothing, but I can see the flash of his eyes, a movement of the mouth beneath a tangled beard.

Moving slowly, I walk towards him.

'Mr Roberts? Len Roberts, is it? I'm Fiona. Fiona Griffiths. From the police.'

Say that last bit with a glance backwards towards the door, my way out. I'm not sure what Roberts's feelings are about me and my kind, but if this encounter gets confrontational, I'd sooner that any rough stuff takes place outside.

He doesn't say anything, but I think his face twitches welcome. His hand too.

He's gutting some kind of animal, I realise. A badger, I think. There's a mess of blood and fur and a loose drool of guts.

'Badger, is it?'

'I took him in the wood there,' he says, gesturing through the wall. 'Proper big 'un, though he's got mange, here look.'

He holds up some scrofulous bit of fur, though what's mange and what's blood and what's just standard-issue badger, I find hard to tell in this dimness.

'You're not in the cottage, then?'

'No, no. No, that's on the . . . on the market now.'

He struggles to find the word 'market'. Roberts, I suspect, is a man who would always have been happier with badgers than property transactions.

'I saw the sign.'

'Aye.'

'Is it with an estate agent as well, maybe?'

'Ah, well, those people . . .'

I take that as a no. Roberts's hands go back to the butchery. He's deft with it. That knife, this carcass, here in the smoky dark.

There's a chair or stool of some kind. I grope for it, checking it's clear. The thing has some padded, velvety surface, like an old piano stool. I sit down.

'You've come about Bethan, I suppose.'

'Sort of. We found a body – not Bethan's – but some other young woman over in Ystradfflur. We haven't been able to identify her as yet.'

'Ystradfflur?'

'In the churchyard there. We found a body.'

Roberts's face moves darkly, but his face is deep in the shadows here and everything is dark.

He finishes his gutting. Stands up, finds a metal bowl from a crude wooden shelf off to the side – planks laid over a couple of old oil drums. Slithers the guts into the bowl.

'For Judy,' he says. 'For later.'

I stare at him, bemused. Then I get it. 'Judy. Your dog.'

'Little Jack Russell bitch. Her mother was a good 'un too. Eager, you know.'

'The woman we found. She wasn't murdered. Just died. Heart attack. She looked completely healthy, but she had a lung condition she may not even have known about. Her heart struggled – and bam! That was it. But somebody laid her out in the bier house in Ystradfflur. Candles, Bible, white dress. No sign of violence.'

Roberts is grinning now. White teeth, white eyes.

'Well, that weren't me. You can't pin that one on me.'

'No, I don't think we can. We're not even going to try.'

'All laid out with candles, you say?'

'Yes. I've got pictures if you want to see.'

He does. My iPad is in the car, so I go to get it. Walking back through these November fields. Bare hedges the colour of mink and woodsmoke. The sheep watch me closely, but are giving up on me as a source of food.

I get the iPad and return to find Roberts in a little allotment behind his shack. Leeks, parsnips, cabbage, kale, carrots. He's digging up a couple of swedes when I find him. Shakes off the loose soil, wipes the rest on his trousers. Holds up the muddy globes against the fading sky and says, 'I didn't know . . . Were you wanting to stay?'

I wasn't expecting the invitation and my reaction is a little slow to arrive. But arrive it does, and it's the right one.

'I can't stay the night, Mr Roberts, but I'd love something to eat.'

Roberts cuts a leek, loosens the earth around his carrots and pulls up a couple of big ones. He's a good gardener. The soil round here is mostly clay, but Roberts has his carrots on a slight bank, loosened with sand for better drainage.

He sees me looking. 'They don't like it heavy. They like it soft. These boys – ' he means the swedes – 'they want it wet and don't mind it heavy.'

He washes his vegetables in a barrel that collects rainwater from the roof. They're not clean, not remotely, but they are, I accept, much cleaner than they were.

We go in.

I'm not sure where the rest of the badger is now, but its two hind legs are in a big metal cooking pot. I show Roberts pictures of Carlotta. Her face. Her corpse. The crime scene photos. Roberts doesn't know how to swipe the screen to flip through the images, so I do it for him. Once, he tries doing it himself, but his fingers are so hardened by this life of his, the thickened skin and accumulated grime, that the screen doesn't recognise there's even a finger there. He might as well be poking with a stick.

'She wasn't hurt?'

'No.'

'No . . . no silly business? Nothing horrible?'

He means rape, I assume. 'No. Not that we can find.'

He nods, relaxes. 'Well. And you don't know who she is, you say?'

'No.'

'Imagine, eh? You being her mother or father. Having a little girl. Looking after her. All the way from a little *babi*.' He uses the Welsh word, not the English. The first syllable rhyming with *Ma* and *Pa*, not *say* or *hay*. 'All that and you don't even call you people when she gets taken.'

'And why would anyone do that, Mr Roberts? Keep their silence, I mean.'

He shakes his head. He doesn't have an answer. Starts cutting thick moon slices of swede into the bowl. The carrot, almost purplish in this interior twilight, follows. Then the leek.

I feel like I stumbled there. Asked the wrong question. But since I don't know the right one, I say, 'I know you were close to Bethan. Her father says you were a real friend.'

'Yes. We were . . . Bethan and I . . .'

He seems on the verge of saying something further, but doesn't. Adds a slop of water to the pan. Salt. Settles the pan on the stove, which is no more than a large, roughly cubic, metal container kept off the ground by a few breeze-blocks. The metal was painted once, but is so time-worn now that only a few flakes of dull white paint remain visible. A bendy metal flue pipe takes most of the smoke up and out of the room. Roberts feeds the fire, poking logs into its red and glowing heart. He adjusts things till he's happy, then steps back.

'He'll do.'

'Mr Roberts, I know we gave you a rough time back then. When Bethan was lost, I mean.'

'You were doing a job. I know it looked funny.'

'That doesn't mean it wasn't hard on you.'

Roberts's eyes flicker, unreadable. I'm very aware that I'm alone with this man. He's bigger than me, of course, and far

132

stronger. Also knows this shack, these fields, this valley. Is a dab hand with a knife.

I change the subject. 'The estate agents, let me guess. You asked them to list the house, but they wouldn't do it.'

'It's been *listed* for two years. Don't think any bugger's come to view it though.'

'And you'd stay here if it sold? I mean, that's the plan?'

Roberts nods, with a kind of muddled approval. As he sees it, I think, he can sell the house, stay living here in this shack, and have enough money for those things – salt, saw blades, nails, winter coats – that he can't make or kill or grow himself. And perhaps, yes, it's true that the estate agents are reluctant to help a local villain, but their task is hardly an easy one: selling a remote and collapsing cottage, whose nearest neighbour is a known badger-killer and suspected child-killer.

'You might want to heat the cottage. It feels a bit sorry for itself at the moment.'

'Yes, she does that.'

'It would look nicer tidy.'

'Aye.'

As we speak, a black, white and brown arrow hurtles into the room. Leaps onto Roberts's lap and vigorously licks the man's face. When the hello is over, another leggy jump takes her up to the shelf with her bowl on it. She slurps up her evening meal then, sitting beside Roberts, starts licking herself.

'Eager,' I say. 'She's certainly eager.'

'Aye.'

Roberts's eyes have a melty quality as he and the dog find their rhythm.

The dog, Judy, must have a good life, I reckon. Everything shared with her master. Same food, same bed, same fire.

Fresh guts for dinner and a whole world to run in.

Man and dog cuddle a bit, until Roberts decides our meal is done.

It's dark outside now and the room inside is almost pitch black. Roberts – for my sake more than his own, I think – fiddles around with an old Petzl headtorch, the kind of thing that climbers use, and plays with some wires down in the corner. To my surprise, a chain of fairy lights comes on overhead, the power coming from an old car battery.

'Get him topped up at the garage. They don't charge me none.'

Roberts hands me a spoon and divides the stew between two bowls, at least one of which, I can't help feeling, was last used by Judy. The meat is gamey and strong, but not unpleasant. Roberts asks, anxiously, if it's OK.

'Mr Roberts, I've never had a better bit of badger in my life.'

He laughs, in relief mostly. Tells me that badger is good, whereas fox, 'You have to lay him in the stream really. He can be a bit ripe if you take him green.'

We eat. We talk. We tickle Judy.

I get up to go. The fairy lights give enough illumination that I can see the shack interior properly for the first time. There's a bed loaded high with blankets and covers. For all that the stove provides warmth, the shack must be icy in winter, unthinkable in any wind.

Also a piano, an object even more incongruous than the fairy lights.

'Bethan,' I say. 'Bethan liked to play the piano. The Williamses didn't have one. You did. It was in your cottage back then, I suppose.'

'I don't play myself, but this was my grandmother's and then my mother's.'

'And you still keep it?' I think of the effort of bringing it down here, from the cottage to its new – and probably final – resting place.

'Oh, aye. Well, it's silly really. But I just think . . . if she ever comes back, I'd like her to know I'd been thinking about her.'

'And you think she could come back? That she's not dead?'

'She was never found, was she?'

I'm uncertain whether that's intended as a rhetorical question. After all, Roberts is isolated enough that he might well not know the answer. 'No, she's never been found.'

His teeth gleam in the light.

'Well, then. She could walk through that door just the way you did.'

'Len, did you sleep with her? Were you and she more than just friends?'

He hesitates at that. Hesitates, but says, 'A couple of times. She gave herself to me. I showed her the way. But we weren't like – a couple. Not that. I knew I was a bit too old for her. Bit wild. A countryman, you know? She wanted something different for herself.'

I thank him. Leave. Walk back through these fields, where a light frost begins to nip the grass.

If he's speaking the truth now, he lied to the inquiry at the time. Despite repeated interrogations, he swore that he and Bethan had only ever been friends. I should really make a written statement, right now, of Roberts's new story. Have him pulled in for another round of questions. But will that bring Bethan back? Explain the riddle of Carlotta's corpse?

I ask the sheep, and they tell me no.

Ask the moon, and it counsels silence.

16

Despite the eye-prickingly intense darkness of Roberts's shack, it's not actually late.

I get into my Alfa Romeo, whack the heating up and wonder what next.

Drive the short distance into Llanglydwen.

The village, such as it is, huddles just below the union of two streams. Waters joining and hurrying under the low, grey hump-backed bridge. Houses, mostly whitewashed. Some newer things in brick. The little village church, St Cledwyn's, and, opposite, one of those tiny pubs. The sort of thing you get in Wales, and maybe in Ireland or the highland parts of Scotland, but nowhere else. The kind of boozer that serves a dozen locals. Where everyone knows each other by their first name. That doubles as a post office and that sells bread and milk and stamps.

I drive the few hundred yards on to the monastery.

Grey stones under silver light. They'll be ringing the bell for compline soon, but I think I'll pass. I'd like to see the pigs again, scratch their piggy bellies, but I'll leave that for another day.

I drive on home.

Or rather: *intend* to drive home. Intend to drive home, have a bath, read a book, go to bed. To do all the regular things that a regular girl does without anxiety or complication. Only, as I draw close to Cardiff, Carlotta murmurs to me through dead lips and we find ourselves heading into the office instead.

Go into the Operation April suite. Check my emails.

I have an email from Aggarwal. The names of thirty-three international clinics, ones that he places at the very top of the rhinoplastic tree. To those names I add another hundred and twelve names from a *Vogue* feature on plastic surgery, and start pumping out emails. Copy and paste. 'Detective Sergeant Fiona Griffiths from the South Wales Police . . . seeking to identify a young woman found dead under circumstances that remain unexplained . . . have reason to believe that the deceased may have been a patient at your clinic.'

Blah, blah. My email isn't exactly truthful, but isn't quite false either.

Copy. Paste. Adjust. Send. Repeat.

Forty-two emails sent. Another hundred-odd to go.

I don't have the main lights on. I didn't want their oppressive overhead brightness. So I work by the light of my desk lamp alone. A quiet pool in this dark room.

And, as I work, I'm suddenly aware that I'm not alone.

Watkins is standing in the light of the open door, a flat cardboard packet in her hand.

'You still here?' she asks.

I wave my hands. Stupid question.

She comes over, looks at my emails.

'It seems like a long shot,' she says, but there's a clear uncertainty in her voice.

'Is it? *Someone* did the surgery. In the end, we just have to knock on enough doors . . .'

Something in Watkins's face softens. It's stupid, but she had an affection for me once, an infatuation even, and I have this idea that she wants to bend down and stroke my nose.

'Aggarwal told me that my nasolabial angle was textbook.' I

show Watkins my face in profile so she can admire it properly. 'That bit there is called the columella,' I add, pointing.

'Well, you're right. It's probably worth a little more research,' says Watkins, struggling to ignore the perfection of my columella.

And as she struggles, my computer bleeps to announce incoming messages.

Twelve unread messages. Eleven automated responses. 'Thank you for your message, our office is now closed.' That kind of thing.

But one that's not like that. From a human, not a robot. From a doctor, not a mere mortal. And from a Hollywood clinic, a proper one. A place that caters to movie stars and the mega-rich.

Dear Sergeant Griffiths

Many thanks for reaching out to us – and I'm only regretful that the occasion is such a tragic one. I can indeed confirm the identity of the deceased as Alina Mishchenko, who was a patient with us just two years ago. She was a beautiful person and touched all of us with her confidence and poise. I'm sure she will be sorely missed. I've attached Ms Mishchenko's contact details to this email and I hope that this assists you in locating her family and breaking the very sad tidings to them.

In the meantime, all of us at the clinic here stand ready to assist in any way that we can – and, of course, we send her family all of our prayers and sympathy in their time of need.

With our deepest sympathies,

Dr. Grant Peterson

Alina. Not quite as good as Carlotta, somehow, but I suppose I should allow her the right to her own name. My own, dear, private Carlotta gives way to the slightly frostier, more public Alina.

Mishchenko. A Ukrainian name. The address which Alina

gave the clinic was in Kiev. Pechersk Raion: according to Google, one of the city's more prestigious neighbourhoods. Google Earth shows me a street of large villas, compounds almost. High walls and security gates.

High walls, security gates and a Hollywood surgery that caters to the super-rich.

With Watkins breathing over my shoulder, I browse further, every inch the modern detective. Google finds me a list of Ukraine's richest people. At place twenty-eight on the list, there is a male Mishchenko in his late fifties. If I understand Google's machine-translation well enough, the guy has two sons and a daughter. Except that, I'm guessing, he now has only sons.

Eleven-thirty.

Lights dim in the corridor outside. Lights dim in the slumbering offices below. In Bute Park, inky and silent, night animals prowl.

Fox. Owl. Mink. Bat. Stoat.

And we have our kill too, our first scent of carcass.

Watkins says, 'If this checks out . . .'

She doesn't finish her sentence.

I nod, but say nothing.

If this checks out then, on top of our various other mysteries, we now have one more: The Mystery of Why a Ukrainian Oligarch's Daughter Should Choose to Die in Remote Mid-Wales.

Watkins clicks around on my computer, trying to find a picture of Alina Mishchenko, but the relevant websites are in Ukrainian and we can't even read the script.

She pushes back from the screen, with a sound that is half tiredness, half that snorty senior officer annoyance.

'Work this through with Burnett,' she tells me. 'It can wait till Monday,' she adds, knowing that waiting is never my strong point.

'Yes, ma'am.'

'And look, I came in to give you this. I was going to leave it on your desk.'

Watkins hands me the cardboard packet she came in with.

I open it up.

Photos. Fourteen of them. Full colour, ten by sixes. Our Operation April targets, the full set of them, A-list and B-list.

'Target practice,' says Watkins, as close as she ever gets to an actual joke.

I say thank you. That and goodnight. Wave to Watkins as she leaves.

At the door, she turns and says, 'Fiona, this . . .' Then stops. Even in the dimness of this room, in the feeble light of the corridor outside, I can see calculation in her eyes. For a moment, I think she's going on to say something further, but then her look changes and she just says, 'This was good work, well done.'

I nod. That wasn't what she'd been going to say, but I think I know what she'd been going to say anyway.

Watkins leaves.

In Bute Park, foxes kill things. Owls devour field mice in a single gulp.

And I'm alone in a dim and silent office, with the corpse of a dead girl, and a conspiracy of photos.

Stay there until something shifts, then drive home quietly, the speedometer needle sometimes within the zone of legal for as much as a minute or two at a time.

Prepare for bed, or try to, but my attention keeps on being tugged sideways by Alina-Carlotta, who seems closer to me now than ever.

I feel her presence so strongly that when I brush my teeth I can't remember whose face I'm looking at in the mirror. Don't know if I'm me looking at Carlotta, or Carlotta looking at me. I know that only one of us is dead, but for a few troubled minutes can't remember which one of us got lucky.

17

Monday.

I'm in Carmarthen shortly before eight. Burnett doesn't arrive until nearer nine. I watch him getting out of his car. There's a heaviness to him sometimes, more strongly present when he's unobserved. When he's with me, or when I see him with other people, he shakes himself into a brighter, lighter, higher-energy self.

I observe him briefly, then bound out of my car to start improving his day.

'Good morning, sir,' I tell him. 'I brought you caffeine, sugar and hydrogenated fats.'

I wave a paper bag at him, full of the kind of baked goods that his doctor probably warns against. A cup of coffee that might still have been warm if Burnett had arrived at a more diligent hour.

'Good morning, Fiona,' he says, capably hiding his excitement at having his day improved. 'To what do I owe the pleasure?'

'Our case, sir. Our corpse. The beautiful corpse of Ystradfflur.'

We go into the building. Up a flight of stairs.

Pausing on the landing he tells me, 'We don't have a case. We don't have a crime. We don't have an investigation. We don't even have any grieving relatives. Not ones who can be bothered to pick up a phone, at any rate.'

'That's harsh, sir. Maybe they're grieving a lot and picking up the phone a lot too. Maybe they're out of their heads with worry.'

We stomp along a corridor to his office. He doesn't invite me to sit, but that's because we're such close colleagues already, he feels able to dispense with the niceties.

I sit. Get horrible baked things out of their paper wrappers and arrange them beneath the glare of his desk lamp. The flaking icing sugar looks like peelings of skin, scabrous and fragile under the light.

'I shouldn't,' he says, but does.

'We've got an ID.'

He stares at me, wondering how come I've got the information before him.

'Missing Persons?'

'Nope. Rhinoplasty.'

I push a bunch of paper at him. The email from Grant Peterson. Bits printed off the Internet. A couple of pages put together over the weekend by some analysts at the NCA.

Not much, but it's a start.

There's a profile of Volodymyr Mishchenko, the man I presume to be Alina's father, taken from a Ukrainian business newspaper and translated by someone at the NCA.

The guy made his money in 'extractive industries', which seems to mean mostly iron ore and a bit of manganese. Estimated wealth: $65 million, but with the comment, 'This figure should be taken as a very approximate guide only. The fact is that there is very little financial transparency in the Ukraine and Mishchenko's real wealth might be a multiple of this figure.' In 2006, the guy bought a house in Chelsea for £6 million.

Pictures too. Of Volodymyr, who just looks ordinary. One of those solid-looking faces. Not chubby exactly, nothing like that, but there's a sort of Welsh stockiness in the bone structure. The sense that you wouldn't have to scratch far back into the guy's ancestry before you found a brood of peasant farmers. Men trudging behind the plough. Headscarfed women bending over the turnip harvest.

The mother – no surprise – is younger. A glamour puss doing her best to keep time at bay. The photo we have of her shows her in a golden dress at some kind of charity event. Not a trophy wife exactly, but certainly one who knows what's expected of her and who does her best to fill the role.

And the daughter. Alina. The NCA doesn't have, or doesn't yet have, a great photo. But from the same charity event, they truffled up a shot of Alina in a little black dress, glass of champagne, laughing at something off-camera. Burnett studies it closely, then says, 'What do you think?'

I say, 'Yes. Not absolutely definitely, but I think yes, that's her.' The girl I spent one beautiful night with.

There's a whole computer thing you can do, forensic facial mapping, which takes a whole host of facial measurements and determines, in theory, whether a given photo is or is not of a given subject. The trouble is that those things only work if you have a half-decent photo to work from, and this one of Alina probably isn't good enough.

Burnett thinks the same.

He turns to a sheet at the back of the NCA package, marked 'Known Travel Movements'.

The whole family entered the UK, travelling first class on British Airways, on 22 August of this year. Father, mother, Alina, the two sons. The father returned briefly to the Ukraine a fortnight later, and the two sons took the train to Paris, but then the two parents spent most of September in London, before flying back on the 29th.

Alina isn't recorded as having left the UK.

I found Carlotta's corpse on 28 October.

'So. Interesting.'

I nod.

Burnett turns back to the top sheet of the package. Grant Peterson's emails with Alina's contact data.

Data that includes a phone number.

Burnett gives a little half-shrug, fills his hand with more pastry, and calls the number, phone on speaker.

A few rings rattle our silence, then a voice answers.

Burnett tells it, 'This is Detective Inspector Alun Burnett of the Dyfed-Powys Police. Is that Mrs Mishchenko?'

It isn't, of course. It's a flunkey. A flunkey who says something to us in Ukrainian, then passes us on to someone else, a higher-up flunkey, one with reasonable English.

Burnett makes his request again. No *please*s. No making nice.

'May I ask what matter this may be regarding?' says the flunkey.

'No.'

The flunkey isn't sure how to react. Has to go off somewhere to consult.

For a full five minutes, we listen to silence. The little gather of electrical crackle which is all that tells us of the fifteen hundred miles, underground and undersea, that separates us.

Then a man's voice, strong and confident.

'This is Volodymyr Mishchenko.'

Burnett re-introduces himself. Says, 'We have information regarding your daughter.'

'Yes?'

Burnett pauses. That little, police-ish squeeze of control, a reminder of where the power lies. Then: 'I'm very sorry, Mr Mishchenko. I'm very sorry indeed. But I have to inform you that we have found a dead body, which we believe to be that of your daughter. In plain English, I believe your daughter is dead.'

There's an *ah* from the other end of the phone. A short,

sharp expression of something inescapable. An expression whose pain travels those fifteen hundred underground miles without losing even a sniff of its energy.

Burnett lets that energy dissipate a moment, then says, 'Your daughter *is* missing, yes?'

'Yes.'

'Has been missing for some time?'

'Yes. Yes, she has.'

Here, in our Carmarthen office, we exchange glances. Until this phone call, it had remained quite possible that our Californian nose doctor had simply misidentified Carlotta. Perfectly possible, indeed, that I'd driven this whole inquiry down a muddy dead-end track, simply because I was too fixed, too obsessive to let a good corpse escape my grasp.

But Mishchenko's reactions more or less kill that hypothesis. It's clear that he had almost been expecting – almost wanting? – this call.

But, though Burnett is good, Mishchenko is hardly a pushover.

He asks for more information, asks to know the details.

Burnett says, 'Mr Mishchenko, I'm very sorry, but we don't yet know that you're the father. I'm afraid we will need you and your wife to give us a formal ID.'

A tiny pause, then Mishchenko: 'Good, OK, I understand. You can send through photo and my wife and I—'

'Mr Mishchenko, we can't release the body for burial without a positive ID. That means – I'm sorry, sir – you'll need to be here in person. Our coroner will insist.'

That's not true, in fact, but it's close enough to serve. And Mishchenko gives way, almost without further resistance. There's a brief pause, one where the silence creaks with his thinking, but when he speaks, he simply says, 'OK. OK, we come.'

Burnett signs off, then looks up at me with a look of

triumph. He wasn't, I can see, expecting this outcome.

Nor was I. As well as triumph, there's a brief dart of something else in Burnett's face. A savage pleasure. I think of Len Roberts as he skinned and gutted his badger. That wild look, that quickly moving blade.

He had his kill and we, for the first time, have the scent of ours.

18

The Mishchenkos come, and come fast. Fly out the next day, Tuesday. Make an appointment to see us on Wednesday.

See us, that is, in Cardiff not Carmarthen, to Burnett's grumbly annoyance. It's ultimately his call, of course, but Carlotta's corpse is still here in the Cardiff mortuary and it makes sense to interview the parents while they're still in the shock of that contact. Not just that, but we have more resources of every sort than does Carmarthen, including – sort of – a Ukrainian speaker, so Burnett arranges things for Cardiff, then grumbles at having done it.

I don't care. He can grumble.

I take the parents to see their daughter's corpse. The parents, Volodymyr and Olexandra Mishchenko, plus a lawyer they've brought with them from London. A British citizen of Ukrainian origin, Anna Tymczyszyn.

The father looks like he did in his photo, the way he sounded on the phone. Confident, alpha-male-ish. Late fifties, but exuding enough authority to make up for any loss of energy.

The mother, Olexandra, is more interesting. She's nervous. Unsettled and unhappy. Plainly dislikes the mortuary's grimly clinical surroundings. The strangely polished, unsettlingly lit rooms where our British corpses come to rest.

For all her grief, she remains self-possessed. She's older than she looked in that NCA folder – our information has her

148

age at forty-eight – but she's ridden the waves of time the way she'd have wanted to. Good skin, good hair. No doubt plenty of surgical support as well. The same blonde roundness as her daughter, though dried out a little by years and sun and diets. She's wearing a dark-grey dress and matching jacket. A black pearl necklace, half obscured.

A mortuary assistant prepares the corpse on a gurney. Unveils her.

That jabbing *ah* again. Volodymyr, and Olexandra too. The mother's shock is almost instantly replaced by a dissolution of tears. An undoing.

I feel a stupid ache of jealousy. This may be *their* daughter, but she is *my* corpse. It wasn't them who kept vigil through that first windswept night of Carlotta's death. Not them who tracked this woman by the rhinoplasty scar beneath her almost-perfect nose.

I want to ask the parents to step back. Want to take my rightful place by the dead woman's hair. Feel its fall again. The icy smoothness of her folded hands.

But I don't. I'm good. Every inch the calm professional.

The parents give us a formal identification, then Tymczyszyn and I stand back. Clones of each other, almost. Pencil skirts, matching jackets, dark court shoes, unfussy white shirts. Tymczyszyn's suit is midnight black, mine only charcoal grey, but we look like what we are. Professional escorts at this grim rite. Sombre, respectful, paid.

The parents take twenty minutes – longer than most, much longer – then pull away. Volodymyr wants to come straight to Cathays, get our interview over and done with, but Olexandra needs time. A fancy lunch somewhere, so she can cry into folded linen, re-do her make-up away from these mortuary smells, the silent dead.

I don't want to pause, but there's no force I can apply so, out in the car park, I negotiate a new interview time with

Tymczyszyn, then watch the three Ukrainians vanish in the lawyer's Audi.

I get back to an angrily impatient Burnett.

He stares out through the internal glass wall of our little conference room, the semi-opened blind. We're on the second floor here, my normal working space, not the upper floor where Operation April once happened.

'Thing is, it's this sort of thing that tends to piss us off in Dyfed-Powys. We get a case. We work it properly. Then all of a sudden the key interviews are happening in Cardiff. The times get changed. I'm kept waiting around. And, in the end, whose case is this?'

He's not angry really – knows I couldn't have done otherwise – just wants to vent.

I say, 'Bethan Williams.'

He stares at me, says nothing.

I go on: 'Because, you see, I could say something a bit similar to you. The file on the Bethan Williams case tells us that the guy co-ordinating the search teams back then was one DS Alun Burnett. And if I were you, I'd have been wondering if the unknown dead girl of Ystradfflur was in any way related to the missing presumed dead girl of Llanglydwen. I'd probably have been thinking that even more, given that the dead girl of Ystradffur appears to have spent time in Llanglydwen a mere day or two before her death. What's more, I'd probably have thought about sharing those thoughts with a keen young detective sergeant from South Wales who was trailing around with me at the time.'

Burnett lowers his eyebrows, till his eyes almost vanish. If the eyes are windows to the soul, then these are gun-slits.

'The two cases,' he says. 'They're not related.'

'Missing girls. Same area. One dead, the other presumed dead.'

'One local girl, a hay merchant's daughter. The other one

some Ukrainian trillionaire. That's hardly the same.'

I don't say anything, but my face doesn't agree.

Burnett waits for me to crumple before his great inspectorial authority but, when the crumple fails to happen, says, 'With Bethan Williams, we basically know who the perpetrator was. We didn't have enough to bring a prosecution, but that doesn't mean the guy wasn't guilty.'

'No body. No weapon. No confession. No evidence. That's a Dyfed-Powys thing, is it?'

Burnett taps rapidly on the table. If he were in his office in Carmarthen, he'd be up, prowling around, fiddling with coffee mugs and drumming at the window. I wonder if it's humane to keep him here, out of his natural habitat.

Eventually he comes to a decision. 'The file. I assume you've read it?'

'Yes.'

'OK. Going on what that says, I'd think the same as you. I'd think, Len Roberts, yes probably guilty, but we can't prove it, so we have to say we don't really know. But the file doesn't tell you what happened, not really.'

'And if it did?' I whisper.

'Look, this is the Breacon Beacons,' says Burnett. 'Home of the Who Dares Wins brigade.'

Who Dares Wins: the motto of the Special Air Service, the country's elite Special Forces unit. The corps is headquartered just over the border in Hereford, but the countryside there is all a bit orchardy and gentle for the games those folks like to play, so they use the Brecon Beacons as their primary training ground.

'OK.'

'And it so happens that Bethan Williams goes missing just around the time that the SAS have a couple of platoons engaged on a survival and evasion training module. Right there, in the hills up around Llanglydwen. Now, we don't

151

have some kind of special hotline telling us what those boys are up to. And vice versa. They don't know what we're doing. So for maybe twenty-four hours, thirty-six even, we're doing our stuff – looking for the Williams girl, going house to house, all of that – and they're up on the hills doing theirs.

'Anyway. It turns out that, back in Hereford, one of those SAS boys actually lives in the real world, because he hears about Bethan Williams on the news and thinks, hang on a bit, we've got two dozen of the country's finest on the hills around that damn valley, maybe we could help out.

'So. Conversations start. They agree to turn their survival exercise into something of practical value. They start looking out for us. They've got nightscopes, cameras, God knows what. And, of course, those boys are expert in camouflage and evasion and all that. They'll find you, but you'll never find them.'

Burnett stops, although his story isn't finished.

I say, guessing, 'They didn't find anything. Bethan Williams never left the valley.'

'Correct.'

'But maybe she left before the SAS started looking. Maybe she just got fed up living at home, hopped on a bus to London, and was a hundred miles gone before anyone put out an alert.'

'That's what you'd think. What we thought. Except those boys on the hills had already collected a whole lot of pictures during their S&E exercise. They passed everything to us. We analysed it and – *bam*!'

'Bam what?' I say. 'Bam who?'

'Bam, footage of Len Roberts with Bethan Williams. Crossing a field up to some woods, at night. That was at a point where we'd already sealed off the roads. The SAS lads were all over the hills. There was no exit from the valley. *None*. Because of the communications issues right at the start of our whole co-operation process – you know, just boring

152

things, like getting new instructions out to their units, getting their pictures downloaded and analysed – it meant we saw the pictures of Roberts and Williams too late to do anything.

'Obviously, as soon as we saw the images, we grabbed Roberts and jumped on him hard. But it was at least sixteen hours after the pictures had been taken. He told us nothing, and those sixteen hours would have given him plenty of time to rape, kill and bury that girl. We kept watching the whole damn valley. Hills, roads, everything, for another two weeks just in case. Did the last week in total blackout, so it looked to every ordinary person like we'd just packed up and gone away. If the girl had just been holed up somewhere, waiting to run, she'd have run then. And she didn't. Because Roberts had killed her.'

I nod.

Roberts is a countryman, of course, and one who knows that valley and those hills better than anyone. If it was just a question of *him* having the skills to evade the SAS – well, you'd have to allow the possibility. But taking Bethan Williams with him? A girl who didn't really like those wilder country things? Not a chance.

I say, 'And the file? The one I read. It's because those SAS boys . . .'

'Like to stay very well under the radar? Yes. Those files basically carry a truthful account of the case, except that they make no mention of SAS involvement. But they were there all right and they're how we know that Roberts was the perpetrator.'

I balance all this out in my mind. It makes sense of why that file felt a bit phoney. It felt that way because it *was* phoney. A careful balance of truth and discretion.

And on the whole, yes, you'd have to say that Roberts was the most likely villain: the odds would certainly point in that direction. I can see that, yes, Dyfed-Powys were right not to attempt prosecution. They just had too little to go on. But I also think that, no, the evidence doesn't prove what Burnett wants it to prove. The evidence only actually proves those things that Roberts has never denied: that he was close to Bethan, that she trusted him, that he sometimes prowls that valley at night.

We coppers like to have facts we can fit together. This man, that crime scene, this piece of DNA. Bish, bash, bosh. Evidence so tight there's no wiggle room.

And here – well, the wiggle room, like it or not, is there. The facts almost, but don't quite, prove a case.

I say, 'You didn't know she was some Ukrainian trillionaire when we found her. Roberts must have flashed up as a possibility then.'

'Yes. But she hadn't been interfered with. There hadn't been violence. Those things didn't sit with the Roberts/Williams case. And – ' he wrinkles his face and narrows his eyes, the classic warning signs of impending Polician Humour – 'she was clean. Clean and tidy. Roberts couldn't have achieved that outcome even if he'd wanted to.'

That makes a kind of sense I suppose, even if I'm still pissed off with Burnett for holding back on me.

We fall into silence.

Burnett prowls. Mutters, 'Wish they'd get a bloody move on.'

The office is mostly empty. An empty whiteboard. A window. Desk, chair, phone. And the phone rings. We both stare at it.

I pick up.

It's the front desk. Telling us that the Mishchenkos have arrived. That they're being directed down to the interview rooms.

I say OK. Hang up. Burnett stares a question at me.

I say, 'We're on.'

154

His grumbly discontent fades into a half-smile.

I say, 'Time to beat up a couple of millionaire Ukrainians. Dyfed-Powys versus South Wales. Bet you we can hit harder.'

Burnett grins. 'Who's on the South Wales team? Who am I up against?'

I show him. Me. Five foot two inches of raw South Wales power.

Burnett laughs softly and play-punches me on the shoulder. It's a push more than a hit and he doesn't use his full strength, or anything like it. Even so, the force of the blow shoves me against the wall and I have to put out both hands to avoid falling.

'Dyfed-Powys against South Wales, sergeant? You're on. You're bloody on.'

19

The interview starts the way all interviews should: with nothing at all.

We gather behind one-way glass and simply watch.

Present on our side of the glass: Burnett, me and a couple of uniformed constables, one from Burnett's force, one from ours. Those people, plus also Tomasz Kowalczyk, our man in the print room. Tomasz is a native Polish speaker, studied Russian at school and university and, though he has no actual grounding in Ukrainian, swears to us that the language is halfway between the two.

We're taping everything, of course, and will get it all properly translated in due course, but for now Tomasz is a more than handy substitute.

After five minutes, he tells us, 'They complain about the chairs.'

Seven minutes: 'Also no window.'

Eleven minutes: 'They not like waiting.' He laughs. 'Stupid Ukrainian fuckers.'

I've never heard Tomasz swear before and I'm not quite sure what to make of it now. Partly, it's just excitement at being allowed out of the print room, but presumably too one of those dark, Slavic enmities. One of those things that originated when some medieval king slaughtered some other king's peasants. Or vice versa. Or whatever.

Something that Welsh history is entirely free of, anyway.

At fifteen minutes, Burnett says, 'OK, let's do it.'

I say to the constable, the South Wales one, 'Get them coffee. Interview coffee, not the real stuff. And get them swabbed.'

He scurries off. 'Interview coffee' means the rubbish sort. A thin, brown, artificial fluid in a plastic cup that keeps looking like it intends to cut and run.

The guy delivers the coffees. Produces a couple of cheek-swabbing kits and asks the two principals to supply specimens.

A brief flurry of Ukrainian.

Tomasz: 'They not like. Want to know what is for.'

In the interview room, Anna Tymczyszyn – mid-thirties, clipped, uptight – says, 'My clients would like to know the purpose of these swabs.'

The constable ignores the lawyer and addresses the parents. He speaks slowly, as though speaking to simpletons. 'It's for identification purposes. To confirm the identification already made.'

More Ukrainian. Tomasz listens darkly but says nothing.

Tymczyszyn consents to the swabs, but tries to stipulate what the data can and can't be used for. The constable gives a that's-above-my-pay-grade shrug and collects the swabs anyway.

Volodymyr says, 'When will this thing start? We've been waiting twenty minute already.'

The constable says, 'Two minutes. *Literally*. Just two minutes.'

We give them another five, then Burnett says, 'Shall we?' and we start for real.

We go in. Introductions. Terse non-apology for the delay.

Volodymyr: 'You can tell us about our daughter? What is happened to her?'

Burnett: 'Yes.'

I get out a notepad and pens. 'Sorry. Some boring

preliminaries.' Roll my eyes. 'Can I have your full names, please?'

Take their names, ask them to spell them out, letter by letter. The name of their daughter. Their sons. Dates of birth. Place of birth. The three kids are born in Kiev, but the two parents were born out of town and I make them spell out their birth-towns letter by letter, make a mistake, then do it all over again.

'Sorry.'

Passport numbers. The Cyrillic lettering confuses me and I take the wrong number and have to redo it.

'Sorry.'

Burnett, who's starting to enjoy this, calls for someone to take a copy of the passports. It takes two minutes for our guy to come back – he's still behind the glass with Kowalczyk, and under strict instructions to do nothing fast. When he arrives, he takes the passports, tells us that the copier is broken but he'll see if he can find one that's working.

I make a kind of *eek* expression and mouth the word, *Sorry.*

Do that, then, timidly smiling, ask, 'Was your flight over OK?'

Olexandra turns to her husband and says something in low, rapid Ukrainian. He doesn't shift his glance from us, but does say, 'We have come here, very open, very fast, because you have information for us. If you need passport and DNA, is OK too. But we do ask you tell us your informations. For many week, my wife is very fearing and now we just want to know everything.'

Burnett: 'Very open? Good. Let's start with that, shall we? In fact, let's start right from the beginning, if we can. When did you last see your daughter, Mrs Mishchenko?'

Glance at husband, then: 'At the end of September. The twenty-eight.'

'Where?'

158

'At home in London. We had a farewell supper. Volodymyr and I were leaving next day for Ukraine.'

'Without your daughter?'

'She is twenty-three. She has her own life.' Her lips move as she realises that she got her tense wrong, but can't bring herself to correct it.

'So she didn't accompany you. What did she do?'

Quick little shrug. A glance upwards and sideways.

'She stays with friend in London. Then they go to Southampton. Idea is they stay on a . . .'

Olexandra doesn't find the word that she wants, says it in Ukrainian, and makes a rocking motion with her hand.

I say, 'Yacht? She boarded a yacht?'

Volodymyr, wanting to take control, says, 'Correct. Yacht is belonging to a good friend, very safe.' Olexandra, relieved to pass the burden to her husband, sits back. Touches the string of pearls at her neck.

Burnett doesn't accept the buck-pass. Directing himself still to Olexandra, he asks for the name of the friend in London. The address. The phone number. How many days Alina stayed there. Whether there was phone contact during that time. When Alina moved on to Southampton. Whose car they went in. Who owned the yacht. The name of the yacht. The name of the owner. The name of the skipper. Who else was on board. Names. Contact information. Any phone details.

Olexandra speaks. I take notes.

We don't go gentle. On the one hand, these are grieving parents and we need to act respectfully. On the other hand, these are parents who never reported their daughter missing and who, far from pouring out their unhappy tale to our open ears, seem unnaturally guarded and strategic about what information they care to give us. If they are withholding something – and it seems clear that they are – we'd be derelict if we didn't work hard to get the information.

Because tired and irritated people are more likely to spill whatever it is they're trying to hold on to, I allow my fumbles and misunderstandings to continue. Once, irritated, Olexandra reaches for my notepad and says, 'Here. I can write.'

Burnett raises his eyebrows to their maximum extent and says, 'You want to write? Do you want to conduct this interview? May I remind you, we're only in this situation because we didn't get a phone call telling us when your daughter went missing.'

He pushes his chair back and offers Olexandra the chance to swap places.

She looks tearful – has actual tears in her eyes – and throws a pleading look at Tymczyszyn. Mutters something in Ukrainian.

Tymczyszyn says, 'My clients are here of their own free will. Please, you have promised to share your information with us. My clients are understandably anxious and they had a long flight to be here with you. My clients want to be as helpful as possible, but they do ask for whatever further information you can offer.'

'For example?'

A quick rat-a-tat-tat of Ukrainian, then, 'Was Alina interfered with? Had she been sexually molested?'

'No. Not that we could tell, and certainly not shortly prior to her death.'

'But she *was* murdered?'

An interesting question that. I feel the sideways dart of Burnett's eyes at me, but he addresses Olexandra.

'Mrs Mishchenko, may I ask why you are assuming murder?'

She flicks her eyes at her husband, who says, 'Our daughter was missing. We were very concerned. We fear the worst.'

Burnett says, enumerating possibilities on his thick fingers, 'Car accident. Heart attack. Drug overdose. Falling off a yacht. Joined a cult. Run away with a new boyfriend. Oh,

I don't know, lightning strike, we've had those before.' He watches the two parents and lets the room swell with silence. 'Yet you assumed murder. Why?'

Volodymyr starts to speak, but Burnett interrupts him.

'Mrs Mishchenko?'

In a tiny voice, she says, 'We don't assume. Just worry.'

Burnett nods, like that was a sensible answer. 'Ah, yes. You were worried, so you naturally assumed your daughter was murdered.' Again, he lets the silence expands. Only cuts it off when he sees Tymczyszyn about to leap in.

'Mr and Mrs Mishchenko, your daughter was not murdered. She had a lung condition which placed a strain on her heart. She may well have felt some breathlessness, perhaps a little chest pain. Then, I'm afraid, there was a complete failure of the right ventricle. Death would have been very swift and, I expect, completely painless.'

There's a quick exchange between husband and wife. Some look, definitely, of surprise, even perplexity. Then more rapid-fire Ukrainian. Then Tymczyszyn comes back with her line about her clients being present of their own free will and listing a whole host of further questions.

Burnett nods. Long you've-made-a-good-point-there nods.

He stares down at her business card. 'Miss . . . Tym Cwsyn,' he says, neatly fitting her name into something Welsh, or Welsh enough.

She wonders whether to adjust his pronunciation, but decides against. A good call.

Burnett: 'Absolutely. You're quite right. Your clients are here of their own free will.' He waves a big hand at the door. 'If they wish to leave, they can do so at any time. In the meantime, if you don't mind, we'll collect the information which would have been very helpful had it been offered at a much earlier stage in our investigation.'

And on we go.

Names, places, phone numbers, dates.

On the other side of the glass, in the viewing room, the two constables will be starting to get those things checked. Seeking to verify facts or prove them false. Their half of this game is at least as important as the one we're leading.

The story, as it emerges, is this. Alina stayed with a friend in London overnight, then drove down to Southampton, intending to cruise down to the French Mediterranean coast, from where she would, when she felt like it, fly back to Kiev.

It turned out, however, that the yacht had a problem with one of its engines and, for reasons that aren't entirely clear, Alina chose to return to London instead, staying partly with friends, partly at her parents' Chelsea house. The Mishchenkos didn't keep close tabs on their daughter's movements. As they say, Alina was twenty-three and perfectly able, in theory, to look after herself. Their last contact with her was 5 October. They say they didn't start to be concerned until 9 October.

'You had no specific reason to fear for her safety?'

'No.'

'None at all?'

'No.'

'Had she ever been out of contact for this long before?'

'Maybe sometime yes,' Olexandra tells us, 'but there was big party on that Saturday – ' she means the 11th – 'and we are mother, daughter. We always talk.'

'About . . .?' Burnett tries to guess what Ukrainian millionairesses talk about together. 'Dresses and that sort of thing.'

'Yes. Dresses and this sort of thing.'

That's Olexandra being snippy, I think, which is good. Her self-control is beginning to fail her.

Burnett thinks so too. He leans forward, pressing. 'So. You're concerned. You make some calls, yes?'

'Of course.'

We take names and numbers of people called. The approximate dates. More grist for our fact-checking mill.

'But you remain in Kiev? You don't return to London?'

Olexandra shoots her husband a glance and runs her hand rapidly down the length of her face, stopping at her necklace. It's an odd gesture. Hard to interpret, but maybe something that combines anxiety and a kind of good-luck gesture to herself.

She says, 'No.'

Burnett picks up the gesture too. He pauses on it.

'You did not return to London?'

'Correct.'

Her mouth is drier than it was and she reaches for some water, eyes still flickering rightwards to her husband. Tymczyszyn is aware of the shift in atmosphere too, but she clearly doesn't know what lies behind it. Her eyes are seeking out clues just the way ours are.

And the thing is, we *know* that they didn't return to London. Not by scheduled aircraft anyway: we've already checked the passenger data. Private jets, the same thing. Either way, passports get scanned and the data gets entered.

Burnett says, 'You stayed in the Ukraine this whole time?'

Olexandra says, 'Yes.' The first time, the word only just clambers out over her perfect teeth and dry lips, so she repeats it, more forcefully, 'Yes.'

Volodymyr, during these last exchanges has been sunk back on his seat. Watchful. Deep in thought. When he hears his wife's second 'Yes,' however, he rouses himself.

Leans forward. Says smoothly, 'You are forgetting, darling. I have business trip to Paris. You also come. We stay at Hôtel Vendôme. Three night, starting fifteen October. Many phone call, of course. Most of them here. You can look.' He pushes his phone across the table to us. 'Then back to Kyiv. Air France both way. If you need flight number, we can find.'

Relieved, Olexandra rushes into the shelter of her husband's slipstream. Corrects her story. *Over*-corrects it. It wasn't really conceivable that she'd simply forgotten a trip to Paris – a recent trip, and one taken during a time of deep concern for her daughter's welfare – but her anxiety to fit in with the new story makes her attempted lie even more palpable.

We probe around a bit more.

Collect more detail. More fact-check fodder.

We ask about the sons, but they're both alive and well. One is a student in Paris, the other doing something with a German-based mining company. Both in regular contact. The Parisian one saw his parents every day during their Paris trip.

Burnett glances at me. Then picks Volodymyr's phone up and says, 'If you don't mind, we will just check the call log.'

He leaves. Partly to get work done on the phone, but mostly to have a confab with the fact-checkers behind the glass.

I check over some of the data I already have, then say to Olexandra, 'That's a beautiful necklace. Black pearls, are they?'

'Yes.'

She puts her hands to the back of her neck. First I think she's intending to unclasp it, so I can see the thing up close. Then I realise, she assumes I'm asking for a bribe. That she's about to hand the thing over. A rapid look and gesture from Tymczyszyn forestalls her and the black-pearl-shaped hole in my jewellery collection remains sadly unfilled.

The three Ukrainians speak to each other in low voices, as I go back over my notes, correcting the messiest bits.

Then Burnett returns. He's brought some of the photos from the crime scene. Drops one of them on the table for the parents. Their daughter in partial close-up. Close enough that the candle-Bible-summer-dress arrangement is mostly hidden from view.

He keeps the rest of the stack face-down on our side of the

table, but says, 'That's your daughter as we found her. She looked very peaceful.'

He makes a show of looking through all the other photos as though wondering how much more to disclose. Ends up revealing nothing more.

Olexandra, at this point, is quietly but profoundly sobbing. Tymczyszyn, after a moment's hesitation, puts her hand on her client's back. Keeps it there.

Volodymyr says, 'Again, I say. We come very fast and very open. We ask you, please, to give us your informations, then we can go and grief in our own private.'

Burnett does the whole police shtick very well. Picks his stack of photos up. Beats it slowly, thoughtfully, on the table. Giving a good impression of a man who is considering the request with an open mind, rather than one who has carefully pre-planned his interview strategy and is now in the course of executing it.

He looks at Olexandra, as though only just now noticing her distress.

'Mrs Mishchenko, do you need a tissue?' Then, leaning back and talking straight into the mirrored glass, 'Please, some tissues for Mrs Mishchenko.'

A uniform comes with a box of Kleenex. Olexandra cleans herself up, not because she really cares at this point, but because she wants Burnett to divulge all that he knows about her daughter and doesn't want to give him any further excuse to prevaricate.

When she's ready, Burnett says, 'Good. OK. That's fair. So let's do this. I will give you my informations. All of them. Tomorrow morning, right here. Nine o'clock. In the interim, I'd really appreciate it, if you could search your memories for any other trips to Paris you might have forgotten. Any trips to anywhere at all. Also, by the way, I don't believe your story. Sorry, but I don't. So if you happen to remember anything overnight that might make me believe it, I'd really, really like to know. Is that clear? Yes? Is that very clear? Yes? OK. Tomorrow morning then. Have a very pleasant evening.'

20

The next morning. Nine o'clock. Same crappy interview room. Same horrible lighting.

We start, Burnett and I, bashing away at that business-trip-to-Paris story. It's perfectly clear that we'd caught Olexandra out in a clumsy lie, one swiftly corrected by her more fluent husband. But now the new story is settled, we can't dislodge it. The little chink we exposed yesterday is closed. The Mishchenkos have gathered confidently behind their new perimeter.

They're right to feel confident. All our overnight fact-checking confirms that, give or take a few minor and excusable errors, the stuff we have now been told is largely accurate. Whatever it is that they're hiding, it looks like it's staying hidden.

So after bashing at them fruitlessly for thirty minutes or so, we relent. That's partly because we don't think we'll get any further information. Partly too that we are all swayed by Olexandra's increasing anger and distress, her husband's pain, their lawyer's increasing assertiveness. But also, we're on thin ice here. Not legally, certainly not that, but in terms of possible public criticism. Coming down hard on people witholding evidence from a serious investigation: well, that's us doing our job. But doing the same thing when the people in question are grieving parents: that's a more delicate proposition. Truth is, if these parents had been more media-friendly – local people, not foreign millionaires – we'd have trodden more carefully still.

So we do as we promised. Hand over our information. The facts, all of them.

Mr and Mrs Mishchenko, we're very sorry to tell you that we found your daughter dead. Lying in a churchyard in Ystradfflur. What's that? You think our place names are hard to pronounce? Oh for fuck's sake: you've got a lawyer called Tymczyszyn. Anyway. Your daughter wasn't murdered. She had fibrotic lungs and a swollen heart. Those two things together: bad news, we're sorry to say. A gasket waiting to blow. There's good news too. No rape. No injury. No evidence of hostile action. No evidence that is, except that little DS Griffiths here would like to mention that your daughter's legs had not been recently shaved and her fingernails could perhaps have been kept in better condition. Of course, there was the little matter of the candles and the Bible and the generally fairly freaky place we found her. Was she religious at all? Yes, sort of? The 'sort of' which means you go to church at Christmas and trace a silent cross when your plane hits a little turbulence? Right. So maybe not the sort of girl to go on silent retreats at remote Welsh monasteries. That surprises you, does it? What about her diet? Would it surprise you to learn she seemed to have an appetite for barley bread? The kind of thing that even pigs find hard to handle? Yes, we thought the same: more a champagne and caviar girl, we reckoned.

That – very approximately – is what we tell the parents. They're frozen. Shocked. In grief. Emotions strong enough and big enough that it's hard to tell what other thoughts or feelings might be moving beneath the ice.

We do ask a few little things. Get useful answers.

Would Alina ever go around with a substantial prickle of unshaved leg hair? No. Never. Under no circumstances.

And her nails? How did she normally wear them? Long,

Olexandra tells us, and nicely looked after, holding up her own perfectly groomed mitts by way of demonstration. 'Ah yes,' I tell her, showing sisterly solidarity. 'Like a Cardiff girl on a night out.'

We give them the details which will allow them to arrange for their daughter's burial. Give them the 'very sorry for your loss' bullshit, which Volodymyr knows we barely mean, but which you still have to say, and go on saying, in case this interview transcript ever ends up in a courtroom.

Then we're done. The Mishchenkos leave, Tymczyszyn with them.

Burnett, his constable and I regroup in a conference room with hot drinks and some food. The constable is called Aaron Hennessey and he has the air of a man always on the lookout for the con, an expectation of deceit.

Burnett glowers at a sandwich. 'As long as it's not fish paste. I hate fish paste.'

I take a bit of the fancy lettuce that the canteen now uses for garnish. I don't eat it, but do wave it. I'm feeling buzzy and strange, but not particularly buzzier or stranger than I often feel.

I hold the lettuce up and it drips beads of cold, clear water onto my thigh.

I say, 'They're foreign nationals. That's a high-risk group. They're *wealthy* foreign nationals. That must make them super high-risk.'

Burnett looks at me, at the lettuce. Narrows his eyes.

Hennessey says, 'High-risk for *what?*'

'Kidnap. High-risk for kidnap. Did you know that more than half of all abductions in London involve foreign nationals? And that's even with a lot of under-reporting, because immigrant communities don't always trust the police.'

Burnett, who I think had already been thinking along these lines, objects. 'Fiona, these aren't a pair of penniless Somalis.

It's not as though the Mishchenkos don't know how things work in the West.'

'But that's the point. They *do* know. I mean, they know how it works for *them*.'

That's not very clear, so I make myself clearer. 'Look, their experience is that the police are corrupt and untrustworthy. Mrs Mishchenko virtually tried to give me her necklace yesterday. That doesn't mean she really thinks that's how things work in South Wales. Probably it was only that she was frightened and not thinking straight. But the point is she's never had to encounter our police service. Her whole life is designed to protect her from that kind of thing.

'Only then she faces a new situation. A horrible one. Her daughter goes missing. She gets – she and her husband get – a ransom demand. A big one, probably. The kidnappers will be looking at the same rich lists as we found. So. You're foreign. You're rich. And someone has your daughter. What do you do?'

Burnett says, 'You dial 999. Your daughter's missing and you're in the United Kingdom. You're not in the Ukraine or Somalia or one of these places. You pick up the phone and call the police.'

I don't agree. 'Really? What do the Mishchenkos *always* do? In any situation, I mean. They get out their wallets. They look for the best of whatever the private sector has to offer. That's their first instinct. The same one that supplies them with hotels and jets and cosmetic surgery and every other damn thing in their life. And when they find the right kind of consultant, they pay some giant retainer and say, "Let's keep this between ourselves." And those people are smart enough, or at least the husband is, that they held those crucial meetings in Paris. Outside our jurisdiction. Nice. Quiet. Tidy. Discreet.'

What I say has the ring of truth. I think we all see that.

Were probably all thinking along broadly similar lines. But it falls to Burnett to point out the obvious flaw.

'Right. Only our girl was praying quietly in a monastery, just a day or so before her death. No ropes. No chains. No thugs with guns.'

Me: 'Was *supposedly* praying quietly.'

'*Not* supposedly. The forensics boys have pinned her to that place.'

'They haven't pinned her to that time.'

'No. But we have the testimony of half a dozen damn monks. I mean – ' he laughs – 'you could think of stronger witnesses, but not really. Six monks, for God's sake.'

That's not quite true, as it happens. As Burnett himself noted at the time, there was something just a bit flaky about the monks' ability to make the identification, to define the exact time frame. But that's not the part I take issue with.

I say, 'Not that place even. What do we have? Really? We have a bit of tissue, some hairs, a cotton thread. The doors aren't locked or monitored. And those hairs and things could have been planted there by anyone at any time. When we examined the shower waste, we found nothing. And there's no way that our Alina wouldn't have taken a shower in the two days she was there.'

'The barley seed,' says Burnett. 'You're saying someone forcefed her with barley to make us *think* she was in Llanglydwen? That's not plausible. She must have been there.'

Hennessey looks at the pair of us sparring. I don't think Burnett even disagrees with what I said about kidnap. He just wants to make sure we've tested out the logic. That we're aware of the holes.

Into the silence, Hennessey says, 'The private sector? What do you mean the private sector?'

Burnett stares, narrow-eyed, at his colleague. 'The K&R

consultancies,' he says. 'Kidnap and Ransom. Control Risks, people like that.'

I don't know if I say or only breathe my own answer. But the answer in my head, the one that hisses down the pipes of my consciousness, the one that chatters in my blood, is 'Yes. *Exactly.* Control Risks and people like that.'

And I think that my corpse – my beautiful, beautiful corpse – has finally found her crime.

21

Two days later. London. The NCA headquarters in Tinworth Street.

There's nothing wrong with the building, really nothing, except it all feels too careful. Disabled ramps and anti-terrorist steel bollards and efficient heating and low-energy lighting.

The whole damn thing feels too safe, too cautious. I'd prefer a building that really went for it, in no matter what direction. Some granite-blocked, carved-lion, fuck-you assertion of state power. Or one of those government complexes that seem barely to have limped out of the Second World War, all crumbling grandeur and tin Nissen Huts. Or, sod it, we're in South London: why not some crappy 1960s towerblock squatting over a retail arcade crammed with Poundstretcher shops and no-brand fried chicken outlets?

Burnett does something with security passes.

I'm feeling spacey, the sharpest attack I've had for some time. I can't really feel my body. I try to act and sound normal. I do whatever Burnett tells me to do. He gives me a sign-in thing and a pen. I drop the pen. Bump my head on the desk when I try to pick it up.

Stand up without the pen.

Burnett retrieves it and hands it to me. I stand there holding it, wondering why he's just given me a pen, and he has to remind me about the whole sign-in thing. Shows me again where I'm meant to sign.

I sign.

Burnett takes the pen and sign-in pad out of my hands. Says, 'You've put your name as "Carlotta". You've just signed in as a corpse.'

I shrug. Like I give a fuck. Like anyone gives a fuck.

Burnett, it turns out, doesn't give a fuck either. He just stares at me a moment longer, then clatters the pad back to the receptionist.

I count my breaths in and out. Try to feel my body.

Meantime, a man – grey suit, calm, sensible eyes – arrives. Shakes hands.

In-two-three-four-five.

He tells me his name. Michael Kennedy.

I tell him mine. The Fiona one, not the Carlotta one.

Out-two-three-four-five.

My Little Miss Normal act is obviously going a bit wrong somewhere, because Burnett says, 'Fiona? Are you all right?'

I say, 'The Lubyanka. The old KGB headquarters. Russians used to joke that the place was the tallest building in Russia. Had to be, because you could see Siberia from the basement.'

I laugh.

Too much, for too long, then notice the two men aren't laughing, so I shut up.

Those male glances pass over my head. The one that asks is-she-always-like-this and the one that says don't-ask-me-mate-I-hardly-know-her.

I don't care. The glances zoom over the top of my head and do no injury as they pass.

I think: the Lubyanka. A place of imprisonment.

That's why I'm feeling weird.

Carlotta was imprisoned. Somewhere, somehow. All the care which had been taken of her in death had not been shown to her in life. I know I've got some data to support that conclusion – those unshaved legs, those scissor-trimmed nails, that uncertainty about the forensics from the monastery – but my conviction runs far ahead of our still-scanty information.

My feeling of spaciness, of outright dissociation, increases. It's one of those times when I feel the dead person almost physically present with me. Her presence more emphatic, more blatantly real, than anything else around me.

I find myself pecking my left arm with the bunched-up fingers of my right hand. It's an old gesture. One I used to use to see if I could locate any inner sensation.

Right now, I think I can feel something, but I'm not sure.

The men stare at me. Their lips move. They're probably saying things.

I think they want me to go upstairs, to some bland conference room, a place of whiteboards and melamine.

I start to follow them but walk straight into a glass turnstile instead.

I don't really feel the thump, but I do feel the glass cold and solid beneath my hands.

'Actually, can we go out somewhere? Get some fresh air? I'm feeling headachey.'

We go out somewhere.

Tinworth Street. The Albert Embankment. A place that does coffees.

The men order grown-up drinks. Coffees. Americanos. The big sizes.

I'm still aiming for normal but, because my compass is spinning, my journey there is more dizzy than direct.

I order coffee, because that's what the men just did and I know it's a normal, everyday thing to do. Only then I remember that I don't like coffee, so I amend my order.

'Only can I have that without coffee, please?' I say, and the man says, 'Caffeine? You mean without caffeine? You want decaf?' and I say, 'Yes, yes, decaf, exactly.'

We step outside.

Red plastic chairs under red umbrellas. Women walking past in padded coats.

Plane trees and traffic and those scuffed-up urban lawns.

Carlotta, grimly, rattles chains at me. Is annoyed with me for having anything to do with this workaday world of the real.

Kidnapped. Imprisoned. What else, Carlotta, what else?

Burnett and the other guy head for a table in the far corner of nowhere, not wanting our incredibly insightful and thrillingly secret conversation to be overheard.

Everyone exchanges business cards, even me. I usually forget to bring them.

Burnett starts talking about Carlotta. He uses that other name, Alina, but at least the gap between what's in my head and what's here in the outside world begins to narrow.

I say, 'Sorry,' but no one listens.

Burnett lays out the facts of our investigation with swift, professional ease.

Kennedy nods. When I manage to listen, he's telling us about a case, 'a few years back. A bunch of Lithuanians snatch another Lithuanian from a bar. They beat him very badly. No particular ransom plan in mind, so they just go to his phone contacts. Put out a ransom demand for two hundred pounds. I'm not kidding. Two hundred quid. By the time we manage to catch up with the victim, the guy's hurt so badly he spends several weeks on life support.'

Burnett says something, I don't hear what.

I sneak a look at my iPad under the table. Get pictures of Carlotta up on screen. The ones I took. They're still probably

176

my favourites. The way the shadows and the pooling blood gather into great clots of darkness under Carlotta's pale skin, her tumbling hair.

Above my head, the red umbrella snaps in this December wind.

I can feel my legs, or think I can. I want to peck my arm again, but think I shouldn't.

Soon enough, Kennedy starts talking about what we came for. An overview of 'high-end' kidnap in the UK.

'OK. The top end of the kidnap scene. That means London, basically. This place has more billionaires than any other city in the world. Way more. Near enough double the number in New York or Moscow, plus loads of super-rich types who aren't quite in the billionaire bracket. These guys are typically foreign-born. They're here part time, most likely, and they're here for safety, for fun, and for business. A mixture of those three.

'The very top end, the billionaire class, they're basically not at risk. They just have too much security. One or two levels down – the Mishchenkos, those kind of people – it's a different story. Yes they have security, but there are limits. And those limits mean there are weaknesses.

'So let's say you decide to target a family like that. You certainly don't take the dad, because he's the decision-maker. He's the one who knows where the money is. You don't take the mother, because for all you know dad is shagging someone else. You don't know if you'd be snatching the love of his life or just solving a problem.

'Result: you take a child, preferably a daughter. Your girl Alina would be a classic choice of target. A party-loving twenty-something. She won't want any heavy-duty man-marking. She doesn't believe London is unsafe. So, one evening, she leaves a party. She hails a taxi and, ta-daa, it's not a taxi.'

A crime so easy, you almost wonder why it doesn't happen more.

I sip my coffee, doing my best impression of Ordinary Girl on Planet Normal.

The coffee tastes a bit like my cooking, like my one-pot tomato-lentil thing when I don't remember to stir the mixture or turn the heat down. The same rubbery burnedness, the same hint of poisoned exhaust fluids.

Burnett asks about perpetrators, their likely profile.

'Two basic options,' Kennedy says. 'One, this is an intra-Ukrainian thing. Some dispute over money or resources or power that just happens to be playing itself out on the streets of London. And if that's what's going on, then good luck. The perpetrators will be abroad. Negotiations will happen abroad. Any settlement will take place abroad.'

I say, 'That's not our thing. I mean, that isn't what we've got.'

The men look at me, so I explain. The Mishchenkos were very quick to come to Cardiff. They were plainly anxious for information. And the fact that they flew to Paris very close to the time of the presumed snatch strongly suggests that the locus of their interest was somewhere in Western Europe, almost certainly the UK.

Kennedy agrees with the logic, adding, 'And the body was OK when you found it. If what we're seeing is the fallout from some power dispute between Ukrainian gangsters, you either wouldn't find the body at all, or it would be a mess when you did.' He shrugs. 'If you're sending a message, you might as well send the damn message.'

Burnett: 'OK, so this isn't an all-Ukrainian affair. Option two?'

'Professional kidnap. That's what this looks like. A well-planned, well-executed snatch for money. Those type of kidnappers generally treat the victim well enough. No rape. No unnecessary violence. Food, drink, housing – all of that stuff usually OK.'

I say, 'Leg hair.'

Kennedy looks at me.

Burnett says, 'Her legs hadn't been shaved for a few days. Sergeant Griffiths here took that as a sign that some kind of coercion had been involved. Coercion up to and including imprisonment.'

The man stares at me, as though seeking to figure out whether I'm a stickler for beautiful legs. Maybe he's wondering whether, beneath my grey woollen trousers, I have the slimmest of slim calves and skin like honey silk charmeuse.

I don't enlighten him. Just do my dating face. The one that's mostly blank, but garnished with random hostility.

I say, 'She'd had cosmetic surgery. She wouldn't leave her legs unshaved.'

'Fair enough. Reasonable deduction.'

Kennedy's calm agreement settles me further. My two worlds sliding into one.

Burnett asks more about the normal practice in professional kidnap, 'if there's any such thing as normal, that is.'

'Oh definitely, yes,' Kennedy says. 'Best practice would be, you take your victim. You get well away from the scene. Get her to a safe house. Check and double-check against pursuit and surveillance. When you're happy, but as soon as you can, you contact the family. Basic message is, "We've got your daughter, don't talk to the cops, start counting your money." If that's what happened here, then the top-end families, the Mishchenko types will go straight to one of the K&R consultancies right here in London. With these high-end incidents, it's very rare for us to be involved before the K&R types get in there.'

Burnett seems surprised at that. I can't tell if I am or not, but I don't think my face has his we're-not-in-Carmarthen-any-more startlement.

Kennedy continues, 'Look, London is probably the world centre for the K&R business. It's got everything. International outlook. Big insurance industry. Lots of money. And any number of ex-spies, ex-Special Forces, ex-law enforcement types keen to increase their income.'

He waves his hand outward, beyond the plane trees and the red umbrellas, over the street.

At first I don't know what he means, but then I do.

Our view is blocked by an old warehouse, but beyond its walls a grey Thames rolls east. Only a few miles now and those cold waters will merge with a chilly ocean. Flat estuary sands and the call of gulls. But on this same river, only a few yards upstream from where we sit, the MI6 ziggurat commands the waves. On the far bank, and only a little way downstream, MI5 has its own glossy offices.

A cluster of spies, a murmur of agents.

Billionaires, spies and secrets.

I say, 'Those K&R guys. Let's say the Mishchenkos hire one of them. Let's assume they have the wit to pick a quality operator. What happens then? Does the K&R guy say, "We have to get the police involved," or does the whole thing happen in the shadows?'

Kennedy laughs. 'Half and half. Look, the K&R people are pulled in two directions. On the one hand, they know us. They work with us all the time. They know we're not stupid. They know we share their objective, which is always, always, always the safe recovery of the victim. Plus they know we have resources that they can't access.'

He waves his hand again in the direction of the river.

Resources: one of the world's three or four best intelligence services. One of its two or three best eavesdropping and

180

decryption services. Access to Special Forces with long experience of hostage rescue.

Resources that would be quite nice to have, you'd think.

I say, 'So the K&R guys mostly want to bring you in . . .'

'Right, but their clients might or might not agree. They don't always trust police forces, even ours—'

'And let's just say that the clients in question flew to Paris to meet their K&R guy, specifically in order to stay out of British jurisdiction, then lied about the trip when being interrogated in a police interview room in Cardiff—'

'Then I'd have to guess that those clients wanted to keep the whole affair nice and quiet and well away from any nasty British coppers.'

And that's it, I think. Our case in a nutshell.

Alina Mishchenko was meant to be on a yacht, but a random engine failure takes her back to London. No parents. No supervision. Any previous security plans thrown into disarray.

And one night, she takes one tiny risk that she shouldn't and learns that, yes, she *should* have listened more closely to Daddy.

Duct tape over her mouth. Ditto with her hands and feet. Change of vehicle. Then, hell with it: you take her anywhere. Not out of the country most likely. Borders, especially sea borders, attract too much attention. But an industrial unit in East London? A Scottish croft. A Birmingham lock-up. Or – why not? – a little farmhouse in the Brecon Beacons.

Shortly afterwards, Alina's parents receive a message. *We've got your girl.* The parents get on the phone. Find a K&R guy they like. An instinct of caution, some ex-Soviet distrust of spies and policemen, makes them hold the meetings in secret, out of earshot, in Paris.

And then – what? Alina's fibrotic lungs aren't enjoying the terror, the change of scene. She's scared, she's breathless, her heart's under pressure. She's all set for total ventricular collapse and a sweet little ransom deal is taken abruptly off the table.

That's a good story, credible in every way, except what kind of kidnappers feed a victim barley-bread still warm from a monastic bakery? Or let her out to pray for a couple of days before dying? There's more to this story than the one we've sketched so far, and much of what we *have* sketched is pure supposition. But still: there's that sense of threads beginning to tie together.

My coffee's cold, but still mostly undrunk. I sip a bit more, but it still tastes like exhaust fluid.

Burnett says, 'Somewhere in town, there's a K&R man who knows a fuck of a lot more than we do.'

Kennedy nods. 'Yes. And given the way this incident turned out, you'd have to say that client confidentiality doesn't have quite the importance it did.'

I suddenly realise that Kennedy has an authority I wasn't expecting. I was expecting some spotty analyst type, and Kennedy has neither the spots nor the lowly demeanour. I sneak another look at his card, my brain clearer than it was the first time.

Michael Kennedy. Head of the NCA's Anti-Kidnap and Extortion Unit.

A unit which is involved in every single case of domestic kidnap.

Which is involved whenever British citizens are taken hostage overseas.

Iraq. Palestine. Mexico. Nigeria. Pakistan. Hundreds of cases a year. Roughly one a day.

One hell of a job.

I tap the card. An Ordinary Girl on Planet Normal. Like that. I tap it the way that girl would.

Say, 'Mike, I've a feeling that Alun and I would quite like a chat with that K&R guy. I think we'd very much like to meet him.'

Kennedy – calm guy, calm face, and as experienced as hell – nods.

'I'll make some calls.'

22

Christmas. I love it. All of it. The lights, the shopping, the whole thing.

I love it the way I love having someone press their face close up to mine and tell me to have a good time, a *really* good time. Like that, only with yellow teeth and garlic breath and a damp, too-long squeeze of my upper arm.

The next day, the day after London, I start my Christmas shopping. Do what I have to do. Make a list of people I have to buy presents for. Think of presents. Buy them.

The actual gift-giving, I like. Thinking of things that my mother would like, or my sisters, or Buzz, or Bev, or Ed Saunders: that part's OK, it's actually nice. It's the process of buying them I don't handle well. Shops always turn me slightly crazy, but then you throw in the glittery Christmas trees, the red-and-green promotional stickers, and the way everything seems to be pawing at me and saying, *buymebuymebuyme*, as though humans were only ever £24.99 away from knowing true happiness – I don't survive that stuff for long.

I shop in forty-minute blocks. When I've reached my forty minutes, even if I have an item in my hand and am next in the queue at the till, I walk outside. Sit under a tree somewhere. Read a book.

The thing I'm reading at the moment – Saul Kripke's *Naming and Necessity* – put a bullet in the head of old, descriptivist theories of naming. So, back in the day, people thought that a name was basically a description. Aristotle? He was an ancient Greek guy, big long beard, top-top philosopher dude, taught Alexander the Great. That was Aristotle. That's what the name *meant*.

Saul Kripke pointed out that this idea was nonsense. What if Aristotle had died in early infancy? All those descriptions would curl up and die, yet it would be daft to say that it wouldn't have been Aristotle who'd have died. We needed, he told us, a different way of thinking about names. A kind of causal harpoon that joined a name to the thing itself. A harpoon whose barb would still bite no matter how things had turned out.

I've read *Naming and Necessity* about a million times and it's still one of my favourite ever philosophy texts.

When I'm not shopping or reading Kripke, I look at my Carlotta photos. Her face, dead. Her body, dead. Photos of her, and of Bethan Williams. Photos taken when she was alive and happy and who is now – what?

'Girl raped and murdered by a wild man of the hills?' Or 'Girl who vanished for no known reason and is now living in London/working as a shopgirl/living under an assumed identity in Albuquerque'? We don't know.

A name without a description.

Kripke's logic is so good, he should have been a detective.

I do another round of shopping.

Downton Abbey boxset for Mam. Pestle and mortar for Ed Saunders, because his current one is chipped.

Last forty-three minutes then run outside.

Sit under a tree.

Read Saul Kripke telling me things I already know.

Also look at my iPad.

My Carlotta photos, my Bethan Williams photos – and a video that Burnett sent me. The SAS one. It's two and a half minutes long. Len Roberts and a girl, Bethan, walking up a field to some woods.

Roberts is in the lead, impatient. Urging the girl forwards. But there's no compulsion. He doesn't touch her, not once, except a time when she half-slips and he catches her arm.

The video is shot at night, and from distance, but Len Roberts is clear enough. I have no problems recognising his figure, black and green in the image-intensifier. He's carrying a bag. Equipment of some sort, but it's totally unclear what. Bethan Williams, I personally can't identify one way or the other, but the images will have been analysed to death and probably shown, confidentially, to family members or school teachers, or others capable of making the identification. In any case, Burnett tells me there was no practical doubt.

The two figures reach the treeline and vanish.

Image intensifiers aren't thermal things. They don't track infra-red. They just take whatever illumination is available and intensify it. When the two figures reached the treeline, what little light there was proved insufficient and the image was lost. The SAS guy in question kept his equipment trained on the area for – Burnett tells me – a further two hours, but saw nothing. No Roberts. No Bethan. No nothing.

I haven't completed my list of shopping targets, but before I know what I'm doing, I'm in my car, heading out of town.

Pontypridd. Merthyr. Glynneath.

Llanglydwen.

Not Llanglydwen proper, but the top end of the valley, higher even than the Williams's farmhouse.

I find the approximate place where that that video was shot. A muddy gate. A sloping field. A fringe of wood, hunkered down against the grey hills rising above.

Park the car. Fleece. Boots.

There's more wind than there was in Cardiff, and it's colder up here, but it's all fine. At least there aren't any Christmas trees. No *Now Only £24.99.*

I walk up through the field. No sheep here now but the weak December grass has been cut and chopped by a hundred sharply cloven hooves. By the time I reach the top of the field, my boots are claggy with dark mud.

A wire fence divides off the wood from the field. There's a stile, but so collapsed, I just climb the wire, using an overhanging ash tree for support.

The wood itself sits in a fold of land just below the main rise of the hill. It's perhaps only fifty or a hundred yards from field to bare hillside, but the trees extend in both directions. More than a mile up to my right. Not as far to my left, but still extensive. Roberts could have entered at any point along the width of the valley. The spot where he was filmed isn't particularly close to his cottage. Isn't particularly close to anything.

I decide to plough more or less vertically through the wood, heading for the hill.

The going gets a bit rough. The parts that aren't thicketed with trees and brambles are a tumble of loose scree and grey rock.

At the upper edge of the wood, I'm stopped by a wall of rock.

The wall is hardly impenetrable. There are places where the rocks rise only a foot or two higher than me, and plenty of places where muddy chimneys sneak up between the little buttresses.

Beyond the rock, a few last trees, hawthorn mostly, slanted and flattened by the wind. No place to hide there and enough starlight to have given those SAS guys a good enough view.

But it's not the hawthorns or the gleam of hill that hold my attention, but a brown pool, stagnant beneath the cliff. The pool is not especially impressive, extending only a few feet out from the rock itself, filling the little dip of land where the ground has pulled away from the stone. The width isn't much greater – twelve feet, maybe fifteen – the sort of feature which might easily be obliterated through the course of a single dry summer.

And yet – it holds my gaze.

The curve of the pool below, the rock above conspire to produce something like a large brown eye. Unblinking. Disconcerting.

We stare at each other for a bit, then I move on. Traversing the upper line of the wood for a few hundred yards in each direction. The little rocky band comes and goes, in some places quite distinct, in others hardly there at all. No other pools. The odd dark band on the rock, where seeping water blackens it, but otherwise nothing.

Why did Len Roberts bring Bethan Williams here? Of all places, why here?

I go back to the pool. The unblinking eye.

The turbid brown is ruffled a little, but only a little, by the tetchily fitful wind.

I prod the pool with a stick. At maximum depth, the water's three feet, no more. But it's not mostly that deep. Mostly, you can see through the coffee-coloured water to the rocks and silt beneath.

The Dyfed-Powys team would certainly have checked the pool for the presence of a corpse. You wouldn't have to drag it, even. Just get your most junior constable to get in there and fish around. It would only take a moment or two to ascertain if Bethan Williams was lying there or not.

So clearly not.

Yet Roberts came here with Bethan and the girl was never seen again.

I poke at the water with my stick. No corpses bob to the surface. Just some bubbles that stink of methane.

I call Burnett. Tell him where I am.

'Why?' he says.

'Look, did you guys drain the pool, or what?'

'Drain it? It's about two feet deep.' He asks me again why I'm there.

I tell him the truth: that I couldn't hack the Christmas shopping. Ask if there's a garden centre anywhere near here. Ystradgynlais maybe.

He says yes. Tells me where. Hangs up.

I drive to the garden centre. Buy hosepipe and secateurs.

Drag both things back to my stupid pool, which looks smaller and more boring than when I first encountered it. The weather has worsened too. A frown of cloud. Quick, sharp scatters of rain, striking my face like flung hail.

I know the theory of siphoning things, or think I do, but the actual practice takes me more time than I expect. Cut my first bit of hose too short. Cut the second bit too long.

But I'm persistent – a pain in the arse, Jackson says – and I get there in the end. My hands are so cold I can't really feel them any more, and I end up getting water over the top of my boots too. But still. I get a bit of hosepipe drawing water up out of the pond and trickling it down the hill instead. Weight my hose with flat plates of rock so it can't move around. Then think, since I don't have long till it gets dark, I might as well get the rest of the hose working for me too. Cut more lengths of hose. Five sections. All properly in place. All drawing water out of the pond.

Six pipes pouring water down the hill.

I start looking for signs that the water level is dropping. Watch to see the soft mud and clammy rocks of the pool bottom rising up out of the murk.

Nothing.

I place twigs and leaves to mark the boundary of the pond. Walk down to my car. Get a joint. Walk back.

The water still pours from my hosepipes, but the water still laps at my boundary markers, just as it did before.

No change.

I smoke my joint. Tuck my hands under my arms in a vain attempt to warm them up.

How long does it take to empty a pond? If the pond is fifteen feet long, by three or four feet wide, by an average depth of no more than eighteen inches or two feet, how long before my hoses drain it completely? Or forget draining it completely: how long before the damn thing drops the two inches that will prove to me the damn thing is emptying at all?

As night starts to thicken around the hills, as the temperature starts to fall further, I see a farmer out on a tractor. Delivering hay, or feed, or something to his sheep. Headlamps in the gathering dark

I go to my car. Get another joint, a torch, a blanket.

I can't see Roberts's cottage from here, but I can see Williams's farmhouse. Lights on, a dog barking.

A rural evening. A Welsh December.

No feed for me. No hay. No tractor.

Climb back up the hill. Smoke my weed. Wish my blanket was thicker.

And still the water drains. And still the pool remains unemptied.

23

I don't go home that night. Can't.

Can't face the drive back. Can't face my house. Can't face all the things which go with that place, that life.

All the same, I can't stay here. By nine o'clock, I'm bone cold. By ten o'clock, I'm even colder yet it's still only a sudden burst of rain, backed by a growl of thunder, that drives me from my spot. Down through the bigger oak and ash trees to the tangle of haw and blackthorn by the fence. Stab myself on the wire as I climb over, then lose my footing and slide several muddy feet downhill on my bum.

By the time I make it back to my car, I'm wet through and stupid-cold.

Engine on. Heating up. Brain off.

When the stony cold in my chest and belly starts to shrink back a little, I start the car, let in the clutch, start to drift down the hill.

I wonder vaguely if I'll head for the monastery. Free bed, free food, and if anyone's pissed off that I'm using the place as a hotel, I'll canticle my way through matins till they're happy.

But that's not there where my wheels stop.

They stop at the bottom of Len Roberts's drive. I don't turn off the engine – I still need that precious heat – but I do bump off the road onto a verge shaggy with long grass and fallen willowherb.

Stay there.

I still don't know if we have one case here or two. Don't know if the Carlotta case links to the Bethan Williams one or not. If had to bet, I'd say yes, but criminal investigation is about evidence, not betting. If the two cases *are* connected though, I'd say they're beginning to knit together very nicely.

These profound thoughts are interrupted by a tap at the window.

A brown finger, horn-nailed in the faint light from my car. Len Roberts.

I wind my window down.

'Good evening, Mr Roberts.'

'Evening.'

I say nothing. He says nothing.

It's still raining. Not hard any more, but with a gentle constancy. Now I'm slightly less cold, I don't mind it. Just let the clean rain wash in through the opening.

'Rain,' he says.

I nod and agree.

He says, 'Maybe that's why she ain't draining.'

'Maybe.'

He knows and I know that it's been dry most of the day. I don't know how Roberts knew I was up by the pond, but if he can move quietly enough to catch badger and fox, he can move quietly enough that I won't see or hear him. It strikes me he could move furtively enough that he'd have been aware of any SAS presence all those years back.

'They looked there,' he tells me. 'Four police in them fluorescent jackets.'

'I don't think Bethan Williams is in that pool,' I say.

'That's what they wanted. They wanted it simple.'

'It's how policework operates, Mr Roberts. Most of the time, things *are* simple.'

He grins at that. White teeth flashing through his beard.

'Things *are* simple,' he repeats. 'Everything is if you looks at it right.'

Silence.

Silence and darkness and the gently insistent rain.

I shouldn't be here, not really. Not having this conversation.

If a police officer has a conversation one-on-one with a material witness, with no recording, no lawyer, no nothing, that conversation is inadmissable in court. Worse still, its very existence risks destroying the usability of any evidence you may collect under proper conditions at a later stage.

When I saw Roberts before, he *wasn't* a material witness to anything. The Bethan Williams inquiry had long since folded its tents. The Carlotta-Alina enquiry had no especial reason to worry about him. But now? With that undraining pool and his flashing smile?

The good DS Fiona Griffiths would say, 'Good night, Mr Roberts,' and drive home to her safe, bland new-build in Pentwyn. Would report her guesses in full to Alun Burnett. Would allow her superior officers to make key operational decisions about the investigation in hand.

Unfortunately, however, the bad DS Griffiths has noticed that her superiors don't always make decisions which accord with the way she wants to do things, and so it's not altogether a surprise that the words, 'Good night, Mr Roberts,' fail to exit my mouth.

Instead, I say, 'Listen, is there any chance I could stay in your cottage tonight?'

I can. He says I can.

The place is as cold and as damp as it was, but Roberts shows me where I can find firewood and matches. Leaves me to make heat, while he goes down to his shack to fetch food. I'm not sure what it is that he brings me – he claims chicken – but it tastes fine. Both bowl and spoon seem reasonably clean. I brought some chocolate out of my car and we sit there in the orange light of the fire, eating it. Judy joins us too, sitting with Roberts but friendly enough.

I don't want to sleep in either of the bedrooms upstairs, but Roberts fetches me some blankets and I pull some sofa cushions down in front of the fire. Apart from the smell of damp things steaming, and mould spores refreshing themselves in the unnaccustomed warmth, it's an OK place to be. Companionable.

Staring into the fire, I ask, 'What was it like? All that time the police were bashing away at you, trying to get a confession. What was it really like?'

He shrugs. He isn't, I think, very introspective. Things happen – rain, wind, sex, police raids – then things change. The sun shines, turnips grow. Badgers either walk into his traps or they don't.

He says, 'I know what I've done and what I haven't.'

That's what everyone thinks of course, what they want to be true. But it isn't. People confabulate. Reshape memories. Take difficult episodes and reconstruct them as narrative. We are liars even to ourselves.

I say, 'Do you have a spade? And, I don't know, a pick-axe?'

'Mattock.'

'Mattock?'

'He's like a pick, only with an adze. You'll want him for lifting stones.'

'And you have one?'

He tells me yes and tells me where I can find it. That grinning intensity is there. Excitement peeping out like a root that's been uncovered, a buried rock.

We talk. We watch the fire. I yawn. Roberts leaves.

The next morning, the weather still looks dour. Trembling on the brink of more rain, more thunder. I do walk back up the hill to my pond. The hoses are still there, still draining. The water level hasn't changed at all.

The two cases. Bethan Williams and Alina-Carlotta. Connected or not connected? Two cases or one?

I still don't know but those hoses say one. The unemptying pond says the same. That unblinking, peaty eye.

I pull the hoses out. Throw them away. Walk down the hill and drive home. Bath-time.

24

Police headquarters, Carmarthen. Monday morning.

I'm there early, as before. A bag of artery-destroying pastries, as before.

This time, though, Burnett half-expects the ambush. Sweeps the carpark with a suspicious gaze and locates me before I've even clambered out of my car.

'Morning,' he says, an observation so obvious you'd think that a professional detective – a detective inspector, no less – would refrain from making it.

'And a very fine and beautiful one, may I say, sir? Carmarthenshire at her loveliest.'

Burnett gazes at a horizon heavy with oncoming rain. A press of cloud, grey-bottomed and laden with threat.

We stomp our way into the building. Upstairs.

'This will be about . . .?'

'Our inquiry, sir. Our happily re-invigorated inquiry.'

On entering his office, Burnett apprehends the bag of pastries and starts to interrogate its contents, with his eyes first, then his teeth.

'This weekend. In Llanglydwen. What the bloody hell were you up to?'

'Taking a look at that pond. I did tell you.'

'Fiona, that pond is about yea long and yea deep. It was fully investigated at the time.'

'I know. Four officers in hi-vis jackets.'

'Well . . .' Burnett is exasperated with me, but hasn't yet detonated. I don't have long, though. I'm like James Bond fiddling with the warhead as the digits count down to zero.

I say, 'If you drain water out of something, and the thing never gets any emptier, what does that tell you?'

'You drained the pool?'

'No. I tried, but I couldn't.' I tell him what I did and what I found.

'Well, I don't know, but it rained, didn't it? The damn thing probably just refilled.'

I shake my head at that. My impatience grappling with his. I don't mention the long hours I sat watching the undraining waters – I try to avoid revealing the depths of my obsessiveness – but I do say, 'Look, maybe that pool is enormous. Like it extends a long way under the hill. Maybe my hoses weren't draining it, because the thing was far bigger than it looks.'

'A giant underground lake? That's your theory?'

'Or it was refilling all the time. Suppose you took a stream and hid it under a mountain of stone. Hid it so effectively, that all you could see is one little backwater. No matter how much you tried to drain that little backwater, it would never get any smaller, not unless you start sucking up the whole damn stream.'

Burnett stares at me. 'I believe you were seconded to the Ystradfflur investigation. The one that has led us to Alina Mishchenko and a possible kidnap case, correct?'

I don't say anything, just let Burnett pin me with his gaze while his hand seeks and finds a Danish pastry. In my opinion, it's not OK for senior officers to give you a bollocking while their bloodstream is being replenished by baked goods of your own providing, but that's my personal opinion only. I don't know how things work in Dyfed-Powys.

'Fiona, does the water-level in a random pool above Llanglydwen have anything to do with a possible – and I'm

197

stressing that word, "*possible*" – kidnap inquiry in relation to Alina Mishchenko?'

Since I don't instantly answer – which is a pity, since the word 'yes' would have been a good, clear, and simple response – Burnett fills the silence by saying, 'At the moment, we have one corpse. *One.* The victim, a certain Alina Mishchenko, died from natural causes, but under circumstances that *might* suggest professional kidnap. We have asked the country's most senior kidnap specialist to investigate that hypothesis using his own extensive contacts in the London K&R community. We will await any further developments with interest but, in the meantime, can I remind you that we don't actually have a case. You know, an *actual* case with an *actual* crime that we can *actually* prosecute.'

I don't really know what people like me are meant to say to people like Burnett after speeches like that. I mean, the gist of anything I say is clearly meant to be, 'You are right, O Mighty One. Before your wisdom, I abase myself. Before your authority, I tremble.' So that part, I get. But how do you say that sort of thing in the kind of English that people actually use? I don't know. I've no idea. On the other hand, since, even if I did know, I'd be most unlikely to say anything of the kind, my ignorance is of that humdrum don't-know-don't-care sort, like 'Why are there glaciers on Pluto?' or 'Why are small boys always dripping with snot?'

Burnett waits around to see if he gets some version of the 'Mighty One' speech.

I try to remember if there actually are glaciers on Pluto, or if that's something I've just made up.

Then everyone gets bored with the moodily silent waiting, so I say, 'I'm very good at boring jobs. The ones with lots of lists and paperwork.'

Burnett nods, but in a way that fails to suggest enthusiasm.

I say, 'I thought maybe it might be useful if I had a look

at car number plates. The ones you collected a few years back.'

'You want to look at lists of vehicle registration numbers?'

I don't say anything. I'm pretty sure I don't even nod. But my face probably does something to signify that Burnett has correctly heard and interpreted what was, after all, a fairly simple English sentence.

He says, 'The Bethan Williams ones?'

'Yes, exactly.'

'Fiona, there are thousands of them. We didn't just track vehicles in and out of Llanglydwen, we had cameras on the A4067 too.'

My face still doesn't say anything, but if it has a look, the look probably says something like, 'Well then. That's good.'

Burnett continues to stare.

'You want to look at a box full of ten-year-old number plates when we don't actually have a live inquiry of any sort and your boss in Cardiff, Dennis Jackson, now, he's happy for you to do that, is he?'

It's eight years not ten years. And Dennis Jackson doesn't know about my number plates or my very interesting Llanglydwen pool, but my face probably looks more yes than no. At any rate, Burnett shakes his head, hollers at someone out in the corridor, and that someone takes me downstairs to an under-lit basement that smells of damp and – just guessing – rats, corpses and mouldering bones. We find a document box containing the registrations collected during that old Bethan Williams inquiry. Burnett has made it pretty clear that if I want to waste my time, he'd prefer me to waste it at Cathays, rather than here in Carmarthen. He also doesn't want me physically removing originals, so I stand over a photocopier for forty minutes shoving bits of paper into its maw.

Then stash the box of originals back in the basement with

the mouldering Carmarthen bones and take my box of copies back with me to Cathays, there to spend a happy day truffling.

Maw. Muzzle. Mouth.

Gob. Gullet. Craw.

25

A happy day truffling. That's the plan, anyway.

But back home in Cardiff, Watkins keeps trying to get me to help with what she calls the 'mothballing' of Operation April. That's work I detest and keep trying to escape from, turning my phone off and sitting in random corners of the office. The strategy is only partially successful, but even when I do get an hour or two alone with my number plates, they grip me less than they ought to.

Just for the hell of it, I do a basic PNC search, looking for daughters of wealthy expatriate Londoners who have been found dead in suspicious circumstances. I find a couple of boring things – motorbike accident, drug overdose – but also come across one instance, in 2005, of a wealthy Swedish-Latvian family whose daughter was found dead in some woods in Suffolk. Cause of death was thought to be suffocation, but the corpse was far from fresh and the indications usually used to make the diagnosis – bloodshot eyes, blood high in carbon monooxide – were of little value so long after death.

I look at pictures of the body. An eighteen-year-old, Linnea Gorkšs. Father a property guy, who'd made a fortune in Latvia's transition to democracy. Mother a Swedish financier who'd become part of the team in more ways than one.

Does Linnea somehow mark the start of our story? It's hard to tell. There was a major police investigation at the time, but one that withered for lack of leads.

I follow the story until I'm sure there's nothing tangible here for me, then just go back to the photos. Linnea made a nice corpse. Pretty. She was found in a shallow grave in a wooded area. Already starting to decompose, but you can still make out that white-blonde Baltic hair, those pale, pale Nordic eyes.

Even those eyes don't hold me for as long as normal, though.

Work is normally a haven for me, a place of calm, but in my current mood nothing holds me for long. I'm a pest and a pain, even to myself. A prickle of misdirected energy.

I email links to the Gorkšs case through to Burnett. Write,

'Another Alina Mishchenko? What do you think? F.'

Ten minutes later, I get a short email back.

'Could be. Very old case, though, and speculative. Leave aside. Alun.'

I search around a bit in the Bethan Williams file. Len Roberts had a brother, Geraint, who left Llanglydwen to go to Swansea University some eleven years back.

I make some calls.

Learn some things.

Start an email to Burnett.

Delete without sending.

I itch around the office. I achieve nothing of value, other than interrupting people, impeding their work, and causing minor disruptions and annoyances wherever I go. I then remind myself that I am now a detective sergeant, trusted by my force with all matters relating to the prevention, investigation and prosecution of crime. It behoves me therefore to repay that trust by dismissing myself from duty before I can do further harm.

I execute my own instruction with alacrity.

I pest, pain and prickle my way downstairs. Drive out of

town. Am actually passing Aberfan before I realise that I don't live out here. I had this weird feeling that I was going home, and here am I – the loom of the Brecon Beacons rising before me – only now realising that I live in a bland little rabbit hutch in Pentwyn and every mile I drive is a mile further from home.

I don't stop driving, though I do slow down.

Darkness starts to seep from the rocks and trees. Leaks from the mountains. Thickens in the fields, the woods, the barns and hedges. It's not dark yet, but everyone knows where it's headed.

I arrive at the mouth of the Llanglydwen valley.

The road up is single lane only. The Welsh version. Hedges rising so close they almost touch the car on either side. About a third of the way down, I park up at a little junction where a muddy track fords a little stream, brown waters over brown rock.

Dress warm, dress sensible.

Coat, scarf, hat, gloves, boots. Torch.

Walk on down the road to Roberts's place. Find his spade and mattock. The mattock is heavy, but not ridiculously so. I lug them up the road, then up through the field and wood to my little pond.

My pond. Roberts's pond. Bethan's pond.

It's full on dark now, and darker somehow beneath these trees, this little cliff. In the light, during the weekend just gone, the water here was the chestnut colour of black tea, but now I can see nothing except the occasional glimpse of silver where a ripple catches a slice of moon.

I start to dig.

I'm small, weedy and unpractised in the use of a spade. A dunderhead in matters mattocky.

But still. If 'dig' is a slightly flattering way of describing my efforts, I do at least start hacking out little spits and clods of earth. Scraping away the surface clutter of leaves and sticks and little splinters of rock that have fallen from above.

My aim is to dig out a V-shaped groove that will pierce the lip of the pool and allow the whole damn thing to drain downhill. My channel will need to be two or three feet deep to achieve what I want, but there's no rush. Bethan Williams has been gone eight years and more. She won't begrudge the odd extra day.

I get stuck in.

Turns out Len Roberts was right about that damn mattock. When I try to stab the spade into the ground, it dings off stone almost instantly. Not that the ground is solid rock, just that the whole bank is a mass of earth, stones, tree roots and larger rocks. The earth and stones, I can work with. The larger rocks, maybe, I'll be able to prise away with the blade of my mattock. The tree roots, I have no idea.

I work for about two hours, propping my torch on a little hillock of new-turned earth. Make use of whatever scattered bits of moonlight find their way down here.

I try to stay clear of the water. My plan is to dig my channel in the dry and breach the restraining dam at the last possible moment. The plan is a sound one, but I still manage to stumble into the pond, getting cold water over the top of my boot. And the earth is wet enough that my boots are soon clodded with heavy clay. My trousers are spattered with mud right up to the waist.

After two hours, I've made a decent start. My arms are aching and, I realise, I've got blisters on both hands.

I didn't know you could get blisters from digging.

I drop my tools, and slip and slide my way downhill.

Roberts's cottage.

No electricity. No running water.

A bathtub, yes, but one so lined with green and brown that it looks like one of those photos you see of foreign torture chambers.

By torchlight, I find some firewood. Make a fire. In the kitchen, there's a drawer with candles, and I light a couple to release me from my torch's blue light.

I have mud on my hands, my coat, my hair, my face. When I lick my lips, I encounter the gritty mineral taste of clay. I fill a bowl of water from the butt outside and do a very basic job of cleaning up. I can still feel where my hair is glued into rat-tails of mud and I slightly doubt that my face is the same colour as it was this morning. But the light is poor and there's no mirror to prove me wrong, so I imagine myself a princess in a crystal palace. A cool light plays on marble fountains and peacocks strut through the gardens beyond.

Food.

It would have been a good idea to bring some but – I confess it – this plan of mine was not well thought through.

I'm not fool enough to open the fridge door, but do rustle around in drawers and cupboards till I find a packet of dried soup. Rice. The soup is more than a year after its sell-by date, but I don't see how anything can kill you if you boil it enough. So I fetch water. Add soup and rice, and settle the saucepan on my fire. Stir with a long stick.

A smell of things scorching and steaming and drying out.

At one point, I have a feeling that Len Roberts is looking in at me from these uncurtained windows. I'd rather he didn't do that, but this is his cottage and I don't much mind.

My riced-up soup boils and burns.

I eat it. Nest up my cushions, my dubious blankets. And stare into the firelight as, outside, peacocks go clucking to their roosts and this cooling marble sheds the heat of day.

26

Morning.

Wake stiff and stupid in the pre-dawn light.

Somewhere down the valley, the first canticles of the day will be sidling upwards. The first few dozen *kyrie eleison*s.

No canticles for me. My eleisons go unkyried.

This aching sinner scrapes a little cold soup from the pan for her breakfast. A little cold rice. Stumbles around, finding gloves and hats. Dresses under the blanket because of the cold.

Walk, fast, back to my car. The temperature's hovering around freezing and the fields are sheeted in white. Hedges stiffened in a white cast that sparkles in the rising light.

Reach the muddy junction where I'm parked. Have to yank at the door handle, because the damn thing wants to freeze itself shut. The windscreen is iced and I don't have any de-icer and my hands, even if I ask them nicely, tell me that they don't want to scrape away at the ice. So I just turn the engine on and the heating up and listen to a farming spot on BBC Wales till the screen clears, or clears enough.

I drive to Cardiff.

My own house – no peacocks, but plenty of mirrors – reveals just how dirty I still am. I wash properly, rinsing my hair until I can no longer feel the fine grit of Llanglydwen mud at the roots. Work at my fingernails till they turn from black, to brown, to almost white.

Get dressed. Office clothes. Smarter than usual. White shirt and a charcoal suit.

My dirty clothes go in a plastic rubbish sack in the back of my car. I drive to the office. Not late, but actually early.

Talk to Burnett. Has he heard from Mike Kennedy?

He has not.

Watkins comes by my desk and tells me things to do with Operation April. Nothing interesting, just things.

I say, 'Yes, ma'am,' until she goes.

Essylt Jones comes by my desk.

She says things. I say things back again. She goes.

My hands are blistered and my arms achey.

I ring Alun Burnett.

'Have you heard from Mike Kennedy?' I ask.

'You already asked me that. About one hour ago. I said no. I also said I would call you when I heard anything.'

'Oh.'

'And I haven't heard anything.'

'Oh.'

We ring off.

Hours kindle and burn. Transform into papery black flakes that float off to wherever those things go when they're done.

I wait until Watkins is out of the office, then slip out. Drive out of town. Up to the little junction outside Llanglydwen, where a muddy track burbles over brown rocks. Change out of my office clothes for the ones I wore yesterday. Crackly with mud, dried-white and cakey. My boots are still wet but, phooey, they're only going to get wet anyway.

Up the hill to my pond.

A brown eye that stares at me. Not angry. Not malevolent. Not anything at all. An unblinking spaniel eye that communicates nothing, that can wait forever.

An eye, a spade, a mattock.

A maw. A muzzle. A mouth.

I dig.

I'm more effective today than I was yesterday, not least because I'm starting in the light. Wear gloves to protect my blisters. Figure out how to let the mattock's own weight do the work for me.

My channel widens and deepens. The light sinks. The moon rises.

And as it does, as I get the first glimpse of that huge orange moon, a great cheese hung implausibly over the north-eastern horizon, I find I have a spectator. Len Roberts's tangled, grinning face.

I tell him good evening.

He asks how it's going.

I point to my labours and say, 'Hard work.'

He nods and laughs and nods again. Two rabbits hang from his belt. 'Hungry?'

'I will be.'

This morning, I drove to Cardiff thinking, 'Must remember to buy food, soap and bottled water.' And, typically, remembered everything except for the last three items on that list.

Roberts tells me to come by later, but he doesn't leave, not straight away. Just watches me work, a chortling laughter dancing in his eyes.

Once he asks about Carlotta. He doesn't use her name, as I never gave him that, but he wants to know.

I say, primly, 'The investigation is still ongoing, Mr Roberts.'

'That means you buggers haven't got anywhere.'

'It means we found a barley seed in her digestive tract. A barley seed that came from the monks down there.'

I point down the valley, where lights are beginning to twinkle. Where vespers are starting to murmur upwards.

'A barley seed.'

'And we know she was there. For a day or two at least.'

Roberts chuckles. 'Oh, a day or two. Yes. A day or two.'

He puts his hands together in prayer, looking up at heaven, then darting quick glances at me to see if I appreciate his humour.

I start digging again.

27

And so it goes. The whole week the same. My days in Cardiff, doing shreds and scraps of work, but mostly just trying to live with my own prickly energy.

I don't mostly last through till five o'clock. Mostly, by mid-afternoon, I find myself in my car again, heading north. Dig every evening. Eat in Roberts's shack at night. Sleep in his cottage. Then get up early, go home, wash, change, pretend to do some work.

Rinse and repeat. Rinse and repeat. The whole week the same, except that on Friday, Alun Burnett says when I call him for the second time that morning, 'Yes. Fiona, yes. I've just heard back from Kennedy. He's got someone for us. A guy called Jack Gerraghty over in Newbury. He's worked for the Mishchenkos and he's willing to meet us.'

Burnett collects me on his way over, then we drive on to Newbury. Not the town itself, but one of the glossy villages that sprout on the North Wessex Downs beyond.

Bare hills and beech trees. Clear streams and, everywhere, the glint of chalk. Roadside banks and cuttings, field margins, the narrow tracks of sheep. Bone white beneath the green. A landscape you can crumble in your fingertips.

Gerraghty's home and place of business is a converted stableyard. Red brick and black timber. A fancy kind of clocktower built over the entrance arch. One part of the complex is clearly a family home – two storeys, windowboxes, curtains, a glimpse of kitchen – but the other two sides of the courtyard are all business. Plate glass. Two or three support staff types whispering into phones. A little conference room built so that the doors open straight onto some shaded decking and some Japanese-style fish pond.

In the yard: a Range Rover, a Jag, a couple of smaller cars.

Burnett parks his Mondeo and lets the engine die.

He says, 'There's a packet of wet wipes in the glovebox.'

That's a declarative statement, but one I choose to interpret as a request or, just possibly, an order. Either way, I'm happy to comply.

I give him the wipes.

He pulls off a couple and scrubs at my ear. The ear itself and the skin just behind.

He shows me the wipe.

Mud.

With another wipe, he scrubs away at my neck, the part of it he can reach. Tosses the used wipe onto my lap. It's streaked with lines of pale taupe.

I realise it is possible that my standards of cleanliness have declined somewhat through the course of the week. I think it is more than possible. It is a hypothesis firmly supported by the evidence.

I use the wipes to scrub away at my other ear, my neck, anywhere I can reach.

My mouth does a kind of sorry thing, though I don't think any words come out.

Burnett takes my hand and turns it over.

Blisters. I also notice, for the first time, that some of my blisters have opened, got mud inside, and now look like little brown molehills of skin, the precursor of some medieval-type disease. I notice that the whites of my fingernails aren't so exceptionally white any more.

'Been digging?' says Burnett.

I nod.

'Planting bulbs?' he says, but his tone makes it clear he does not think I've been planting bulbs.

'That pool. Up in Llanglydwen. I think you should see it.'

'I *have* seen it. I was there, remember?'

'Sorry, sir. I think you should see it *now*.'

A short pause, then, 'OK. OK, then.'

We make a date. It's Friday today and Burnett isn't the work-all-weekend type, but we agree to meet tomorrow morning. I'm relieved actually: making my excavations official seems like a good thing.

We get out of the car.

I smooth myself down. Try to disentangle the professional police sergeant from the semi-feral ditch-digger. Last night, Roberts fed us fox, and I have the taste of it in my mouth still. The gamey density of venison, but with something doggier about it. Sharper. The choking scent of chicken going bad.

I blink myself into the right frame of mind, or something close.

Burnett inspects me a moment in the clear light. I don't know what he concludes, or if he concludes anything, but his face moves in a certain way and he walks us both over to a doorway.

Black painted. Glass either side. Brass plate saying, 'Gerraghty Consulting.'

Burnett is about to knock, but the door opens before he can reach it. A secretary says, 'Inspector Burnett, is it? Please come on through.'

She seats us in a conference room. Mildly pressures us into taking hot drinks. She asks, 'All ready for Christmas, are we?' and I can't find a single thing that connects me to the ordinary world of Christmas. My head is full of a small, brown pool in the Brecon Beacons. A young woman in a white dress, laid out dead on a wild October night. And a small monastery

212

in a nearby valley, where the doors are never locked and the prayering never ends.

Gerraghty arrives.

Handshakes. Business cards. Smiles.

Gerraghty has the confidence of a successful man. Nothing showy. Nothing braggy. But that clear cold edge of steel all the same. He looks fit enough, but not Special Forces fit. If you were told that he was a successful IT entrepreneur, or a high-earning London lawyer, you'd believe it.

Burnett starts us off. A quick case overview, concluding, 'We only got the ID because this one – ' jerking his thumb at me – 'doesn't know when to leave something alone.'

Gerraghty looks at me.

Blue eyes under sandy hair. A steady gaze.

Burnett: 'I understand from Mike Kennedy that you worked for the Mishchenkos.'

Gerraghty: 'Yes.'

'You flew to Paris. They met you. Signed a consultancy contract.'

'Yes. Look, before we go on. I have permission from my clients to speak to you, but on the understanding that nothing here is to be presented in an English court. Nothing will be shared with a foreign police force. Nothing that I tell you can be used in evidence against my clients should they be charged with any matter related to their daughter's abduction.'

He pushes a draft letter across the table. A letter for Burnett to sign that says the same things but in proper legal form.

Burnett says, 'I can't sign that. I don't have the authority and I highly doubt that—'

Gerraghty nods and completes the sentence, '—that it would hold up in court anyway. Sure. You have to say that. Call Kennedy.'

'Look, Mr Gerraghty, I understand that you—'

'Call Kennedy.'

213

Gerraghty pushes his own phone across the table. He's got Kennedy's number up on screen. His mobile, not his office landline.

Burnett's mouth moves a couple of times before any words come out, but he makes the call, via his phone not Gerraghty's. Goes outside so he can speak to Kennedy in private. First Kennedy then, I expect, his own chain of command.

Gerraghty brings a cardboard document box into the room. Leaves it on the side. Pours water.

Looking at my hands, he says what Burnett said. 'Been digging?'

'Bulbs,' I say. 'I've been planting bulbs.'

His face doesn't say 'Yes, I accept that as a highly plausible and socially satisfactory answer,' but neither does it say, '*No!* I accuse you of an approach to police work so obsessive that it borders on mental illness.' It's just a face.

We watch Burnett through the glass walls. Talking. Gesticulating as much as a heavily set Welshman of middle age ever does.

I say, 'That document. Would it even stand up in court?'

Gerraghty laughs and shrugs. 'Maybe. Don't know. Never tried.'

Burnett returns. He has some quarrels over some of the wording in the document. Minor stuff. He just has to fight something to avoid feeling pushed around.

The two men agree a compromise. A secretary removes the document, then brings back a replacement with the wording corrected. She wears a grey skirt and a navy top. When she walks, she makes almost no sound.

Her hands are not dotted with little brown molehills.

Burnett signs. The secretary leaves.

I have a notepad on the table. Burnett has a phone. Gerraghty removes notepad, and phone, and asks me for mine

214

too. 'No recording devices of any sort,' he apologises without apologising.

Then Gerraghty kicks out his legs. Says, 'Good. OK. The whole story, right? From the top.'

And he tells it.

Alina Mishchenko stayed on in London after her failed yacht trip and the departure of her parents. Friends, parties, lunches, visits.

On 10 October, she left a nightclub in Mayfair in the company of a couple of friends. 'Old friends, perfectly trustworthy as far as we know.' They hailed a taxi to go in one direction. She took a taxi to her parents' home in Chelsea. 'She never arrived. The house had CCTV mounted to sweep the entrance. It's possible the audio captures the sound of her taxi arriving at about 1.30 a.m. – that would fit with the times we've been given – but in any case, she never made it as far as the front door. Never appeared on camera.'

The next day, the eleventh, the Mishchenko parents were contacted in Kiev. They were told their daughter had been kidnapped. That she was unhurt. That she was being kept in good conditions. Told also that a ransom demand would be made. No mention at that stage of any price.

Burnett: 'So far, so standard, is it? I mean, for this type of high-end, professional kidnap.'

Gerraghty nods. 'Yes. The whole thing was clearly professional. No ears being sent in cardboard boxes, nothing like that. The first contact communications contained a link to a private page on YouTube that showed the victim speaking in English and Ukrainian. The girl was cable-tied to a chair. Black cloth backdrop. No clues to location. No abductors, not even in partial view. Her words were obviously pre-prepared. Basically, confirmation of abduction, a request for help. Victim was tearful, but not visibly hurt.'

I say, 'Communications? What – phone, email?'

'Email and fax. Faxes give you a return receipt automatically. An email could easily end up in spam.' He shrugs. 'There were several unusual features of that early approach. One, the communications explicitly advised the Mishchenkos to hire a K&R consultant. Two, they provided a list of names. Four names, I was among them.'

Burnett: 'Go on.'

'I don't know in detail what contacts the Mishchenkos had with the other consultants – all known to me, all well known in our little industry – but they settled on me. We met up in Paris. I went over the terms of our normal consultancy arrangement. They hired me. Then, we did as instructed, and placed a comment on that private YouTube page. Basically, just confirming that I was involved. Asking for next steps.'

Burnett: 'That YouTube thing. That's usual?'

Gerraghty: 'No. It's slick. I mean, it's all easy enough to arrange. You just have to make sure you don't use any IP address that can be traced. But still. The whole thing was slick. Very well planned. And that's a good thing. I told the clients as much. You'd much rather deal with pros, than people who don't know what they're doing. You'll get squeezed harder financially, but you're more likely to see the return of your loved one.'

Gerraghty's face changes. He's plainly not a man who gets surprised all that easily, but there's a wry acknowledgement in play as he says, 'And one thing I hadn't seen before. *I* get contacted too. Email and fax, same thing.'

From the document box on the side, Gerraghty extracts a sheet of paper and floats it over to us.

Dear Mr Gerraghty,
Congratulations on your recent appointment as advisor to the
Mishchenko family. For examples of our previous work, please
contact one or more of the consultants below using the codeword

jr5v7k.

We look forward to a fast and satisfactory resolution of this matter.

There was, of course, no name in the place you'd normally find a signature. The 'sent from' field is some made-up Gmail thing. And the place where the email implies we should find a list of names is as blank as the chalk downs themselves.

Burnett puts his finger on the empty spot and raises his eyebrows.

Gerraghty says, 'Sorry. There were four listed consultants. They all spoke to me on condition of absolute secrecy.' He shrugs a get-used-to-it type shrug, and continues, 'The gist was they had all handled nearly identical cases. All abductions from London. All the same approximate family wealth: tens of millions, maybe just scraping into the hundred, two hundred million bracket, but no more. Foreign citizens. Three adult daughters taken, one teenage son. Two of those successfully returned. Two not. Presumed dead.

'The purpose of getting me to talk to these guys was partly to confirm that we were dealing with experienced pros, but also to set some "house rules". That's the term the kidnappers used. Rule number one. No negotiation on price. The ransom amount was set at one seventh of the family's publicly estimated wealth. So, in the case of the Mishchenkos, we received a demand for a little over nine million dollars. That same proportion had been applied in each of the other four cases too.

'Two, no contact with any law enforcement body. The first consultant advised his client – as I would have done in his place – to talk to Mike Kennedy's crowd. The client agreed. And that was that. There was no further communication from the kidnappers. Not even an updated ransom demand. No news of the victim. Missing, presumed dead.

'Three. Kind of the same as two. No contact with any law enforcement body *ever*. No matter if the victim is returned

217

alive or not. No matter what happens. We were told that *any* contact with *any* law enforcement body at *any* time would result in a further family member being abducted or killed. In theory, the Mishchenkos broke that deal by flying in to see you. They're a brave couple, actually. And they loved their daughter.'

Burnett's throat rumbles. I think if the rumble could speak its name, it would call itself something like *fuck-a-duck*.

I'm somewhat the same as him, except that I don't rumble.

Once he's done, Burnett asks, 'And the other one. The other missing presumed dead?'

'The family was short of funds. They *needed* to negotiate on price, or claimed they did. Same thing. No further contact of any sort.'

Burnett: 'Jesus. So the kidnappers are basically using your K&R colleagues like professional references. Take a look at our previous work. Please notice that we mean what we say. We look forward to doing business.'

'That's about the long and short of it. I talked the case through with those four colleagues, the "professional references". We agreed – the Mishchenkos and I – that we'd play it straight.

'Volodymyr Mishchenko isn't in fact worth what those public figures say. I mean, he may have been once, but the guy's in a country whose eastern half is fighting a civil war. The western half is peaceful, but bankrupt. Commodity prices are shite. And Mr Sixty-five-million-dollar Mishchenko probably isn't worth half that today.'

I ask, 'His house in Chelsea? That must be worth the ransom money on its own, or almost.'

'Yes, except he'd remortgaged it. Put the cash back into his business. I've seen the paperwork. There was maybe a million pounds of equity in that house. Maybe one and a half, but Mishchenko was in a tough spot, no question. And, not that it matters in a way, but he loved his daughter. He'd have sold everything.'

'So your role here . . .?'

'Was to negotiate on timing, not price. We said, nine million dollars, OK. Explained about the mortgage. Sent bank statements and financial accounts from the Ukraine. Said we'd get the money but to give us time.'

'You sent financial statements? Literally? You sent audited accounts?'

'Not just that. We gave them the login details that would enable them to view the firm's own management accounts. It would be easy enough to fabricate something on paper, but to reconstruct the firm's entire financial management system? Impossible. We wanted to show that what we said about the money was true.'

'And you think those accounts made sense to them?'

'Oh, no question. They came back to us with questions on things like the way Volodymyr's firm accounted for iron ore inventories. Things that made no sense to me. These guys were very financially sophisticated. Volodymyr commented he'd want them working for him.'

I ask, 'These professional references. What were the dates of the cases they handled?'

The first case was 2008. The most recent case was 2012.

Burnett goes back to Gerraghty's role. 'So, you negotiate. You ask for time to pay. They say yes, but you need to show us your financial circumstances. Did they ask for anything upfront?'

'Two million. We paid it.'

'Pounds or dollars?'

'Dollars.'

'Did you ask for proof of life?'

'Yes, of course. The response was, we have the girl. You've checked our references. You know that we return our victims in good condition. You don't need proof of life.'

'And you accepted that?'

'We had no choice.'

We talk more, but Gerraghty has little more to give.

Only one more question. As we get up to go, I ask the thing that's missing.

'Jack, you told us that these kidnappers promised to abduct or kill another member of the Mishchenko family, if they spoke to us. Yet they *did* come to Cardiff when we asked them to. They *did* authorise you to talk to us. They didn't have to do those things.'

My question *why* hangs in the air. A puzzle that clusters with all the others which ghost through this inquiry.

Gerraghty doesn't answer. Just passes across the document box, which isn't as heavy as I'd like.

'There's not much here,' he admits. 'Any evidence we collected. Email exhanges, faxes. Anything we could get from the Mishchenkos' own security systems. Anything we could do on IP addresses and that kind of thing.'

He grimaces, telling us not to expect much.

Burnett, ever the gent, takes the box and Gerraghty walks us both to the front door and outside. We stands together in the cool air. Damp brick exhales softly in the pale December sun.

By the fish pond, a black ceramic jar sits on an iron stand. Gerraghty lifts a lid, takes a small handful of powder and scatters it on the water. Gold flashes beneath the black. A brief, splashing frenzy.

We all watch the water as the ripples subside.

Burnett says, 'It's a lovely place this. I'd love a fish pond.'

Gerraghty ignores Burnett, answers me.

'Why? Why did they do it?' His faces changes, gets more serious. 'We think of these Soviet Bloc oligarchs as terrible people. Thugs who cheat and bully their way to success. But

220

it takes all sorts. The fact is, Volodymyr and Olexandra loved their daughter. They needed to see her body. Claim her. Mourn her. Take her home. Find out as much as possible about how her life ended.

'And it was more than that. Volodymyr thought that pulling nine million bucks from the business now, of all times, might drive it over the edge. Into bankruptcy or forced sale. But he was prepared to do that. And, after it was too late, after you confirmed her death, he decided he didn't want any other family to suffer. He wanted to do the right thing.'

We go over to our car. The crappy green Mondeo that seems even crappier here, in these surroundings.

Gerraghty says, 'Andriy, the son who was studying in Paris, has terminated his studies. He's now living in Kiev under a twenty-four-hour armed guard. Roman, the other boy, is still in Berlin, still working for the same mining company, but he too is under twenty-four-hour protection. Volodymyr and Olexandra, the same. They have a bullet-proof car. Armed guards on duty all the time. It's a fucked-up way to live and it's fucked for ever.'

He tails off, but he isn't done.

Blue eyes, steady gaze.

'Unless you get the bastards. You want to know why they came to Cardiff? Why they let me speak to you? So you can do your job and get the bastards.'

28

Get the bastards: if I had a motto, it would be something like that, only in Latin of course. Posh but violent: I'd like that.

For now, though, our efforts at getting the bastards are focused on a muddy bit of hill above Llanglydwen. The next day, Saturday, I arrive before Burnett.

Get a torch and a joint from the car. Climb up through the sheep-chopped field, the wire fence, the overhanging tree, the wood which thins out as it rises.

When I arrive at my pond, its unwinking brown eye has changed. Somebody has been here. My excavations have been cleaned, tidied, deepened. The little bank that retains the pool is still there, just, but a neat V-shaped channel is ready to spill the waters downhill. The mattock and spade aren't where I last left them – muddy-handled, lying on the ground – but leaning up against a tree, their handles shining in the half-sun.

It's Roberts, of course, and I can't help looking around to see if I can see his chuckling smile, his wild beard. I see nothing, though that doesn't mean he's not here somewhere.

I climb down the hill far enough that I can get a view of the road below. Sit there smoking and watching, just happy to be here.

It's beautiful. On days like today, you notice that nothing is ever only brown. You can see where bare branches are budding purple or green at the tips. The bronze of bracken, the blue light in the shadows of stone walls.

A kestrel floats into the wind, riding the rolling level. Sandy feathers tipped with black.

Down below me, a Mondeo arrives. Parks up. I flip my joint – only three-quarters smoked – away. Wave at Burnett as he steps out, finds his bearings.

He trudges up the field towards me and I take him over the fence by the ash tree. Up to the pond.

He surveys the excavations.

'Bloody hell. You have been busy.'

I wave a hand at the tools. 'Do you want to do the honours?'

Burnett says yes, which is just as well because my hands have the dull red fire that, I now know, comes from having too many mud-filled blisters.

He starts to hack away at the last little wall of earth.

There's not much to do now. The job's already mostly done. A few good blows with the mattock and the water starts to spill. The pond, for the first time since I've seen it, drains a few inches.

Burnett keeps going. He doesn't avoid the mud any more than I did and it's worse now because there's more water around.

Burnett hacks. The pool drains.

But even as it drains, the water keeps coming. The pond refills from somewhere we can't yet see.

Eight inches down.

Half the surface area of the pond is now exposed, or almost. Soft mud open to the unfamiliar sun. Tiny worms wriggling away from the air.

Burnett keeps going.

Eighteen inches down and only the deepest part of the pool is still closed to us.

Burnett doesn't talk now. Partly the effort, but also that he's in the grip of this same thing. I badly want to go and find the joint that I flipped away, but don't do it. Once I think I do see Roberts peering at us from the undergrowth to our east but, if so, he vanishes again when he sees me stare.

And, finally, we do it.

Drain the damn pond.

A stream tumbles away from us down the slope. Not a huge one, but a steady one. A stream that comes from beneath the little cliff itself. With the water gone, you can see the thing. There's a little black-shadowed overhang right at the bottom. A litter of loose rock in its mouth. Water burbles out from around the rocks. A trickle that never stops.

Burnett says, 'If that stream keeps flowing now, why wasn't it flowing before?'

I say, 'It was. But it was flowing somewhere else. Underground. It just found some other exit.'

'Do you know where?'

I shake my head.

Burnett digs until the pond no longer exists. Aside from a few little puddles of water, the original pool has disappeared. Burnett gets down on his hands and knees in the mud and drags the loose rock away from beneath the little overhang.

It doesn't take much dragging.

Burnett peers into the opening he's created and says, 'Fuck.'

I pass him my torch. He shines it into the opening, repeats the swear word, then says, 'Take a look.'

I step down into the mud. Hands and knees. Peer along the line of the torch beam.

A low, black tunnel retreating into the bowels of the hill.

You couldn't see the tunnel before, because it was blocked by a mouthful of water and rock, the way water fills the U-bend under an ordinary domestic sink. Now that we've drained the water and cleared the rock, we see the whole length of tunnel shining clear.

There are no bones. No corpse-of-Bethan-Williams. Just wet rock, shining like whale flanks in the torchlight. I can't even tell how far the passage extends. At the limit of the torch beam, the rock seems to turn. Into a dead-end, perhaps. Or possibly not.

There's only one way to find out, but it's not a way that appeals to us right now. Not without preparation. Not without equipment.

Burnett looks at me.

He says, 'The passage was flooded.'

I say, 'Yes, they'd have had to get wet. They'd have had to go underwater.'

'Right. But what then?'

I pull away from the mouth of the hole. Pull well away and say, 'You're closer.'

'You're smaller.'

'You're the senior officer. This is your investigation.'

He says, 'Right. I'm senior. Exactly. So look, just . . . just bloody do it.'

I just bloody do it.

Squelch down into the soft mud. I'm lying on my belly, eye-level with that darkly dripping opening. I squirm through. It's tight, but not ridiculous.

From a dark slot at the back of the tunnel, a bubbling spring produces a little stream that rolls out to the clear air. I'm not quite sure where those waters drained before we cut the hillside open, but there are any number of cracks and fissures which could have provided drainage.

From outside, Burnett's voice asks, 'Well? Can you stand?'

He wants to know if the passage was flooded to the roof – in which case, it's inconceivable that Bethan Williams ever voluntarily made this dive. But the line of the water is clearly marked on the walls. A light-brown silt mark rippling along the rock. And though I can't stand, I can kneel upright with my head only half-bent under the low roof, well above the level of that now-drained water. The rest of the passage varies in height, sometimes higher, sometimes lower, but was never wholly submerged.

If Bethan Williams did make the dive that dark night, she only had to duck down under this one canopy of rock – the dip of the U-bend – before emerging again. Beyond that point, she'd have been able to squat or crawl or kneel, her head in the air, able to breathe normally.

I tell Burnett what I've found.

My voice echoes in here like a sound chamber, a pebble rolled in a stone bucket. Burnett's voice, by contrast, comes from another world. A world where the light hovers blue and green and dusty gold.

From that far-off planet, the voice says, 'And the tunnel? Does it go further?'

'I thought I was only checking head heights, sir. Did I mention that you're the SIO?'

'Fiona . . .'

That's his just bloody do it voice, so I just bloody do it.

The passage has an inch or two of cold water burbling through it, but I crawl on through.

My stupid, crappy LED torch in my right hand. Silver-blue light on black rock. Jonah crawling in the belly of the whale.

Those Aberfan schoolchildren, buried under rock.

I get to the end of that first straight run. The tunnel does a dog-leg, but continues. Behind me somewhere, twelve yards and a million miles way, Burnett's head looms at the little opening, blocking the light. I feel a sudden rush of terror, as though someone were stopping the passage.

I jerk instinctively in alarm and hit my head sharply against a shark's fin of projecting rock. Get that temporary white-black flash which accompanies head pain. Disorientation. Drop my torch, rub my head, feel what I think is a red wetness of blood, though since I'm wet enough already, it's hard to tell.

I crouch there, swearing as my pulse rate calms.

A cool air moves against my face. Burnett is saying something, but I can't tell what.

After a bit, I call to him. 'Yes, the tunnel goes on, and no, I'm not going further.'

He says something else, but I can't tell what.

I move to come out, but realise that the passage is tight enough, I can't simply turn. I can't raise my head above a kind of high-crawl position and the passage is narrow enough that I can't twist round that way.

I feel a tide of panic. That quick, dark surge.

Take control, woman. Get a grip.

I get a grip.

Crawl backwards a yard or two, until I'm in a place where I can rise into a low crouch, twist round and head back for the light.

Squeeze out into the golden world, this blue-green planet spinning on its own in the darkness. Get far enough out into the opening, that Burnett can get a big hand under my arm and haul me out and upwards.

He says, 'Are you OK? Did you bang yourself?'

I don't answer. Just clamber back out of the dank pond-bottom. Sit on a pile of grey scree looking down into the hole. My whole front is wet. Muddy and wet.

I wish, I really wish, I had that joint with me now. Without the calming, collecting weed, my thoughts feel scattered. A field of sheep, disturbed by foxes.

Burnett looks at me closely. Says, 'Go on. Talk to me.'

I say, 'Um.'

That, and possibly, 'Uh.'

Burnett looks at me like he wants more and, eventually, when my brain sort-of catches up with my body, when it re-orients itself in this world, I say, 'Look, Bethan Williams didn't leave the valley by road. She didn't leave it over the hills. This whole damn place was surrounded by the best damn surveillance team you could ask for and she just vanished.

'So, OK, so Roberts could have killed and buried her – but buried her where? He didn't have much time and you guys put massive resources into finding any grave, any place of deep water or disturbed earth. And how often does a body actually vanish under those circumstances? I'm going to say, just about never.'

I continue. Set out the various thoughts that led me here.

Tell him that Len Roberts still keeps a Petzl headtorch. That's the leading lighting brand for extreme sports. The brand used by any serious caver.

The neoprene too. Wetsuit material. Cavers always keep spare, so they can mend any snags and tears in their suits.

And this pond itself. Why did Roberts take Bethan Williams to this particular section of hillside? It's not especially close to his cottage. The rocks and the hills and the woods extend along the valley for a mile or more. If he just wanted a patch of woodland, this section here had nothing much to recommend it.

I say, 'When I came here to drain it, I assumed the water would just empty out. That I'd get a chance to take a proper look. But when it didn't drain, that proved to me there was a lot more happening here than we could see. Something like that, for example,' I add, pointing at the tunnel. 'And you know, your officer, Ceri someone-or-other, the one who told us about the monks. He reminded us that Llanglydwen is only a few miles away from Pen-y-cae, the caving place.'

Burnett swears gently to himself. I know the feeling: when a clue thumps you in the nose and you don't even notice because you don't know how to recognise it for what it is.

He says, 'Pen-y-bloody-Cae. The caving place.'

'The main cave there is called Dan-yr-Ogof. And I've been doing some research on these places, these last few days. You want to guess how far Dan-yr-Ogof extends underground?'

'I expect you're about to tell me.'

'Seventeen kilometres. Eleven miles. One of the main explorers of that system reckons the whole thing will run ninety miles once it's fully mapped.'

'You're saying this . . . this . . . tunnel here connects with Dan-yr-Ogof?'

I shake my head. 'Maybe, I've no idea. But this whole area is hollow with caves. Ogof Draenen measures seventy underground kilometres. Ogof Ffynnon Ddu runs to almost sixty. Agen Allwedd runs to over thirty. And there are dozens more as well, a whole sweep of them. The whole southern edge of the Brecon Beacons and Black Mountains. The chain runs all the way to Abergavenny. Fifty or sixty caves easily and that's only the ones we know about.'

Burnett joins me on the scree. Says, 'Fuck.'

Says, 'Times like this, I'd kill for a cigarette.'

I tell him he doesn't have to kill anyone. Also – and this is really Murder Planning 1.01 – he shouldn't announce his intentions beforehand, particularly to a detective sergeant whose specialism is in major crime.

I go to my car. Make a roll-up for Burnett. Make a roll-up for me, and sprinkle just the wee ittiest bit of resin over my tobacco. Take my booty uphill.

We sit on rocks and light up. Once we have our favourite addictive substances floating in our bloodstream, Burnett says, 'So. Your theory?'

I shrug. Don't have one, not really. But I do say, 'Bethan Williams didn't walk up this hill unwillingly. She didn't *think* she was walking to her rape and murder.'

'Plenty of victims don't.'

Which is true. But how many rapists get their victims to crawl through an underwater opening as a prelude to their crime?

We both feel the pressure of the dark tunnel which snakes

into the hillside behind us. Our duty will require us to crawl that route. Not this morning. Not today even. But sometime soon.

Burnett shudders. Asks, 'How are you with enclosed spaces?'

'Fine.'

'Really? The thought of that thing doesn't creep you out?'

'I'm fine with enclosed spaces, so long as they're lit, heated and in possession of doors, windows and, ideally, tea-making facilities. That thing creeps me out like all seven shades of fuck.'

Burnett laughs.

Flips his ciggy away into the damp leaves curling up against the tumble of scree below us.

'How did Roberts even know it was there? I mean, you dug for a week to find it.'

'The water level. If that pool is effectively just part of a stream that drains away somewhere else inside the hill, then its water level would never change. If there was a drought, the water level wouldn't fall because the stream would replenish it. If it rained all month, the water level wouldn't rise, because the stream would go on draining the excess in the normal way. Most people wouldn't notice those things and wouldn't be able to make sense of them if they did. But Len Roberts and his brother knew this valley, every inch.'

'That's still theory. You don't actually *know* that Roberts knows anything about caving.'

'Which Roberts?'

'Len Roberts.' Burnett shoots me a look. 'What do you mean which one?'

'Len always stayed here in this valley. Never moved. But his brother went on to Swansea University. Became a regular member of the South Wales Caving Club. They tell me he was among their most active members. Geraint died a couple of years back in a cave diving accident in Austria. No funny circumstances, as far as I know, just a dangerous sport claiming its victims.'

'Fuck.'

For a while, we just sit there. Enjoying the free air, the empty air, the gold, the blue, the green.

Burnett says, 'They're connected, aren't they? The Bethan Williams case and this Mishchenko one.'

I nod. Take away the Roberts-as-rapist theory, and what do you have left?

He grimaces. Gropes as though looking for another ciggy, then moves his hands in an oh-sod-it sort of way.

He says, 'So, eight years ago, when Bethan Williams vanished, we thought we had a simple little case. We assumed we were looking for a child-rapist-murderer type, and we just went about that investigation in the normal way. But now we know about the kidnap, and we know from Gerraghty that these kidnaps have been going on for years, so that obliges us to consider an alternative hypothesis. A hypothesis such as, for example, Bethan Williams stumbled on some information regarding the Welsh end of this kidnap operation and was either silenced or forced to run.'

I nod.

Yes. I always like the moment when senior officers come round to my way of thinking. I should find some way to mark the moment. Ring a silver bell or strike a small commemorative medal.

Burnett sighs and continues. 'And your idea is that if you'd been running the London end of this kidnap operation, you'd have some natural concern about Bethan Williams. You'd want to know whether she had any incriminating information. You might even want to try finding her before the police caught up with her.'

231

'Exactly. In any case, I'd be pretty damn sure to come up here and check things out.'

'And you wouldn't especially be worried about being seen by local police, because we were all so busy looking at what we took to be a child abduction case we wouldn't have any interest in any Londoners dropping by for a visit.'

I say nothing.

Burnett says nothing.

The air moves and kestrels glide and water burbles and drips.

He says, 'Those number plates . . .'

'Yes.'

'How far have you got?'

'I've done about half the data, sir. Isolating number plates registered to London addresses. I've only got three London-based vehicles entering this valley. Many more if we look at the A4067 in total but, even there, and excluding goods vehicles, I have only eighty-seven movements.'

Burnett nods. 'Good. Those are manageable numbers.'

'Yes.'

'And you've done about half?'

'About that, yes.'

'OK. Good. Keep going. Thank you.'

I shrug. A *de-nada* type thing.

He says, 'And we've got that box of stuff from Jack Gerraghty.'

'Yes.'

A case that had no leads at all – a white dress and an undigested barley seed – is beginning to thicken with the kind of operational data that police inquiries are made of. This case still has plenty of don't-knows. Plenty of need-to-find-outs. But the biggest one yawns just behind us.

A dark opening.
A black tunnel.
A maw. A muzzle. A mouth.
A gob. A gullet. A craw.

29

Cardiff. Not my house, but Watkins's. Hers and Cal's.

It's Cal who answers the door. Welcomes me. I've left my boots in the car, changed into something less clumpy, less heavy with clay. But the rest of me has still been squelching around in old pond mud and Breconshire streams. My hair is matted. I am not fragrant. I look like something rescued from a storm drain.

Cal chides me gently on the doormat. Makes me take off my trousers. Picks at my jumper until I release that too. She coaxes me to take a shower and I do. Stay under the streaming water till the water gurgling off me runs clear. Dress in some clothes which Cal lends me: a pair of navy leggings and a thick patterned jumper which somehow expresses a wholesomeness that my own wardrobe sorely lacks.

I'm then hustled, nicely hustled, through to the kitchen, where Watkins sternly bustles. She's pleased to see me – she's always telling me that I should come round more often – but she's awkward enough that her pleased-to-see-you expression appears only flickeringly, one short spasm of discomfort, before giving way to the inevitable default glare. I don't mind. It's not often that I get to be the more socially sophisticated half of a pairing and I welcome the change.

Cal, immune to her partner's idiosyncrasies, asks if I want anything to eat. When my answer is a bit vaguer than it should be, her tone changes and she asks – sternly, suspiciously –

'Have you actually *had* breakfast, Fiona? Have you eaten anything today?'

I fess up. Admit my fallibility in the remembering-to-eat department. So Cal starts offering me things and I say no to everything until I realise that I'm meant to say yes to something, so then I say yes to whatever the last thing was that Cal offered, which turns out to be some granola-y thing so frighteningly wholesome that it looks like it could split a lip or crack a tooth.

Cal says, 'Coffee?' and, because I'm trying to be good, I say, 'Yes, please,' prompting Watkins to say, sharply, 'But you don't like coffee,' and I'm forced to admit that, no, I don't like coffee, sorry, and could I please have some peppermint tea.

Anyway. Gradually, everyone sorts me out. My head returns to normal, or as close to that happy place as I ever get.

And I realise something. This nice, ordinary house. Its tidy kitchen, its scrap of lawn. Its apple tree pecked about by birds. I'm here because these two people actually like me. I don't know *why* they do, but they do. It's why they invite me round, why they ply me with tooth-crackingly fierce granola. And the truth is, it's nice. I like it.

I realise something else too. Watkins and Cal are too old to have kids and maybe that wouldn't have been their thing anyway. But for them, I'm a kind of substitute. A slightly too-vulnerable young woman in need of adult protection. In need of love.

I'm a bit old, of course. Really, I should be a dewy eighteen-year-old just off to university and rushing back home every time I broke up with a boyfriend or needed my clothes washed. But if you're two lesbians who found love relatively late in life, maybe you're good at making the best of what you're given. Since I'm as close as they may ever get to that dewily hypothetical daughter, perhaps they'll just make do.

And I like it. I think I like it. When Cal steps next to me, bringing cold milk for my, genuinely quite hard-core, granola, I lean my head against her. She's wearing one of those super-soft woollen jumpers – containing mohair or angora or something of that sort – and I just lean in, against her side, against that soft, ticklish warmth. She puts her hand to my shoulder and squeezes. No one says anything and the moment doesn't last more than a couple of seconds. But's that it, I think: a contract sealed. They've invited me to be their sort-of daughter and I've said yes. It feels odd, but good-odd, definitely good.

We eat. We talk. My head becomes more normal.

Watkins says, 'Fiona, the mud?'

I check that it's OK to talk about a live investigation in front of Cal, and it is, so I tell them. The pond. The digging. The tunnel.

The pond that was really an entrance. The dead end that was really a door.

'Does Burnett know?'

'Yes. He was with me when we made the breakthrough.'

'We'll have to investigate.'

By *we* she means *you*.

By *investigate* she means *crawl into a tiny enclosed space knowing that there is an entire moutainside of rock and earth above your head.*

I say, 'Yes.'

'It's turned into a good case, though.'

I nod. Yes, it has. It really has.

Watkins looks for a moment like she's going to say something further. She looks like that time at night in the Operation April suite, when she stopped at the door to say something, then turned that something into a bland 'Well done.'

Once again, though, she pulls back. Just does one of her

strange faces at me. It's like some team of nerdy NASA engineers has been commissioned to convey warm, human emotion using nothing other than remotely controlled facial muscles and carefully calculated eye contact. The operation is sort of successful, if judged in narrow, technical terms, but still mostly serves to remind you that NASA isn't that great at everything.

I smile back.

Watkins says, 'We've had the new budget through on Operation April.'

'Oh.'

'Dennis pushed for the maximum he could get.'

'And . . .?'

'There's no budget. They haven't given us one. They've just folded what's left of the operation into Major Crime's ongoing remit. There'll be an announcement in due course, but . . .'

I don't actually say anything, but I don't need to.

'I know,' says Watkins, 'I know,' as her tear-stained and unboyfriended daughter comes home from university with a bagful of wash.

I accept her commiserations, but mentally log the fact that I have a new item for my To Do list, a list which now contains two items:

(1) Find, arrest and prosecute Carlotta's kidnappers.
(2) Revive Operation April in order to find, arrest and prosecute all its principals.

And, in the end, that two-and-a-bit item list reduces to one.

Nail the fuckers, what it always comes down to in the end.

30

I don't go home.

Should, but don't.

Should, because it's Saturday. Because I'm meant to restock my fridge, do some cleaning. Tidy my kitchen, my car, my house, my life.

Should, because I've got a bin liner full of clothes that want washing.

But don't, because that's not the way the wind blows for me today. Not the way this breeze breezes.

I sit in my car and call Bev. She's pissed off with me because I forgot our swimming date this week. Forgot to let her know I wouldn't be there. So I call her. Say the right things – the sorries, the promises. Ask about her and Hemi Godfrey.

She gushes about how well things are going, but adds, 'Fi, he does talk about himself a *lot*. I mean, it's early days and maybe he's feeling a bit insecure, but do you think I should say anything at all?'

What I think is that Hemi Godfrey looks handsome enough, but that he's a self-absorbed arsehole whose conversation would bore a tree stump. I dilute that sentiment down to some homeopathic quantity and deliver it gently. Bev instantly starts defending her beau and I say yes to everything she tells me.

We talk for thirty minutes then ring off.

Bev is too nice, really. There should be some protection service you can get. Someone to keep the arseholes away.

I think that, then wonder if I'd make it through the net.

I sit a bit longer to see if I feel like doing the Saturday cleaning/food-buying/laundry thing but find I still don't. That breeze just ain't a-breezing.

Think, *I should probably get something to eat.* Then remember I've just eaten.

Delete the thought.

Scrap it, release it, let it go.

I have, I think, one of those time-slippages like the one I had that first night at Ystradfflur, under the tower of the church. Detach briefly from this place and time. This quiet car, this peaceful street. A bare-branched cherry tree alone under the sloping light.

I can't, for the moment, tell what's alive and what's not. The tree, the car, the street, me. I know Carlotta is here somewhere but know I won't find her if I start to look.

Who? Where? What? When?

At times like this, I don't know anything at all. Feel nothing. Think nothing. Know nothing.

Then something changes again. The tree is just a tree. The car is just a car.

I start the engine and drive slowly to Penarth.

The seafront first. Iron railings and Victorian lamp-posts. A frill of cafés and beachside things, all empty now. Closed shutters and vacant car parks. A brown sea snapping at this iron shore.

I watch the sea for a bit, then drive up the hill to call on my friend, Ed Saunders.

Reliable Ed. Safe Ed. Good and kind Ed.

Ed who once tended to my angrily psychotic teenage self.

Ed who was – years later – my lover. My sort-of-but-never-quite boyfriend.

He comes to the door wearing dark jeans and a shirt in sky-blue that makes his eyes pop.

I poke him in the tummy and say, 'That shirt makes your eyes pop.'

Say, 'Any room for random waifs and strays?'

Would go on with the patter, except that he's opening the door wide and welcoming me and saying, 'No, it's fine, come on in.'

Come in to meet a woman uncrossing her legs from his sofa. Skinny trousers in, I don't know, amethyst or something like that. Blue jumper, loosely cool with a Jackie Onassis collar. Patent-leather slingbacks glossily discarded on the floor.

The woman stands. Taller than me, but everyone is. Shinier than me, better groomed, but again, ditto, ditto, ditto. Everyone is.

Ed is doing the socially graceful thing. The person-meet-person thing. Names, introductions.

I do my best to be Little Miss Normal greeting my fellow guests at Château Average, but it's not a great act.

'Milly, did you say?'

'Jill. Or Jilly. Whichever.'

'Jill. Jilly. Jilly. I'm terrible with names.'

The sort of thing you say when you're being introduced to five people all at once, but doesn't work so well when there are only three people in the room and you're one of them and your best friend is one of the others. Cal's thickly knitted jumper is a bit bigger than I am and hangs low enough over my bum that it looks like a slightly questionable sort of mini-dress. One I can't slip out of, because the T-shirt underneath isn't as clean as it could be.

Also: I can't wear slingbacks because they either fall off or lacerate my tendons.

Also: I'm not one hundred per cent sure that I don't still have mud in my hair.

The woman is nice. She doesn't bite me, anyway. And Ed is used to me. Settles me down. Calms me. Equips me with a plate of salad and apple tart to follow. Water.

The grown-ups drink espresso from tiny Spanish-patterned cups and make smiley eyes at me.

This, I realise, is A Date. Part of Ed's settle-down-and-get-married campaign which he's been running with increasing seriousness for about a year. In that time, he had one quite committed relationship with an Australian colleague, a blue-eyed, blonde-haired woman who said 'Grrreeat!' a lot and showed her very even, very white and very large teeth when she did so. The relationship did OK, I think, but she wanted to return to the land down under and he preferred to stay the right way up. To remain with these Welsh winds. Our brown seas and chilly rains.

This woman, this Jill, this Jilly, this possibly-Gillian or possibly-just-plain-old-Jill, is clearly a fairly serious proposition, because first dates have to happen in restaurants – that's the rule – and even second dates don't normally mean lazily casual Saturday lunches at the guy's house.

Conversation happens.

Ed says, 'No, it's great. Jill, Fiona is one of my most important friends.'

The yes-she's-a-girl-I-once-shagged conversation is presumably something that happens after I've gone. Jill asks about my morning.

'You know. Same old, same old. Crawling into caves. Searching for corpses. Smoking dope in front of a detective inspector.'

Jill doesn't know what to say to that. Looks over at Ed. A look which confirms to me that this pair have already crossed over into whatever number date it has to be where you sleep

241

with each other. I realise – stupid me for being so slow – that, most likely, they're here now because they were here together last night.

Ed says, 'This is Fiona. She's probably telling the truth, unfortunately.'

Jill does the 'Gosh, that must be an interesting job' thing at me, the sort of shiny conversational tuppences you throw to people unable to manage a pair of slingbacks. Alms for the poor.

I eat my salad. Eat my tart. Go moodily to Ed's fridge so I can steal any good leftovers he has. He finds some Tupperware for me and watches me steal.

He's got a new pestle and mortar, I notice. Uncracked.

Jill stands in the doorway, checks her watch and darts a look across at Ed. He does a Roger Wilco look back again, but no one has to hustle me anywhere, because I'm going to leave this place of my own free will, magnificently knitted mini-dress and all.

Say bye to Ed without poking him in the tummy. Say to Jill how *great* it was meeting her. Say I *must* get the pair of them over to mine, a promise which Ed will know for the untrustworthy lie that it is, but which Jill or Jilly or Gill or Gillian is gracious enough to accept at face value.

Leave clutching Tupperware.

Drive away, brightly waving.

I don't think I'm weirded out because I'm secretly lusting for Ed and have just managed to suppress that feeling for the last however many years. I *am* weirded out, though, and I think it must be because I can see that the Good Ship Ed Saunders is starting to steam away from me. Not away-away: never that, I hope. Just – he's becoming the sort of person where I can't simply turn up unannounced and slightly pongy on his doorstep. Can't poke his tummy, make comments about his shirt and march on in as though he had nothing better to do than cook me proper food and talk me into becoming something like a passable human being.

I drive home, annoyed with all tall dark-haired women with a loosely cool Jackie Onassis vibe. Annoyed with Ed. Annoyed, most of all, with myself.

I go home.

Go home and, for one short afternoon, comport myself like a model citizen of this difficult planet. Clean. Buy food. Do laundry. Pay bills.

Do those good things, then drive over to my Uncle Em's house. Not a real uncle, just the very closest of Dad's partners in the dark days of their mutual past. Em was always the first to arrive, the last to leave. My dad and Em often slightly withdrawn from the crowd, Em muttering to Dad behind his glittering, signet-ringed hand. If criminal gangs had handed out titles in the manner of some American corporate, I think Uncle Em would have been the chief operating officer. Not the strategist, but the engineer. The fixer.

I've asked Em for photos before, and he told me he had none. But that, I'm certain, was just a reflexive, precautionary no. So I let it be. Allowed time for him to check in with my father. And when I asked again recently if anything had come to light, he said, as a matter of fact, yes. Invited me round to take a look.

So I sit together with Em. A slow man now, attentive and kind.

He teas me. He biscuits me. He gives me a little china plate, decorated with miniature dogs, 'for the crumbs'. And we sit on the sofa and look at pictures of Emrys's past.

A christening, two weddings, a funeral.

Something on a boat.

Because Em will have checked all this with my dad beforehand, I know I'm looking only at approved photos, ones that tell me nothing.

But Em has always liked me. And as we sit and chat and eat butter-rich shortbread from a dachshund-rich plate, the conversation spills over to the races. That's a topic that never fails to engage Em, and at one point he stands up and says, 'Hold on, I wonder if . . .'

If he has more photos.

His face does that security thing. That checking-against-risk thing that was the iron discipline of my father's inner circle. But his face clears the checks. Even then, when he locates a fat paper wallet of his racing photos, he doesn't hand it to me, but scrutinises each photo first before handing it over, slowly, formally, like a parole officer checking a discharge order.

Horses. Men. Women.

Most of the photos, he just hands over. But one arrives with an odd gesture beforehand, a quick brush of the fingers against the photo's rightmost edge. A flick which was, you'd say, an attempt to get rid of a speck of dust, except that this photo had lain sandwiched in a group of forty or fifty others, in a closed envelope, and none of the others have been even the slightest fly-blown or dusty.

There's nothing on that right-hand edge though. The photo is a nice-ish one of my dad, close by a bay horse, with Howie Jones and, I think, the arm and half the face of Gwion Cadwalladr's wife. On the right-hand edge of the pic, there's nothing but the horse's bum and a man's arm in a blue Prince-of-Wales check. I take that photo as I take the others, with a bit of chat, a bit of daughter-ish interest in my dad's old life.

That photo and the ones that follow. These clues that are either not clues at all, or ones so deeply hidden as to pass my understanding.

When I ask Em if I can take these photos to make copies for my dad's Christmas present, he hesitates only a moment before telling me yes. Yes, of course.

And, as evening twinkles from the street lamps, from this

violet sky, I say goodbye to Em. Say my thank-yous, and drive over to my parents' home in Roath Park. My parents: who love me and welcome me and care not a damn that I am an imperfect human struggling for goodness in this corrupted world. We watch Simon Cowell on the TV and I fall asleep amid the coppery burnish of my mother's scatter cushions, the metallic cutwork of their brocade.

31

Monday. Carmarthen.

Tuesday, Carmarthen.

Wednesday, Carmarthen.

For the first time, we have a proper inquiry, a proper incident room, a proper commitment of resources. I'm given a uniformed constable to direct, and set him to work completing my number-plate-sifting assignment.

Meantime, Burnett and I dig into Gerraghty's box of evidence.

A wodge of emails: the ransom demand and the correspondence that followed.

The proof-of-capture video.

CCTV from the Mishchenkos' Chelsea house, a recording that shows nothing on video, but might contain an audio recording of a taxi stopping, just outside the sweep of the cameras at 1.30 a.m.

A few other bits and pieces.

We jump on the emails first, hoping for an easy win from the IP addresses. Send our data to tech analysts at the NCA, who come back to us within the day with bad news. The IP addresses come from some proxy server based in Mexico. No particular reason to believe that the kidnappers have any physical presence in Mexico, just that, as the NCA analyst put it, 'It's an easily managed location. Chances are, if we could unpick this whole thing, we'd find there was a proxy server in Mexico, sheltering a proxy server in Gibraltar, sheltering a proxy server in Russia, and so on. Our chance of unpicking it? Oh, I don't know. Somewhere between zero and none at all.'

Better news elsewhere. We send the audio recording from the Mishchenkos' CCTV to a specialist lab. They confirm that the beat of the engine is 'highly consistent' with that of a London taxi, and the guy who calls us with the news tells us that what they mean is, 'It basically *is* a London taxi. We just can't say so in case we're wrong and some idiot ends up suing us.'

We track use of Alina Mishchenko's phone to see if, by any crazy stroke of fortune, her kidnappers forgot to turn the thing off when they grabbed her. But no. Her phone pinged the mast closest to her parents' Chelsea house at about 1.28 a.m., then nothing further. Phone turned off, battery most likely discarded.

Slim pickings, slim pickings.

On the Tuesday, Burnett puts on a rain mac and does a televised appeal for information. He stands on the little hump-backed bridge above Llanglydwen. Two streams merge behind him, hurtle through the stone arch beneath.

Kitted out in his long coat and serious, official face, Burnett narrows his eyes to gun-slits and tells a spatter of journalists that 'some very significant breakthroughs have been made in relation to the very sad disappearance of young Bethan Williams, abducted from this village more than eight years ago. We also have to take seriously the possibility that Bethan's disappearance is connected with the strange death of Alina Mishchenko, who may have spent a day or two in this area in the period immediately preceding her death.'

He appeals for information. Promises total confidentiality, total commitment.

I'm not there, but I watch his performance on BBC Cymru Wales and think he's pitched it just right. The very picture of the dogged rural copper.

Those media appeals always generate a surge of calls, or at least they do when both victims are reasonably photogenic young women, but we've had nothing helpful yet. May get nothing ever.

In the meantime, we have another angle to explore, a dark, wet and dripping one.

Burnett makes contact with one of the people who runs the South Wales Caving Club. Tells him we want to investigate a cave in Llangattock – a good distance from our actual location – and can he recommend someone to guide us. Also: can we borrow whatever equipment will be needed. The answers to those questions are yes and yes. Not even just yes, but yes certainly. Yes, definitely. Yes, nothing would be easier.

Burnett, who was expecting a boring negotiation over consultancy fees and risk assessments and insurance arrangements, is surprised by this. I would be too, except that last year I worked with a couple of rock-climbers on an assignment and they had the exact same attitude. One of genuine surprise that someone might want to offer them cash to do something that they'd enjoy doing in any event.

'They're nuts,' I tell Burnett. 'That's the thing you have to understand. They're crazy people. We should probably lock them up for their own safety.'

He doesn't let me lock anyone up. We do, however, meet a guy called Rhydwyn Lloyd at the SWCC hut in Penwyllt, a row of old stone cottages that's been converted into a base for cavers returning from the dark below.

Lloyd is brightly cheerful, like a spaniel puppy. He has an open smile and blond curls over a broad forehead. An instantly likeable man. He riffles through a cupboard full of kit, adding junk from his own collection when needed.

Helmets are easy enough. Mine comes in fetching yellow, Burnett's in dayglo-green. When I tell him he looks like a radioactive apple, he tells me to find a mirror.

Boots are also easy. The ones I have, the ones I used when I was doing all my night-time digging, are fine. As Lloyd comments, 'They're trashed already.'

It's not hard kitting Burnett out with all the other bits and pieces. Except that his waistline has a comfortable midde-age swell, he has a fairly regular build and Lloyd doesn't have a problem finding stuff to fit.

I'm a bit more of a problem. Lloyd finds me a fleecy one-piece undersuit in 'Small', but it still flops down below my ankles and hangs in bags around my waist. Lloyd picks at the flaps as though that'll make them vanish. Then looks at me as though I've done something wrong.

The oversuit, a waterproof thing in blue and black, fits a bit better and by the time Lloyd has found a belt and punched an extra hole in it, we find a way to pluck, fold and buckle me into shape.

Lloyd adds gloves, neoprene cuffs, and torches to a mounting pile.

I tell Burnett he looks like a sewer maintenance guy.

He tells me I look like I had a fight with a tent and came out second.

Lloyd shows us our lamps, how they work. Gives us each a 'dry bag', in which we'll carry food and anything we might need for police work: latex gloves, cameras, evidence bags. Fills a couple of bigger tackle bags with ropes, karabiners, belay devices, ascenders, spare torches, batteries and other stuff I don't recognise. The bags look heavy and I'm happy to leave them to the men.

Safety.

Lloyd talks us through the basics. Keeping contact. What to do in case of injury. Keeping warm. How to avoid getting lost.

'The main thing is a Disaster Alert Plan. Basically, we need to tell someone where we're going, how long we're going to be gone for, what to do if we don't come back.'

Burnett shrugs. Starts to say he'll just tell his boss, but I intervene.

I say, 'I'm not sure,' which is me-code for, 'I think that's a terrible idea.'

Burnett says, 'Fiona . . .' in that warning voice of his, which is him-code for, 'Do you remember I'm the boss?'

'Sir, these kidnappers got inside Mike Kennedy's unit. Or had a mole planted in the Met. Or had the systems expertise to hack into police systems remotely. Do you really want to bet that Dyfed-Powys is proof against attack?'

That pauses him, so I whack him with my follow-up while he's still reeling.

'Or, to put it another way, do you want to be crawling around a tiny little hole in the ground, uncertain about whether a highly professional kidnap gang might know exactly where you were? And if that gang knew you were on the hunt for Bethan Williams, a girl who might still be alive and who might, in that case, still have evidence that could compromise the entire kidnap operation, would you feel confident that they would not attempt any countermeasure?'

Burnett thinks about that.

Thinks about that, scratches his jaw, and says, 'Ah.'

We have a brief discussion of alternatives, but Rhydwyn Lloyd knows this territory well and calmly proposes a solution. We'll simply act like any serious caving party, and leave a detailed plan here at the caving hut in a sealed envelope. If we're not back by 8.00 p.m., Lloyd will ensure that one of his fellow cavers opens the envelope and organises a rescue. Simple, sensible, foolproof.

A plan that can't possibly go wrong.

32

Friday morning.

A shallow frost crisps the fields and hills. A blue and yellow light falls over a sparkle of silver, white and the palest winter green.

Burnett and I arrive at Penwyllt first. Smoke outside in this frozen dawn. We ask each other about our Christmas plans. Our answers are absent-minded, distracted. Knocked off course by the anticipation of what lies ahead.

It's not long before Lloyd rolls up, driving a much-travelled Ford Fiesta in muddy claret. He says no to a ciggy and stands as the two of us blow smoke upwards into the rising light.

'So,' he says. 'The big mystery. Where we're going.'

Burnett says, 'Not far,' and waves his DAP envelope in the chilly air.

We go inside. The boys get changed in the changing area. I change alone in the long common room. Twenty easy chairs, a pile of mags, a cast iron stove. Two or three tattered boxes containing board games. I undress as far as my knickers. Then climb into my undersuit, which feels furry and nice. Waterproof oversuit. Nylon belt. Thermal socks. My already trashed boots.

To my dry bag, I add a tin which holds twenty roll-ups and a lighter. Half the roll-ups are tobacco only. The other half aren't. Not standard caving equipment, but I like to be prepared.

I join the boys, who are already dressed.

Lloyd leaves the envelope in the hut's little office. We put our names, the date, and an 'Is it after 8.00 p.m.? Please check our DAP!' message in huge red letters on the whiteboard.

Burnett adds 'Don't forget us' with a picture of a Christmas tree. That's a bit girly for him, so I know he's nervous too.

Lloyd promises that he's got two separate cavers charged with checking whether we're back on time, adding, 'Cavers are serious about that kind of thing. They won't forget.'

He sees we're nervous. I like that.

We drive up into the mountains. Lloyd's car, because it's the one with all the kit. Burnett gives directions. I sit silent in the back.

A pale sun starts to tackle the frost. The lines of white are hardest and deepest in the north-facing shadows of walls, hills and hedges.

We get to the Llanglydwen valley, its mud and its mists lost beneath this scattering of diamond.

Climb up to our little hole. Our underground burrow. The little trickle of silver water spilling out.

'Oh cool,' says Lloyd, seeing the entrance we've uncovered. 'That's really cool.'

He wants to take a quick recce before committing us and dives into the hole, feet thrashing briefly in the light.

'Crazy,' I say to Burnett. 'Locking them up would actually be kinder.'

Ten minutes go past. Fifteen. Twenty.

Burnett says, 'Do you think he's OK?'

'No, I think he's crazy.'

Another fifteen minutes pace anxiously past, before we hear a dim echo, stone on stone, followed shortly by Lloyd's helmet and excited face.

'OK,' he says, 'it goes. I mean, *really* goes. This isn't one of those things that just goes a few yards then peters out to nothing. It's a biggie and it's a goodie. That's the good news. The bad news – bad if you're you, good if you're me – is that the entrance crawl is fairly tight. Four, maybe five hundred yards before you get to a real chamber. Basically, it's on your face and belly to start with. Proper caving. Now, how we're going to approach this is . . .'

Confident and in command, Lloyd lays out the plan. He's going to escort us on the entrance crawl, then come back for the tackle bags. 'We'll establish base camp, basically. If the system looks really big, we can bring sleeping gear and food and set up shop.'

At that phrase – 'sleeping gear' – Burnett and I exchange glances. Ones that mean, no way, no chance, you can completely one hundred per cent forget that idea.

We say nothing.

Lloyd says, 'Smallest first, Fiona. Then me, then Alun. I'll help out if either of you have trouble. About a hundred and fifty yards in, we'll have to pass through a choke. That's an area of unstable rock, the result of a breakdown in the passage itself. Don't worry too much about that. The breakdown might have happened a hundred years ago for all you know. This is geology we're talking about. Just move carefully and stay focused.'

We enter the cave.

I squirm on my belly through that narrow entrance. Remember that Bethan Williams did this once at night and through a barrier of cold water. What she could do then, I can do now.

The light changes as soon as I duck into the tunnel. The light and colours. The walls here are a deep blue-black, crossed with lines of wavy red stylolites. The voices and colours from outside are immediately lost, or so dwindled that they might as well be from another world.

I crawl far enough down the tunnel, as far as the first bend, that the others can follow in after me. I wait in a kind of crouching kneel as Lloyd adjusts the settings on Burnett's torch. My head is bowed under the roof above and I think: this is how people kneel in those hostage videos. Waiting for the jihadist's axe.

Behind me, I hear Burnett say, 'Fuck.'

Lloyd says, 'It gets better.'

It doesn't get better. It gets worse.

The dark roof lowers, pressing me down. Mostly, I'm able to look ahead, following the line of my torch beam forwards. Black rock. A trickle of water. The incipient white of stalactites. But there are times too when my helmet bangs against the rock, forcing my face down and flat. When it's like that, I thrutch forwards like those soldiers on their mud-and-wire assault courses. My torch illuminates nothing except wet stone, my moving arms. And all the time, my head and back feel the scrape of rock, the press of mountain.

I started out wearing my dry bag, the one with food and other bits, over my shoulder. But this new posture means it keeps catching and I have to shuffle it down, clipping it to my belt, and wriggling my hips to free it any time it catches on the stone above.

Back in Penwyllt on Wednesday, Lloyd asked me if I wanted knee guards, a kind of hard-compound neoprene thing. I said no because I didn't want to look wussy, but my knees are already beginning to question the wisdom of that decision.

No corpses.

No Bethan Williams.

No trace of previous passage.

Onwards.

Because I can't turn, I can't even turn to see the others are still following. I do sometimes catch the dart of their torchlight. Lloyd's, 'OK, doing good.' Burnett's peppery *fuck*s.

We get to a place where the passage is blocked by fallen stone, its largely smooth walls interrupted by a crashing intrusion from above. My instinctive thought is, 'Oh, that's stupid, it's a dead-end after all.'

I shout something to that effect, but Lloyd just says, 'Yep, don't worry, this is the start of the choke. It's a bit of a dog-leg here. There's an opening up and to the right, but then you've got to fold over on yourself and go back down and to the left.'

My helmet scrapes the ceiling as I try to figure it out. I can't get used to the fact that my eyes can't see anything outside the line of my torch beam, which means I've got to skew my head sideways and flat to get my torch pointing the right way. There is an opening, yes, but fiercely tilted, like a shark bite angling in from the side.

The stone looks ridiculously loose – a pile of tumbled packing cases – and Lloyd is asking me to plunge down into it. I'm hopelessly aware that even the smallest of these rocks could, if they slipped just a little, kill me or trap me beyond hope of recovery.

I have those thoughts and can feel my breath coming stupid-fast and have to remind myself what Lloyd already told us: that passages like this form over millions of years. Collapse over thousands. Nothing I do will leave more than a temporary thumbprint on either of those processes.

So I do as Lloyd tells me. Sideways and up. Then fold over and down. Diving down into stone. A wilderness of rock. The one time I get a proper view of the tunnel above, I see it's a mass of sharp edges and hanging masses.

The three of us kick, slide and pant our way through. There's a moment when one of the two men behind accidentally shifts a rock and we hear that terrifying sound of stone moving on stone. A sound that, blessedly, soon ceases, leaving the tunnel echoing in its own silence and Burnett's swearwords.

When we break into open tunnel again, the relief, at least for me, is tremendous. There's only one other moment of real tension. A place where the passage is half-filled with water, or more than half. A 'duck', Lloyd calls it. Cold stream water slops to within two or three inches of the roof, and only a narrow ginnel of air snakes over the top.

Lloyd says, 'OK, roll over onto your back. Keep your mouth and nose in the airway. Don't splash too much, or you'll scare yourself. You won't be able to see where you're going, but just keep going anyway.'

I trust myself to his words.

The air in the cave isn't warm – a near-constant nine or ten degrees, Lloyd told us earlier – but the water feels colder. Instantly penetrating my outersuit. Turning my furry inner into a wetly sodden mat. The chill of the water and the cold stare of rock an inch above my eyes does scare me and, sure enough, I move too fast, inhale a mouthful of water, metallic and sharp, and scare myself again as I jerk my head up, looking for air, and succeeding only in rapping my helmet on the roof.

Slow down. Calm down.

Steady breathing and steady movement.

'Easy does it,' says Lloyd, 'Easy does it.'

And, not-easily doing it, I pass on through.

Lloyd follows easily behind. A sputter of self-reassuring swearwords from the rear says that Burnett is also through. The number of grey pies and questionable pastries to have descended that Carmathenshire gullet won't have made that last little experience much fun for him.

On we go. The roof starts to lift. I'm on hands and knees now, exhilarated by the sudden freedom of movement.

And then – I'm crawling along and the roof vanishes. Soars away above my head. My torch beam, so close and constricted in its bluish brightness, suddenly cuts a long swath through the inky dark. I stumble to my feet, feeling that odd gravitational shift, the way you do when you clamber out of the pool after swimming a long time. The chamber we're in isn't vast by the standards of vast. It's perhaps twice the length, height and width of that common room at Penwyllt, but it feels cathedral-like to me. Lofty and aerial.

I sit on a hunk of rock and wait for Lloyd (grinning) and Burnett (muttering) to appear. We congratulate each other. Learn to keep our torch beams angled slightly away from each other's eyes, so we can see each other without dazzling ourselves.

Water pools in places on the floor, but is nowhere more than a few inches deep. Somewhere there's a drip of water against rock. A faint draught.

Burnett sits next to me, mixing blasphemy and old-fashioned cursing in a way that is both dully conventional but also pleasingly heartfelt and direct.

Lloyd bounces round like a puppy. Splashes to the end of the chamber. Points out that the passage continues on from there. Pokes around a rubble of loose rock along the chamber's right hand edge, muttering to himself.

When he's done, he trots back.

'OK? OK? You both all right? You've done well. That was a good crawl. Not as good as Ogof Daren Cilau, but still a good 'un. A really good 'un. Now, OK, take a break. Have a rest. I'll get the sacks and we'll set up base camp.'

He gives us instructions not to leave the chamber. Not to fool around with the loose rock. Tells us to sit still and be good, basically, an order which neither Burnett nor I feel inclined to disobey.

Lloyd crawls off in the direction we just came from.

Burnett looks at me.

Says, 'Fuck.'

Says, 'It's all right for you. You're not old and fat.'

Says, 'You honestly still think they came here? Did all that?'

I don't answer that. It's a silly question. We know Roberts was a caver. We know he took Bethan Williams to a pond that was really a cave. That she vanished from under the eyes of one of the best surveillance teams in the entire world. What else could have happened?

I grope around in my dry bag. Find my tobacco tin. Offer Burnett a ciggy – a regular tobacco one – and we light up.

In the silence between our low conversation and stiff nylony movements, we hear nothing except the drip of water and, just occasionally, the sound of Lloyd receding.

Minutes pass.

I say, 'Are you cold? I'm freezing.'

'Well, not freezing exactly, but . . .'

We tell each other that next time we'll come in wetsuits, but both hope there won't ever be a next time.

My own watch isn't particularly waterproof, so I left it in Penwyllt. Burnett wears one of those chunky masculine things, all dials and knobs and pointlessly excessive chrome, and he checks it every few minutes.

'He's been half an hour,' he says.

'He was a bit more than that last time. And he's got those bags to deal with.'

Ten more minutes.

Burnett says, 'Our last CID briefing in Carmarthen. You know, one of those where everybody's there.'

Those don't seem like questions to me, or even sentences, but I say 'Yes' anyway.

'I gave you a good old plug. Said how much you'd done to get us this far.'

I stare at him. Or sort of stare. Keeping the torch beam angled up over his helmet. Catching his face in the periphery of my beam.

I say, 'Thanks,' but don't mean it.

He shrugs. 'These things get back.'

259

Meaning that his bosses will speak to my bosses. Meaning that he'll look after my promotion chances if I look after his.

I don't tell him that I don't want to be promoted. Didn't want the elevation to sergeant.

I say, 'It's better to keep this quiet. Everything. Loose talk costs lives, and all that.'

He shrugs in a have-it-your-paranoid-South-Wales-way sort of way, but I don't think I'm paranoid.

Another ten minutes.

I say, 'Your media thing on Tuesday. How many journalists were there?'

'Oh, I don't know, six or seven.'

'And you knew who they were, yes? I mean they had credentials?'

Burnett shrugs. 'Why wouldn't they? I mean, who turns up to one of these things if they're not running a story?'

I stare at him.

No one. That's the answer. No one turns up to these things except journalists. Journalists and just possibly criminals seeking direct access to the officer leading the investigation.

Burnett, following my line of thought, shifts uncomfortably.

'It's not like I gave them anything that wasn't pre-planned. I stuck to our agreed disclosures. I answered nothing that went beyond that list.'

He means, he said nothing about this cave. Nothing about the nature of our new leads on the Bethan Williams case.

I say, carefully, trying to be every inch the model junior officer, 'And this cave itself. The entrance. There was nothing that would have indicated . . .'

'No.' Burnett's face is grimacing, though, and he soon corrects that answer to, 'I mean, I gave instructions . . .'

'Sir?'

'I didn't want anyone fooling around with that cave.

I wanted a man in a car down below, doing nothing, just reading a paper, but keeping an eye on things.'

And, in Dyfed-Powys, with its tiny rural force, its general absence of major crime, its limited CID resources, that instruction might very well end up being executed by a uniformed officer.

I stare at Burnett.

He says, 'Look, as soon as I got away from that media thing, and saw that we had one of our damn patrol cars on the job, I got things changed around. I put a man in plain clothes, in an unmarked vehicle there instead.'

'The patrol car, sir. How long was it there for?'

Burnett nods. An 'all that morning' kind of nod.

We stare at each other.

Burnett says the same thing as I'm thinking. 'Where the fuck is Lloyd?'

He goes to the mouth of the tunnel and yells down it. 'Rhydwyn? Rhydwyn, man, are you there?'

The sound booms and echoes around our little sarcophagus. It presumably travels some way down the passage too, but we hear nothing back.

I don't think that means much. If Lloyd is pushing one tackle bag ahead of him and dragging another one behind him, and if he's in any of the more constricted points in the tunnel, I don't think he'd hear anything much beyond his own breath, the struggle of boot against rock.

On the other hand, I'm not at all keen to be here now. We entered this cave quietly, without a wall of police protection around our entry, because we were pretty sure that we were entering it undetected, unwatched. All of a sudden, I'm no longer so certain.

More minutes pass by. Glue-footed. Leaden.

'How long has he been?'

Burnett checks his watch. 'Fifty minutes. Maybe a bit more.'

261

'Sorry, sir, would you mind calling him again? You've got a louder voice.'

Burnett looks at me, almost more disturbed by my quiet 'sorry, sir', than he would have been by my normal knotty awkwardness. But he's thinking what I'm thinking. He goes to the mouth of the tunnel and yells. Really yells. Gets nothing back.

Too much nothing.

Much too much.

'Sir, I think maybe we should fuck off out of here. I think we should do it now and I think we should do it as fast as we possibly can.'

Burnett looks at me. A swift, hard, appraising look. In normal police situations, we'd discuss things. Balance odds, form strategies. We'd do those things, then the senior officer – Burnett – would make the final call.

This isn't one of those times. He just nods. 'OK. Let's do it. I'll go first. You follow. If we meet Lloyd, we re-appraise. OK?'

That sounds good. We hurl ourselves back into the tunnel.

Burnett has the fear about him now – perhaps I do too – and we move faster than we did before. Even when we get to the duck – when we're on our backs sucking that flimsy inch or two of air – we move fast. Don't even care when we splash ourselves, those drowning mouthfuls. I stay close to Burnett. Close enough that a couple of times I get a faceful of his boot, and find it almost comforting: a reminder of human presence.

Only then we get close to the choke, that place of tumbled boulders.

Those suspended rocks, a collapse running in slo-mo geological time.

And only there does the darkness of this nightmare truly start to close.

Lost in that wicked tangle of stone, I hear Burnett saying, 'Rhydwyn? Rhydwyn? Are you OK, man?'

I can't see, not really. There's not enough room to look. But Burnett mutters a commentary. 'Fuck, he's hurt. He's . . .' I think Burnett's initial assumption is that Lloyd has been injured by one of those rocks, something fallen from the unstable mass above. An injury in this place would be bad enough, but as Burnett gets closer in, his tone changes, darkens. 'Christ, Fiona, there's blood here. Oh, Jesus. Oh, Jesus. He's had his throat cut. Somebody's come and killed Lloyd.'

Burnett's first thought is flight.

Get out. Get out. Get out. Get out.

That's my first thought too, but I've a different idea about the direction of travel.

As Burnett lunges forward, I grab his ankle.

'The other way, sir. It's not safe.'

'What the fuck do you mean, it's not safe? Of course it isn't. Let's just get the hell out of here.'

'Not that way.'

Burnett is plenty stronger than me, but he can't move forward with me hanging onto his ankle.

I plead. 'Look, just come back a way. We'll make a plan. Let's not panic. Let's not rush things.'

That logic works with Burnett. Calms him down a bit. Maybe calms me too. We work our way slowly backwards, until we get to a temporary bulge in the passage. A place where we can just turn about and kneel, albeit still with that awful lowered head.

'Sir, we need to get all the way back to the main chamber. I need you to trust me on this.'

A moment's hesitation. His panic against my insistence. My flat, unyielding face.

'OK.' He says, 'OK,' and we track back. Fast, scared, unhappy.

263

We're most of the way there. Done the hard yards, the long ones, when our world detonates. A flat *boom*, without tone or pitch. A blast of air and flying particles. The crump of rock crashing behind us. Air hardened and dense.

Something moving hard and fast hits my helmet, but doesn't split it.

Then a too-silent silence that leaves our ears ringing with the echo.

That silence doesn't last long. A few moments later, dimly, there's a second hard thump. Much fainter. No blast of baking air. No rush of wind.

Two blasts. The first one nearer, the second one further. The two together blocking our exit completely. Somewhere, close to us, there's the soft tinkle of settling rock. The faint thickening of loosened dust.

Then, for a long and awful moment, everything is completely still.

I roll around trying to check myself for injuries. That's always harder than it sounds: shock deprives people of fine sensation and I find physical dissociation much too easy at the best of times. But stuck on my face and belly as I am, I can't see myself. Can't make a visual check. Can't bend most of my joints.

I *think* I'm OK, but it's an unconfident thinking.

Shout back, 'Are you OK?'

Burnett says, in a voice that's weirdly tight, 'Let's just keep going.'

We keep going.

No more blasts, or none that we hear. The air is strangely, uncomfortably still. My face is gritty. Dust crunches between my teeth.

We move on.

At one point my torch cuts out. It's a moment of terror, almost worse than the blast. The abrupt movement into darkness that would be total, except for the shreds of light from Burnett's torch behind.

I jiggle the battery pack on the back of my helmet and the light comes back on, but goes off twice more on the journey back.

When we emerge into the main chamber, I see that Burnett's face is strained and white. Streaked with lines of pain as well as fear. When the roof heights allow us to stand, I do and he doesn't.

'I took a knock,' he explains. 'Probably need to rest a bit.'

'Arms and legs? You can move everything fine?'

'Yes. I just need . . .'

'And breathing. You can breathe OK?'

He makes a gesture with his hand, which says, 'What do you think?'

I'm reserving judgement on what I think, but what I say is, 'Is there blood? Can you find any blood?'

He just lies there, turned on his side. He's in shock, for sure. So am I. But still, police training says look for blood. Close any wounds. Stanch the flow.

Burnett doesn't answer my question, but the hell with it. I'm an investigator. I'll investigate.

With a quiet, 'Sorry, sir,' I shift his position just enough that I can reach the zip of his nylon outer suit. Pull it all the way open. Then do the same with the inner suit. His face is pulled tautly away from me the entire time. Something much too rigid in the pull of his neck.

When I get the inner suit open, I find the fall of Burnett's belly. White Welsh skin and a scramble of hair.

No major wound. No blood to speak of. But already a vast discolouration. A purple-black mottling all down his left side.

'I'm going to palpate, sir. Let me know if—'

If it hurts. That's what I was going to say. If it hurts.

But I only just start my palpation, the heel of my hand

exploring the base of his ribcage, when he lets out a bellow of pain, a bellow that only causes more pain. His body stiffens and his breaths shorten as he tries to manage the rush of sensation.

Once he's somewhat under control again, I murmur, 'Sorry, sir, but I think we need to know.'

I continue my exploration. As gently as I can. Soft hands.

Get no more bellows of pain, but only because Burnett is virtually biting down on rock to keep himself from yelling out. The ribcage on his left hand side is pretty much staved in. I don't know if there's a single rib there which isn't cracked or outright broken. That in itself isn't life-threatening. Plenty of rib injuries are managed by doing nothing at all. The sheath of muscle all around acts as its own natural sling, and bones can be naturally reset without need for surgical intervention.

But the ribs aren't the problem. If there's internal bleeding on any scale, we just don't know what the consequences may be. If there's bleeding plus a punctured lung, then Burnett may, even now, be starting to drown in his own blood.

He needs a hospital and he needs it fast and we have nothing at all, not even a first aid kit, because the stupid tin box with first aid stuff in it was in the haul bags that Lloyd was going to collect when someone slit his throat and mined the tunnel.

I put my ear to Burnett's chest. Want to see if I can hear the bubble of air rising through blood. I can't, but my ear's not a stethoscope, Burnett's chest carries more insulation than is ideal, and I don't really know if punctured lungs bubble or not.

Burnett: that could have been me, I realise. If I'd gone down that passage first. If I hadn't had Burnett's ample body in between me and the blast.

Burnett says, 'They dynamited the fucking passage. Killed Lloyd and then they dynamited the fucking passage.'

I nod. Don't even have the words to agree.

'Our Disaster Alert message . . .' says Burnett.

'Is fucked,' I say.

A whiteboard and an envelope. We couldn't have made it much easier to erase or destroy those things. Our DAP plan was made on the basis that no criminal gang could have known what we were up to. Our plan was to enter quietly, leave quietly, keep our movements as private as possible.

But since Burnett and his police force, in a forgivable-except-unfortunately-lethal oversight, sent a massive visual warning to any bad guys – 'Yoo-hoo, guys! We're watching something in this deserted location in this quiet-looking valley. Bet you can't guess what it is!' – and since, additionally, any bad guy exploring the hill above that police car would have seen an extremely recent excavation and a tunnel winding back into the hill beyond, I think the plan we chose was quite possibly the shittest possible plan we could have come up with.

I've more than a suspicion that Rhydwyn Lloyd's soon-to-be-grieving family will come to agree with that assessment.

I've more than a suspicion that Burnett, with his shattered ribs and anguished breathing, would concur.

Game, set, match to the bad guys.

Or, in older language, we're fuckety-fuckety-fucked.

Burnett says, 'An ordinary tunnel collapse. That's what it'll look like. Stupid coppers barking up the wrong tree. Too dangerous to pursue that line of inquiry any further.'

I nod.

And yes: if our colleagues dig the whole damn tunnel out, they'd sooner or later find traces of explosive. But who would authorise that dig? Who would authorise it in circumstances where two officers and one civilian have already died and where the whole damn tunnel will now be acutely unstable? It'll be one of those cases where, at best, there'll be a few days of mostly-for-show rescue work, before a grave-faced emergency worker announces that efforts have had to be abandoned.

That wouldn't even be the wrong thing to do. I'd make the same call myself. No point in jeopardising further lives.

And it's a Friday morning, the weekend before Christmas. We're unlikely even to be missed until Monday, and then perhaps only in a knowing must-have-pulled-a-sickie sort of way.

Burnett does the same maths. His sums add to the same bitter conclusion.

'They've blocked our fucking exit,' he says. 'They've blocked our fucking exit and they're leaving us here to die.'

33

First things first and second things second.

Although the chamber here is high enough, the floor is broken and wet. A bad place to lie. Just twenty yards from us, there's an area of floor of gently sloping mud, almost cushiony in its comfort.

'Can you get over there?' I ask.

He nods. Does so.

As his shock wears away, the pain will be starting to come full force. It's actually painful watching him move. The difficulty he has with even minor movements. The gasps that self-release when he can't block them.

But he gets there. In the dry. Comfortable enough.

That done, I say, 'Alun, I've got a tin of cigarettes with me. Do you want one?'

He says yes.

I open my tin and explain, 'These ones contain tobacco only. These ones contain certain herbal additives which may not be strictly legal under the law of England and Wales.'

'You came here with some *joints*?'

'You never know when you might need one.'

'Well, fucking hell, I need one.'

We light up. I breathe my smoke out. Watching it hang and slowly dissipate in the unmoving air.

Burnett says, 'Those Chilean miners. They got them out.'

'They had food. Not much, but some.'

And the people on the surface knew where the mine was. They knew where to look. We're, what?, maybe half a kilometre into a mountain and no one has any idea where we might be. You could drill thirty holes, a hundred, without managing to find us.

Also: that Chilean mine was warm, I don't know why. All the TV shots were of miners bare-chested in the heat. Our dank little hole sits under a Welsh mountain. We're soaked through and the cold is already chilling. It's not lack of food that will kill us, it's the cold.

I sit with my helmet on my legs. Burnett shines a light on it. The plastic battery pack is split. Not about-to-fall-apart split, but loose enough that the battery connections have become uncertain. Burnett's helmet is too big for me, even with the headband tightened to the max, and the battery packs are integrated into the helmet.

'Oh piss,' I say, and Burnett doesn't disagree. I turn my torch off. Spare the batteries.

We smoke.

The sweet, sweet weed of Pentwyn. Cardiff's finest.

'Where did you get these?' says Burnett.

'I made them. I grow the stuff at home.'

He looks at me like I must be joking, then realises I'm not. Gives me a you-South-Walesers headshake but goes on puffing.

I move fairly fast onto a second joint. Offer another to Burnett but he just shakes his head.

We smoke, or I do, in silence.

When I'm halfway into my second joint, something loosens. The shock of that blast dissipates a bit. The shock and the fear.

I look at Burnett. His face is mostly dark under the rim of his helmet, but he looks drawn, wrung out, as though he's been crying.

He says, 'What a place to die, eh? What a place to fucking end it.'

I don't say anything.

He says, 'Thanks for getting us out of that tunnel. I mean, thanks, I *think*. I'm not sure which would have been worse.'

I realise – stupidly, belatedly – that he hasn't got it. Hasn't really understood any of it. I'd assumed that all his 'leaving us here to die' stuff was simply the rhetoric of a frightened man. A rhetoric I could more than understand, more than sympathise with.

I say, 'Why do you think we're here?'

'Looking for Bethan Williams, I suppose.'

'Really? What did you think we'd find – a corpse? A pile of bones?'

'Don't know. But we had to look.'

'No, don't you see? We've found *exactly* what we expected to find. I mean, *exactly*.'

'We haven't found anything.'

I rub my face with my hands.

I wish I wasn't so cold. I wish I wasn't already achey and tired. And, most of all, I wish Burnett was uninjured and intact, as I really, really don't want to do this next part alone.

'Look, we've found a cave system. Not a small one. Not just a little passage running into the hill. But some major system that could even be as extensive as one of the real monsters around here. We've got all that and, so far, no Bethan.'

Burnett stares. Stares directly enough that I have to close up my eyes against his torch.

'Now watch this.'

I show him my joint, make him observe it, pay attention to it, then take a deep puff of the good weed. Hold the breath long enough to get the best of it, then blow it slowly out, a long tube of smoke.

'What do you see?' I ask.

'I see a possession offence, minimum.'

'You see smoke, yes?'

'Yes.'

'Moving or not moving?'

'Not moving.'

The smoke dissipates, but doesn't rise, isn't pulled to one side or the other. It just slowly spreads out, fading to black.

I say, 'Before they blew up that tunnel, there was a draught in here. A wind. You must have felt it on your face. Now, when I first felt that wind, I assumed it must be blowing through the tunnel. From one entrance point to another, an exit point somewhere else completely. But I don't know caves. I don't know how these things normally work. Maybe they have their own air currents. Only then, they blocked one entrance. The one we came in at. And the draught ceased. I mean, from the moment the tunnel was blocked, the draught stopped.'

I stare at Burnett. Because he's now wearing the only light, I can't see his face well, but under the dark rim of his helmet, his lips move silently in shadow.

I whisper, 'So that proves it. The wind *was* blowing through the tunnel. There *was* an entrance and an exit. Our job now is to find the exit.'

'Bloody hell, woman. You find me that exit and I won't bust you for growing weed.'

I grin at him.

He grins back.

Deal. We've got a deal.

'And you're saying that Bethan Williams has already been out that way? That Roberts took her out of the valley right under the noses of the SAS?'

'Yes.'

That 'under the noses' thing is a weary old cliché, of course, but in this case you can't beat it for accuracy.

'And who would do that?' Burnett continues. 'I mean, who

would leave their mother and father, make a new life under a new name? And who would do those things like *this*? A teenage girl, crawling through that bloody tunnel . . .'

'Who would do it? Someone who had very, very strong reasons. Someone who feared for her life. A very brave girl under one hell of a lot of pressure.'

'She found out about the kidnapping? Was scared they were on to her.'

'Or something like that. I'm not psychic.'

I'm a bit snappy because I've got to the end of my second joint and am not quite feeling cooked through. Stupid, really. I made the joints quite weak, because I was worried I wouldn't get the chance to smoke them next to a detective inspector, and brought some tobacco-only ciggies in case I had to share them. Now here I am, sharing my joints and wishing I'd brought a bloody great lump of resin to juice them up.

Burnett is staring at me.

'Rhayader. That van in a barn in the hills above Rhayader. The one that was burned out with a corpse inside it.'

I don't say anything. More of those non-sentences and non-questions. I don't know how these people expect to get a conversation going.

Burnett says, 'You. You were involved, weren't you?'

I make a face. Wave my hands. We're buried alive under the Brecon Beacons and he wants to know my backstory.

He says, 'Bloody hell, *and* Nia Lewis. There was South Wales involvement in both of those.'

I pick up his roll-up. Inspect the stub. He didn't smoke it right down to the cardboard the way I do, but there's not enough juice there to be worth relighting.

I say, 'I'm going to need your batteries.'

'What's your plan?'

'I don't *have* a plan. My plan was kind of fucked when the tunnel came down.' I stand up. 'And your watch.'

'My watch?'

'Yes.'

He gives me his watch, which is just stupid-big on my wrist, but which fits OK if I wear it over my various caving things.

I turn my light back on.

It's hard for him giving me his batteries, but he can see why I need them. He takes them out of his helmet and his light goes dark.

I listen to his chest again. It sounds OK.

I ask him to breathe in as far as he can. It's painful for him that. Pretty much any movement is painful. But when I ask whether he feels short of breath, whether his breaths feel shallower than normal, he shakes his head. 'No. I'm just a fat bugger who should take more exercise.'

But I don't know what that means, not really. Do people about to drown in their own blood know that's what's happening? Is it one of those things that either happens fast or not at all? I don't know. Nor does Burnett. And the questions are theoretical only. Nothing we do here can make a difference. Nothing except getting the hell out.

I say, 'Make your Christmas lists. People you haven't got presents for yet. It's what I do.'

'Wife does all that.'

'Well, I don't know. Christmas cards you ought to send and never do. Something to keep your mind away from all this.'

He gives me a grin. An I'll-be-fine number. Big, bright and shiny. But his task will be to wait here, in this cold and total darkness, with a chest smashed to buggery, and no way of knowing where I am or how I'm getting on. Not easy. Not fun.

Burnett gestures at his dry bag with a finger. 'There's food in there. Take it.'

I'm about to demur, but he's right. I'll need the energy

more than him. He'll get out of here only if I do.

I take the food. A sandwich, a chocolate bar, a banana.

'Thanks.'

'Ogof Draenen. How long did you say that extended underground?'

'Who cares? It's just a big stupid hole.'

The truthful answer is seventy kilometres, but I don't see that Burnett's life will improve if I tell him so.

I'm cold, achey and scared, but as ready as I'll ever be. Food and batteries in my dry bag. A messed-up torch on my head.

A last check of the cavern. There's one entrance, one snaking exit.

I point to the exit. The only tunnel that isn't blocked.

'I think I'll go thataway,' I say.

And do.

34

Thataway.

Walk through this dark cavern to a passage, even more emphatic in its blackness. An angled cleft which presses me over to almost forty-five degrees. Brown minerals chalk the wall, like the runes of a forgotten people. I squeeze along, face pointing upwards at the swell of the mountain above. I have this crazy feeling that the mountain is alive. That a sudden out-breath from it, a sudden flexing of these rocky arteries, will squeeze me to a pulp, unremarked and unnoticed. A little flesh-and-nylon footnote to a much older story.

To start with I focus on making progress, then remember I need also to be looking for any passages forking off from this one. Not only left and right, either, but above and below. Anywhere that could lead to new rooms, new passages.

A labyrinth, yes, but one built crookedly, and in three dimensions.

Knowing that makes my progress stupidly slow at times. Once, for example, I see a dark hole looming, somewhat beyond the reach of my torch, perhaps twelve or fifteen feet overhead. I don't want to scramble up there. I want to move on, but I also know that Len Roberts wouldn't have left that kind of gap unexplored, so I kick my way upwards – curling my body like a comma, jamming up against these tilted walls, moving my legs and feet to a new position, then fighting on up. I get there. Reach the damn hole, but its dark mouth retreats only a few feet, the stone fractured, hanging and lethal. I slip-slide my way back down.

A dead end, but one that was costly to reach in terms of time and energy, and I'm short of both those good commodities, dammit.

Continue.

Get to a proper fork.

A larger tunnel continuing with the line of the rock strata, heading right and slightly down. Another tunnel, much smaller, like the gurgling head of an old streamway coming in from the left.

Eeny-meeny-miny-mo.

I take the larger tunnel.

Flowstone, or something like that. Tubes of brown and beige and a calcified pale white. Minerals laid down over the centuries. Bulgy and alien in the damp.

Even where the tunnel is broad enough and even enough to allow something like an ordinary walking movement, I have to inspect every inch of it as I go. The inky shadows at the base of a wall might hide a tunnel, an exit, the thing I'm looking to find.

I do what I can. Inspect as much as I can while continuing my forward progress. It's hard work. Physically demanding. I'm always bending, twisting, stooping, crawling, slithering, climbing. Shifting loose rock and double-checking tunnel walls.

Hard work. Relentless.

Work that will kill me if I get it wrong.

Onward.

Another cavern, water pooling to the side.

An awkward, small, constricting passage writhes up and to the left. One whose muddy slopes and dark shadows retreat beyond the reach of my lamp. Another tunnel, one of those smooth whale-flanked crawls, takes a stony path twisting and down. My torch fails a couple of times as I explore, but always comes back on when I jiggle it.

I do realise, though, that, give or take the odd bit of flowstone, the occasional unusual formation, these passages look all alike. The next black and watery cavern blurring into the one before, the one after.

When I try to picture the route back to Burnett, I'm already pushed to do it.

Which tunnel? Which rocky, uncertain path?

I don't know. I've a moment of sheer terror when I see how this plays out. Me, with a failing torch, crawling around. A blind beetle in this buried labyrinth. Crawling slower and slower, colder and colder, until my limbs no longer function.

A bad way to end.

A stupid way to go.

So I stop. Three joints smoked. Seven joints left. I light up, lying back against the cavern wall.

The jolt of my head on rock kills the light again and I leave it dead. Nothing in here but rock, darkness, water and the sweet red glow of my roll-up.

Stupid, stupid.

Crawling around like this, no plan, no vision.

The stupidest thing of all: doing this like I'm a regular sort of person. Doing this the way Burnett would. Not that there's anything wrong with him, or his natural process. Just – I'm me. I need to do this my way.

I think: *I need to commit this cave to memory.* Map it. Figure it out.

I'm not particularly good with spatial things. Give me a book of criminal law or a list of vehicle registrations to memorise and I'm your girl. Ask me to steer my way from one part of a shopping centre to another and I'm your classic female incompetent, saved only by my magical womanly ability to ask directions.

There's no one to ask in here, no maps, no GPS.

But – play to my strengths – I do happen to be familiar with the story of Simonides of Ceos, a poet of ancient Greece. It's told that Simonides happened to exit a crowded banqueting hall shortly before it collapsed, killing all the remaining guests. Afterwards, Simonides was able to recall the name of every stricken guest by calling to mind their original seating position and finding the face associated with that position. His method – making associations between places and the things to be memorised – became known as the method of loci and is still the primary tool used by memory champions today.

I realise I need to apply that method to my own situation. A modern memory champion places objects in a mental map: perhaps the rooms of their house, or their walk in to work. My issue is almost the opposite one. I *have* the places – these caverns, these walls – but I need to find a way of making them memorable, one from another.

Make a map. A mind map. A picture of this maze.

That's what I need to do and I start to relax. Partly with the joint, but mostly with the sense that this thing is doable. That I have a manageable task to perform.

I start with the choke where Lloyd's corpse lies buried, exploded, and slit-throated. Think of the tumble of rocks that is even now squeezing him out like a sponge.

I give Lloyd that crush of rock. Let his soul inhabit that space. Spend long enough with his squeezed-out corpse that I feel it, feel him, feel the press of that little dark tunnel.

Once those things are firmly in memory, I move on to the cavern where I left Burnett. Him with his broken rib cage, his shattered chest

That place is easy too. The last big case I worked on featured a guy called Derek Moon, who was struck on the head, then pushed off a cliff. His battered body, half stoved in, lay on the rocky beach below, head staring up at the blue and glassy sky.

Burnett doesn't have the same wide view, but his little muddy beach, his stoved-in ribs are the same.

So I give that first big cavern to Moon's staring corpse. Allow him to merge with the cavern. With Burnett's figure patiently waiting in the darkness.

I move on down the cave in my mind. Reach that first crucial fork. The larger tunnel continuing on, and the smaller streamway emerging from above.

That's a mother-daughter arrangement, I think, and with a pang of feeling, give the smaller streamway to little six-year-old April Mancini, my first ever proper corpse and still one of my all-time favourites. I hesitate about giving the larger tunnel to Janet, April's mother, but Janet had lovely coppery hair and I can't quite fit her with that other tunnel, so I leave her be. I'll find something better for her in due course.

And so it goes. The most significant landmarks, of course, I want to reserve for my best corpses, the ones I've encountered through my work in CID. But a career in policing gives you enough traffic accidents, enough stabbings and GBHs, that I'm able to endow even minor features of this midnight world with a victim. A chattering crowd to map out this catacomb.

And so I smoke my joint, map my cave, and feel the spirits of the dead cluster round.

Carlotta is here too, of course.

She's my most recent corpse and, perhaps, my most importunate, the most demanding. She doesn't want to be left out of my map, but at the same time I can't think it's right to give her any old junction, any bit of dried-out streambed or muddy rockslide. So with her, I hold off. With a little luck, I'll find something really good for her. Her own echoing chamber. Something grand. Something special. I look forward to finding it.

And when I'm done – joint smoked, map made – I crawl

on. Not frightened any more, but excited. Keen to populate my new world.

Reach a place of complex, fractured passages, a kind of meeting point of three or four lanes, one of them emerging almost from the roof and accessible only by a mountainous, lumpen stalagmite. The floor of that meeting point has a litter of smooth black stone, evidence of some old streambed, and I almost yelp in excitement when I remember that Mary Langton's severed head had just such a black pebble clacking in her mouth.

Mary too joins our throng.

I work for two hours. Probing these passages. Peopling them.

I eat a sandwich. Drink water from a pool underfoot. My light, I think, is dimming, but it's good enough to work with. I'm just getting used to smaller and smaller amounts of light.

Two more hours. More food. A cheeky little top-up joint, which I know I haven't quite deserved.

My light is now fading to a silvery-blue nothing. It's strange. The torch still beams. There's an impression of illumination, but nothing is actually lit enough for me to properly make it out. It's like a slow blindness, the last glimmer from a dying star.

I've got Burnett's replacement batteries with me, but I don't know how long *they'll* last and I can't afford not to squeeze the very maximum from the ones I have.

A slow blindness.

A gathering chill.

It's nine in the evening, a full twelve hours after we first entered the cave, when I come across Carlotta's cavern.

It's a really good one. Huge. So long that my limping torch can't even find the end, perhaps not even the middle. The cavern is wide too, broad enough to swallow a church. Up at my end, the cavern floor is rocky, but further on there's the glimmer of water.

Carlotta and her family lived life on a big scale. A cut above ordinary folk. Kiev, Paris, London, New York, Hollywood. That kind of girl, that kind of life. And as soon as I find the cavern, start to understand its true size, I feel Carlotta sauntering down to take possession. I'm thrilled, actually thrilled, to be able to hand it over. My gift to her in exchange for that lovely first night she gave me.

I think, *Silly, whoever it was who laid her out.* Silly to have placed her in a modest little churchyard. Carlotta always wanted something grander. A cathedral perhaps. A saint's resting place. But here, in my torchlit underworld, I've found her the perfect crypt, a place to rest forever. I'm pleased about that. Contented.

I eat the last of my food – half a banana and the last of the chocolate. Think about smoking, but decide against. Then stumble forward to explore my find.

35

High stone arches.

The plop of water falling somewhere out of sight.

The stone, where I can see it, is mostly black, or very dark grey, plentifully intermixed with shades of iron and calcite. Further ahead, water shimmers on the tunnel floor. The blue-white of my torch strikes a temporary silver from the ripples.

I walk on into the cavern, echoey and vast. Walk on until I reach the water.

At that shivering brink, I hesitate. I'm cold and tired. I really, really don't want to enter this water alone. Perhaps I could rest? Stop for the night. Sleep. Start again, revived, in the morning.

I don't quite make a decision, for or against. Prevaricate by deciding to reconnoitre further. I continue into the water.

Ankle-deep, calf-deep, thigh-deep.

There's been plenty of water on my journey already, but nothing at all on this scale.

A giant underground lake? That's your theory?

Yes, inspector. It turns out we have a fair few of them in South Wales. If my researches on the Internet were anything to go by, this particular cavern is large, but would be dwarfed by the much bigger chambers at Ogof Ffynnon Ddu and some others around here. The quantity of water is also unremarkable. Water, after all, is what makes these things in the first place.

I go on until the water level reaches my mid-thigh, then stop. This cavern is too big to explore with the light I have. I can hardly see the side walls properly, and the chamber's end is still in darkness.

I start to track back, so I can replace my batteries on dry land, when my light goes out. It's not just the loose connection playing up again, because when I jiggle frantically at the back of my helmet, nothing happens. Nothing at all.

The darkness is extraordinary. So total, so sudden, that it's like being transported at once to the bottom of the ocean floor, flung to orbits beyond the solar system.

Something flutters in my chest, my freezing hands.

A quick, elusive flutter of feeling, like a small animal scurrying for its burrow. A quick movement of grey-brown, then nothing.

That movement is a feeling, I know that. One I should capture and figure out.

First, I think it's excitement. To be here, in Carlotta'a cavern, standing in this lake, inky and cold, beneath the mountain. To be in a place like this and to know that your footsteps are the first, or among the first, to have trodden here? Well, it's a rare and special thing. A privilege.

But even as I think those thoughts, I feel that quick dart of feeling again, more strongly this time, and realise, *This feeling. I know it. It's fear. Yes, maybe an explorer's excitement too, but that's not the main thing. The main thing is fear. The growing hunger. The gathering cold. The knowledge that this clock is ticking and the endgame is already here.*

But that insight also tells me something further. To explore this cavern in all its chill enormity or not? The answer is that I have no choice. By this time tomorrow, I'll be too weak to crawl, too cold to swim.

I also know that I can't change my batteries here, in the middle of this lake. My hands have long lost all sensation. I

284

can't see what I'm doing. And if I drop Burnett's batteries, the good ones, then I'd never be able to retrieve them.

Here, in this dark place, light is life. Those batteries more precious than gold.

I start to go back the way I came, but that's far harder than it sounds. Within a few paces, all sense of direction vanishes. The lake's uneven bottom means that I'm constantly stumbling and, when I right myself, I'm uncertain about which direction I'm now facing. For perhaps ten minutes, I try simply to walk back to the start of the cavern. Then trip on some underwater hazard and only just manage to stay upright. By the time I've regained my balance, I'm thigh-high in water again and I realise that, for all I know, I'm back standing exactly where I started.

Not good.

The fear isn't fear now, it's terror. To die here, in this place? With Burnett dying slowly of pain and cold all that way back in that first big cavern? Not good. Not good at all.

An unthinkable place to die.

I mutter a swear word. 'Fuck it.' The cavern walls bounce it back at me, in multiple fading copies.

Think, Griffiths, think. It's the only thing you're really good at.

Think. Use your brain.

So I do. I stop to think and it occurs to me that if I'm as blind as a bat, I may as well try to navigate like one.

I whisper, 'Carlotta,' and the sound, too quiet, barely travels over these gently rippled waters.

I try again.

'Carlotta!'

Louder this time, and an echo bounces back. Compacted, close, almost claustrophobic.

Turn my head through ninety degrees.

'Carlotta!'

Another echo, but this time tubular and distant. Remote. I realise that I'm now facing down the length of the cavern, hearing the echo return from a far-distant end wall.

Turning the other way, I try again. A long echo – another end wall – but I think the echo here is less remote than the one before.

I don't think I'd explored more than a third of this cavern before losing the light. I want an end wall, yes, but the nearer one, not the further one.

And so I do it. Navigate my way back by echo. Checking every two or three yards. Keeping the compact echoes of the side walls to my left and right. Checking the sounds to front and rear.

Gradually, the water drops down to knee height. Mid-calf. Ankle.

Then nothing at all.

I'm on dry land, and my panted 'Carlotta, Carlotta, Carlotta', is now no more than a prayer of relief to the dark deity of this cavern.

I change the batteries. My numb fingers do drop them, several times, in the process, but find them again almost instantly. And with new batteries, my lamp comes back on. Full brightness, the way I started this morning. The length of the torch beam is almost shocking. Unreal. Searchlight-bright.

And this cavern is a true monster. My lamp can't pick out the far end. The light just dissolves into a kind of misty blackness.

I'm shivery with cold and I really, really don't want to go swimming in this. On the other hand, I'm not going to be in better shape tomorrow, so I do what I have to do. Walk back to where I was and only when the water is again thigh-high, do I see the far end of the chamber dimly visible in my beam. Dark walls, rising from water.

For a while I just stand, beaming my torchlight at the cavern ahead, looking for exits, but torchlight is a fickle companion. Any outward projection of rock casts a huge shadow which could conceal any number of tunnels leading out. The simple truth is that if I want to check this cavern properly, there's only one way to do it, and that's by exploring its full length.

I try moving closer to the side of the chamber, to see if the water gets shallower. The water *does* get a little shallower, but then I catch my foot on a submerged rock and fall over.

Ah well.

Since I'm now soaked anyway, I just swim in slow strokes the length of the chamber. Black waters, blue light.

From above, Carlotta looks down with grim satisfaction. Relishes this pilgrim prostrate in her dark crypt.

Swim on. Reach the end of the chamber. The water is bitterly cold. The walls rise in a smooth slab overhead. When I test the shadows with my torch, I find nothing. Some broken rocks and fissures, yes, but nothing that a human could walk or crawl along. Nowhere for Bethan Williams to have exited this place.

Nowhere for *us* to exit. Burnett and me.

I've reached a dead end.

The blindest of blind alleys.

Bumping up against the wall, looking for a resting place in this smoothly curved rock, I feel almost furious with frustration. It wasn't meant to be like this. If we'd just come in here with four uniformed policemen guarding the entrance, we'd have had no problems at all. Or Len fucking Roberts could just have told me what he did. He knew I'd found his damn cave. Knew that his secret was out. He could just have told me, instead of bringing me bloody badger stew.

Angry, scared and cold, I swim, stumble and walk my way back to the head of the chamber.

I sit on a stone, while water pours out of my outerwear like someone emptying a wellington boot.

Cold shivers inside me. Cold and fear.

I need to finish this. Bring this little adventure to an end.

I call to mind my map of the cave. The system is a tangle of passages, caverns, crawls and ducks. A system I can make sense of only with my population of corpses, each one lighting up its own little area, its own little catacomb. As far as I can tell, the system is roughly Y-shaped. That long entrance crawl formed the lower tail of the Y. The fork in the system guarded by April Mancini is the crux of the Y. This blind cavern forms the end of the left arm. The right arm is made up of a long series of passages and caverns with countless side-arms and twists and loops and dead-ends, each of which now has its own guardian corpse to identify it.

But if I'm right, I've explored the entire cave system. Looked for the exit and failed to find it.

I go back to my earlier logic, the logic I gave Burnett. Test it. Think it through.

And it's not wrong, I'm certain. Quite apart from anything else, I *haven't* come across the corpse of Bethan Williams and that says, as strongly as anything could, that she entered the cave and *left it again*. Since she didn't leave it, only to re-enter Llanglydwen and the world she'd left behind, that says I've missed something.

Something, somewhere.

I look again at my watch.

The cold is intense and I'm not drying out, not really. Long shivers run through me, ones that are systemic now, that I can't shake off.

I hesitate a moment, then make the walk, crawl and stumble back to that first chamber where Burnett still lies. The journey takes two and a half hours, and I'm numb with cold, the creep of exhaustion.

But I arrive.

When I do, Burnett doesn't instantly move, his body crunched and somehow wrong-looking.

As I draw closer, though, he moves – a bit, not much – and greets me. Asks if I've got anything.

Nothing, I tell him. Say I'll start again tomorrow.

He's positive, encouraging. Tells me to come in beside him and get warm. But I can tell: he thinks we're dead. Him and me. Trapped down here for ever.

He could be right. I think we'll manage one night down here all right, but not two. In twenty-four or thirty-six hours, we won't be dead or anything like it, but I'll be too weak to move and Burnett isn't healing any time soon.

There's no food, so we just talk ourselves through dinner. A huge pile of roast chicken for Burnett. My mam's cottage pie and lots and lots of chocolate cake for me.

I tell Burnett that I'm meant to be home for dinner with my family tonight.

'They won't raise an alarm, will they?' asks Burnett with a flicker of hope.

'Nope. Just think I'm a useless, forgetful idiot, like normal.'

'Oh, well. Pass the gravy, would you mind? I shouldn't really, but these roast potatoes are just too good.'

I pass the non-existent gravy. He eats his non-existent potatoes. We talk rubbish and think our own thoughts.

Burnett manages a belch. Says, 'I can't eat another thing.'

'Me neither.'

'I fancy vegging out in front of a movie now. Coffee?'

I say no to coffee and we bicker about what movie to watch. Settle for an old Connery-era Bond movie, I forget which one.

I offer Burnett a ciggy. He takes a joint and smokes it. I smoke two.

He says, 'Connery is still the best, isn't he?'

I don't really have an opinion on that, but we snuggle

together. I lie on Burnett's right side, the one that doesn't make him yelp with pain if it's touched.

His lungs are OK, I assume. If there was a meaningful puncture there, he'd have been dead by now. He's stiffening up, though, the pain getting worse now that the shock has dissipated. I'm pleased that I'm not him.

And that's how we spend the night.

Burnett's big paws around me. Like an embrace of lovers, except that our bodies are too cold and our minds too distant for anything at all like that. I borrow usefully from his warmth, spooned up inside his curl. He won't get as much from me, but I'm still better than nothing. Even so, and doing everything we can to conserve the heat, we feel, all night long, the cold ground beneath us, draining our heat.

A few times in the night, I feel Burnett shiver. Or maybe I start shivering and the act is contagious. But I feel him try to suppress the shakes. He's awake, but trying to let me sleep. A little act of courage.

I don't sleep, not really, but sleep and me are not always close friends, even at the best of times. So, instead, I just think myself a cheeky midnight snack – one of those lovely gooey chocolate puddings that you can microwave and eat with cream – and think through my long day's journey underground. Walk those dark tunnels again in my head. Corpse after corpse, chamber after chamber. Checking my map in my head. My memory.

I think it through, test it, check it – and feel increasingly certain of my conclusions. I want to wake Burnett and tell him not to worry. Want to tell him how I've peopled these caves with corpses. How I can travel it from place to place in my mind. That I've got it all figured out.

But I don't do that. Partly because I *am* half-asleep and don't want to wake enough to tell anyone why everything's going to be OK. But also: courage is a virtue. Something to

290

keep hold of. Dying well is an achievement, a thing to be proud of, and so far Burnett has handled himself impeccably. It would somehow be letting things down, giving away his treasure, to tell him that he doesn't have to worry, that it'll all be OK.

So I lie in his arms and wait, shivering, for morning. And when morning comes – the luminous tick of Burnett's stupid watch creeping round to seven o'clock – I know what I'm doing.

We wake.

Talk ourselves through another meal, this one a huge cooked breakfast with side-orders of everything. Coffee for Burnett, tea for me, but the real sort of tea, caffeinated and everything.

'Go crazy, why not?' says Burnett, approving of my recklessness as he eats another farmhouse sausage with his fingers.

'You've got bacon fat on your chin,' I tell him.

'I haven't finished eating yet. Food tastes better from your fingers.'

Then – serious face – he wishes me good luck. Tells me with a tone that has already given up. Is already preparing for death.

I say, 'Good luck yourself, mate.' I can't stop myself from grinning.

'You're cheerful.'

'Don't know about you, but I'm planning to fuck off out of here.'

I have another joint. I've not smoked as much as this in a long old while, but I've not lost the knack, it seems.

Burnett wants to know why I'm in a good mood. I show him his watch. 'It's morning. A bright new day.'

When I stand up, I stumble. Light-headed from cold, from lousy sleep, from lack of food, from too much ganja. Burnett watches my stumble. He says nothing, but recalculates his odds. Revises them down from puny to nothing at all. His face saddens but stays brave.

'When you get out,' he says.

'Yes.'

'Forget the Christmas turkey and all that. You can order me a plate of roast lamb. Spuds. Veggies. Bottle of wine. One of those old-fashioned puddings to follow.'

'Treacle sponge?' I say, 'That kind of thing? Spotted dick, rhubarb crumble, bread and butter pudding?'

'Oh yes. Yes to all that. And cream and custard and ice cream and coffee, please. You can bung the lot on expenses.'

'If you don't mind me mentioning it, sir, your arteries won't thank you for that. Maybe lighten up on the dairy products?'

'Bugger my arteries, sergeant.'

'Bugger your arteries. Yes, sir. They're your blood vessels after all.'

We say goodbye. One of those adventure movie, stumble-out-into-the-night goodbyes, the sort of thing that makes my father cry every single time.

I walk off down the cavern.

Burnett thinks he'll never see me again.

36

But it's not hard. If Burnett hadn't been preoccupied with his own demise – or his own demise plus lots of puddings – he'd have seen it too.

I get to April, her forking little chamber. Blow its guardian angel a kiss. A fond smile. Then take the smaller passage, the left-hand fork of the Y, the part I explored yesterday evening.

Yesterday. December the nineteenth. Near enough the shortest day of the year. And I was here in the hours of night.

I head for Carlotta. Her grand chamber. Her rippling, silent sepulchre.

Stand there on the edge of the black water.

It's ten o'clock, or almost.

Broad daylight outside, wherever outside may happen to be. Birds cheeping. Trees waving. Sheep baa-ing.

Outside.

Murmuring a little prayer of hopefulness, I close my eyes. Turn my torch off. Keep my eyes closed long enough for them to become accustomed to the absolute dark.

In my explorations yesterday, I explored every damn yard of this whole damned cave system. Perhaps something, some minor little tubule, evaded my attentions, but I don't think so. I truly don't think so.

And how do you hide an exit? The same way you hide an entrance.

And how, from the inside, do you figure out what's entrance

and what's exit? Well, sometimes the best answers are the simplest and I'm about to try the simplest method of all.

I count one minute. Then two minutes.

I want my eyes to have the absolute maximum sensitivity to light.

And when I reopen my eyes, I see – *something*.

Not an absolute blackness, but, for the first time, a shimmer of something like silver in the dark.

Walk towards it.

Ankle-deep. Calf-deep. Thigh-deep.

I struggle out of my blue-and-black nylon outer. Leave it floating on the water. A shadow corpse, the ghost of me.

When I start swimming, I barely even notice or care about the water's cold embrace.

The silver thickens. Brightens.

As I approach the end of the chamber, Carlotta watching in silence above me, I see a split in the roof. The split was there last night, but its interior, its further end, stood invisible in the darkness.

It's not invisible any more. Through that rift – high, narrow and inaccessible – comes a glitter. I can't see the sky directly, but through that narrow opening comes the reflection of the reflection of the reflection of daylight.

Roberts came to this chamber and he saw that glitter too.

Knew that this chamber was butting up close to the flank of the mountain. Knew that if he could find an exit from this chamber large enough to take a human, that exit would quite likely emerge into the open air.

How do you hide an exit? The same way you hide an entrance.

I reach the end wall on its leftmost flank. My torch back on now, I swim cautiously round the rim searching downwards all the time.

And see it. By the light of my torch, I see it.

An orange rope.

Underwater.

Four feet down.

I take a deep breath. Ask Carlotta to guard me. And dive.

37

Dive down, grab the rope.

My light fails the moment my head goes underwater, but I don't need light now. If I'm right, I'm about to get as much light as I can handle.

I grab the rope. Let my body settle into a roughly horizontal line. Then gently pull.

The rope is anchored to something. To what, I can't see. But I pull gently, sliding myself along. From above, the line looked like it was running straight into the wall of the chamber but, though my helmet scrapes scarily on a low ceiling, my forward movement is unimpeded.

I move, slowly, hand over hand through the cold water.

After – what? – four yards, five?, my head raps against stone.

Panic, instant and complete engulfs me. I yank hard on the rope. I tug at it, thrashing around to see if I can evade the rock that's now obstructing me.

I can't. The rope is fixed to some underwater block of stone and there's no way round, or none that I can find.

The panic lasts only a moment.

I laugh at myself, or would do if that wouldn't mean swallowing a few pints of cold, Welsh hill water.

Instead I ease myself up. Let go of the rope. Allow myself to float upwards.

Once my helmet hits rock, nudging me sideways. There's a momentary *ding* of alarm, but not the panic there was before.

Carlotta can't follow me here, but she's laughing. Gently sad to see me go, but pleased for me as well.

I open my eyes. There's still water above me, but it's not black, not the colour of water rising into rock.

A thin plate of grey, glazed with silver.

I swim up and burst through.

Into air. Into light.

I'm in a little pool encased by a low cave tunnel. The pool is small – a few yards across, nothing more – and I swim and stumble to the little shore.

Lie down, panting. *Thank fuck*. That kind of panting. I can't yet see the outside world, but its light fills this little place. Grey and silver and with shades of green and gold and every good colour that exists in this world above ground.

I feel Carlotta now only as a faint regret. A lingering sadness.

When I'm done panting, I crawl slowly to the exit. Stand when I can.

Stand in the mouth of this short and stubby cave – this cave which looks like a dead-end, closed off by this flat, unimportant bit of water – and look out at an ordinary Welsh scene. Winter fields, their grasses bleached by time and frost. The brown studs of molehills, prickled with silver. Winter trees, leafless, but beautiful. And God's own sky, arched and blue and puffy white and everywhere.

Downhill from me, there are some men planting a hedge. Ripping out some old, dead stumps. Planting saplings that will live another fifty years. They have a Land Rover and a wood-chipper and what looks hellishly like a flask of hot tea.

38

It takes four hours to assemble a rescue team. That's slow-going in one way, but it's the weekend before Christmas and the resources needed are fairly specialist.

Two cavers up from Swansea. Both seriously skilled. Each with a ton of experience in cave-diving and cave rescue. Both of them friends or, at any rate, good acquaintances of Rhydwyn Lloyd. Speaking of him with the solemn respect that only the newly dead enjoy.

Also, a paramedic with expedition experience. Karakoram. Himalayas.

A collapsible stretcher. Sub-aqua gear. Pain medication. Some kind of full-torso strapping, heavily padded. A 1000-lumen halogen lamp, in addition to top-end Petzl head-torches and extra thermal clothing for Burnett who'll be very cold by now.

And food. Because I didn't have much to do for those four hours, I spent the first one getting warm. The hedging guys, having heard some fraction of my story, made me sit in their Land Rover under a blanket that smelled strongly of dog, but with the heating switched to max, and hot tea in my hand, and eating the sandwiches that they'd brought for lunch.

My first phone calls, made with a borrowed phone, were to Jackson. Protocol probably required me to speak to Carmarthen but, sod that, I don't know anyone there, not properly, and if I wanted anyone to arrange a complex rescue operation at short notice, and on the weekend before Christmas at that, it would be Dennis Jackson.

Thereafter, and with Jackson's growly, commanding energy on the case, I knew I could take it easy.

So – bandying Jackson's name around as needed – I got two uniformed constables from Neath to take me to an M&S store. There, I bought a packet of slow-roast lamb shanks with honey-glazed root vegetables and a red wine *jus* that presumably just means the same as juice. And a portion of ready-made mashed potato, with a cheddar cheese crust. And a bottle of Aussie plonk that's on special offer. And a chocolate fudge pudding that serves three to four. And a bread-and-butter pudding with cinnamon and nutmeg and sultanas and candied orange peel. And an apple crumble, because they didn't have rhubarb. And a pint of double cream. And a pot of fresh custard. But no ice cream because, in all sober truth, ice cream seemed like a quite impractical request on Burnett's part and I don't think he'll be cross with me if I substitute with custard. And I sent one of the constables to buy some proper metal cutlery from a kitchen shop down the road, because the stupid plastic things that M&S offer me are no use to man or beast, as I told the perfectly nice headscarfed woman who serves me. Get the same copper to buy a flask and have it filled with coffee at one of those chain coffee shops, with plenty of milk and sugar and cream, as I don't want the boss to get snarky with me just because I have a natural and – just my view – appropriate concern for his arteries. One of the coppers drops by at a friend's house and comes away with a little camping stove and some basic cooking equipment, which means Burnett will be able to eat his goodies sort-of hot instead of cave-interior cold.

I put my booty in a bag, along with the various receipts, so Burnett can start my expenses claim promptly.

When I meet the rescue team up at the exit chamber, I

make them stuff the whole lot into their tackle bags and tell them to serve it properly, and to mind he gets the paperwork.

The rescue party wants to know where it's going of course, and I sketch the cave out for them. The whole system. Every chamber, every turn, every forking twist.

I don't think my map is to scale, but it has every notable feature marked and I can see one of the cave-divers is looking at me quizzically.

'You've been in this cave *once*?' he asks.

I ignore the question. I want to tell him to go gently at April's little junction. She's only six, now and for ever, and she needs gentleness, but I don't know how to say that in a way these guys would understand.

The first diver – properly wet-suited, no furry undersuits for him – drops into my little hole, finds the rope and disappears. A minute later, he's back again, confirming that what I'd said about the underwater tunnel was all correct. Then the two divers negotiate the stretcher and various tackle bags through the tunnel. Come back and escort the paramedic.

I wave them off.

The two uniformed constables from Neath are in a car on the lane sixty yards below me. They thought they should stay with me, as though I were some precious vase with complicated insurance. But I want the solitude, not the insurance.

The solitude, the silence, and a final joint.

Lean against the little cliff and smoke.

Sheep, fields and hedges stretched out under this chilly northern sun.

When you have things, are used to always having them, you forget to value them. Greens and golds and blues and the faint violet buds on these bare December branches. Those things and this freely moving air. These scents of freedom.

I'm still in my stupid furry suit and nylon belt, but I now have a thick police jacket over the top and my legs have dried out and a nice female police officer from Neath lent me a bobble hat that is red and white and has a Christmas tree stitched in green.

I think about our case.

The thing about making a big move, the way our kidnappers did when they blew up the tunnel, is that you have to get it right. Get it right and the kidnappers would have wiped out the two lead investigators. The whole cave thing would have looked like a distraction: the system clearly too dangerous to allow safe passage. Bethan Williams: she too would have looked like a red herring. The kidnap ring itself, well, presumably, for safety's sake, they'd uproot the Welsh end of the operation and replant it elsewhere in Britain. Everything else would go on as before.

But screw things up, as these guys did, and the situation looks very different.

With only a little luck, we'll be able to identify the explosive used. Try to track a supplier. Attempt forensics at the mouth of the cave. See if we can pick up traces of someone other than myself, Burnett and the poor, dead Rhydwyn Lloyd.

Those things, plus there are now two police forces who will be super-committed to deploying every possible resource to catching these bastards.

And Bethan Williams. It's pretty much certain now that she made it out of Llanglydwen alive. Unless something strange happened thereafter, she's more than likely alive now. Getting on with her new life, under a new name, that old past already fading into something a little like barely plausible myth.

Will we find her? Get her to tell us what she knows?

I don't know. Eight years is a long time, but I'm more optimistic than not.

In the lane below, a car stops.

A police Range Rover. One driver. Not in uniform.

It's DCI Jackson. He's about to ask the two uniforms for

help, but peers up the hill first and I wave at him. He waves back.

Reluctantly, reluctantly, I take a last drag on my joint and flick it away from me. Get out my boring tobacco roll-ups.

Jackson doesn't smoke normally, but he makes an exception when it comes to corpses and we're near enough corpses here, I reckon.

He stumps up the hill, looking his age.

'Afternoon,' he says, when he comes into range.

'It's a nice one,' I agree.

'You in one piece?'

I nod. Give him a ciggy. We light up. Backs against Welsh rock looking out over a world full of good Welsh light.

For a while, a good while, we don't speak.

'Christmas shopping today. That's what the missus had planned. You got me out of that one.'

I give him a *proud to serve* sort of gesture, but don't really put my back into it.

Christmas shopping: what I should have been doing too. And I should have been with my parents last night. My mam will have been upset with me.

Oh, well.

'Your man, Burnett. He'll be OK, will he?'

I say, 'Yes, I think so.'

His rib injuries looked horrendous, but in the context a few painfully broken bones hardly signify. And I'm fairly sure that if he had a punctured lung, we'd have known all about it by this morning.

'Cold?' asks Jackson.

'Yes, he'll be cold. But – ' I shrug in that way you have to do if you're saying something a bit delicate about someone's weight – 'he carries more padding than I do, and I survived.'

Jackson asks a bit more, then dismisses the issue. Nothing to be done but wait.

He bums another roll-up.

Lights up, inhales, exhales.

'He's worked with you, but lived to tell the tale, eh? That's not bad going, considering.'

We talk about Rhydwyn Lloyd, who suffered worse than one shattered ribcage. It won't, thank goodness, be either of our jobs to break the news of his death to his family. Not us who'll be knocking on a well-garlanded door to smash every peace-and-goodwill sentiment within.

'Poor sod,' says Jackson, but there's a grimness around his jaw which says that his thoughts are running on more polician lines. *Get the bastards* lines.

I say, 'We should probably get the bastards, sir. You know. Arrest them. Prosecute them. Convict them. That sort of thing.'

'That'd be good. You should look into that.'

'Yes, sir. Will do.'

'Got any leads?'

I talk to him about getting Forensics on the cave entrance. The one we entered by.

'If we can find what sort of explosive they used, we might be able to trace any recent purchases. And of course it's hard enough getting in and out of those damn tunnels as it is. Doing so in a way that avoids leaving any trace forensically must be just about impossible.'

'Whoever did it would have worn gloves, presumably . . .' says Jackson, uncertainly.

'Yes, but . . .'

I don't answer, or not properly, but latex gloves would have torn to shreds within seconds. And, in any case, DNA-testing is sensitive enough these days that any drop of sweat can be tested for skin cells. A single broken hair. There's just no way a person could kick and thrutch through those tunnels without leaving a trace. And, with its cool, constant temperature and absence of sunlight, that cave isn't far from being an ideal place to keep those traces in a perfect state of preservation. Whether our guys can find those traces, and whether the resultant information will be any use to us if they do – those are open questions, of course.

Jackson says, 'I'll get Carmarthen on to all that. Offer our resources if they need support.'

I nod. Good.

'This'll stay in Carmarthen, of course.'

He means the inquiry. Means that, even minus Burnett, and even given what's looking like an increasingly onerous workload, the inquiry will remain a Dyfed-Powys-led operation.

I mutter something vaguely polite. I don't really care who runs the damn inquiry. Don't care, as long as the person in charge isn't terminally stupid and as long as I'm left with a little freedom of action.

'Rhiannon said to pop in later. If you can. If you want to.'

I nod. I will if I can.

'And well done, I suppose. I can't think of any other officer of mine who'd have got themselves into that situation. But I can't think of anyone who'd have got out of it either.'

Is that a compliment? A Jacksonian compliment? It's not quite clear, but I say, 'Thank you,' anyway.

Jackson stands. I stand. We walk together down the hill.

39

Saturday, what's left of it, is a day for home and hot baths and speaking to my sister on the phone and padding around in bare feet with the room thermostat turned up so high that even though I'm in knickers and a dressing gown, nothing else, I still feel too hot.

Call my mam. She's out, but I leave a message apologising for my no-show last night. Tell her I'm looking forward to Christmas Eve, the start of our family Christmas.

Go to sleep early that night. Sleep well.

Sunday starts out slow. I sleep in, pad downstairs for some peppermint tea, then go back to bed and spend two or three hours on the Internet. Wikipedia: the source of all good policing.

When I'm done, and still in my dressing gown, I go down to the kitchen to make myself a huge breakfast – huge by my standards, that is: tea and toast and bacon and a three-egg omelette which I make by trying to fry three eggs in the same pan, making a mess of it, then stirring it all together and wondering how come the bottom starts to char before the top part has managed to cook.

I think I should eat it all, that I must still be hungry, but I'm really not. I eat most of the middle layer of egg – the bit that's neither burned nor raw – but the truth is that the itch of impatience is on me now, and I leave my toast and most of my bacon. I don't even want the egg I do eat.

Hat, coat, scarf. Car keys. Phone. Bag.

Gun.

I'm actually standing in my hallway, checking my bag, having that know-I've-forgotten-something feeling, when I realise that the thing I think I've forgotten is a handgun. Except that British police officers don't ordinarily carry guns. I'm not a firearms-trained officer and my supervising officers would refuse point-blank ever to authorise me to carry a weapon.

Also: most people don't need guns when making an ordinary set of house calls.

Not for the first time, I wonder why I have a thing with guns. Why I sometimes grope for a gun which isn't there. Why – at one time during my life – I slept with a gun by my bed and why I slept like a baby as long as it was there.

Don't know.

Don't know, don't care. Glaciers on Pluto and small boys with snot.

Gunless, I jump in my car and see where it wants to take me. To hospital, is the answer. Not Carmarthen's Glangwili General. Burnett's injuries necessitate the kind of complex surgery that only the University Hospital here can offer. So we pootle up Eastern Avenue, my Alfa Romeo and I. Park. Locate Burnett: the prize exhibit of the orthopaedics ward.

He's looking fine, basically. Cheerful.

Of his ribs, he says, 'Smashed to buggery, but everything basically fixable.' He shrugs a bit, with his right shoulder only, and gives me all those surgical details that are so involving if you're the patient and somehow just gibberish if you're not. But ribs are quite easy, surgically speaking, and he somehow managed to avoid lasting internal injury.

'I'm a fat bugger, see,' he tells me, contentedly. 'Carry my own anti-blast padding.'

I say the things I think I'm meant to say, then his face goes flat and shiny and he says, 'Thanks for getting us out of there. I won't forget what you've done for me.'

I tell him, OK. No worries.

He thanks me for the food.

I tell him *de nada*. Ask if he's processed my expenses yet.

He starts thanking me for something else. I don't really hear what.

I change the subject.

We talk a bit more until Burnett's earnestness and his smashed ribs and these hospital smells – these careful nurses and squeaky vinyl floors – send me running again.

Running for the hills.

Neil Williams first.

He's in his farmyard, tinkering with his tractor. Flat cap. Tweed jacket so grimy it looks like it's grown over him, woody and mossy and smelling of green.

He straightens when he seems me. Mostly pleased, part anxious. Asks me if I want to come in.

I do.

He lets me in and stands back, a marine recruit readying for the sergeant's inspection. And I play my part. Do actually inspect every room of the house. For clutter. For damp. For cold. For grime.

It's about a hundred times better than it was. Maybe a thousand. There are still a few little drifts and piles of clutter, which I point out sternly. Williams promises to shift them.

The first time he makes the promise, it sounds like one of those things that people say and don't mean. Like me telling the glossily slingbacked Jill how I couldn't wait for her to come round to mine. So I don't leave it there. Make him actually assemble all the crap on the kitchen floor, and tell him I want it all properly sorted by the next time I come.

He nods and promises and this time he means it.

Good.

The house remains colder and damper than any city-dweller would keep their home. The kitchen still has a smell of sheep and mud that perhaps is endemic to any farm of this size and type. The living room has walls painted a pale bathroom blue. The sofa is old and its threadbare flowered weave is covered by a blue throw, which is itself balding and puckering with age.

I stand in the doorway between kitchen and living room. Revolving between the two. Trying to figure things out.

Say, 'Mr Williams. If Bethan returned now, if she walked through that front door today – or not today, but in two weeks' time, four weeks, or I don't know, some time soon – what would she think? What do you think she would think?'

He's unsure. He's not a particularly verbal man and has trouble articulating his thoughts, but we get there. She'd find it a bit 'country', a bit wild. 'She liked things, not all pink and frilly exactly. But she liked things right. Done proper.'

I try to figure out what that means, but I think I know. I think Bethan would like a more contemporary version of anything my mother likes. Cream walls. Sofas from John Lewis. Side lamps with silk shades. Prints or photos on the wall.

'Mr Williams, I think we need to get at least one room properly ready. This room. The living room. New paint. New carpet. New furniture. Everything done right, top to bottom.'

He nods. Can't speak. His eyes are bright and overfull.

'I'll arrange for someone to come here and sort things out. But you'll have to pay. Do you have the money?'

He nods. Pawing at his eyes. Not knowing what to do.

'It'll be thousands. And I'm not promising that she'll ever come back. You do understand that?'

He nods. Says it's fine. His voice is choked but I pretend not to notice.

I make him show me photos of Bethan. All the ones he has. Her, and Joanne, and him too. Their shattered family.

He's got quite a good collection, in fact. Wedding photos. Baby photos. First day at school photos. We make a pile of the best ones and I tell him he needs to get them professionally framed.

He blots his eyes and promises me yes. He says, 'Before. Those other police. They weren't like this. I'm not saying they didn't try their best, like, but . . .'

He stares with puzzlement into the ashes of his life. How the man in that wedding picture, the proud father of that little baby girl, became this man alone on a lonely hillside.

I tell him, 'That lot before were Dyfed-Powys. I'm South Wales. Part of the Life Reassembly and Home Decoration Team. And I want you back on track. If your Bethan ever does walk back through that front door, I want her to think this is a place she'd like to come and stay in. The kind of home she might create for herself. And I don't want her to think of you as the angry father she left behind, but as a loving one waiting to welcome her back.'

He promises me, again, that he'll do everything I say and I leave him there, in his living room, looking at photos of Bethan.

Leave the house. Drive down the hill.

Roberts.

Len bloody Roberts.

March into his damn shack. Kick off the well-meant assaults from Judy. Stare at the old villain with blazing, angry eyes.

'Well?' I say. 'Well?'

At first he says nothing.

Then he says, 'Look.'

Then he says, 'I'd of come to get you. I wouldn't of left you in there. I didn't even know about the collapse till the day after.'

That puzzles me a moment. How come people didn't hear the bang? Say something to that effect.

Roberts replies, 'There weren't no bang. I mean, up close, if there'd been anyone there, then maybe. But what I'd have done – and it weren't me who did it – would be set off a charge, only a little one, in that boulder choke.'

I interrupt. 'There were two charges, not one. Two detonations.'

'OK, so two small charges, both ends of the choke. Just enough to bring him all down. Anyone looking wouldn't even think about a bomb. They'd just see a tunnel collapse. Prob'ly blame you for entering where it weren't safe.'

I nod. That makes sense.

Too much sense. A plan almost perfect in its conception. Almost perfect in its execution.

Roberts continues, justifying himself. 'I knew you'd gone in there. Was expecting you to come bouncing round as normal after. Had stew ready, and all. Then when you didn't . . .'

He goes on to tell me that the next day he tried entering the tunnel the normal way, found it blocked, realised what must have happened and went over the hill to the cave exit on the other side.

'I'd of got you out,' he says, 'but I saw the ambulances and all that and realised you must of found the dive already. Good going that,' he adds. 'Took my brother and me more 'n' a year to find him.'

'You could just have told me about the cave in the first place. You could have told the police all those years back.'

He shakes his shaggy head. Mutters something that doesn't get further than the thick furze of his beard.

310

I say, 'That cave almost killed Inspector Burnett. It *did* kill Rhydwyn Lloyd. I don't know if you knew Lloyd, but he'd have known your brother.'

Roberts nods, admitting the acquaintance, but says, 'It wasn't the *cave* who done it.'

'I know. And I know it wasn't you who blew the tunnel.'

He says nothing, so I push.

'Len. The cave. You took Bethan Williams out that way because you knew the valley was being watched? You knew there were men on the hills?'

'SAS, them boys were. They're the only ones as could hide like that.'

'They were SAS, yes. And they were there to protect Bethan. To find her. To take her back to her family.'

'That's not protecting her.'

'Oh really? How did it work out then, your plan? How many corpses so far, Len?'

He scowls. His look is blazing and dark, but also furtive. Temporary. A look that grazes my face only briefly, then hides back in its own shadows.

'I hope you get them bastards,' he says.

'I will get them bastards, but you could just have told us. You could just have told the damn police at the time. Like, when someone said to you, "What the fuck did you do with Bethan Williams?", you could have given them the fucking answer.'

'I couldn't. I promised.'

'Promised who? Bethan?'

He nods.

The stupid sod is still in love with her, I realise. The one true relationship of this man's life is still alight in him. Preventing him from engaging in any further adventures in the world of the ordinary, the loving, the human, the connected.

'Mr Roberts, I want you to come to a police station with me now. I will interview you on the record. And you will tell me every damn thing that happened. You will not face charges. But you will tell me every fucking thing that happened and every fucking thing you know.'

Roberts's face changes. Becomes mobile. Flickers sideways. And, for a moment, I think I have him. Think I've got the stubborn bastard to relent, to allow change.

But if he relents now, what have the last eight years been for anyway? This stupid, impossible love of his, this pointless sacrifice – what do they become if he just leans forward into a police microphone and tells us everything?

So he says no. Says sorry. Apologises and means it. Wishes me luck. Offers me tea and a ladleful of God-knows-what from the black pot of sin on his stupid homemade stove.

I turn down the food, the drink and the apologies. 'Promises are for helping people. If they don't help people, they're pretty fucking stupid.' I tell him if he ever grows up enough to change his mind, I'll drive him over to Carmarthen and we'll do things right.

He watches me go with Judy in his arms, that tangled beard, those flashing, unreadable eyes.

The stupid sod. That thwarted, idiot heroism.

I'll talk to Burnett about all this. We could just send a squad car to pick Roberts up. We can't, as it happens, arrest him, as we suspect him of no crime, but we could try intimidating him into giving us a proper interview. Personally, I don't think that option has a hope of working, but it'll be Burnett's call, not mine.

I think he'll agree with me.

I get back into my car and drive – freewheel almost – down the hill into Llanglydwen and the further few hundred yards that lead on to the monastery.

Those quiet walls, that peaceful courtyard.

312

Matins. Lauds. Terce, sext, nonc.

Then vespers, compline.

I've missed none and it's not yet vespers. I search out Father Cyril, the tall, blue-eyed, smiling abbot with that more-than-human grace.

Find him talking to Brother Gregory in the tool shed. Ask for a few moments in privacy.

He takes me not to the farmhouse's main reception room where Burnett and I first interviewed him, but upstairs to his study. Small. Not much by way of creature comforts. A lot of theological work. Bibles and prayer books. Plus an accumulation of the sort of paperwork that this life, this monastery entails.

Bills for oil, electric, water. Diocesan correspondence. Ministry of Agriculture grant application forms for certain works connected with one of the barns. Veterinary certification for the animals. Most of the paperwork is filed in lever-arch files with their contents marked in felt-tip on their sides. Some of it spills over the desk. The detritus of a lived life.

Above the abbot's desk, two little prints. Icons, I suppose he would call them. A male figure and a female one. The male one is standing on a green hill and has a white dove perched on his shoulder.

He sees me looking.

'You'll recognise our patron, of course?'

It takes me a second, but I realise he's talking about St David, a Welsh bishop of the sixth century and the patron saint of Wales.

'David,' I say. 'A local boy.'

'Local enough. He was preaching at the Synod of Brefi to a large crowd. Because those at the back couldn't hear him, a small hill rose up beneath him. The dove here settled on his shoulder.'

'That's his big miracle?' I ask. 'Making a *hill?* In *Wales?*'
It's hard to think of a more superfluous achievement.
Making ice for the Inuit or sand for the Bedouin might just
about top it.

Cyril laughs. Indicates the other icon. The image shows a
woman in bed – sick, or dying, or maybe just asleep – and all
manner of heavenly wonderfulness breaking out in the room
above her. Cyril's long finger keeps pointing and he has his
eyebrows raised.

Wants to know if I recognise the image.

'No idea,' I tell him. I'm not really au fait with medieval
saints. Just know that most of the women ended up
being broken on wheels, or purged by fire, or dying from
exceptionally holy self-imposed starvation.

Cyril says, softly quoting, '"And He showed me something
small, no bigger than a hazelnut, lying in the palm of my
hand. In this little thing I saw three properties. The first is
that God made it, the second is that God loves it, the third
is that God preserves it. But what did I see in it? It is that
God is the creator and protector and the lover. For until
I am substantially united to Him, I can never have perfect
rest or true happiness, until, that is, I am so attached to
Him that there can be no created thing between my God
and me."'

That's nice, I think. More compassion than hellfire. I say
as much.

Cyril nods, like I've just passed a test. 'Mother Julian of
Norwich,' he says. He shows me a small leather-bound volume
and adds, 'Her little book, *Revelations of Divine Love*, is the
first book in English known to have been written by a woman.
And it is one of the greatest. You should read it.'

'Maybe sometime.'

'That sounds like "probably never".' He laughs at me but
it's a generous laugh.

Across the yard, the solitary bell starts to toll. Cyril glances over and apologises.

'I will have to go in a moment. You didn't come to learn about Mother Julian.'

'I want to know about Alina Mishchenko. The girl you gave shelter to. She didn't stay in that room. The room where we found the genetic material.'

Cyril, shortly: 'I don't know which room she was in.'

'She wasn't in any of them.'

Cyril is irritated with me now. It's one of the holy things about him, this lack of concealment. Like he doesn't have to play games of pretence, he can just be himself and trust that the result will be a good one.

'I'm not a forensic expert. All I can tell you is that she stayed with us for a few days. Then moved on. Why you did or didn't find anything, I don't know. I couldn't tell you.'

'A few days? Before, when we first interviewed you, you said two days. You and your colleagues.'

'Two days, then. What I said then would have been right. It was nearer the time.'

The bell's tone has changed now. A long, slow beat through the twilight. Cyril stands.

'I'm sorry. I need to go.'

'*I'm* sorry. I need a truthful answer.'

Cyril laughs. There is something intensely seeing in his eyes. And compassionate. And as patronising as fuck. And I don't like being patronised.

On an impulse, he gives me the *Revelations* book. A gift.

'If it's truth you seek . . .'

He leaves. Starts to walk downstairs.

'Father, you must answer my questions. I'm going to have to insist.'

315

He reaches the turn of the stair. Broad oak treads. That deep patina that only old wood can achieve.

'I "*must*"? You "*insist*"?' That damn smile again. Then, 'There is compulsion in religion too, in the sound of that bell. And its summons weighs a little greater.'

He goes on down.

Over the banister, I shout, 'There's more compulsion in a pair of fucking handcuffs, Father.'

My voice sounds sweary, and stupid, and aggressive, and thin, and pointless. The abbot just raises a hand and disappears. I hear the front door open and close.

The low bell sounds another twenty or thirty seconds, then silence. Cyril will just about have made it in time.

I go back to his study. Poke around in his things for no particular reason except I'm feeling pissed off and there's no one here to stop me poking. I find nothing of interest. The study is just what it looks like.

Go out into the courtyard.

Dusk. A violet light, speckled with stars.

A free air moves.

I move with it, over to the pigsty. Lean over the wall and grunt at the pigs until I get a hoggy sound of happiness back.

They're happy pigs, these. Peaceful. More peaceful than me.

I feel like – no, I *am* – the least peaceful human here and, to my own surprise, find myself pushing at the church door, joining the evening service.

I sit at the back. The Carlotta position. I'm wearing an ordinary woollen scarf, but adjust that over my hair so that my scalp won't afright the gaze of the Lord. There are a few others there. Spiritual seekers getting a dose of the hard stuff. Just pre-Christmas: boom time for the God industry.

Cryil clocks my entrance – the monks all do, probably – but he and his brothers carry on their chants without pause.

316

I join in, or do mostly. When the monks whack out their *kyrie eleison*s, I come right back at them with my *christe eleison*s. No one's going to out-*eleison* me and no one does. We get to forty each, at which point the *kyrie* camp folds its tents and moves on.

A psalm. A reading. A canticle.

Prayers.

Lighten our darkness, we beseech thee, O Lord; and by thy great mercy defend us from all perils and dangers of this night; for the love of thy only Son, our Saviour, Jesus Christ.

A good prayer that.

I think of Len Roberts hurrying a terrified Bethan Williams up a hill at night-time. Saving her from something, but condemning her parents. A failed marriage, a lifetime of regret.

I think of Burnett and me in that damn cave. *Lighten our darkness, we beseech thee, O Lord.* We could have used a little holy fire in that place.

And Carlotta. Those first hours we spent together in Ystradfflur. *All perils and dangers of this night.* And what a night it was.

I'm intent enough on these thoughts that I hardly notice when the service ends. Hardly notice when the monks do their business with the icons.

The church empties till only Father Cyril and I remain.

He lays his hands on my head and murmurs, 'Go in peace to love and serve the Lord,' and my lips answer, 'In the name of Christ, Amen.' He doesn't move his hands straightaway and I don't move my head.

We stay there for I don't know how long before something shifts and I stand and we walk outside together into the night.

He invites me across to the farmhouse for dinner, but I shake my head. I still want answers to my damn questions, but those will have to wait. Right now, I'm tired. I want to go home and say as much.

I say, 'Sorry.'

He waves my sorry away. Not needed, not wanted.

I hold up the *Revelations* book. 'And thank you. I'll read this. Actually read, not pretend-read.'

He whops me one of his courtly smiles. 'Peace be with you.'

He goes his way and I go mine.

40

Monday morning, Carmarthen.

No Burnett, of course. His boss, a DCI Jimmy Pritchard, is running things for now. He's old school. Ramrod straight. Grey moustache. Doesn't like me. Somehow wants to blame me for injuring Burnett, for making this case complicated, maybe even for finding Carlotta on his patch in the first place. It's as though finding a London kidnap ring operating in the heart of Dyfed-Powys is all my fault. Me, my force, my big-city ways.

But I'm a good girl. Arrive on time. Say, 'Sir' when I'm meant to. Break nothing. Don't swear. Shoot no one.

And I protect the case. Against Pritchard's dislike. His depredations.

'What's all this business with the Bethan Williams number plates?' he asks tetchily. 'That data's eight years old.'

I say, carefully, 'Yes, sir. Inspector Burnett saw a possible link with the Mishchenko case.'

I explain our thinking, making it sound entirely like Burnett's ideas.

Pritchard rubs his moustache with the back of his hand and says, 'Long shot.'

'Yes, sir.'

'What else did Inspector Burnett have you working on?'

I tell him. Our other leads.

Thanks to Gerraghty, we now have a very full picture of

Alina's movements prior to her disappearance and, because of the kind of girl she was and the kinds of place she frequented, most of those movements would have been covered, at some point, by private security cameras. We started soliciting the relevant data in that week before our caving adventure. Material is coming in now and we need to start sorting through it. In particular, we'd strongly expect the Mishchenkos' own house to have been surveyed, and carefully surveyed, by the kidnappers in the week or so before Alina's abduction. We have some possible shortcomings in the CCTV set-up – the system was optimised for the view of the stairs up to the front door itself and offers only a partial view of the street – but these things are never perfect.

We also have those IP addresses, the ones used for the kidnappers' email correspondence. That line of attack remains unpromising, but we have the NCA's tech unit doing what they can.

Then we have that tantalising bit of audio of a London taxi arriving at the Mishchenkos' house at 1.30 of the day Alina was snatched. Not all taxis carry CCTV or systems that monitor locations in real time, but plenty do. We've asked our colleagues in the Met to ask the major taxi firms for help. They've told us fine, no problem. For them, that kind of enquiry is routine.

I talk everything through with Pritchard, including the early forensics work on the cave tunnel.

The entrance tunnel has become unsafe after just a few dozen yards and the forensics boys have been unable to collect any blast residue. They can't use robots to push further in, because they lose radio contact almost immediately.

Pritchard says, 'Where was the blast exactly? How far in?'

'Well, I didn't measure it, sir, but two or three hundred yards, I'd guess. And the tunnel walls were very tight in places. And very twisty.'

Plus the explosive was placed in an area of geological instability anyway. My guess is that the device was fairly small. Just large enough to set off a collapse that would have happened at some stage, no matter what. If it weren't for the direct evidence of Burnett and myself, no one would ever guess that an explosive had been involved. Just an ordinary rockfall in a cave that should never have been meddled with.

Pritchard glowers at my answer, like it's all my fault the blast wasn't bigger, louder, bangier.

I say, 'But whoever placed the bomb didn't have much time, sir.'

'Hmm?'

'Well, sir,' and proceed to offer the fruits of my Wikipedia research yesterday. 'Look, if you want to throw a bomb together quickly, and if you don't have the materials already to hand, you're probably going to choose an ordinary ANFO explosive. That's a mixture of ammonium nitrate and fuel oil, both of which are easy enough to come by. That's the low-tech explosive of choice in all those improvised explosive devices in Afghanistan and the rest.'

Pritchard latches on to that.

'OK, so let's go with that idea. Let's assume that's right.'

I nod. 'The timing is this. Somebody in this kidnap ring saw Burnett talking to the media last Tuesday. That's also the moment they spotted a police patrol car guarding something up on the hillside outside the village. Someone went up to investigate and found the cave. So between Tuesday lunchtime and our entrance into the cave first thing on Friday morning, someone bought or made some ANFO, presumably secured some kind of detonation device as well, placed the cave under some kind of surveillance, and had the materials and personnel in place ready to take action as soon as they saw the three of us enter. That's fast, that is. *Too* fast. I just don't think you can act that fast and cover your trail effectively.'

Pritchard says, 'No, no. When the mines were active, laying your hands on some explosive would have been possible enough. Maybe not easy to get hold of, even then, but now . . .'

Now all the mines are shut and the ex-miners are either coughing black stuff into their old men's handkerchiefs or they've retrained as plasterers or motor mechanics or forklift operators. Either way, none of them are chucking explosives around with the merry abandon of old.

I say, 'Yes, sir. I'm sure you're right.'

Pritchard's face tries out a few different possible looks. Settles on a 'Well, OK then, keep going' one. A face that seeks to convey, 'It sounds like you and Inspector Burnett have been handling things very much as I'd have done in your place.'

I say, 'Yes, sir. Of course. Thank you,' but I can't help remembering Mervyn Rogers's comment back when he stood back to let me into all of this. He said he hated these country crimes: 'You just tramp around in mud, knocking on doors till you find whichever lonely nutter chose this particular moment to go round the twist.' As it turned out, he was wrong about that, very wrong, but I can see that Pritchard is used to one type of inquiry, has spent his whole professional life figuring out how to work those inquiries as efficiently and effectively as possible – and now his DI is blown half to bits and is recovering in a Cardiff hospital, he has fifteen officers, mostly constables, absorbed in work which is mostly to do with data analysis and hardcore computer stuff, and he's having to deal with a load of other forces and agencies – us in South Wales, the Tech people at the NCA, the chemical reporting crew at the Metropolitan Police, a heap of other specialities too. That's not what he ever asked for, ever wanted. But it's what he's got.

And as it happens, we're doing OK, not least because

Burnett, though now at home, is on the phone every hour, issuing instructions, receiving reports, and generally marshalling the whole op.

I have a new respect for him, actually. Case management of this sort is a skill all of its own. Burnett has it. I don't and never will. A police force needs people like him a whole lot more than it needs people like me.

And as we do our work, in this stub-end of a week, this sawn-off Christmas week, the first little nuggets tumble into our lap.

Yes: the Metropolitan Police have located the taxi driver who arrived outside the Mishchenkos' house that night. An interview is being arranged.

Yes: we've made good progress on those old Bethan Williams number plates. During the time that movements in and out of the Llanglydwen valley were being monitored, there were only eight number plates that could be traced to a London owner. Research on those eight owners has given us probable negatives on five of them: four had friends or relatives in the area. A further one was travelling to a holiday cottage rental. That gives us three names where we can't locate an innocent reason for travel. We haven't yet pulled anyone in for questioning, but we don't want to go in hot and heavy until our evidence base is stronger.

On the explosives front, then, no, we haven't yet been able to source any unusual movements of high-explosive or detonation devices, but we have found an agricultural merchant in Brecon who reports a possibly suspicious sale of ammonium nitrate fertiliser. The purchase was on the Wednesday before we entered the cave. It involved just a single sack and was a cash purchase by an unknown customer. Obviously ordinary householders might well use those agricultural merchants, if they need a new spade, say, or some fencing materials, but sackfuls of agro-industrial chemicals are generally only bought by farmers, and those guys are all repeat customers, known to the vendor, typically buying in bulk – and during the growing season at that. Who needs fertiliser in December?

No in-store CCTV, but the till log gives us a precise time for the transaction and there were exterior cameras surveying the car park and timber store. We have yet to acquire and process the data, but the pieces are there.

Monday, Tuesday, we work hard. On the Wednesday morning, **Christmas Eve**, Burnett comes by. He's in a wheelchair and his bloodstream is still groggily high with heavy-duty painkillers. But he's OK. Pleased to see me. Pleased to be on the ship's bridge again, of this inquiry which now looks like a proper inquiry.

He says, 'When Bethan Williams ran, presumably the kidnappers knew why. Wouldn't they have been worried about Roberts too? Wouldn't they have wanted to kill him?'

'Mmm. Maybe. But who actually knew about the Bethan/Roberts relationship? I mean, not even her mum or dad really understood that.'

'That's true.'

'And let's say the kidnappers didn't know about Roberts until you guys started trying to pin a sex-killing onto him. At that point, the kidnappers have to think, maybe we got lucky. Maybe this girl we were worried about got killed, totally at random, by somebody else. Or if not that, then – somehow, we don't know how – she ran away. But since she obviously hasn't told the police anything and since this guy Roberts obviously hasn't told the police anything, even under very strong pressure to do so, maybe we're OK? And if we suddenly decided to kill Roberts anyway – a better-safe-than-sorry thing – then the police would all of a sudden have to think about totally other hypotheses for the two deaths and we'd be at risk of making ourselves more visible not less. I mean, I don't *know* how these things worked, but it seems to me that the fact that Bethan had gone and there were no police officers battering any doors down must have seemed like a sign that everything was OK.'

'Yes. I suppose. Fair enough.' He grimaces. 'It drives you mad, lying in hospital, thinking about these damn things and not actually able to *do* anything.'

'Yes.'

I've been in hospital more than once myself following incidents in the line of duty. It didn't drive *me* mad, but I know what he means. When a big case is heading for its endgame, you don't want to be anywhere but in the thick of it.

Burnett, thinking something similar, says, 'This is shaping up, isn't it? This is shaping up.'

'Yes.'

'We might actually have a case here.'

'Yes.'

'Jimmy Pritchard didn't manage to bollock the whole thing up, then?'

'DCI Pritchard was very helpful, sir.'

'Bet he was.'

It's Pritchard's job that Burnett wants.

He stares at me.

I don't know what he wants, what he expects.

I don't say anything. I don't think my face does anything in particular. His gaze blows over me like wind over barley. Ripples on a midnight lake.

'Fiona, go home. It's Christmas Eve. Take the rest of the day off. You work too bloody hard and, a few days ago, you were almost killed. Take a break.'

I open my mouth to protest. To argue back. But he pre-empts me.

'Go home. That's an order. Fuck off right now, or I call your Dennis Jackson and tell him that you grow and smoke your own cannabis. And I will bloody do it.'

He moves towards a phone.

OK, OK. I wave meek surrender.

I get my bag but, before I go, I check that he knows where we are with the explosives stuff.

He does.

Check that he knows who to call at the Met on the taxi things.

He doesn't but, he points out, his indexer, Ffion Harries, certainly does.

I start to talk through the cave forensics, but he says, 'Fuck off. Right now. If I don't see you in that car park in one minute, I call your boss. Starting now.'

I fuck off.

Get to the car park in less than a minute.

See Burnett's wheelchaired form in the incident room window. He has a phone. Is waving it. Threatening the call.

I do meek surrender hands.

Get into my car.

Sit. Door open. A brisk wind blowing up the River Towy. A chill wind, a chattering wind. A wind born of the wild Atlantic, now blowing over this garrison outpost.

Civilisation's furthest frontier and the first line of her defence.

I do nothing.

Feel the wind. Feel myself.

Have I been overworking? Maybe. Quite likely yes.

The wind blows. The Towy flows. I count breaths.

In-two-three-four-five. *Out*-two-three-four-five.

Part of me agitates to get back into that incident room. To stay on top of that flow of data. To check that neither Burnett nor Pritchard makes a move that I wouldn't.

But Burnett is a competent guy and also, sad but true, he's told me to fuck off.

And off, reluctantly, I fuck.

On the way, I call Ed Saunders. Ask, timidly, if he has the day off work and if, by chance, he'd care to spend a couple of hours Christmas shopping with me.

'Leaving it till the last minute, Fi? Sure you don't want to wait till last thing this afternoon?'

'Not completely the last minute. I got you your present early, only then I saw you'd got yourself it already.' I explain about the pestle and mortar.

He tells me, gently, that the new pestle and mortar had come 'from Jill, actually', but it would have been a wonderful idea. Says he'd love to meet up. We agree to meet at one o'clock on the Hayes.

I call Bev. Ask if she's at home later. She is.

I say I'll pop round.

Call my mam. Talk about Christmas arrangements. Say I'm looking forward to seeing her later.

Meet up with Ed.

He helps me get the last few bits I need. Going round the shops is easier with him there. I have less need to run out screaming.

I tick off all the last people left to do, except Ed.

I don't know what to get him, except then I do. Waterstones doesn't have what I want, but then I remember a Christian bookshop on Wyndham Arcade and I drag a surprised Ed in there. I find a copy of *Revelations of Divine Love*. Buy it. Write 'To Ed, Happy Christmas 2014, Fi xxx' inside it and hand it over.

He takes it, looks pleased but also puzzled.

'Not your usual reading matter.'

'No. But an abbot gave me a copy and then I swore at him and then we just kyried ourselves into a holy coma.'

I tell him that thing about it being the first book in English known to have been written by a woman. I don't tell him that I read the entire thing, cover to cover, last night. Don't tell him I started reading from page one again when I woke this morning. That I have it in my bag right now. The book has a short biography of Mother Julian in the front of it, a few pages of historical context. Those things disturb me more than a little, but the text itself is solid gold.

Ed gives me a chaste kiss on the cheek and says thanks.

We go to a café. Orange juice and a salad box for me, juice and a toasted panini for him. The panini when it comes is way better than my salad, so I keep begging nibbles from him and, because he's nice, he lets me have them.

He gives me my present. A pair of gloves in soft brown leather.

'You're always complaining you have cold hands. From now on, I'm not going to listen.'

He's right, of course. I do complain. But that's not because I don't have gloves, it's that I almost always forget to wear them or carry them with me in places I might want them. But I don't have any gloves as lovely as these and I put them on and wiggle my fingers and tell Ed that I *love* them, which – in so far as it makes sense to love a pair of gloves – I do.

'How is it going with Jill? She seems really nice.'

'It's going great. Really well.'

'Is she The One?' I ask. A question which is permitted me by virtue of being Old Friend and Former Lover.

He nods. Not a 'yes for sure' nod, but a 'definitely possible' one.

'You won't stop being friends with me? You're not going to be one of those awful, terrible, wicked people who ditches all their existing friends just because they've found someone they're going to be with for the rest of their lives?'

He shakes his head and reassures me, but some women just don't handle the presence of former lovers in their partner's life. In the end, Ed's loyalty to Jill will be – should be – greater than his to me.

Not a thought that hugely cheers me.

I also realise that though I've given Ed books for Christmas before, I've never dated them like that. With the year as well as the season. I think it's because I know that things between us are more fragile now than perhaps they've ever been before. Under threat.

I sigh. A big let-it-all-out sigh.

I remember Father Cyril's hands on my head, and the way I leaned into those hands, and the way that time and the world vanished as I did.

Ed says, 'You've got mozzarella on your cheek.'

I remove it. The café is heaving because it's Christmas Eve and people with trays but no tables are circling us the way, I imagine, hyenas circle a limping wildebeest.

I wiggle my gloves and point at the hyenas.

'Let's get out before they eat us.'

We do. Say goodbye and Happy Christmas.

Ed goes back to Ed-land. I drive across town to see Bev.

Give her her present: a DVD of *Water for Elephants*, which looks terrible to me, but stars an actor called Robert Pattinson on whom Bev has a major crush. She gives me a little tower of books, the Fifty Shades trilogy, and explains, 'You love reading and, I don't know, I just thought this would be really *you*.'

I don't entirely know how to respond to that, but we end up laughing a lot anyway.

'Bev, I know I've been a bit useless these last few weeks. Sorry about that. It will get back to normal.'

She looks stern for a moment. 'Not a *bit* useless, Fi. *Completely* useless.'

I mutely agree and she looks stern another second or two before relenting. 'Anyway, you're always like this when you're on a case. You always come back, though, so I do forgive you.'

I ask about Hemi Godfrey and she scrunches her face up and says, 'Well, he *is* nice, but . . .'

I listen to her mount the case for the prosecution. A case so hemmed around by qualifications and denials that it sometimes sounds like the opposite. I don't comment except to say, 'Bev, I'm sure you'll make a good decision. Just listen to your heart.'

We kiss goodbye.

Then home to change. I wear one of Kay's cast-offs, asparkle with gold at the neck. More attention-seeking than anything I'd normally wear, but nice, definitely nice.

I go crazy and wear a pair of heels too. Make-up. An itsy-ditsy dab of perfume.

Then on over to my parents' place. That tinselled, fairy-lit, carolling, glittering, and much mince-pied, abode of glad tidings and Christmassy good cheer.

My father tiggers around like an over-excited eight-year-old. As he does most years, he's just invented a new tradition. On Christmas Eve every year from now on, we will have fish pie and champagne and what he promises will be the 'world's biggest trifle'. He opens the fridge to show me the trifle, which is a mighty confection indeed, implausibly yellow on top and so spectacularly towered with cream that my mam has had to remove the shelf that would normally sit above.

Meanwhile, Mam scolds us, peels potatoes, shifts things in and out of ovens, and plucks at my waist, complaining that I can't have been eating.

'And where were you on Friday?' she asks. 'You were supposed to be coming over.'

'Sorry, Mam. It was a work thing. I was just totally buried.'

My younger sister, Ant, assesses the presents under the tree. She wants an iPad and worries that there's nothing iPad-shaped for her there, which indeed there isn't because Dad has hidden it, saying, 'She'll be absolutely blown away, she will, it's the top one for iRAM or whatever, top of the range everything, and I can't wait to see the look on her face.' My other sister, Kay, is in a mood where she's decided that she and I are the only grown-ups in the house and she snugs up to me on the sofa, poking me with her stockinged feet, and tells me in a low voice why she's going to 'do New Year' with her on-off boyfriend Cai, whom we all thought had now been permanently ditched.

Kay is doing a course in fashion retail at Cardiff Uni. She's messed around with other jobs and courses in the past, but this one, I think, has a chance of sticking.

I ask her if she has ever thought of interior design at all, whether that's something she might turn her hand to.

She shrugs. 'Yes. I mean, if you're a visual person . . . But it wouldn't ever be my main thing.'

'What if I had a client for you? A paying one. You wouldn't just have to choose everything. You'd also have to get it done. You know, get workmen in, all of that.'

She scrabbles at me with her feet, working herself upright. Sticks one of Mam's brassy cushions behind her head so she can see me better.

'How much? I mean, like how much per hour?'

'I don't know. What do you charge?'

She aims at thirty pounds. A look in her eye wonders whether she should have said thirty-five.

'Kay! You don't have any experience. This is a CV-building thing.'

We bicker companionably. She comes down to twenty. I say, 'Eighteen and I give you an amazing foot massage.'

It's a deal.

Then the fish pie is done and the champagne is opened and dad whacks up the carols so loud that I can feel the vibrations through the floor. I shout at Kay that she can have her massage tomorrow and we both dive – dive happily – into the full disorder of our family Christmas.

This is happiness. Rowdy. Human. Impermanent. Sufficient.

41

Christmas comes and Christmas goes.

I give Mam and Dad their big gift, the photo album. Not just photos either, but mementoes. Orders of service from friends' weddings and christenings. Ticket stubs from our days out at the Barry Island Pleasure Park. Film mementos: a poster of *Beauty and the Beast*, which I remembered loving at the time.

They both love it, of course. Dad, being Dad, gets teary and hugs me until it actually hurts. Turning the pages, Dad has a fond, nostalgic eye but – unless I'm wrong, unless I'm just projecting – he's also slightly wary of the gift. Checking, as ever, that this is a gift which comes with no dangerous reveals.

And there are none. None that I can see. This whole effort to uncover some revelatory corner of my father's past has failed.

Except.

Except, except, except.

That one photo that caused my Uncle Em to see invisible specks of dust had the exact same effect on my father. A quick brushing motion at the picture's right-hand edge.

It can't be the horse's bum that caused that reflexive pushing-away motion, so it must be that man's arm. An arm in blue Prince of Wales check.

That's not an insight I can do anything much with now,

but it doesn't vanish. If anything it hardens. Becomes smaller, denser, more solid.

An arm in blue Prince of Wales check.

An arm, which even sawn-off, even twenty-five years after the event, causes my father and Em to want to brush its memory away.

A clue. One hell of a puzzling one, but a clue for sure.

And, as it happens, I have a contact from a previous case, Al Bettinson, a racecourse photographer with a massive archive of his own and access to the archives kept by most of the bigger local courses.

I have a date. A horse. And a blue Prince of Wales arm. It'll be a ton of work, but I think I'll find that arm.

That, however, lies in my future. For now, I just plunge onwards in this family Christmas.

Ant gets her iPad and is as thrilled as everyone wanted. We all eat too much and then Dad forces us to watch an old DVD of *Beauty and the Beast*, which somehow worked better for me when I was seven and whose relevance to Christmas I find hard to discern.

On Christmas afternoon, a terrible time to choose but I can't help myself, I get Dad alone in his 'studio', his grown-up playroom. He wants to white noise me. To continue with his Christmas prattle.

But I say, 'Dad, I've got a big question to ask. One you won't like.'

'Don't ask it then.'

'I've got to.'

'Then ask it.'

'Murder. Did you ever kill anyone? Have anyone killed? Issue the orders, do the deed, I don't care which.'

He wants to intervene, deflect, move us down a different road, but I can't do that. I hold up a hand.

'Dad, if the answer's yes, just say so. I won't investigate.

Won't share anything with my colleagues. If I have to, I don't know, join a different force, then I will. And if there were other crimes, even serious ones, then I really don't care. I mean, what's a bit of arson between friends?'

'You want to know if I've killed anyone?'

'Or if you ordered it. Or conspired to have it happen. Anything like that. I'm not a lawyer. I'm not after some legal definition.'

He shakes his head. First I think that's a refusal to answer. A reference back to the long 'Don't ask, don't tell' pact that has got us this far together. But then I realise it's not that. He's not saying that.

He says, 'No. Not that. There was plenty of rough stuff, for sure. You know, I was building up. I had to show I was serious. But murder, no. Not that. Never.'

'That's real?'

He nods.

'Dad, if that's not true and one day I come across some evidence that says otherwise—'

I don't finish my sentence, because I don't know what I'm saying, but Dad interrupts anyway.

'It *is* true. Plenty of rough stuff. Some of which your people knew about at the time, a lot of which they didn't. But no killing. I'd never have allowed that.'

I want to believe my father is telling the truth. His face says, yes, he's telling the truth, but there's an expression there I don't understand, can't read, won't be able to get to.

Then his face changes. He says, 'That was it? The big thing? I thought you were going to tell me you were pregnant.'

He bellows with laughter at his own joke, whacks carols on the stereo, tells me about a bar he's bought up. How he's going to redevelop it as a private member's club. 'Really exclusive. High-end. Not like my normal rubbish.'

The conversation spins on and forward, as it should, and I let myself go with the flow.

Did I get an answer to my question, or only a polished lie? I don't know. But that's for the future. Carlotta is my now.

On Boxing Day, the Friday, I'm impatient, but mostly good. I do a little research on medieval religious traditions, but nothing too heavy.

Burnett has suspended all work until Saturday. Won't ramp up to full speed again till Monday.

I hate that, of course. Hate it. But the man's right. We won't get proper support from the Met, the NCA or anyone else until Christmas has tinselled itself into oblivion. Burnett knows he won't even get proper commitment from his own team until they're sick of the sight of mince pies.

And I'm good.

Not just good-for-me – a weak-enough compliment, alas – but actually good. Aside from my week or so of obsessive excavating around that now-vanished brown pool, I've been really well behaved on this case. Not too obsessive. Not especially crazy. I've not even smoked all that much. My mini-binge down in that damn cave was a rare, and more than permissible, exception.

So I keep the good habits. Stay disciplined. Let work be work and holiday be holiday.

On the Saturday morning, I go up to my Aunt Gwyn's farm with the rest of my family and we all have another mini-celebration there. I like Gwyn. A proper good 'un, she is. Say hello to Iestyn and the dogs. Go for a super-massive walk on the hills, roaming the long north-western rampart of the Black Mountains to the Twmpa or, as the English weirdly call it, Lord Hereford's Knob.

Sandstone and mudstone. A prominent limestone interpolation.

I think of what those things do below ground, unseen.

Water acting on rock over the millennia.

On Sunday, unexpectedly, Cesca calls, and we end up driving up to the monastery.

Spend six hours there. Eating, working, praying. Cesca's still serious, but less intense than she was the first time. Shirking work for a moment, sitting on a stone wall and eating cheese and apple, she says, 'Yes, I'd still love to do a retreat, I suppose. But things are really busy for me in London. I'm feeling super-motivated at the moment.' Her dark eyes flash a smile at me. 'Is that really shallow?' and we both laugh.

She asks how my case is going. I say, 'Um. Nothing definite yet, but I think we're getting there.'

After vespers, I ask Father Cyril about the thing with the icons at the end of each service. He's happy enough to show me. Saint Hilarion. Saint Osmanna. Saint Aurelia. Saint Anthony.

'They have chosen our community and we choose to honour them.'

There's an empty spot further on down the same wall. The same darkened glass and an inset ready to take a candle, but no candle, no icon.

I say, 'You're waiting for another?'

Cyril smiles and deflects. 'Not *waiting*, no. That would be presumptuous. But if we are *chosen* again, we are ready.'

I don't ask about the choosing, because I know he'll just lift his eyes upwards and wave a hand. We stick around for supper, then compline, then leave.

On that post-Christmas Monday, the 29th, I zoom over to Carmarthen super-early. Work is work and holiday is holiday all right, but nothing in that slogan says I can't start work at 6.45 a.m. if I want to.

I bring myself up to speed with what's been happening in my absence. Not much, the simple answer. Check lists of actions. Emails. Data.

But still: those scraps of progress are accumulating.

Our number plates team has found that one of the three potentially interesting London-registered vehicles belonged to a woman then in her late sixties, now in a home for dementia sufferers. We can't very well interview her, but she doesn't seem like a likely prospect. Two number plates left.

The explosives lead. Late on Christmas Eve, the team obtained the CCTV from the agricultural merchants' car park. We have almost decent pictures of our suspect. The images have gone off to a specialist lab for amplification and analysis. Results required back as urgently as possible.

Eight in the morning and I'm still checking these things, when there's a scrabbling at the incident room door. It's Burnett. Still in a wheelchair, but looking much better than when I last saw him. I let him in. The chair is motorised, driven by a little joystick. Burnett wears heavy strapping and padding round his torso, but his face and eyes are brighter, much brighter, than they were.

We how-was-your-Christmas each other but soon give way to the dark hunger which drives us here.

Burnett does something with the coffee machine to produce the highest-octane brew known to industrial science. He gazes at the dark brew smouldering in his mug, takes a pill of some sort, then hurls the lot down his throat. One gulp, two gulps, done.

As he does that, I go around the incident room ripping down tinsel. Destroying foil stars.

Then we're done.

Off to the side of our little suite, there's a little conference room. Burnett wheels over. I help with the doors.

'So,' he says. 'So.'

We start big picture. A case overview.

I stand at the whiteboard, mark out the headings that Burnett gives me.

KNOWN FACTS.
CONFIDENT ASSUMPTIONS.
HYPOTHESES.
QUESTIONS.

Burnett says, 'OK. Here's what we've got. We know about five kidnaps in total. The Mishchenko one, plus the four that Gerraghty was told about. That's five, minimum. Maybe plenty more besides. Five kidnaps, plus at least one murder, that of Rhydwyn Lloyd. Two attempted murders, you and me.'

I mark that down on the board under 'known facts', though personally I don't count attempted murder on the tally. A murder without a corpse isn't much of a murder at all.

I don't say that, though, not with Burnett still in a wheelchair. Not with the coffee-'n'-painkiller diet he's on.

Burnett: 'These kidnappers are highly professional, enough to impress a man like Jack Gerraghty. They're financially sophisticated, operationally sophisticated. They have the capacity, or have had the capacity, to infiltrate police systems. They're looking at very high payoffs per operation. And they're ruthless. Ruthless enough that they aimed to solve a possible problem with a sack of explosive.'

I write, 'Sophisticated, ruthless, ambitious.'

Burnett waits to see if I write anything further, but I don't.

'OK, then, here are two more pieces. One, obviously, we're dealing with some kind of local connection here. We found Alina Mishchenko in Ystradfflur. She appears to have spent time in Llanglydwen, though we've got some uncertainties about exactly where, how, and for how long.

'Two, we're basically confident that Len Roberts spirited Bethan Williams out of the valley at the time she went missing. How he did it was remarkable, but it was remarkable mostly because a fifteen-year-old girl, without any strong interest in adventure sports, was willing to enter a flooded cave, traverse a long way underground, then emerge by a different exit, also flooded. Yes, she was with a man who knew that cave extremely well. And yes, he placed a rope to help with the second, and more difficult, of the two dives. But all the same, we have to believe that Bethan Williams was in fear of her life. That strongly suggests she had stumbled onto some aspect of the kidnap operation. Those things together – the Mishchenko sightings plus the Williams case – imply that the Welsh end of this kidnap operation has its centre in Llanglydwen or somewhere very close.'

I mark the board as Burnett talks. We're seeing the case the same way now. No points of discord.

'OK,' he says. 'That's known facts and probable assumptions. Hypotheses?'

It's my turn, it seems, so I say, 'Well, we can't be sure, but we presume that one of the houses in that valley has been used as a safe house to store our kidnappees. So someone there has a secure cellar. They have, or can arrange, a black cloth backdrop, and a video camera. Enough stores of food that they don't all of a sudden walk into the village shop and start buying for one extra person. Those things are noticed in places like that.'

Burnett nods and agrees.

I write, 'SAFE HOUSE = LLANGLYDWEN'.

Burnett says, 'And what do we think? The gang who makes the snatch?'

I shake my head. 'No. They're London. Different skill sets. Very different territory. The London end has to make the grab, then deliver that guy or the girl to whoever runs our safe house. If I were doing it, I'd make the swap somewhere completely random. A truck-stop on the M1. A bit of woodland outside London. Anything neutral and meaningless.

'That way the London end has one job to do. They do it. Get paid. Move on. They know everything about the target – who she is, where she lives, all that – but nothing about what happens next. The Llanglydwen end is the exact opposite. It's perfectly possible that whoever runs the safe house doesn't even know the name of whoever he's got. He just keeps that person locked up and fed, clean and warm. What happens next depends on the victim's family. If they pay the ransom and follow the rules, he just drops the victim in some random location and simply drives off again. Or, if the family breaks the kidnappers' rules in any way, he kills and dumps the victim.'

Or doesn't kill them and doesn't dump them.

I'm not sure we're looking at killers here, but what evidence do I have for that speculation? None at the moment and Burnett is a man who likes to take things one step at a time. Evidence first, conclusions second.

I keep my mouth shut, my speculations silent.

Write, 'SNATCH SQUAD = LONDON' before shifting my pen rightwards to the heading that says, 'QUESTIONS'.

Burnett says, 'Still the same one as we started with.'

I write, 'WHY A.M. TO YSTRADFFLUR?'

A.M.: Alina Mishchenko. My dead Carlotta.

And why the Bible? The candles? The dress?

Write: 'WHY BIBLE? WHY CANDLES? WHY DRESS?'

Burnett says, 'The monastery? What do we think about that?'

I shake my head. I don't know what I think. What I say is, 'The monastery pretty much has to be involved in some way. The barley-seed doesn't prove it, because anyone held against their will in Llanglydwen might well eat bread that's been baked and bought locally. And our forensics don't quite do it, because anyone could have planted the things that we found. But the monks *do* acknowledge that she was there and the whole set-up at Ystradfflur smelled of something religious. So,

341

yes, on balance, we have to guess the monastery is involved in some way.'

I suddenly think of the pigs, oinking in their hoggy happiness. Think of the way the world vanished when I leaned into Father Cyril's blessing.

Burnett – trying out a hypothesis, no more – says, 'So what if we say that the monks are all phoneys. *They're* the safe house. They keep their victims in a barn or a cellar or something, and either collect their share of the money or just kill them.'

I shake my head, and this time it *is* a no.

'I've gone to and fro on this, I really have. But I just can't make it work. For one thing, these monks *aren't* phoney. They're always praying. Always on silent retreats. Always giving shelter to the needy and all that. They work damn hard and there's no money there. I mean, nothing's uncomfortable or badly made, but there's just no mismatch between their visible income and their visible outgoings. No hint of luxury. They're basically vegetarian. They've got one van and that's a piece of crap. And then . . .'

'Yes?'

'Well, they don't do locks. Not that I've seen. Not in the guest house. Not on the front door. When I was there before Christmas, Father Cyril just left me alone in his study. Alone in the whole farmhouse. I could have gone anywhere, looked at anything. And remember, they have strangers floating around all the time. I mean, yes, the whole place is big enough that you could certainly find, or build, a decent hiding place. But it would be a weirdly complicated set-up if all you need is a quiet safe house.'

Burnett fires a look at me. 'You were there before Christmas?'

Interviewing material witnesses without another police officer present. That's a massive no-no. A career-ending one.

I say, 'I went to church there. While I was there, I talked to the abbot. He mostly told me about medieval saints of theirs.

If he'd even started to tell me anything that was inquiry-relevant, I'd have told him to shut up and taken him off to Carmarthen.'

Burnett rumbles at that. A not-how-it's-done-in-Dyfed-Powys rumble. I get the same rumblings in South Wales too.

We talk a bit more about those monks, and while nothing coalesces, our unease remains. Burnett's and mine. Under 'QUESTIONS', I write, 'MONASTERY???'

If I could, I'd want to smash that monkish serenity. I'd want to detain each one of the monks and interrogate them under caution. Have a team search every damn inch of that monastery. Guest rooms. Monks' rooms. Communal areas. Barns and outbuildings. Say to Father Cyril, 'So, Father, what does Mother Julian mean to you?'

It's not even that I think those guys are killers. I don't. Their air of godly gentleness isn't faked. It just runs too deep. Yet that same basic evasion that Burnett and I detected on our very first visit has never quite gone and that's been an itch I've not been able to scratch into submission.

Burnett grimaces. It's frustrating to be this far into an inquiry and to have quite such an unquenched sense of unease around a major piece of the investigation. But we have nothing to justify a warrant – nothing, remotely, to justify an arrest – and we're forced to leave it. The law of England and Wales doesn't allow us to kick doors open, just because those doors happen to annoy us.

Stupid laws. They should make me prime minister.

'OK,' says Burnett. 'Actions.'

I write, 'ACTIONS', lettered in blood.

We go through the various strands of our inquiry. The progress that we've already made. The bits that need more attention.

We go on talking. As we talk, people start entering the incident room behind us. A couple try to barge through.

Want to exchange Christmas chat with their heroically injured and now heroically returned boss. Burnett's look tells them to fuck off, though his actual lips just ask someone to get him more coffee.

We go through our lists. Talk things over. A plan evolves.

Burnett is really impressive in command. He's just better at this, the leadership thing. Flashes of insight and occasional obsessive brilliance: that's what I bring to the party. But effective policing is about much more than that, and Burnett's skills in managing this operation show why he's heading for DCI, and I never will.

I say, 'Bethan Williams is still alive. She's out there somewhere.'

Burnett nods. We've already put out all the media appeals that make sense. No useful response so far, but we just might get something now that Christmas is gone.

I say, 'Her dad still wants her back. It's like his life has been frozen for eight years.'

Burnett nods. 'I'm sending a couple of officers to re-interview the mother. See if we get anything further.'

I write, 'WHERE IS BETHAN?' on the now-crowded whiteboard. The only part of it that holds my attention, however, is the single word, 'MONASTERY???'

We fall silent. Burnett's face changes, getting himself ready for that incident room.

His change of expression: it's as though he's buckling on his armour, readying himself for battle. The burden of leadership. Rather you than me, mate. Rather you than me.

And as I'm thinking those excellent thoughts, I realise that Burnett is looking at me with a certain intensity.

He says, 'Go on.'

'Go on, what? Go on where?'

Burnett gestures at the whiteboard. Says, 'Fiona, this lot, it's all important, it all has to be done, we know that . . .'

'Yes.'

'But you're not engaged, not really. When we were talking all that through, you didn't stick your hand up for any of it. You're normally biting my hand off to do the next thing.'

I make a face. I don't like being so easily read.

'Sorry.' One of my not-sorry sorries.

'So?'

'Sir?'

'Fiona, I know you. Somewhere in the recesses of what you're pleased to call your brain, you'll have something you want to do. Chase a barley seed, talk to plastic surgeons, start digging in the hills above Llanglydwen. I have no idea, I have absolutely no idea what that thing might be. But I would quite like it if you told me. You know, told me before you started doing it.'

I make my face again. The one about not liking being so easily read.

'Yes, sir.'

'So? Fiona . . .'

That's his warning *Fiona*. His rumbly, growly one.

'Bethan, sir. Bethan Williams. I'd like to understand more about Bethan.'

'Go on.'

'Look, she learned something. Something that no one else in the valley knew. Where did she go? What did she see? Who did she talk to? When did her behaviour change? Why did she trust Len Roberts and no one else?'

Some version of those questions were asked in the original Bethan Williams inquiry, of course, but only in a context where the investigating officers knew nothing about kidnap and had strong reasons to suspect Len Roberts of being the killer. Asking the same questions but from a different position of knowledge could – just could – yield remarkably different results.

Burnett nods.

A slow nod. A good one.

As he stares at me, I write the question in letters as large as our now-crowded whiteboard will allow.

'WHAT DID BETHAN SEE?'

What did Bethan Williams see? What did she learn? How did she come by the knowledge that sent her scurrying for her life through the wet and gloomy labyrinth that all but killed Burnett and me?

Burnett says, 'OK. Bethan Williams. How do you want to play it?'

He means, do I think we should pull Neil Williams into a police station and give him a formal interview?

But the answer to that is clearly 'No', and Burnett, for all his instinct towards tidy police procedure, sees that too.

I say, 'I've got a good relationship with him. I'll just go over for cup of tea and a chat, sir. See what I can get. It's intelligence we're after, not evidence.'

Burnett nods. 'OK, good. Do what you need to do, Fiona. Just do what you need to do. Stay in touch.'

I say all the things I'm meant to say. Hold the door open as he buzzes himself through. But all I can think is, *Bethan Williams. I'm going to meet Bethan Williams.*

The teenage girl with the answer to everything.

42

Credit where it's due: and Kay exceeds expectations, not least in looks.

She's beautiful, Kay, much more so than me, but her wardrobe is usually stuck in Late Teenage, a range that extends from Darkly Moody through Sulky to Stupidly, Wildly Sexy.

Not today. She wears a floral dress in black and white. ('Ebony and natural,' she admonishes me. 'That's not a hard black and that's more like a really soft lime-white than an actual white-white.') Either way, it's a nice dress which she teams with a tailored jacket in very dark grey, the sort of thing that I used to wear to interviews, and smart shoes, and she's tied her hair in a bun.

Gone is my sulky teenage sister drifting from job to temporary job. Here instead is a self-confident young woman who looks like she's already interior-designed a few dozen homes into carefully managed beauty. Kay looks like a young woman who knows who she is and what she wants from life and, if that's the case, I wish her the very best of Welsh luck. Hope that the hounds of Luck and Providence and Good Fortune yap always at her heels.

In the back of the car, three 'mood boards' rattle and shake.

Kay has assembled these things with astonishing speed – astonishing to me, that is. She says, 'It's mostly just a couple of catalogues. It's called cutting out pictures.'

'You've got actual fabrics there too.'

'A shop? Called John Lewis? You ask for samples and they give them to you.'

There are paint cards too, but I don't ask about those. I've been put in my place and there I'll stay.

The mood boards have titles. One is '1950s retro/cool'. The second is 'Contemporary neutrals/textures'. The third is 'Classic', which, Kay tells me, is her way of saying 'incredibly boring and safe'. I think I know which one Neil Williams will choose, but he's the client.

We arrive at the farmyard. I'm in jeans and old shoes, but Kay has to find a way to tiptoe and jump through the mud and the dung and the puddles and the coarse granite chippings to the relative safety of the cracked concrete paving that runs down the side of the house. I carry the mood boards and offer her an arm when she has a long step to make.

We go on in.

Neil Williams is visibly impressed by Kay. Calls her 'Miss Griffiths' and pulls a chair out for her and asks her, three times, if she would like tea. At the sight of the mood boards, he says, 'Goodness gracious' and 'Well I never', even though he's only a little past fifty.

I think part of him thinks that the mood boards *are* the product. That it'll be down to him to reproduce those colours, those fabrics, that look in his living room. He has a daunted, even terrified, expression locked away behind that armoured politeness. But Kay says no. Explains it all to him. How he has to choose a look, then she'll take it from there, and in stages.

Scared of giving offence, Williams spends a long time admiring the 1950s retro board and even longer with the contemporary neutrals, but he heads for 'Classic' with the certainty of a pointer on a grouse moor. Kay, privately, rolls her eyes at me, but takes out a tape measure and starts to measure up.

Williams, relaxing now that it's just me and him in the

room, starts to talk. About Bethan. About him and Joanne. About all the things his life once was and the mess it's now become.

'I see now that I shouldn't have asked Jo to stay up here. Be a farmer's wife. We'd have been OK in Brecon or Carmarthen, but she just wasn't cut out for this kind of life. She said that, you know, in her way, and I just couldn't hear it. Stuck in my ways, I was.'

I nudge him about Bethan and her music. That first time I met him, he said that things would have been all right if Bethan had lived in Brecon or Carmarthen or St David. That didn't echo much the first time I heard it: Brecon or Carmarthen are simply the two nearest towns of any size, and St David would be a nice place to live if you wanted to avoid the bigger cities.

'But were you saying it was church music that she loved especially? St David is tiny, but it has a cathedral. A choir. Is that why you mentioned it?'

'Oh yes, she loved singing. The organ. All that church stuff. She used to play the harmonium in St Cledwyn's' – that's the village church – 'but the monks had a harmonium too, and a piano and they helped her with lessons and harmonies and things.'

'Did she feel a sense of vocation? Was she religious at all? Even just one of those passing teenage things, a temporary infatuation perhaps?'

'Oh yes. She liked her music. That was probably the main thing, but she really got into the church stuff too. She could get quite intense, I suppose. Like you say, it was probably only a phase.'

'The monastery? She spent real time there? She liked it?'

'Oh yes, until she took up with Roberts, she probably spent more time there than anywhere.'

'Evening services too? Compline, for example?'

He says yes, and why not? He's somewhat defensive.

349

Protective even. He starts telling me that the monks keep their farm 'very tidy'. Tells me that he once bought a load of hay from them, 'Really beautiful it was, cut just right, good bright colour, nice sweet smell and absolutely no dust.'

I nod, as if I care. Then ask, 'It's a fair way from you to the monastery. How did she get there? Was it you who drove her? Joanne maybe?'

'Oh!' Williams laughs at my city-bred assumptions. It's three miles by road, he says, 'but only two if you take the back way.' He jerks his finger at the back of the farmhouse, indicating a footpath, I assume, that must run roughly parallel to the road. 'Bethan never minded pulling her boots on.'

We talk more, but I get nothing that I much value.

Kay comes in from the living room, all clicky-heeled and in control.

'Mr Williams, would you just like me to measure up elsewhere? The bathroom, perhaps? Your daughter's old bedroom?'

He would, yes, is the answer. He stands up and straightens as he delivers it. Escorts Kay to the bedroom door, throws it open for her and stands back, chest puffed out like a guardsman on parade.

I don't think Kay will do her job better if she has Williams puffing anxiously at the door, so I drag him away again.

He and I sit in the kitchen drinking tea, while Kay clicks around with her tape measure, makes notes. She photographs the rooms on her phone.

Then she's done. She goes over the next steps. Promises to provide a 'budget for your approval'. Says she'll get started as soon as possible thereafter.

I realise I am extraordinarily proud of my sister. A feeling that has no basis in reason. I've done little enough to make her like this, after all. But I sit at the table and listen to this beautiful and self-possessed young woman explain how the

350

lamp shades will be chosen to complement the curtains and feel quite unjustifiably proud that that a sister of mine should become this person.

And then we're done. I walk and Kay precariously hopscotches to the car. She's seeing a friend in Swansea after this, so I drive her there. Kay's elated by her first taste of the interior decorating game. She relishes it the way she enjoys a new dress, a new look.

'I'm not saying I'd go for interiors over fashion,' she tells me. 'But I could maybe see it as a second string to my bow.'

I laugh – she has a *bow?* – but encourage her. Tell her I think she'll do a great job, which indeed I do.

I drop her in Swansea.

My phone jabbers with texts and emails from Burnett's team. Most of them just FYI-type stuff, some good, some bad.

They've sent two uniformed male constables down to the south coast to interview Bethan Williams's mother. A lousy move. I know Dyfed-Powys struggles with resourcing these bigger enquiries, but the interview really needed two women in plain clothes. Two burly Welsh coppers, in full uniform, filling Joanne Williams's kitchen – that's just not the way to tease out any long-concealed secrets.

There's better news too. The taxi driver who dropped Alina Mishchenko off on that fateful night has been interviewed. He correctly picked her photo from a set of six different mugshots. And he remembered, or claimed to remember, the moment of her arrival. Said there was a dark-grey BMW waiting, lights on and engine running, just a little further on down the road. Said someone came out of the car and spoke to Alina. She walked on to the car, hesitated, then got in.

You wouldn't normally believe an account that detailed three months after the event, but those black cab drivers have spent years honing their memories and, as the driver said in the interview transcript, 'She was a pretty girl, nicely dressed, and you do remember those ones, I suppose. But also – well, I don't know. There was something odd about it. She obviously wasn't expecting anyone to pick her up. She was going home after a party. And there was just something about it. It was like she didn't know this guy, but she went over to his car anyway.'

I wonder just how it worked. Presumably BMW guy said something – anything – to get Alina over to his car, then, once there, pulled a gun or a knife, and forced her to make the last, tragic misstep. We may never find out exactly, but that dark-grey BMW may be traceable. Burnett, needless to say, is already on the case.

He wants me back in Carmarthen, wants me to report back. Phooey to that.

Do what you need to do, Fiona. Just do what you need to do. I opt to give that instruction priority over the rest.

Turn my phone off. Listen to my cooling engine.

Things appear differently depending on who's observing them. Neil Williams would have told the original Dyfed-Powys inquiry something very similar to what he just told me, but they'd have heard it very differently.

Dyfed-Powys would have heard of a studious, rather earnest girl, who loved music and was a little enamoured of the religious life. They'd have heard of that girl being led astray by a man, ten years older than her, and a rough sort, a wild sort, an untamed man of the countryside. It's little wonder they came to the view they did.

But we now know different. Bethan ran because something terrified her. And whatever that terrifying thing was – and I think we're looking at more than simple kidnap – it has its epicentre at that damn monastery. There are simply too many paths leading to those same too-open doors.

I get out my copy of *Revelations*. Re-read the little bio of Mother Julian.

Almost nothing is actually known about her. She was an anchoress at the church of St Julian in Norwich. She was born about 1342 and died about 1416, though there's uncertainty around both of those dates. Indeed, we call her 'Julian' because we don't actually know her name, just use the name of the church she was attached to. She wasn't a mother either, for that matter. Unmarried and never formally a nun.

Bethan never minded pulling her boots on.

I've never minded that either and, phone still silent, I drive back towards Llanglydwen.

From the coast to the mountains.

From the flatlands to the high ones.

From this clamorous twenty-first century city to the quiet timelessness of deep Wales, old Wales. A Wales where old habits, old beliefs can live for ever, if they want to. Len Roberts and his way of life. The monks of St David and theirs.

Miles and the centuries fall away as I drive.

I don't drive to the monastery. That place scares me now. I don't go to Williams, to Roberts, or the cave.

Instead I park up at my favourite muddy junction. Where a little track fords a stream. Brown waters, brown rock.

It's three o'clock in the afternoon. I put my walking boots on, dried out now after their adventures beneath ground. Coat, scarf, gloves. My ordinary woollen ones, not the lovely ones Ed gave me.

Binoculars.

I wonder about taking a torch, but I'm not going to be out long, or go far. This track, I realise, runs all the way down the north side of the valley. The road, taking a more circuitous route, takes the south side. This track will pass just behind Williams's farmhouse and head on into Llanglydwen proper, coming out on the road about halfway between the village and the monastery. It's the track Bethan would have taken to go to her music lessons, to come back from compline.

If you want to know what Bethan saw, then try walking in her footsteps

I do just that.

Walk briskly to begin with. The track is rutted and wet. Choked with long grass and brown-stemmed dock. Hedges to either side. Hawthorn and elder and hedge maple. The hawthorn berries seem particularly abundant this year. Swagged in purple. Gifts left over from a generous autumn.

I walk for thirty minutes or so until I see the lamps of Williams's farmhouse two hundred yards below me. There's an easy path from there to here. In summer, especially, this must have been a lovely place to grow up.

I walk on, slower now. Towards Llanglydwen. Towards the monastery.

Bethan Williams walked this route frequently. She walked it, sometimes, at night. Coming home after compline.

She'd have been in a part of the valley where no one would have expected a pair of eyes, not here, off the road, after dark.

Walk on.

My view is occluded by the hedges, and the occasional bigger tree. An oak or an ash. But there are gaps in the hedges, or changes in the level of the ground which afford me the chance to look around.

And it's obvious really. A cottage. Two-up, two-down. Whitewashed. An ordinary rural scramble of stone-built outbuildings around a little yard.

A Mitsubishi Shogun, or something of that sort, parked outside.

Somewhere, out of sight, a dog yapping in this air that is starting to grow heavy with the approaching dark.

And a driveway. Formed of some grey aggregate crush.

Leading up from the road to the cottage. Intersecting my track. Bethan's track.

Interesting.

I walk right on down to where my track disgorges into Llanglydwen. There are other farmhouses and cottages dotting the valley, but none where Bethan's vantage point would have given her nearly such a clear view. When I hit the road, I walk back the way I came.

It's after four now and lights are beginning to twinkle up and down the valley. We're not long past the shortest day of the year, and you feel it here. This rural nightfall. Sheep bleating over damp fields. The burr of tractor.

I get back to the intersection between my track and that heavy driveway. The little cottage whose whitewashed walls might hide a deep interior darkness.

I clamber up a little bank, thick with the wands of dead willowherb. Press up against a tangle of elder and blackthorn and train my binoculars on the house.

The upstairs windows are dark, which doesn't help. If I saw any children's toys or posters in an upstairs bedroom that would, most likely, kill my theory, but I can't see enough to know.

Downstairs, someone moves in a kitchen window. People are allowed to move and kitchens are a natural place in which to do so, but the person is a man and, as far as I can tell, he's alone.

My theory stays alive.

Look at the Mitsubishi.

Again, hard to tell because of the light, but I think its rear windows may be tinted, perhaps even darkened.

My theory isn't just alive, it's starting to awaken. To gather force.

I don't like being here now. The sense of peril is just too strong. I stuff my binoculars into my coat pocket and start to disentangle myself from the bank and its knotted trees.

Slither down. Fall. My binoculars go tumbling beyond my reach.

Land, as a savage ill-luck would have it, at the feet of a man.

A man I know well.

Father Cyril, Abbot of the Monastery of St David at Llanglydwen. He's here with Brother Nicholas, possibly my least favourite of the monks.

I say, still stumbled, still fallen.

'Evening, Father. It'll be a beautiful night.'

The abbot picks up my binoculars. Slowly folds the leather strap round the hinge and focusing ring. Once he's happy with his arrangement, he hands it to me, saying, 'I think perhaps it will be, yes.'

His eyes are serious, clever, full of thought.

I say, 'We don't get walks like this in Cardiff. You never escape the neon.'

'No.'

I start to say something else. A tra-la-la-la whistle of innocence. An I've-no-idea-what-dark-game-you're-playing tune. I keep it light and bright and, as far as my shaking fear permits me, normal.

The abbot says, 'You were taking a look at the cottage. That's Dylan Parry's place. We were just going to visit him.'

He gives me a come-with-us wave. One that is simultaneously gracious and commanding.

One that issues an order.

I say no. Say I need to be getting back. Say, 'My boss was on the phone just now, yelling at me because I'm meant to be interviewing with him in forty minutes.'

The abbot looks at me. Says, very quietly, 'I don't think so.'

Brother Nicholas, meanwhile, is starting to work his way round me, cutting off my exit route.

I don't let him.

I run.

Run like I have all the hounds of hell on my tail. The horsemen of an apocalypse in which these men believe and in which I never have.

I run for the road. The sweet road with its rare, but occasional, traffic. The road which might offer me safety.

Because the driveway offers the shortest way there, it's the path I take.

My headstart is almost nothing at all. A couple of yards plus just a half-second of surprise. I'm much fitter than I ever used to be. Fitter and faster. All those good evenings spent with Bev at the swimming pool.

But a million evenings spent swimming couldn't turn me from a woman into a man. Don't suddenly turn me into some turbo-charged va-va-vroomy super-athlete.

As it happens, I do OK. Make a good twenty yards. Think that perhaps, just perhaps, I'll make the whole distance, when Nicholas just catches my trailing leg.

It's not a big touch. Just enough to throw my balance. I stumble once. Lose an ounce of speed. Feel Nicholas's crashing force slam into me from behind.

I go flying.

Scrape along the drive, winding myself. My face protected only by my outstretched hands.

Nicholas, panting heavily, drags me upright.

Even then, I'd fight him. Guys – perhaps especially if they happen to be monks – don't expect women to come at them like a bagful of angry cats. Still less will they expect that this particular petite and unimpressive woman has received many hours of combat training from Lev, a guy who used to teach for the Russian Spetsnaz.

I'm just gathering myself for a hard blow upwards to Nicholas's jaw. The sort of savage first move that can give

357

a second or two's space in which to figure out the rest, but Father Cyril has reached us now. Grabs my scarf from behind. Twists and pulls till I start to see black. Choking.

I wave my hands in failed surrender.

Nicholas removes my coat, then puts it back on again, zipped up, but with my arms straightjacketed inside. It's a very simple, very effective ploy. I can't fight without arms. Can't even run sensibly.

Cyril hands the twist of my scarf to Nicholas, who keeps an ungentle hand on it.

Cyril leads us to the little cottage.

The yard, the car, the barking dog.

I'm stupidly scared now. 'I almost peed myself in fear.' That's what they say, don't they? It's not an experience I've had before, but I have it now. A kind of draining, shaking, emptying feeling that sucks at me. Weakens me.

When Nicholas pulls too hard at my neck, Cyril chides him, 'There is no need to hurt her, Brother.'

The Shogun, I notice, does have darkened rear windows. Blacked out. How's my theory doing now, I think. Evidence for and evidence against?

Some of the evidence for comes to the door at Cyril's knock.

Dylan Parry. The intense tweedy guy from that day with Cesca at the monastery. He recognises me, with an 'Ah! Our little police girl,' and his dark eyes have a glitter that I do not love.

I'm bundled inside. An ordinary cottage kitchen. Tidy, homey and warm.

I'm squished down on a chair.

Nicholas keeps a hold on my throat as Cyril fishes in my coat for my phone. Finds it. Sees that it's turned off.

Places the phone and my car keys on the table.

There's a short and wicked silence.

Parry says, 'All right. Let's do this properly.'

He steps out into the hall. Comes back a moment later with cable ties. Binds me at the wrist.

At the ankle.

I say, 'I don't have to tell anyone what I've seen. I really don't.'

Cyril says, 'And could we trust that, officer? Would we wish to?'

I don't answer.

On the wall above the small kitchen window, there's an icon. Gold-framed. Precious.

It's the same as the one in Cyril's study. Mother Julian of Norwich and all manner of heavenly wonderfulness.

My mouth is almost too dry to speak, but I do say, 'Father, I am not ready and I am very unworthy. I—'

He interrupts. 'No one is ready and no one is worthy.'

Parry takes my phone and car keys.

He doesn't say anything, but doesn't have to. I know what he'll do next. What I'd do if I were him. Drive far enough that he'll be sure my car is getting picked up on cameras. Turn my phone back on again somewhere random – Leominster, Bristol, Whereverthehell – then drive a bit more. Create a trail. Send some texts to DI Burnett – brilliantly labelled as such in my phone book. Cute little texts. 'Got something really interesting. Brief you properly in the morning.' That kind of thing.

Fiona Griffiths: last seen in Swansea.

Next recorded in Leominster, or Bristol, or Whereverthehell. Absolutely no reason for anyone to suspect I'd been anywhere near Llanglydwen. I even parked well away from the village so if by any chance Burnett has officers out here, they won't have seen my car, won't have logged the number plate.

Brilliant work, Griffiths. You're lost, forgotten, unknown.

When we first met Cyril, he told us about the 'refugees from the world' the monastery sought to help. He told us,

There are people who might look happy and successful to you. Perhaps, I don't know, they have money, jobs, boy- or girlfriends, whatever they want. But they have lost their connection to God. And without that, what are they? Souls in trouble. People who need our help. Sometimes they know that. Sometimes they half-know it. Sometimes they have to learn it, or re-learn it. We are here for them all.

I think I'm in for a learning experience myself. About to learn precisely how far these monks were prepared to go in their soul-rescue mission. And I'm not sure I'm going to appreciate the ride.

As I'm thinking those thoughts, Cyril places a glass of water in front of me. A pill. Red and white. The polite little medicament that smooths this coercive trail.

I start to shake my head, but Cyril says, 'My daughter, if you resist, we will force you. And I don't want to force you.'

I nod, acknowledging the logic.

'Father, this pill . . .?'

'Will quieten you. It's only for while we prepare you. You will be alive and unharmed and perfectly conscious.'

'Thank you.'

I open my mouth. Cyril places the pill inside, where I hold it on the tip of my tongue. He raises the water to my lips.

'Pray for me, Father,' I say, and drink.

I swallow the pill. Ketamine, I imagine, or one of its many bedfellows.

Cyril places his hands on my head, as he did that time in church. There is something wonderfully peaceful in that touch. Brother Nicholas and Dylan Parry kneel down facing me, their heads bowed. Cyril says a prayer, quietly and repetitively. It's in Greek, I think. Not English or Latin at any rate.

Unconsciousness starts to nibble at me. A darkening and slackening. An easy road, not a scary one. I can't resist and I don't try to. Wait for the blackness to rise and claim me.

And DI Alun Burnett, my doggedly capable boss, has absolutely no idea where I am.

43

Dreams.

Turbulent and confused. A rushing upwards. Like a diver breaking for a distant spill of brightness.

A brightness which spreads and dazzles.

I keep my eyes closed, but start to feel my body again. The loll of my head. The pull of my limbs.

My tongue is clumsy and oversized. A cow's tongue in a lamb's mouth.

There are voices around me. A low, murmuring chant. I'm shivery, but I can't tell if I'm cold. I try moving my arms, my legs. No dice.

'*Do what you need to do, Fiona.*' Burnett said. '*Just do what you need to do.*'

For once in my life, I've pretty much done things by the book. Cut some corners, yes, but not many. Worked a little hard, a little obsessively at times, but I've always brought my findings to one of my many bosses. I've kept them in the loop. I've not gone crazy. Not sworn at the wrong times or deliberately messed up things I was told to do.

I've played this whole case as cleanly as DS Griffiths of the South Wales Police is ever likely to play it – and here's the result.

'*Do what you need to do, Fiona.*'

Steps. A man approaches.

Brother Anselm. 'Are you waking?'

My ox's tongue lashes around in its little space. Asks for water, or tries to.

Anselm's voice moves in and out, but he comes back with a glass of water.

Drink some, spill some.

My eyes are still gummed shut.

Anselm tells me that what I'm feeling is normal. That it takes time to clear the muddiness. He places his hand on mine and lets me lean my head against his arm.

Days or minutes pass.

Seconds or centuries.

I ask for more water. Drink. More effectively this time.

My head and arms, body and legs feel like they belong to me. As much as they ever did anyway.

I open my eyes.

I'm in the monastery's little church, of course. Where I knew I'd be. The view is blurry though. Hazed out. At first, I think that my faculties are still blunted by the drug, but then I realise my faculties are just fine.

I'm wearing a veil. A white veil that falls below my shoulder. An appliqué hem of lace and beads brushes my bare arm.

I'm wearing a dress. A white dress.

Cottony pintucks and broderie anglaise.

My wrists and ankles are cable-tied to a chair, but tied with gentleness. Cloth pads stop the ties from cutting into me.

Cyril approaches.

'How are you feeling, my daughter?'

'OK,' I say. 'I'm OK.' Then, because he doesn't respond to what is transparently a lie, I add, 'I am very frightened, Father. I am very frightened indeed.'

Cyril says, 'Can you find the voice of God within you?'

I shake my head. Mam used to drag us to chapel when we were kids, but I stopped going as soon as I could, allying with my dad, who was bored by the whole thing. Me and God are like kids who used to know each other, vaguely, in a junior school playground. Him playing footie with the big boys. Me playing skipping ropes and clapping games with the girls. We hardly knew each other then. We're near-total strangers now.

I don't know how much of that my headshake conveys, but Cyril just smiles sadly and quotes, '"Our Lord said not, *Thou shalt not be tempested*. He said, *Thou shalt not be overcome*."'

Mother Julian of Norwich. That's one of her zingers.

I do a sad smile of my own and whisper back. 'It's one heck of a tempest.'

He nods.

I say, 'Where are we?'

In time, I mean, not place.

The abbot catches my meaning, and says, 'We have just celebrated none. We keep vigil for an hour, then mass, then the ceremony of enclosure.'

I nod.

Stupid.

Clues right in front of me the whole time. Literally from the first day I stepped foot in this monastery. Me too blind to see them, because I thought we were investigating a modern crime committed by modern criminals. Which we are and were, except that when the crime entered this valley, the crime morphed. Turned wickedly. Changed direction, losing six or seven hundred years in the process. Clues that would have blazed like beacons to the medieval mind almost entirely hidden from ours.

I ask for more water.

Drink it.

Smile thanks.

Up at the altar, Brother Gregory flashes a look down at us. I'm on a red and gold seat – a throne, if you like, a throne – at the head of the nave, just below what I think is called the chancel. Gregory's look is nudging a reminder at Cyril. The vigil, I guess, is due to start.

I whisper, 'Sorry.'

My lips shape the word anyway. I don't know if anything comes out.

Cyril's eyes stay on me. Intent, serious. Loving.

'Father?'

'Yes?'

'I know I have no choice in this. That is: I have no choice the way I used to mean it.'

He inclines his head. He knows what I mean. Neither of us especially want to touch on the dark heart of what is being done here.

I continue, 'But perhaps there is a choice of the heart. I don't know if I can make that choice, but if it's possible, I would like to try. I would like to go into this knowing that, at the very least, I did try.'

'You do know the door here is locked? The windows have bars?'

'I've already tried escaping. That didn't work out so well.'

Cyril looks at me. His eyes are oddly ambiguous. By day, in sunlight, his eyes have an extraordinary paleness and clarity. In the weaker light of this chapel and with his eyebrows, as now, drawn forward, his pupils are open and cavernous and dark.

And then – I don't know. There is a shift between us. A melting. Like some intense wave of compassion, almost physical in its force.

He grips my hand and says, 'Daughter!' There is nothing fake about his emotion.

He calls for a knife. Someone gives him one and he cuts my ties. Rubs my wrists and helps me to stand.

I'm wobbly to start with, but find my balance.

365

At the back of the church, there's a metal basin and a jug. A ewer, I think you'd call it. Soap.

I walk, shakily but unaided, to the basin. Pour water. Wash my hands.

The soap is heavily scented. My hair is too, I realise. That same dusky scent that Carlotta wore in hers.

'Frankincense?' I whisper.

Anselm, who is with me, nods.

I turn back to the altar.

Cross myself. Genuflect.

I almost fall when I genuflect, but Anselm's strong arm catches me and raises me up.

I steady myself and walk up the nave. My shoes are wedding shoes. Satin lace with a tiny white bow. A sweet little kitten heel. They're not hard to walk in, but hard enough that I need to take care with my steps, my still-muzzy head.

At the altar, I genuflect again and kneel before the cross. The six monks flank me, three and three, sitting in their regular places in the little choir stalls.

Someone rings a small handbell. The start of the vigil, I assume. I bow my head.

Pray.

Not fake-pray, even. Real-pray. To who, to what, for what purpose – I couldn't say. With what words, or meaning, or intent – that too, I don't know, can't tell.

All I know is that there is a roar, an intensity of purpose in this space. A purpose whose object and plaything I am. I don't surrender to it, but nor do I fight it. I bob on its current and it hurtles me forward, taking me where it will.

Time detaches. We slip its feeble moorings.

It's like that time under the church tower in Ystradfflur again, except that these infinities are greater. Their wash runs deeper.

When someone rings the little handbell again to mark the

end of our vigil, I am genuinely startled that an hour has gone by. I'm almost frozen into position. One of the monks, I don't know who, thinks I'm resisting the next bit and comes forward to move me on, but I gesture him back with a hand.

I've never knelt this long in my life and, now that I notice it, my back is a red flare of pain and stiffness. My attention dwells on the pain for a moment, then simply glides off again. I'm having difficulty anchoring myself in anything like this time and place.

Anchoring. People think that the word 'anchorite' derives somehow from 'anchor', but it doesn't. It derives from a Greek word that means to 'withdraw.'

To withdraw from temptation. From the world. From all things human.

Again the monk behind me moves forward.

Again I gesture him back.

I stand up, staggering as I do. Partly the ghost of the ketamine still in me. Partly just my stiff and unresponsive muscles. I hold the altar rail to steady myself, then turn.

What next?

What's next is that throne again. Red and gold. Placed at the end of the chancel, facing the altar. Candles lit on either side.

Still veiled, and walking unsteadily but without support, I walk to the chair.

Sit.

I'm not normally a graceful sitter. Not the skirt-smoothing, dress-adjusting kind of girl. But I am now. Tweak my dress as I sit, smooth it after. Check and adjust the fall of my veil.

Then – nothing. There is nothing more to be done. I sit with my legs together but uncrossed. Place my hands on my lap. Look up, find Cyril's eye, and nod once. As the monks rise to begin a chant in plainsong – a psalm, I think, but don't quite hear – I stare forward at the altar. A golden cross on a white cloth. The whole church has been kept quite dim, candlelit for the most part, but a bright halogen spot keeps the cross bright and ablaze.

I can't keep my eye on anything else.

Psalms and canticles.

Prayers of penitence and praise.

I don't participate, or I don't think I do. Perhaps my lips form a few *amen*s, a *christe eleison* or two. Mostly, though, that timelessness seizes me again. There is me. There is a golden cross on a snowy altar. Everything else passes in a haze.

And the strange thing is: I feel this as I think I'm meant to. Feel bridal. Like a consecrated, beautiful object being passed from one honoured hand to another.

It's partly the clothes, of course. That whole white veil, church music thing that almost no woman I know is wholly immune to. But it's more than just that. More than this setting, these monks. There's something – *something* – in this wash of ceremony that invites my participation.

Invites and secures it.

Then, as a psalm ends, Cyril steps forward. He wants me to stand. Gestures me forwards towards the altar. I do as he wants. He asks me to prostrate myself.

It is hard to obey, as hard as anything so far, but I do as he asks. Lie face down before the altar as the monks chant and sing above me.

Then I rise.

Cyril is asking me questions. I give responses, I think, but there are only two parts of the ceremony I really hear.

The first is where I am asked to renounce the seven capital sins. *Luxuria. Gula. Avaritia. Acedia. Invidia. Ira. Superbia.*

Lust. Gluttony. Avarice. Sloth. Envy. Anger. Pride.

I renounce the first five with barely a tremble. But on number six and seven, the words don't come to me. 'Father, I cannot.'

Cyril doesn't answer. Just waits. Then nudges again. Then again.

And on that third time, I say, 'Anger. I renounce it. Pride. I renounce it.'

Then the final question and my final response. The question and answer that makes this whole ceremony binding and for ever.

'Do you withdraw from the world? Do you renounce it?'

'I do.'

Then someone raises my veil. Folds it back over my head. I am given bread and wine. Flesh and blood.

I am very shaky. So much so that I can hardly stay standing. Indeed, when Cyril withdraws the goblet from my mouth, I do actually buckle at the knees. A half-collapse that I parlay into a further act of submission. A deep, penitential kneel and I feel a wave of surprised approval from the men around me as they watch.

I stay kneeling for five minutes, perhaps ten or twenty. Then rise. Anselm's hand supports me as I do.

He escorts me to the first icon, the first piece of darkened glass, the first inset candle.

The glass isn't there to reflect the candle. It is one-way glass, arranged so that the person on the other side can always see the altar, that golden cross.

I say, 'Saint Hilarion?'

Cyril says, 'Halarion the Anchorite lived in the desert in the fourth century. Lived alone in a low-ceilinged cell that was more like a tomb than a house. Fasted often. Prayed always.'

I can't tell if the person on the other side is watching me. There's no flicker behind the glass, but I don't think there would be no matter what.

I wonder why the person doesn't tap, if he's there. Then realise that perhaps he *is* tapping. Perhaps there are two or three or five thicknesses of glass. Whatever is soundproofed enough.

I cross myself in front of the man's cell.

God help you, I think. *And God help me.* Then – and this isn't premeditated, just the most natural thing to do, somehow – dip into a deep curtsy. Again, I feel that wave of monkish approval.

The next icon.

Osmanna.

I glance sideways and Cyril says, 'In the seventh century, an Irish woman of noble family chose to retire to France to live in solitude with the Lord. She died aged about seventy.'

Cross myself. Curtsy. Move on.

At the next icon – Aurelia – I don't know why, but I have a powerful sense that the woman on the other side is looking at me. I wonder what I must look like to her. What my face conveys. I must, at a minimum, remind her of her own strange journey to this place. The dress. The veil. The pale shock of what's been and what's coming.

Cyril: 'Saint Aurelia of Strasbourg. Lived for fifty-five years as an anchoress in the praise and service of her Lord.'

I don't quite know how to honour the face I feel watching me from the glass. Don't know how to communicate, or even what message I want to pass on.

You and me, Sister. We're in this together. Sisters now and sisters for ever. Something like that.

I cross myself and curtsy – a deeper, longer curtsy than the others received – but it's still not enough.

I say, 'May I have a candle, please?'

I need to say that twice. Wet my lips and say it twice, because my voice is little more than a croak. A wooden spoon, stirring ashes.

Someone brings me a candle and I light it from the flame

that poor Aurelia gazes on. Set the second candle in the same little niche.

Something in the interaction still feels incomplete, but I don't know what would complete it and, in any case, Saint Anthony – the bearded, haloed toughie who, in an only somewhat different life, could have been one of those seen-it-all, done-it-all big city DIs – now claims my attention.

I stare at the darkened glass.

Feel some kind of gaze, perhaps, but nothing like what I felt from Aurelia. There's something wolfish perhaps. I have the sudden creepy sense that, if there is someone watching me now, they're masturbating as they do so.

I do the cross and curtsy bit again, but no candle for you, Anthony, mate. Not that I exactly blame you for taking your pleasures where you can.

The fifth pane of glass. The blank wall. The empty niche.

I stare at the wall. A nail has been placed to take a picture.

Cyril murmurs, 'We have prayed and we have chosen. In your case, the choice was easy.'

He settles a little icon on the nail. Mother Julian of Norwich.

He gives me a candle. Wants me to light it myself, but my hands are shaking too much to do so. Someone lights it for me and helps me settle it in front of my own little bit of darkened glass.

'Mother Julian,' Cyril murmurs. 'Anchoress at the Church of St Julian in Norwich.' Then, quoting her, adds, '"For I saw no wrath except on man's side, and He forgives that in us, for wrath is nothing else but a perversity and an opposition to peace and to love."'

I cross myself and curtsy. Curtsy so deeply, so shakily that this time I can't get up. Need to be supported up, Brother Anselm on one side, Brother Thomas on the other.

I say, 'May I please have something to eat? I feel very faint.'

Cyril: 'Sister Julian, your first day will be a day of fast and penitence. There will be ample food thereafter.'

Brother Nicholas's barley bread, and plenty of it.

But they bring me water and I drink it and the water helps. I feel weak, but ready. I nod to indicate as much.

I'm escorted to the back of the church, where a little door leads into a vestry. Vestments and hymn books. Packets of communion wafers and cardboard boxes of candles. The room looks like just another version of the vestry at Ystradfflur. Smelling of plaster and damp and last Sunday's incense.

But this room has a second door. One you hardly notice, stuck behind the angle of a cupboard.

They don't do locks. That's what I told Watkins, but I was wrong. You only need one lock, after all, and here it is. Brother Nicholas unlocks that second door and leads me through. Three monks passing ahead of me, three behind: an arrangement that is ceremonial but also carefully security-aware.

We enter the lean-to that runs the length of the church. This lean-to that has a woodstore at the far end and which, I'd always assumed, was simply storeroom or barn all the way along.

And it *is* a storeroom, of sorts.

It stores people.

Within the large room, there is a chain of smaller ones – cells – built up against the church wall. The cells have no doors. They have no windows. A small opening at the bottom of each cell allows food to be passed in and any waste to be passed out. Those openings are, for now, shuttered with thick iron plates, heavily fastened and bolted.

But it's not the chain of four completed cells that claim my eye, but the one on the end. The one that currently stands open and incomplete.

Its walls are thick. Two feet at least, I estimate. Solid Welsh sandstone. A lime mortar mix with plenty of cement.

Most of the masonry work has already been done. The side walls come out and join at the front. The little food tunnel has already been constructed. The iron plate isn't yet in place, but the fixings are there.

Above that, though, there's a kind of ragged opening of unfinished stone. An opening that widens as it rises towards a half-domed, almost beehive roof.

The opening is big enough to admit a human. Particularly, a short-ish, slim-ish human wearing only a thin white dress and veil.

The monks, or some of them, are impatient for me to move forward. To enter my cell.

One of them, Thomas I think, touches my arm in the hope of nudging me forwards. But I shake him off. Angrily. My first outburst of petulance.

'By. Choice,' I say. 'By *choice*.'

My voice is a useless thing. A broken toy. But the monk steps back.

I stare at that little stony opening. It stares back at me.

My legs, without any conscious volition from me, carry me over to the spot.

Inside: a stone cell.

About six foot square. The roof, when it is finished, will be perhaps eight or nine foot at its highest. The walls are unplastered. There is a low stone bed, with a thin mattress. Two grey blankets. No pillow. A small pile of clothes, neatly folded. A metal basin and ewer. A bar of soap. A tin cup. A little straw brush for keeping the cell tidy. A chamber pot.

And, of course, that one-way glass.

From where I am, I can't see the church altar, but I know that if – when – I kneel in front of that glass, my gaze will be directed, through the light of the candle, to that golden cross on its snowy altar.

On this side of the glass, there is a little step, equipped with a tiny cushion, on which to kneel.

Also: a palm cross, a Bible, a string of beads.

I stand at the threshold, gazing at my future.

Saint Aurelia. Fifty-five years in the service of her Lord. And, dear God, I'm young enough and healthy enough that I might live that long.

I step right up to the opening, resting my hand on the rough stone.

There are loose blocks here. Some of them small enough that I could carry them in one hand. If I were Lev, perhaps that would give me enough of a weapon. But even he, I think, might struggle, one against six. And I'm a pretty feeble one.

I move my hand. It comes away with a little grey dust, which I brush off. A hand-washing movement. A cleansing.

I put my hand up to my head and find the little comb that secures the veil to my hair.

Look at Cyril, who gives me a tiny nod.

I remove the veil and fold it, taking care that the lace hem shows properly, that it's folded, not crumpled. I take my time, not because I am ordinarily careful about such things but because the veil is, in its own idiot way, a beautiful thing and I may not see many more such things.

It is hard to hand the veil over to Cyril, but I do.

By choice.

I will do this by choice.

Shoes next. Those are still harder to relinquish, because their lace and satin curves, their tiny flirty kitten heels, those adorable foolish bows have a hold on me that I can't quite describe. I'm not a shoe girl, never have been, but this pair seem now like the loveliest objects in the whole universe.

But I relinquish them. Trembling, but I do.

The next step is to cross that stony threshold. To surrender this dress, so white and pretty. To don whatever clothes lie

374

folded on the bed. To do that – and what? – kneel? pray? scream? fight? – as these men wall me in, stone by everlasting stone?

I crumple. A full-on, legs-give-way crumple. I end up kneeling, if only because it's all my body now seems able to do. Knees on the bare stone floor. Head on the ragged open wall.

'I can't do it, Father. Sorry.'

'You can. You have done so well already. The others, they were not – they were not like this.'

I bet they weren't. I try to imagine those rudely abucted kids. Rich kids, moneyed kids. Perhaps – who knows? – selfish and brattish kids. Imagine them as they saw these walls for the first time. Understood their purpose.

I hope those kids fought and swore and kicked and screamed.

I hope they hurt someone.

But that was them and that was then. This is me and now and here and inescapable.

'I don't know how to pray. I've never learned.'

'The Lord will teach.' I think the abbot wants to dish out more of the *tempested/overcome* stuff, but something tells him now isn't the time.

He waits. We all wait.

I shake again. Not just my head, but my whole body. A long, shuddering *no* of refusal. 'I'm sorry.'

The word is a mouse that skitters a foot or two across the floor, no more. A whisper's echo.

Am I faking this resistance?

I don't think so. I feel it as real and as hard as a stone in my belly.

Again, I think one of the monks comes towards me, intending some form of physical compulsion. Thomas, I expect. Or Nicholas. I never liked those two.

But again, some signal from Cyril, perhaps also Anselm, heads off whatever was about to happen.

More waiting.

I say – the scratch of an echo of a murmur – 'This first night, this first day. May I have guidance? Someone with me? Support?'

That sends a ripple round the group. I don't know what form this ceremony of enclosure takes, but not this. Their whole ordered life has just hit a little obstacle. A tiny boulder just peeping above the current.

Thomas starts to say, 'It is not—'

But Cyril, bless him, bless his monkish wisdom, cuts the man off. He says, 'My daughter Julian, if that is what enables you to make this a choice of the heart, then so be it. This first night only, one of us will keep vigil with you. In the morning, we will celebrate matins, then complete the Enclosure. Is that acceptable?'

Still kneeling. Still breathing into the soft mortar dust and cold stone, I say, 'Yes.'

'Can you make the choice?'

'I can.'

Someone helps me stand. I am cold and shaky. Long waves of fear that ride through me leaving me breathless.

I take the abbot's hands. Both of his in both of mine.

'Peace be with you, Father.'

'Peace be with you.'

Each of the others, the same, except that I call them Brother and they me Sister.

I stand at the opening, bare-headed, bare-footed. 'Pray for me, Brothers,' I say, and step through into my cell.

Outside, a couple of the monks put some kind of board up over the opening. A piece of ply they've been using to mix their mortar on, I think. I use the privacy to step out of my dress. Explore the clothes on the bed.

There's a loose linen shirt. I put it on.

Then some kind of dress. Long, loosely gathered at the waist, sleeveless. The kind of thing that needs something underneath. The dress is heavy, woollen, scratchy. I search my memory for the right term. A kirtle, perhaps. Pale grey. Chaste, but also plain. No temptation here to vanity.

I put it on. It ties up at the front with a cord almost like a bootlace. Thick enough, perhaps, for me to hang myself, except that there's no place to tie the other end. The skirt reaches almost to the floor.

Grey woollen stockings. Warm and thick. Sandals.

Then, great heavens, something that is surely a wimple, a headcovering. I try to figure out how the thing works, but can't, so I tap at the board and say, 'I am clothed.'

They move the board. Through the gap, I hand them my white dress, neatly folded.

'The wimple. I'm sorry. I don't know . . .'

Brother Thomas who, I am increasingly sure, gets a savage, sadistic and – I'll bet – sexual pleasure from this thing, ties the thing tight over my head and neck as I lean forward. I loosen it as I withdraw.

My cell, my rules, buddy.

There's one more item of clothing too. A short cloak. Also grey. Also coarse. A crude tie at the throat, but the damn thing is heavy and warm and my chilly arms are happy to welcome it.

I put it on.

Not a cloak. A mantle, or perhaps a mantelet. That's the right term, I think.

Fully dressed now, prepared and fitted for my new life, I turn to the men.

To my surprise, they kneel. Cyril speaks some Greek prayer, honouring me, I think, for my holy vocation. I don't know what to say. What response is called for. But when they rise, I curtsy.

Wimpled, kirtled and mantled, I curtsy. An anchoress who has stepped, of her own volition, into this cell, these clothes, this life.

When, behind me, they start to build my cell's walls, I don't watch.

When, behind me, they start to chant the funeral service that marks my ceremonial death, my death to the world, I hardly listen.

I just kneel at my little pane of glass. My eye fixed the only place it can: on the golden cross burning on an empty altar.

Kyrie eleison.

Lord have mercy.

Christe eleison.

Christ have mercy.

And all the time, behind me, the stone walls rise.

44

Stonework is a physical business, of course, and these walls are thick.

But the mortar is already mixed. There are six men gladly at work. The stone lies ready. And, of course, these monks are practised at this work and the wall flies up.

When the opening is closed all the way up to head height – more than, more than my height – I turn from my prayer and throw a desperate look up at Cyril.

He wipes sweat and building dust from his face and says, 'I haven't forgotten. We keep our word.'

The walls rise to eight foot. Most of the ceiling is completed too. An arch that leans up against the church wall. The gap that's left is about the size of the little loft hatch that led to Lev's attic. Wider than some of the tunnels in that damn cave.

And Cyril keeps his promise. Asks me who I would like to accompany me, this first night of the rest of my life.

I don't know. I should have an answer, but I don't.

Thomas, the little bastard, is nasty, but I'm nasty too and I reckon, with the power of surprise and desperation, I might, just might, win a physical contest with him. But Cyril is a wise old sod and he hasn't been running this game so cleanly and for so long without plenty of operational savvy.

'Anselm,' he says. 'You have always got on well with Brother Anselm.'

I bow my wimpled head in acceptance.

Anselm is indeed my favourite of the monks. He has an easy kindness and earthy humour, which is, I think, real enough, for all that I don't share every last one of his religious beliefs.

But he's also the strongest. He's late thirties, perhaps, or early forties. Not huge. Not one of those sixteen-stone rugby types who could walk through a brick wall and not notice the difference. But he's strong, all the same. I've seen him lifting one of those big hay bales and tossing it, actually tossing it, onto a handcart. Seen him working on the dry-stone walls in the fields and he picks up stones, even big ones, with a single powerful hand.

They drop a ladder down from the roof. Anselm squeezes through the hole and climbs down. They hoist the ladder back up. When they were working on the wall, a couple of monks stood on my side, building the cell up from within, tidying up the pointing. When they left, they left a couple of small bags of lime and cement. Those things and a trowel.

Metal-bladed. Pointed. Long enough.

Anselm chuckles at me. Winks. Corrects a few places in the wall where he's not happy with the pointing – he loves his stonewalling – then tosses the little trowel up through the gap in the roof. We hear it tinkling down the other side.

He scrunches his eyes up at me. Friendly. A laugh, only part suppressed.

We sit beside each other on the bed.

'I have never prayed.'

'You will learn.'

I pick up the chain of beads. 'This? It's a rosary?'

'Yes.' He starts to explain it. One prayer per bead. Each set of ten – a 'decade' – preceded and completed by a different prayer. He tells me of the Joyful Mysteries, the Sorrowful Mysteries, the Glorious Mysteries. 'But there are no rules. You will find your own rhythm. Your places of peace.'

We start.

I kneel at the little window. He kneels beside me.

We recite prayers – simple ones, short ones, things that I can quickly pick up. We recite prayers and the beads click round. A decade first, then five decades, then fifteen.

We pause. I take some water. The church clock above us chimes midnight as we pass over into the last day of December. The last day of this expiring year.

I offer water to Anselm but he says no.

I ask if there'll be any chance of getting any reading matter in here. 'Devotional texts, I mean,' I add hurriedly. 'To support my reading of the Bible.'

He nods. 'Of course. To start with, we do encourage a devotion of the heart, not the brain. But after a year or two, if all goes well, there might well be writings that would support your journey.'

He tells me that some anchoresses used to embroider things. 'Perhaps when you enter mid-life,' he says placidly. 'You are still very young. It would not be wise to be too distracted by things of the eye.'

Oh sweet Lord. Two years before I get something to read. Fifteen or twenty before I get to distract my eye with a little holy embroidery.

'I would like to sew kneelers,' I say. 'For the church.'

He smiles at me. In fifteen years, I might get my wish.

We pray again.

And it's true. The strange thing is that it's perfectly true. These prayers, this repetition, even the knowledge of this long, strange anchoritic tradition – these things help stabilise me. Bring a kind of uneasy peace.

We complete another fifteen decades, but we go round again. Then round again.

I pause for rest.

Sit on the bed.

'If the others call to me, can I hear them?' The people in

the other cells, I mean. My fellow anchorites and anchoresses.

'We encourage silence and silent contemplation. If you need counsel in matters spiritual, you can speak to any of us when we bring your food and water. If you need to make confession, we will always accept that, of course.'

'But if they call, will I hear?'

Anselm smiles. 'We place a high value on silence. If they are noisy, and some of them have been, we place a bale of straw in front of their hatches.' He looks at me and, with gentle eyes, says, 'No, you will not hear them.'

We rest a bit more. Then pray again.

Two o'clock.

'Anselm, will you always tell me about the pigs? I want to know they're happy.'

He laughs. 'I will always tell you about the pigs.'

Rest a few minutes, then kneel again.

Three o'clock.

Rest.

'Anselm, my brothers and sisters in these cells. I know why you chose me, but why did you choose them?'

'Why them? Unlike you, they all grew up in the bosom of the Mother Church. They knew God. Knew what it was to worship. And they strayed. Lost their souls. For money. For things of the world.' He looks at me with a grave face. 'We pray every day for their redemption. We *work* for it. It is our honour and our duty.'

That's how they justify all this to themselves, is it? *Yes, walling people up in tiny stone cells might look bad to you but, hey, we're trying to save their immortal souls. And, OK, it might look like we're hypocrites, wandering around in the wind and sunshine, living a free life under the stars, but* we really care. *We feel for these people. We pray for them. We're saving them, don't you see it, we're saving them.*

Bollocks to that. Bollocks to it all.

382

Carlotta, I presume, died in Parry's cellar. Her kidnap negotiation was still ongoing. Even so, her fibrotic lungs, her endangered heart couldn't take the strain of that place. What would they have made of this? How long would they have lasted here? And how exactly would any of that have helped her hypothetically immortal soul?

In a grim way, however, I like it that I have taken her place. My living corpse taking the place of her departed one. Entering the tomb that had been readied for her.

Anselm interrupts my thoughts. 'But you are wrong. You *don't* know why we chose you.'

'I found Parry. You knew I'd understood the set-up.'

'Yes, and in a way that forced things on us. But it was still *you* who chose us.'

I shake my head, resisting, but he continues, 'The first time, yes, you came because your investigation brought you here. But the time after that? And the time after that? And the time after that? And when you prayed, we saw a soul in trouble. And when you swore at Father Cyril, he heard a soul in trouble. And when he gave you the *Revelations of Divine Love*, you read it, every word. And when he placed his hands on your head, your troubled soul felt peace.'

I stare at him, mouth open.

In a very gentle voice, he adds, 'And what happened in there, in our church tonight: can you really tell me that you did not feel the spirit of the Lord moving within you?'

I don't answer.

Can't.

'You chose us. It was you who chose us.'

I bow my head.

'Forgive me, Brother.'

'You are already forgiven.'

We move to the glass and pray again.

Five decades. And five more. And five more. And yes, I say, can we do five more?

Four o'clock and Anselm yawns.

It's one of the things about the monastic life. We're so regular in our timings that when we reach the midday dismissal, our bellies start to rumble. That's what the abbot told us when Burnett and I first met him.

My own relationship with sleep is so impaired, so strange already, that a night spent awake hardly signifies. But Anselm is different. His monkish body-clock is all askew. Kneeling all night when he should be asleep, and these hours of prayer are hard on any bones, old or young. This isn't the first time he's yawned, but it's the biggest so far.

I yawn too. Amplifying that contagion of tiredness.

'Excuse me, Brother, I need to use the chamber pot.'

And do. I've been drinking water half the night and have a whole bladderful of urine to release.

I squat over the little pot and pee, as noisily as I can.

Use the sound to cover me, as I empty the little ewer of water out over the floor.

Use the sound to cover me, as I take two handfuls of finely powdered lime.

A natural product. Beautiful when used right, and one that does all those good things to do with letting old buildings breathe, that sort of thing.

But also caustic. Fiercely, dangerously caustic.

When wet, lime is one of the most strongly alkali substances available outside a chemist's laboratory. One that will react, and react strongly, to moisture of any sort. The cornea of the eye, for example. The soft linings of the nose and mouth.

Stepping up behind Anselm, I give him one handful of lime in his eyes, the other over his airways.

He gasps in pain and surprise and the gasp allows me to shove a whole big handful into his open gob.

There's no treatment for caustic burns, except plenty of fresh water and I've just emptied all the water we have.

Stepping quickly back as Anselm roars and flails, I snatch up the chamber pot. Smash the thing over his saintly little head. Which stuns him, if only a little, and makes more of him wet. I take the bag of lime and pour it, throw it, scatter it over him.

He's a man powdered and, beneath the powder, burning.

When he opens his mouth, it's white and void inside. The same thing with his eyes. It looks like they're closed, but they're not. They're open. Just white and grey and staring.

He tries to clean the lime away with his robe, his hands, but he's like a fish trying to wash away the river. Whether he's permanently blind, I don't know, but he's functionally sightless.

He thrashes around. Cries out, I think, saying 'Sister! Sister!', but his mouth is full of a powder that burns and his roar is the roar of a beast.

I stay clear of his arms, ducking and weaving as I have to, but I don't actually think he's trying to hurt me. To restrain me, yes, but not actually to hurt me.

Choose the fight you want, not the one they want. If you can't win, don't start.

Any time before now, those monks would have had the fight they expected – and that Brother sadist Thomas wanted. Right now, I've got the fight *I* want, and one that takes place when and where and how I want.

A strong, blind man whose instincts are for gentleness versus a petite, but seeing woman who has her entire life hanging on the outcome.

No contest.

I wait until Anselm is a little off-balance – skidding on china and urine – and kick hard at his only standing leg. He starts to fall.

As he goes down, I grab his head and throw it downwards

against the stone. It bounces horribly, but just once.

He starts to move, just a little. Not in combat mode now. Not even restraint mode. More am-I-still-alive mode. I put in a few more considered, disabling kicks and stamps, then leave it.

That brother ain't gonna bother this little sister no more.

I step up onto the bed. I can't reach the gap in the ceiling like that, but my little glass prayer-niche gives me a foothold and – clumsily, clumsily – I scrabble up to the roof and through it.

Look down.

Anselm is dragging himself upright, or sort of upright. But he's not trying to stand, he's trying to kneel. My kicks were scientific enough that he's going to have problems with his ribs, knee and testicles, but he somehow accomplishes a kind of lopsided lean up against the wall.

His burned hands search for and find the little palm cross. The bit of glass through which a pair of seeing eyes would find the altar.

I leave him at it.

A basic clip-together tower scaffold provided support for the monks as they built the roof. There are stones still here. Some mortar left overnight with a square of plastic keeping it moist. I add a few more stones to the roof. My stonework is of the very crudest sort – Anselm would hate it – but it doesn't have to hold for long. There's still a gap here, but not one that a man could climb through.

'So long, Brother,' I call down. 'You were always nice to the pigs. I'll remember that.'

And leave.

Out of the room, its row of cells. The door into the vestry is locked, but it's not much of a door, not much of a lock. It was only ever needed to keep out the idly curious. I give the thing a couple of good kicks and it pings right open.

Then out through the vestry and church into the courtyard. It's asparkle with frost and moonlight, the way it should be.

I feel a bit wobbly, a bit light-headed: the after-effects of the ketamine, that strange and scary night, eighteen hours or so without food, a blast of adrenaline from the fight I've just had. None of those things are particularly disabling, more that their cumulative effect leaves me feeling a little delicate.

I want a joint, want some warm food, want to have a long, hot bath and a cuddle from someone friendly. All those things will have to wait, though. For now, I have work to do.

I start walking out – to the road, to freedom – when I see that there are several cars parked in the little visitors' area.

Of course. This is the week after Christmas. There'll be plenty of spiritual seeker types who want a nice little jolt of religion to get them through the holiday season. I don't know how the monks explained that the church was out of bounds yesterday evening, but they'll have found some smooth lie to get them through.

I pad over to the visitors' block. The one whose doors are never locked, where Carlotta never stayed.

Open a couple of doors at random – empty – then find one where someone is sleeping, but don't see what I'm looking for. Then open another and there, on the little table, are some car keys and a phone. Also – praise be – a cheeky packet of chocolate digestives that whoever this is has already half-eaten.

I take the phone and the biscuits. Creep out.

Walk far enough that my voice won't disturb anyone and call Burnett's mobile.

'Who's this?' His voice, grumpy and asleep.

'It's me. Do you still want that promotion?'

'Yes.'

'Then you should probably make some arrests. People won't just arrest themselves, you know.'

I tell him where, tell him how. Make him play it back,

because I don't want him to screw this up because he's sleepy. He's on the case, though. He'll do fine. When he asks do we need an ARU – an Armed Response Unit – I say no, then change my mind and say yes. 'For Dylan Parry, yes definitely. For the monks, probably not, but I'd have something in reserve, if you can.'

If you can: Dyfed-Powys isn't the sort of force that can assemble many firearms-trained police officers at a moment's notice. Burnett says he'll get on to it.

'And communications,' I say. 'You have to get Dylan Parry before he can get to a phone. If you need to block signal or whatever, then do it.'

It takes Burnett only a moment to figure out what I'm talking about, but says, 'I'm on it. What's wrong with your voice?'

'I'm eating biscuits.'

'You're eating biscuits?'

Burnett is obviously still a bit sleepy, since I couldn't have made myself much clearer. 'Yes, sir. I'm eating biscuits. Stolen chocolate digestives. Oh, also, we're going to need some ambulances.'

'Ambulances?'

'Sir, is this a new game where you repeat everything I say?'

'OK. Ambulances. How many?'

'Um, one actual hospital case, but we probably better have paramedics as well. Four possible cases of shock.'

Burnett, I think, is about to say 'Shock' or something like it, but he bites the word back and just says, 'Fine.'

Adds: 'You better not be screwing around here. This better be for real.'

He says that when, unfortunately, I have quite a lot of chocolate digestive in my mouth so although I do say, 'It's for real, don't worry,' it does sound quite a lot more chocolatey and biscuity than it should.

Burnett wonders whether to growl at me some more, but decides against. We ring off.

I call Cesca.

She answers, sleepily.

'Cesca, it's me. Your strange detective.'

'Ess? Hi. Are you OK?'

'I'm fine. Where are you? Right now. Where are you?'

Plas Du, is the answer. Her mother's house near Llantwit.

'Good. That's good. Then do you want to see how this ends? This investigation of mine.'

She does.

I tell her to shift herself over here. 'And, Cesca. That little hippy-dippy box of yours. Do you still have it?'

There's a short pause, then, 'You want me to bring you a *joint*?'

That High Rising Terminal. A generational thing.

'No. Not *one* joint. Bring everything you've got. I'm not in a one-joint place right now.'

She says OK. Says it enthusiastically enough that I can actually hear her leaping out of bed, starting to get organised.

I ring off.

Walk out into the dark road. Keep my arms well tucked into my mantelet. Keep my wimple on because, much as I dislike it, it keeps my head warm.

Try eating more biscuits, but I'm feeling a bit sick.

The first patrol car arrives in about fifteen minutes. No sirens. No noise.

Two officers, neither armed but both competent enough. They park well back from the monastery, not wanting to give anything away just yet. A radio burbles.

I ask one of them for a jacket. One of the uniforms gives me his. One of those black and neon hi-vis things.

'Thanks.'

I pull my wimple off my head but keep it as a thickly folded scarf.

'Were you undercover?' asks the uniform curiously.

I don't answer.

Another car arrives, then an ambulance.

Two officers stamp up the road a little way and have a cheeky ciggy. They don't offer me one, I think because they're still slightly intimidated by the pious and virginal nun who first greeted their arrival.

The radio tells us that an ARU is in place outside Dylan Parry's house, which is good. He's the one most likely to give trouble.

Then Burnett arrives. Tracksuit bottoms and an old jumper pulled straight over pyjamas. A thick coat over the top. No wheelchair.

He stares at my socks and sandals and long skirt. At my hi-vis jacket and wimple-scarf. Opens the jacket enough to see my kirtle in all its glory.

'What the fuck are you wearing?' he says.

I shake my head. Don't even ask.

A bell starts to toll for matins.

'We could take 'em now,' says Burnett, but I say not. It's better to collect everyone in the church and make arrests as they leave. Besides which, a van full of officers up from Neath is due here any minute.

The matins bell slows to longer, single beat, then falls silent. A uniform with a night-vision scope, trained from a distance on the yard, reports that the monks 'appear to have entered the church'.

The van arrives from Neath. Ten officers. More than enough now. A second ambulance too, with three paramedics and a bleary-eyed junior doctor.

We allow another few minutes to take care of any stragglers, then our little force enters the yard. From the dim church interior, the first psalm.

The little quadrangle fills and thickens with our booted, jacketed, batoned presence.

Burnett radios someone. Tells them to suspend phone lines. Landline and mobile. Cutting the valley off. Once he gets the confirmations he needs, he tells the ARU at Parry's house to move in and move in hard.

Hard, loud and nasty.

I know how those things go. Steel ram on the door. Lights ablaze. Police megaphones at maximum blare.

It's not the cuffs that make the arrest. It's the noise and commotion first. Get that first blazing intro right and the bad guy knows he's defeated the very same second that his door bursts open. That's the moment his freedom ends.

Three minutes later, Burnett gets a call back. Parry under arrest. No weapons discharged or even taken off safety. Parry neither made nor attempted any phone call, but his mobile has been seized and is already en route for the tech team at Bridgend.

Burnett tells someone to get the phone lines turned back on.

Three minutes after that, another call. A cellar found in Parry's place. Multiple locks on the doorway in. Black cloth backdrop. Video camera. Ditto a cache of tinned and dry food that would, at first estimate, feed one person at least two months.

Burnett tells them to sod off out of the cellar. Tells them to get the forensics boys in there immediately. He's got one hand on his promotion and he'll be damned if he pisses it away now.

Burnett wants to enter the church, make the second set of arrests. No operational reason why not, but I say no. It's just not how I ever pictured it and I like to do things, when I can, the way they always looked in my head.

We hear the last sounds of matins inside the church. A silence – that'll be Cyril giving the blessing, then the whole business of honouring the anchorites, me included. I imagine Anselm on the other side, tapping on the glass.

> *Tippy, tappy, by the way,*
> *Sister Julian's run away.*
> *Tippy, tappy, tap, tap, tap.*
> *I've gone blind, my life is crap.*

Sounds that no one in the church can hear.

Then the movement of the congregation outside.

We don't use rams or batons. No lights. No blare of megaphones.

Just quietly detain each monk as they step out into this still pre-dawn frost. Handcuffs and the caution. Our own sweet litany of detention.

The men are surprised – startled – but their monastic serenity remains remarkably unperturbed. The civilians – the two men and four women who were in the visitors' rooms – are unhappy and perplexed, but they exhibit that wonderful British trustfulness. That belief that, if a uniformed copper wearing the Prince of Wales's feathers on their badge arrests someone, that person almost certainly deserves it. We could probably arrest the Pope, the Archbishop of Canterbury and a whole shower of bishops and archimandrites, yet receive no more reaction from the Great British Public than a quiet, muttered, 'Goodness gracious.' That, followed by a quick, polite search for a nice cup of tea.

We take the five monks. It's me who gets to do the honours with Cyril.

Don't swear. Don't shout. Don't use one of those whoops-a-daisy tricks of violence that leave no mark and which no court ever needs to hear about.

I don't speak even.

Just hold up the cuffs and let him place the bracelet on his own wrist. A burly uniform from Neath, every inch the rugby-playing type, completes the process, delivers the caution.

Cyril holds my eye, every moment, but I can't read his expression.

He's led off.

Someone tells the civilians that they should go to their rooms and remain there until otherwise instructed. I find the person whose phone I've got and give it back. I tell her that I stole her biscuits as well, and she says, 'Oh, that was you was it?' and gives me a strange look.

Then Burnett says to me, 'Five men. We've only got five.'

'That's why we need the ambulance.'

I take Burnett and a couple of others round to the vestry. Through the door that leads to the cells.

I explain what they are. Point to the one on the end of the row. 'That was mine. Sister Julian. That's what they called me.'

Burnett face goes pale white in shock. I don't think he even went quite that colour down in the caves. He says, 'Fuck.'

Burnett can walk OK, it seems, but bending isn't his forte. So it's the two men with us who throw open the iron hatches. They start shouting, 'Police. We are here to release you. Please . . .' I think they want to say, 'hold on', but holding on is the forte of these particular guys and girls. They've been holding on for years already. Were expecting to stay holding on for the rest of their prayer-achened lives.

Burnett starts to radio for help with demolition. One of the guys tries to gauge the depth of the walls by looking along the little food tunnels. Says, 'Fuck.' Looks pale.

A babble of accents – Slavic, Russian – comes out of the

tunnels, weirdly warped and still muted by the stone.

A uniform tells me there's a girl outside. Asking for me by name.

Cesca.

I tell him to send her in.

Stand there with Cesca. Show her the cells. The iron hatches.

She stares.

We go round into the church, where someone has had the wit to smash those glass windows with a police crowbar. Five heads in the openings.

Two men, heavily bearded, wild-eyed.

Two women, shocked, but somehow looking less bestial than the men, perhaps only because their faces are smoother.

I catch Aurelia's eye – not that she'll stay 'Aurelia' for much longer – and we stare at each other, recognising that moment we had last night. Me, enrobed as bride. She, kirtled and mantled and seeing herself in me.

Our eyes touch and I catch myself having the strangest thought. That I ruined this thing for her. Smashed her anchoritic freedom. As though I wanted what she had. I wonder if Anselm – the fifth face, at the fifth window, sightless but still praying by the shattered glass – was right. That something in me chose this place, this life.

The junior doctor comes to Anselm's little window and starts to see if he can do something for his eyes. My guess is yes. My hope too. I wanted to get away from Anselm, not blind him.

At the other windows, an official clutter of paramedics checking on the kidnappees. Coppers trying to get names and next-of-kin information.

I watch for a second, then say to Cesca, 'I really, really, really need that smoke.'

We head out.

Burnett yells, 'Fiona, where are you off to? I still need to know what the bloody hell this is all about.'

'Sir, I am going for a smoke and when I'm good and ready, I might come back.'

He does a short double-take. Shakes his head in disbelief. And lets me go.

45

Up on the hill, Cesca and I smoke.

Her joints are thin, weedy, useless things. Rolled too thin and with too much corrupting tobacco. But, three joints in, I feel almost calm.

As I light my fourth, the sun rises over Pen-y-fan and a plane of sunshine tilts and gilds everything with its touch.

Rose and gold and this sparkling diamond frost.

Cesca says, 'Ess?'

'Sorry. I'm OK. Really.'

'If you want to talk . . .'

Because her serious, dark eyes still hold mine, I say, 'Technically, I'm dead. They held a funeral service for me last night. It just takes me a bit of time to . . .' To what, I don't really know. But I raise the hand that has the joint in it, to the hills, to the valley, to the sun. 'I wasn't sure if I'd see any of this again.'

'You said they were – anchorites?'

'Yes. An anchorite – more commonly an anchoress – is a person who chooses a life of solitude and union with God. It's a spiritual tradition that dates back right to the start of the Christian era, but probably reached its peak in the twelfth and thirteenth centuries. For some reason, England and Wales seem to have had more anchoresses than anywhere else.'

'And they were forced into it? It was a punishment?'

'Oh no, they chose it. Absolutely no compulsion involved.

It used to be quite a big deal. You had to ask your bishop for permission and there was a whole big process of prayer and reflection while the thing was being considered.'

'OK.'

'But assuming your bishop said yes, you could go right ahead. There would have been a vigil, a fast, a mass. Then the enclosure ceremony itself. The anchoress was taken to her cell and there'd actually have been a funeral service held for her. Not because she was dead, but because from now on she would be dead to the world. She'd have had her funeral service and then – at her request, this is precisely what she wanted – she was walled up. There was a window through which she could receive food and water. And, this bit was crucial, she had a little window, a "squint" it was called, that gave her a view of the church, the altar.'

Cesca is listening intently, but she's also opening up her hippy-dippy little Indian box to get at the hash and tobacco and Rizla papers within. Starts to make a joint, because I've smoked all the ones she had pre-made.

'Anchoresses would have had what I had, basically. A mattress. Plain clothes, rather heavy and scratchy. A Bible. And as much opportunity for prayer as you could wish.' I grimace. 'A girl can never have too many canticles, right?'

Cesca: 'What if one of these people changed her mind? Tried it for a year and found she missed things too much?'

'No dice. She'd made her vows. There was one anchoress who *did* change her mind. She got someone to open her cell and she left it. When the bishop heard, he flew into a rage and made her go back. Once you were inside, you were there for ever.'

Cesca looks hard at me, and I say, '*I* was. I'd made my vows. Knelt as they gave me a funeral service. Prayed as they walled me up. I was there for ever. That was their plan.'

Cesca, who doesn't swear much, swears softly under her breath.

She wants to know how I got out, but I won't tell her.

That old anchoritic tradition, it seems to me, was holy enough, good enough. Life back then was hardly easy, no matter where you were. And most anchoresses came to be seen as holy people, sources of wisdom, whom people would travel to see and consult. Theirs was a strange calling, perhaps, but not a crazy one.

And it happened by choice. Real choice. A choice where people could say yes or no. For all the crap and the earnestness and the theological justifications that Cyril and friends no doubt have up their monkish sleeves, they took away choice and forced phoney vows into unwilling mouths. Vows that any self-respecting deity would see for the trash they truly were. Those monks deserve to pay the heaviest of prices for their crime.

Deserve to, and will. It would be hard to think of a simpler case for the prosecution.

We smoke a bit more, and the brief sun vanishes behind cloud, and the rose and the pink fades from the air – except that it doesn't, because it's still there, dancing and for ever – as Cesca and I walk back down the hill through the baa-ing sheep.

46

By the time we're down, the clean-up is in full flow.

Fire crews and a team of coppers are whacking at those damn cell walls with picks and sledgehammers. I don't think I've ever seen a group of men work so hard. One guy stands and assaults his piece of wall with massive, repeated blows until his arms shake and his face and back are running with sweat. Then he stands back and his team-mate takes his place. Ripping out those stones, block after block, blow after blow. Somewhere down the far end, a guy with a power tool stands in a rain of stone dust, a pile of broken stone at his feet.

Almost nobody speaks but there is a tremble of rage in this room, the like of which I've never experienced.

I say to the crew attacking the third cell, Aurelia's, 'I would like to speak to this woman, please. When she is out and safe.'

They nod, wipe their faces, return to their task.

Burnett is busy with a million things. The whole machinery of arrest and charge. Assigning bodies to tasks. Approving interview strategies. Resolving problems. Keeping intact anything that's forensically important. Handling the exhibits officers, the SOCOs, their questions. I don't disturb him.

Someone's got a van up from Carmarthen that's doling out hot drinks and bacon butties.

I butty up. Drink a weak tea.

I'm on my second butty when Burnett finds me.

'You still here?'

'Yes, Brother Alun.' I fold my hands in front of me and bow my head, anchoress style.

'Don't start that. Here, give me two minutes, can you?'

We sit in his car as he eats his bacon butty. His face has a kind of taut rigidity as he lowers himself into his seat, but after that one moment he seems comfortable enough.

I wonder if he's remembering that first grey morning at Ystradfflur. He was slow to handle his butty then, but he's making up for it now. Massive bites. A greasily gleaming maw.

He says, 'My ribs hurt like buggering hell. I'm only on aspirin and paracetamol now.'

But he's OK and getting better, so I say nothing, or nothing much.

He takes a monster mouthful of butty and says, through the mush, 'OK, there's a kidnap ring. I understand that.'

I nod.

'Dylan Parry. He was the Welsh end of the operation. The one who held the kidnappees. The one who fed them, took care of them, and handed them back over if the ransom was paid. I get that.'

Nod.

'But if you don't get your ransom money, why the fuck do you do that?' He jabs his butty at the monastery walls. 'It's not tidy. It's not a safe way to dispose of your victim.'

I shake my head. 'Really, are you sure?'

Burnett looks uncertain, and I follow up.

'Remember Linnea Gorkšs? The girl found in that Sussex woodland?'

'What about her?'

'OK, from what we know now, today, she looks like a match. Russian Orthodox upbringing. Wealthy parents. Mysteriously dead. Killed efficiently enough that a major inquiry found no leads they could progress.'

Burnett stares at me and completes the train of thought.

'So let's say this kid, Linnea, was one of the very early targets. Family doesn't pay up, the victim gets killed, but then – whoops – her corpse is uncovered. Massive police inquiry. A ton of publicity. And the people behind the kidnapping realise that corpse disposal isn't actually all that easy or safe. They're worried that the whole operation will be sprung into the open.'

'Exactly,' I say, 'Exactly. And, look, I don't know everything. But I imagine that Parry would have started out every inch the professional criminal. He was fine with kidnap. If that meant he had to murder an eighteen-year-old and dump her in a Suffolk wood, well, hell, that was in the job description. He just got on with it.

'But then – I don't know. Parry's living in this valley. Maybe starts going to one or two services in the monastery just for the hell of it. Or because he had a guilty conscience. Or to build himself some cover. Who knows? Anyway, he gets talking to the monks. He realises these guys might be highly spiritual in some ways, but they're also psycho-fundamentalist nutcases. Let's say, for example, he hears Father Cyril letting rip on how today's young and over-privileged are endangering their immortal souls. Maybe Cyril goes on a rant about how the true Christian soul longs for nothing more than silent communion with the Lord.

'So Parry says, "Hey, guys, do I have sinners for you." He explains that these monks would actually be saving lives. After all, if the monks don't take the kidnappees, Parry explains, sorry and all that, but he'll be obliged to kill them.'

'Oh, bullshit,' Burnett interrupts. 'Why don't the monks just go to the police?'

'Why would they? They don't regard *our* law as having any real validity. The only law *they* care about is the Word of God. And, in any case, if Parry made his proposal by way of a formal confession, I don't think the monks *can* divulge his secret. I mean, legally, yes of course they can, but not under the rules they live by.'

'That's fucked-up.'

'Fucked-up, but sweet, no? Basically, Parry makes a "confession" that the monks can't do anything with. And he says, "Now, look, either I go on killing these people – who will, by the way, be damned for ever because of all that terrible soul-imperilment of theirs – or you get to save lives *and* save souls. How about it, Father?" Whether that's exactly how it happened or not, I'd guess it was something along those lines. And the monks did really believe their own shtick. They thought they were doing a good thing here.

'And in terms of cover, it couldn't really have been better. A bunch of monks, who worked and prayed and were openly, obviously committed to a life of prayer and charity and poverty. All those things plus walls two foot thick. No doors or windows. From Parry's point of view, it was like burying his corpses without the trouble of killing them. Nothing for us to find and if we *did* ever stumble across the victims by accident, we'd have rounded up the monks in a flash, but – unless any of those guys volunteered a full confession – we would have no way of working back to the ultimate perpetrators. What's not to like about that?'

'Fucking hell,' say Burnett.

'Yes,' I say. 'Fucking hell.'

'Weird to think that all that was going on – ' he gestures over at the now rapidly vanishing cells – 'when we were in here that first day, chatting with the abbott and drinking their damn soup.'

'Yes.'

Burnett never went into the church that first day. I did. Saw the icons and didn't recognise their message. Looked in through those little windows and, for all I know, was witnessed by four pale-faced victims looking out.

402

'Do you think Parry was actually religious?'

'Don't know. Probably not. I know he came to occasional services, but maybe that was just to keep in with the monks. Or maybe he just got a kick from thinking about what was happening behind those little panes of glass.'

'Last night. Was he there as you . . .?'

'No. I presume he was busy ditching my car, which we still need to find by the way, but I'm pretty sure he'd have been there otherwise. Apart from that, I had essentially the same treatment as the other four. I was heading the same way.'

'Fuck.'

I'm still wearing my kirtle and Burnett's face is sombre as he looks at it. He doesn't even know about the bridal wear. The candles and the prostration and the funeral.

'You're OK, are you? Really?'

'No, I'm not OK. Everyone keeps asking me stupid questions.'

Burnett focuses back on the case.

'Bethan Williams,' he says.

'Yes, Bethan,' I say. 'A serious girl. Musical and religious. A bit infatuated maybe, the way some girls get into boy bands and some girls get into God. Probably infatuated enough and serious enough that the monks might have thought she had a vocation.'

Burnett: 'A vocation for . . .?' He nods at me. My anchoress garb.

I nod.

'Yesterday afternoon, I walked the path that Bethan used to walk. I saw Parry's place and realised that if Bethan *had* seen something, it was most likely here that she saw it. Perhaps a victim being taken by Parry and the monks together down to the monastery.

'Whatever. But the point is, she figured it out. Realised who these people really were, what they were up to. She realised

403

that these were astonishingly dangerous men and that she was at risk of going the same way. Perhaps she already knew a little too much. Perhaps one of the monks, convinced of her religious seriousness, told her more than he should have done. Or perhaps they saw her, just as they saw me, as someone who might want to do this thing for real.

'Any case, she ran. At that time, her parents' marriage wasn't good. They were angry and arguing. They didn't seem like a safe refuge for her problems. Len Roberts – who, by the way, *did* have sex with her a couple of times, but never forced, always consensual – he seemed like the obvious refuge. He sheltered her for a while, but then there was a police manhunt and, Roberts realised, SAS men out on the hills. Both of them felt, Roberts and Bethan, that she couldn't go back to normal life. There was simply too much danger. And they were absolutely right. If Bethan *had* gone back, she'd have met with an accident.'

Burnett, who's finished his butty and is now licking his chops and exploring his fingers, objects to that. 'Right. Or she could just have reported the whole matter to the police.'

'Really? Only to find that there's nothing in Parry's cellar except for his porno DVD collection? And nothing in that storeroom except for some sacks of grain and loose firewood? These were the very early days of the whole operation, remember, and the monks didn't have much to clean up.'

Burnett follows that logic. Agrees with it. 'OK, so she runs. Roberts gets her out of the valley via those damn tunnels. Kisses her goodbye. Off you go, lass, you go get yourself a brand-new life. He comes back. We give him a hard time, but he says nothing because that's the deal.'

'Yes, exactly,' I say. 'And years pass, no problem. Only then Carlotta comes along. A police inquiry gets going. And when we start to open up that cave, Parry sees what we're up to. Now, he presumably didn't know there was a cave there at all, let alone a second exit. But once we'd found the cave, Parry realises that Roberts somehow used that cave to shelter Bethan. In which case, she's probably still alive. And if he's figured that out, then *we've* figured it out, and all of a sudden there's an active police investigation aimed at finding her and getting her story. And if we get her story, then the whole little operation is well and truly screwed.'

Burnett: 'Bloody hell. So Parry thinks he has to stop that investigation.'

'Correct.'

'Bye-bye Rhydwyn Lloyd. And almost goodbye you and me.'

I nod.

Burnett: 'You think it was Parry who placed the explosive?'

I shrug. Don't know.

'Hope we get that bloody murder charge.'

He always wanted a murder conviction from this case, but Carlotta wasn't killed, Bethan isn't dead, and the missing-presumed-dead kidnappees are now neither missing, nor dead.

I say, 'No maximum sentence for kidnap. If a court wants to hand down a life sentence, it can.'

'Ha! That's true. Six monks, plus Parry: seven.'

Burnett computes what seven life sentences on a single case translates into. The answer is Detective Chief Inspector, minimum.

'And you'll get Inspector,' he says.

I make a noise with my throat and nose that, translated, means approximately, 'I bloody well hope not.'

A uniform knocks at the car window. Starts asking some boring question about some boring evidence-handling issue.

Burnett's attention starts to float away.

I call it back. 'Boss?'

'Yes?'

'Bethan. Bethan Williams.'

'What about her?'

'She's alive. Somewhere. She doesn't have to run any more.'

'OK. So she can come home.'

'What if she doesn't know it's safe? We need to find her.'

'It'll be all over the papers. She'll know.' He shrugs.

A police shrug. A not-my-problem shrug.

His attention starts to shift away again. Before it quite vanishes, he says, 'Look, Fiona, we're here to solve and prosecute crime. Bethan Williams is an adult woman who can make her own free choice about how she wants to live. Those choices are no business of ours. It's not a police matter.'

No business of ours?

And Neil Williams with his ruined life. And Len Roberts, a crazy but brave and resourceful man, with his.

If Bethan isn't part of Burnett's business, I think she might yet be part of mine.

I get out of the car.

Burnett yells, 'Fiona, we're going to need a statement from you.'

'Now, sir? It's been a long night.'

Burnett wavers. On the one hand, he wants to get every last shot in the can now. To run this case so tightly no defence barrister in the world will be able to raise a quibble.

And on the other hand . . . me. My kirtle, wimple and mantle. Those cells that are still in the process of being pulled apart.

'OK, then. Tomorrow first thing. Now go home. Get some rest.'

I raise my hand in acknowledgement, but walk away.

Into the courtyard. Am going over to the church, when a constable, younger than me, says, 'Sarge? We've got Miss Zhamanakova for you.'

Because my face doesn't do an oh-yes-Miss-Zhamanakova thing, he says, 'Cell number three? You asked.'

Yes, I did.

Cell number three. Aurelia.

I find her in the farmhouse living room. Those panelled walls. A fire roaring in the hearth. That oak sideboard with its water decanter, its glasses, its heap of fruit.

Those things and Aurelia. Two uniformed officers are talking to her. A paramedic. The junior doctor just finishing up some tests. Blood tests. Blood pressure. Heart. Other things. I don't know what. There'll be more tests, hospital tests, after this. Burnett has a Family Liaison type working to make arrangements with the medical team, the victims, the families. What those arrangements are, I neither know nor care.

I say something.

Nobody hears.

I try saying something again, but no one's listening, so I just say, 'Look, fuck off. All of you. Just fuck off out of here.' Say it grimly enough and repetitively enough that they all do, except this pale woman in her grey habit.

Someone closes the door and the two of us are left here. I shed my borrowed jacket in the hall. Aurelia has laid her mantelet I don't know where. She's still wearing her wimple, but aside from that we're the same.

Give or take the odd electric light, we could be two women from a painting five centuries old. Even the air is quiet at that thought.

I say, 'Sister Aurelia.'

Her lips close several times on air before they form an actual word – I know what that's like – but I know what she's going to say before she says it.

'Sister Julian.'

We sit.

Opposite each other at a short refectory table. Like staring into a mirror, except that she is taller than me, and very pale.

The skin and eyes of a land close to the High Arctic.

Her kirtle is beaded around the neckline, where mine is plain, but the bootstring lacing at the front is the same. The grey cloth is the same. The weight of scratchy wool. The thin, almost sheer, undershirt.

I say, 'Last night. You saw me through the glass? I thought I felt it.'

'Yes. That evening. They told us you were joining. You made cross and, I don't know, this.' She crosses herself and, as far as you can while sitting, bobs.

'I curtsied. Yes. You got the best one.'

She smiles, but there's no happiness in the smile. As far as there's anything in her eyes, it's shock. A sense of danger.

I say, 'All the brothers are under arrest. Father Cyril, Anselm, Nicholas, all of them. Dylan Parry too. The man whose cellar you stayed in.'

'Thanks you.'

'They will go to jail and never come out. We've swapped places, them and us. It's their turn now.'

She shakes her head. A tiny shake and a real one.

She does that partly because no British prison would reproduce the kind of confinement that this woman has endured. But mostly because imprisonment is an inner thing more than an outer one. Part of Cyril, I think, will welcome the chance to withdraw. '*I myself have just finished four weeks in which I spoke not a word. I'm afraid elephants might have walked through that courtyard without me noticing.*' Perhaps he half-wanted this outcome. Perhaps they all did.

Aurelia says, 'You are a police?'

'A police officer. Yes.'

'Last night, when I see you, I— '

'Yes?'

I think this is what I wanted to know. The reason I asked

to see this woman. I want to understand what she felt. What she saw.

She says, 'I don't know.'

I feel a quick rush of disappointment black-tipped with anger, but she hasn't finished speaking.

'I don't know. I have two thought. One is, you are real one. You are really here to do this thing.' She sweeps her hand from wimple down towards the hem of her skirt. 'You have this in your face which say, "Yes, I am come to really do this." But also, I think, this woman make us free. How, I don't know, but . . . this woman make us free.'

I say, 'What did you do?'

She snorts at that. Dismissively. A stupid question.

'What you think I did? What is to do in there? I prayed. For you, I prayed.'

'All night?'

'Yes.'

'On your knees?'

'Of course.'

My mouth moves in a 'thank-you' shape, but says nothing.

We're silent a few moments. A merest speck of the silence that Aurelia has known these last several years.

Then she says, 'I was almost ready for my third dress. You spoil this. I don't get my dress.'

I don't know what that means. Say as much, and she tells me.

When things wore out, the monks weren't mean or stupid about replacing them. When Aurelia's undershirt disintegrated with use, they simply replaced it, no questions asked.

But then her dress, her kirtle, started to collapse.

'Here is bad and also here.' She indicates where seams started to go at the neck and side. 'Also,' she says, fanning her hands under her nose, 'I don't think it is good.'

'So?' I ask.

'So I say I am ready for new dress. They say yes, no problem, please to pass out. So I give them. Wait for new dress. But all they do is sew here, here,' she mimes the same seams. 'Not even clean. I cry. Am angry and they just say, "You must pray, Sister. Pray for dress." So I do. Pray real . . .' Her hand raps her chest.

I say, supplying the words that, in English, she doesn't have, 'So you prayed with all your heart, and all your soul, and all your mind, and all your strength.'

'Yes. This. Exact.'

'And?'

'I wear my dress out. Not here.' Her hand waves around her neck and upper body. 'But here.' She points down to her knees, hidden beneath this refectory table. 'Both knees, holes. And then I say, "Brother Monk, dear fellow, I am ready for new dress," and I pass it out and, same day, is come back new dress. Brand new. Same . . . same . . .'

'Any colour you like, as long as it's grey. Any fabric you like as long as it's wool.'

'Yes. But also this.' She runs her hand around her neck, that beaded collar. 'This beads. Little silver bead. And I am so happy I cry, really, for three days. When I sleep, I touch, touch, touch. But also one other different. The cloth here,' she indicates her knees, 'is more thick than first dress. Only here on knee. Everywhere else the same. And I understand. I can get third dress. Third dress even nicer. Maybe more bead. Maybe, I don't know, belt? But I have to work hard. More hard than first time.'

'So what did you do?'

'I pray on my knee every day. All day sometime. At night, if not sleep, then also pray. One knee already – *phwoot!*' She makes a noise and gesture as of a knee popping through cloth. 'One more knee and I get my dress. Then you come.'

She stands and shows me. One knee worn through. The other not far to go.

'From now today, I will have new clothe, every day. Father has money, so best clothe of anywhere. And all I really want is to see that third dress. See if it have more bead.'

I stand up.

'Aurelia, your wimple. Your headcovering. May I?'

It's hard for her, but she nods. Says yes.

I untie her wimple. Drop it on the table next to her. Comb out her hair – which is very long, very blonde – with my fingers. She looks like a beautiful, frightened princess from a Russian fairy-tale.

'It's over, sweetheart. It's really over.'

I hug her head against me and she cries. Long, trembling sobs which I understand because I have known them myself, albeit that my eyes never manage to produce tears.

We stay hugging. She stays crying. Human and human alone in an empty room.

After a while, and when I can sense she's almost ready to pull away, a black Rolls-Royce glides into the courtyard outside.

'Aurelia, sweetheart. Your family. Are they in London?'

'Mother and brothers, no. They are in Moscva. But your policeman, he said, my father yes, my father in London, my father they call.'

As she speaks, she looks up. Looks into the courtyard. Sees a man – silver-haired, burly, pinstriped, Slavic – step out of the car.

She dissolves. 'Papa. Papa.' Her face is a mess of tears and love and her first real sense that her old life might yet grow again.

I rap at the glass. Attract his attention. But the young constable who directed me here is directing him too. He breaks into a heavy trot.

My cue to leave.

I take Aurelia's hands – these hands which are no longer Aurelia's, but which belong to a Miss Someone Zhamanakova, a person with whom I have a vanishingly small amount in common.

'Peace be with you, Sister.'

She peaces me back, but her attention is elsewhere.

As it should be. As it should be.

I leave them to it.

I walk through the whole house. Searching through the monks' bedrooms. Their music room. Their linen room. Every sodding room in that light-filled and handsomely appointed house.

I find it in the attic. A linen chest. Some sheets and blankets on top, but beneath them, clothes.

Undershirts. Wimples. Stockings.

Another plain grey kirtle, like the one I'm wearing. But some others too. I spread them all out on the bare boards of this little room.

I can see which dress was coming next. Sequins instead of beads. A silver tassel on the bootstring tie.

It's clumsily done and not particularly attractive. Not by any standard that would have made sense to the Miss Zhamanakova of old. But there's another dress here too. One with gold lace at the collar and a polished leather belt and just the merest whisper of black velvet at the hem.

That was certainly not dress three in the sequence. I doubt if it was even number four. It looks more like five to me, even six. Thick padding at the knees. Padding so thick, they had to quilt it.

Long years of prayer needed to get through to the frock after this one.

I take the dress. Stealing evidence, in theory, except phooey to that, those boys are going down. The only evidence that mattered was ripped apart with picks and sledgehammers earlier this morning and a million people watched it happen.

Using pen and paper from the abbot's study, I write a note.

'Dear Aurelia, This was the next dress. Call me any time. Fiona (Sister Julian)'.

Add my home address and a phone number.

Down in the courtyard, the Rolls has long gone, taking father and daughter back to the life they once shared. I shove the dress and the note in a plastic evidence bag. Find a uniform and tell him to post it to Miss Zhamanakova.

'Post it first class. No, actually, special delivery. Do it right now. Don't mess up.'

The uniform jumps to it. *Leaps* to it.

I glimpse myself in the hall mirror. I look like an angry nun. Never say no to an angry nun: first rule of policing.

Burnett sees me.

'What the hell are you still doing here? I told you to go.'

'No vehicle, sir. The senior investigating officer hasn't bothered to give me wheels. I'm not sure this inquiry is being very well run, to be honest with you.'

Burnett yells at someone outside. Tells them to bring a patrol car.

As they go, he says to me, 'The dead house in Ystradfflur. Why that? I can see they had a body they weren't expecting. They're religious guys, so they don't just want to drop Mishchenko, the one you call Carlotta, into a lake. But why there? Why not at least drive her to some other part of the country altogether?'

I chide him. 'You're thinking modern again, inspector. You need to think medieval.' That doesn't illuminate things for some reason. So I explain, 'This is the monastery of St David. He's their patron saint. Now David's big thing, his signature miracle if you want to put it like that, was raising a hill at Llandewi Brefi—'

'A *hill*? In Llandewi? Why would anyone—?'

'I know, don't ask. But Llandewi is the place for anyone who venerates St. David and I think that's where they wanted to take Carlotta. Far enough away that she's off their turf and a reverential place to lay her out. A nice compromise. Only, that night, there's the tanker spill on the A40. Emergency vehicles everywhere. And no safe route through to Llandewi. Whoever's carrying Carlotta basically panics. They decide they need to dump her and dump her fast, but still somewhere respectful and preferably somewhere that—'

Then Burnett gets it. 'The Church of St David at Ystradfflur. The same bloody saint.'

'The same bloody saint. Exactly.'

The weird thing about this whole case is that, if I'd been wearing my medieval glasses from the start, I'd have got the whole thing more or less straightaway. Those five panes of glass in the church: there'd have been plenty of medieval peasants who'd have understood them for what they were. The icons above: any medieval churchman would have known that these were saints revered for their feats of godly isolation.

I think Cyril even took pleasure at laughing at my blindness. 'There is compulsion in religion too,' he told me. As he told me about David's miracle at Llandewi. As he handed me Mother Julian's *Revelations*. As he sized me up for that final cell.

The patrol car arrives. Burnett tells the driver to deliver me home. 'If she tells you to go anywhere else, to make any kind of stop or detour, you say no. And you actually wait long enough to see her in through the front door. Yes? Have you got that?' The driver yes, sirs him and looks fiercely at me.

Then, to me, Burnett says, 'Go home. Go to bed. Get some rest.'

'Yes, sir,' I say.

And obey to the letter.

47

We get the gang, or Burnett does. London and Wales, both damn ends of this operation.

Parry's phone gives us contact numbers. One of those numbers connects to a man who owns a dark-grey BMW, a BMW that we can place on the King's Road in Chelsea at 1.10 a.m. on the night Alina Mishchenko was taken. And, joy of joys, that same BMW owner once owned a pale-blue Audi, which was one of the two unaccounted-for London number plates in Llanglydwen, that week after Bethan's vanishing.

Those things gave us enough, more than enough, for a search warrant. One of those steel-ram, siren blaring, you're-so-totally-fucked raids that every copper loves more than anything, me included.

The man involved, our target and now our prisoner, is called Michael Nugent. The guy owns a couple of fancy restaurants in Hammersmith, London. Lived in a big, leafy house in Chiswick worth maybe three million. His home computer was encrypted and secured, but wasn't encrypted enough. Not when pulled apart at a GCHQ lab in Cheltenham, staffed by the best minds in cryptography and computer tech.

And the computer reveals – everything. I don't understand the process, but our techie guys can basically connect that computer via a whole chain of proxy servers to the emails sent and received by Jack Gerraghty and the Mishchenkos. Not just those emails, but others too. Nine kidnaps in total, Aurelia –

Ekaterina Zhamanakova – being one of them. Four of those kidnappees ended up buried in the walls of that Llanglydwen monastery, and are now out and free. Poor Carlotta never survived Dylan Parry's cellar and her ghost now broods over the black and silent waters of that underground lake. In the remaining four cases the ransom money was paid. Money totalling somewhere just north of forty-five million dollars, or about thirty million quid.

A bit of further truffling – phone records, computer stuff, some clever analysis of car movements by a specialist team in the Met – gives us a further two people. Thugs for hire. London muscle. Those two, Don Devonish and Jackson Small, we also collect.

So much for the London end.

The Welsh end is also nicely tidy.

The monks are behind bars, never to emerge again.

And Dylan Parry. We have him for multiple kidnap, yes, but also for murder.

Our forensics guys found remains of homemade ANFO explosive in one of the guy's outbuildings: he'd mixed the stuff in a plastic water barrel, stirring with the shaft of a wooden yard brush. He'd cleaned out the barrel carefully enough – though we found traces in a drain – but the grain of the yard brush was still dense with the stuff. Since analysis has demonstrated that Parry is also the man on the agricultural merchant's CCTV, our case against him is already pretty much secure.

Also – a curious point, not really relevant in evidential terms, but still a little missing piece of the whole puzzle – it turns out that Parry and Father Cyril went to school together. A Catholic, all-boys boarding place in Shropshire. At one time it must have looked like the two boys took very different paths away from that place. Now: not so much. And the little coincidence helps answer that question of how come Parry felt able to broach the whole anchorite thing with Cyril. The two men weren't strangers. They knew each other from way back. Felt able to talk without constraint.

But that's a by-the-by.

Truth is, our evidence comes in so sweetly that, for once, our interviews won't make much difference: we can build a watertight case with or without a confession. But still: you work through the hard bits, so you can enjoy the fun bits, and Burnett and I intend to have some fun. And not just that but, as I say to Burnett, there are still some unsolved questions. Big ones. Ones that matter.

We run the interview in Carmarthen. Nugent has some fancy-shmancy London solicitor to advise him and we make a big show of welcoming him to the town. Showing him the views of the River Towy. Asking if this is his first time here, all that rubbish. Give the guy as much time as he wants with his client. 'Don't rush. Take your time. We like to do things right here. If you need teas or coffees, just shout.'

Nugent's hair is short and already grey, though he's only forty-seven. But he's lean, and fit, and has the kind of tan that you only get from skiing and swimming and sailing, not quite year-round but regularly enough that the tan never really fades. The guy is with his solicitor for four hours. Burnett and I just piss around upstairs, doing little scraps of work from time to time – taking phone calls, responding to emails – but mostly just talking bollocks.

When we start, as the clock draws close to three in the afternoon, Burnett just drops a file of paperwork on the table and says, 'Well, Michael, nice to have you here. Just . . . well, we wanted to give you the chance to talk to us. Tell us about things.'

He spreads his hands. Friendly. Welcoming. A conversation between friends.

Silence. Nothing. In the corner of the room, a video camera winks red.

Burnett waits. A full minute. That's a hell of a long time. Even a ten-second silence seems long, but one minute filled only with waiting – that seems like for ever.

Nugent strokes the underside of his nose with his right hand index finger, but otherwise just toughs it out. Stays silent. Shows no anxiety.

Burnett: 'OK, then. How about you tell us about the abduction of Alina Mishchenko? We could start there maybe. You could talk to us about how you identified her, abducted her, removed her to Dylan Parry's cottage over here in Llanglydwen, then contacted Mr and Mrs Mishchenko with a demand for money. Why don't we start there, maybe?'

Burnett glances at me, as though seeking my approval. I give it with a shrug and a nod. Yep. Good place to start. Nice idea, boss.

We each turn a friendly face to Nugent.

Another minute drags itself through the room, embarrassed.

Burnett tuts a little. 'Maybe it's the Welshman in me. The Celt, you know. We love a good chat, like after a rugby match, you go down to the pub and talk everything over. Every move, every play, every player. For me, that's even better than the game itself.'

I murmur, 'Boss . . .'

'Quite right, Fiona, yes, quite right. I'm off topic, aren't I? So, let's start really simple. Just get the conversation started. Now, then, Michael – Mike, Michael, Mr Nugent? – we'll settle for Michael, OK? So, this is your house, yes?'

The first item in Burnett's stack of paperwork is a full-colour photo of Nugent's house, with the address printed in block capitals underneath.

Nugent glances sideways at his solicitor, who just gives a half-shrug and opens his hands.

Nugent says, 'Yes. Of course. That's my house.'

'And this would be your living room?'

Another photo. A nod from Nugent.

The camera captures Nugent's nod anyway, but I say, 'Mr Nugent nods in response to the question.'

Burnett says, 'Yes, good catch, Fiona. Michael, if you speak your responses, it does help with the transcript. Would you mind? Thanks so much.' He pauses before tossing another photo over and continuing, 'And this is your home office, yes? And on your desk there, that's your computer?'

Nugent shifts in discomfort, a movement he half-suppresses when he catches me watching.

He says, 'Yes, correct.'

'OK, good, this is really good. We're making progress. Now, obviously we turned your computer on and took a look at things, and we found these emails. I mean, lots more of course, but these ones, for example.'

Burnett throws a few stapled pages across the table. Just subject headers, dates, sent from details. Ordinary things, restaurant business mostly, nothing encrypted.

'Yes, you recognise these?'

Nugent nods.

I say, 'Mr Nugent nods in response to—'

Burnett: 'Yes, sorry, Michael, would you mind—?'

Nugent, loudly, irritated: 'Yes, yes, these are my emails.'

'Thank you. Yes. Your emails. Good.'

Pause.

Burnett again: 'So what you're wondering, what you're sitting here wondering, is whether your encryption held up. I mean, you're a restaurant guy, yes? I mean, give you, I don't know, a steak and ale pie to make, and you'd whip the thing up, no problem. Or get someone to do it. Anyway, a task like that, you'd handle it. Computer encryption, though. That's hard. Technical, now. And for a long time, it didn't really matter, did it? You just ran your little operation, and nothing went wrong. So maybe you got a little sloppy. Or maybe your techniques didn't evolve to keep pace with new technology. And, right now, you're wondering whether you slipped up. You're wondering whether our case against you is purely circumstantial or totally overwhelming. That's right, isn't it? I'm right. I should be a mind reader.'

Nugent has a frozen, almost spacey quality. When he moves, and he doesn't very much, there's something both jerky and gluey in his movements. Like some rusty machinery trying to rediscover its action.

The lawyer just sits there pressing the pads of his fingers against each other. Slowly, repetitively, wondering quite how fucked his client is.

Very fucked, the short answer.

After Burnett has waited long enough, he starts floating more papers out of his folder. The encrypted emails, decrypted. Page after page after page.

Burnett releases the papers one by one. Some of them land on the desk, some on Nugent's hands or lap, others go fluttering past his head or float off the table completely, landing on the floor.

A snowfall. A drift. A whitening.

Nugent makes almost no attempt to look at the papers. He glances at one or two, but a glance tells him all that he needs.

The solicitor grabs for individual documents. Reads them. He's not seen this stuff before and it takes him time to understand quite how incriminating this snowfall is.

After a while – papers all over the table and floor, more papers still in Burnett's folder, one or two sheets still floating through the air – I say, 'Boss.'

Burnett stares at me. He says nothing, but he stops pulling pages out of the folder. He stays totally still until the solicitor has stopped reading whatever lethally damning piece of evidence he's currently on. Waits until both men, the prisoner and his lawyer, have his full attention.

Then: 'Mr Nugent – Michael – did you send these emails?'

No response. None.

A sideways glance at his solicitor. A small swallow. A look around for water, but though there's a half-empty plastic coffee cup at hand, he doesn't drink.

Burnett: 'Remaining silent?' Nods. Almost approvingly. 'We're governed by the laws of England and Wales. You have the right to remain silent. That's your call.'

I say – and this whole thing has been pre-planned, the whole strategy chucklingly arranged while we were pissing around upstairs – I say, 'Yes, but, boss . . .'

Burnett stares at me. A what's-this-woman-on-about-now stare.

And then he remembers.

'Oh.' His face changes. Looks crestfallen, worried. 'If you *don't* say anything and then you come up with some trumped-up bit of nonsense in court, people wonder why you didn't just tell us right now. When we're asking. So: if you want to produce some kind of excuse in court, you really need to come up with it now. Like, *right* now.'

Pause.

A long one. An empty one.

One that rings with the clang of prison gates, the shriek of the prison yard.

I say, 'Mr Nugent makes no response to the question.'

Burnett: 'Michael, I'm asking you again. Did you or did you not send these emails from the computer in your home office?'

No answer.

The solicitor, clearing his throat, says, 'Perhaps if my client and I—'

Burnett, interrupting: 'Bollocks to that. You had a full

four hours in which to prepare and I'm asking your client a perfectly straightforward question to which he knows the answer. Mr Nugent, did you, yes or no, send those emails?'

We leave it a long time.

After thirty seconds, I say, 'Mr Nugent does not reply within thirty seconds.'

After a minute, I say, 'Mr Nugent makes no response within one minute.'

Burnett looks at his watch, at Nugent, then makes a noise in his throat. 'OK, we're done.'

Starts scooping up papers. Not even doing it properly. Just stuffing the most accessible ones back, any old how, into his folder, then tucking the whole messy sandwich under his arm.

I scrabble around on my hands and knees picking stuff up from the floor. Nugent is almost frozen into position. The solicitor, unable to overcome his own instinct of politeness, helps me gather up papers, but does so stiffly. Never shifting from his chair.

Burnett stands angrily at the door, and says, 'Kidnap. Murder. Attempted murder of two police officers. It's life. Multiple, multiple life sentences. Category A all-male prison. And the age you are, the seriousness of those crimes? You'll never get out. You'll never, I don't know, sit under a tree again. Have you thought of that? They don't have trees in prisons. You'll never see a fucking tree again.'

I say – still scrabbling after those fallen pages – 'There's mitigation, sir. He could try to mitigate.'

'Mitigation? Bollocks. What is there to mitigate? Even if he made a full confession. Even if he told us every last thing, it's too late. We don't need a confession.'

I get up, hands full of paper.

'Money. There's the money.'

'What? What do you mean? The Proceeds of Crime Act covers all that. We'll take the house. Take the car. Take the restaurants. Take the fucking lot.' Then, pointing down at Nugent, says, 'You won't just be a prisoner. You'll be a bankrupt prisoner. A bankrupt prisoner for the rest of your life, trying to remember what a fucking tree looks like.'

'Sir, actually though, there's a lot more money.'

'What?'

'Mr Nugent's assets, sir.'

'What?'

'They're not enough. Not nearly.'

'That house of his? Do you have any idea how much those things are worth these days?'

'Sir, Mr Nugent extorted almost thirty million pounds. I mean, that's the part we know about. The part we know about *so far*. And his assets are worth maybe a third of that amount, probably less.'

Burnett pauses at that. Seems to really pause, I mean. Not the tactical, obviously stagey pauses that this interrogation has been full of so far, but one that looks genuine – even, almost, to me.

He thinks a moment, then says, wearily, 'Mr Nugent, where's the money? You've got some offshore stash that you don't want us to find? I can tell you right now, you will never get out of jail to spend it.'

Nugent's eyes are flickering now. A foot taps rapidly against the table's iron leg. His finger, unreadable, traces shapes on its melamine top.

I say, 'Mr Nugent, what's your accountancy background?'

'What?'

'Your accountancy background. Are you a trained accountant? Do you have finance training?'

'No. I run restaurants. I— '

'You are not a trained accountant?'

'No.'

'Would you be capable of understanding, let's say, the

management accounts of a Ukrainian manganese mining firm? Would you be able to discuss alternative approaches to the valuation of iron ore inventories?'

Here, for the very first time, there's something like a smile at the corners of Nugent's mouth. Not a proper smile, nothing like that. But a ghost of muscle memory. The recollection that things like smiles were once possible.

He says, 'No. I wouldn't understand those things. I have no background in that kind of thing at all.'

Burnett pulls away from the door. Drops his folder on the table.

'Mr Nugent, who were you working for? Who was your boss? It's that person we want in jail.'

Nugent covers his mouth with his hand. Doesn't even bother to conceal the calculation in his eyes.

Thinks for a moment, and says, 'Inspector, may I have some time alone with my solicitor?'

Burnett pauses – grins – then punches the prisoner softly on the shoulder. 'Take as much time as you want, Michael. Take as much time as you want.'

48

We leave them to it, Nugent and his solicitor.

On the way upstairs, I call Watkins.

I say, 'Nugent's going to tell us. He's strategising with his solicitor now.'

Watkins thinks a second, then says, 'OK, I'm coming over.' Says that, which is nice, then to make up, adds, 'But it's a long shot, Fiona. Really long.'

Is it? I'm not sure. But she'll be here in about an hour and we'll find out soon enough.

Burnett goes out for coffee and something to eat. He doesn't really care about this next bit. But me, I have my To Do list still:

(1) Find, arrest and prosecute Carlotta's kidnappers.
(2) Revive Operation April in order to find, arrest and prosecute all its principals.

Item (1) is nicely ticked. But item (2)? Just exactly where have I got to on that?

We're about to find out.

After about an hour, we get a call from downstairs telling us that Nugent is ready. Watkins is still about fifteen minutes away. She tells us to go ahead anyway.

We go back to the interview room. Burnett carries a cardboard tray with doughnuts and hot drinks. And we haven't even sat down, haven't even shared our bounty, when Nugent says, 'I'll give you everything. Everything I have. Everything I know. But . . .'

Burnett: 'No *but*s, Mr Nugent. Everything needs to mean everything.'

There are no plea bargains in Welsh or English courtrooms. Prosecutors can't go easy in exchange for information. The way we look at it, arrangements of that sort create an almost intolerable incentive for a suspect to deliver the evidence he believes the prosecution wants. They rob the court of its power to choose its verdict and its sentence.

Even so, Nugent has something real to play for. He'll get a life sentence, almost for sure, but the judge will still have to set a recommended minimum tariff. Given the nature of Nugent's crimes, he's looking at anywhere from thirty years up to a whole life term. Since his crimes include conspiring in the attempted murder of two police officers, most judges would be looking to sentence at the upper end of that range.

All of which means that if Nugent ever wants to remind himself 'what a fucking tree looks like', he needs to give the court some damn good reason to find clemency.

A damn good reason such as giving us everything.

No ifs, no buts, no exceptions.

Nugent whispers – croaks, 'I've got everything except a name. "John Jones". I never had a real name.'

'"John Jones", you say? He was Welsh?'

'Yes.'

'And, to the best of your knowledge and belief, he was the principal owner and beneficiary of this kidnap operation?'

'Yes.'

'Him alone, or him in collaboration with others?'

'Alone. At least, as far as I know.'

'And what was his role? What did he do?'

'Everything. Chose the targets. Gave me instructions. Handled the whole money thing. Receiving the money offshore, hiding it, making my payments to a Cayman Islands bank account. My job was to oversee the actual implementation. Arranging the snatch. Getting the target over to Parry. All of that. But the big decisions were John's. He just paid me my share.'

'Which was?'

'One third. Always one third.'

I see, or think I do, Burnett supressing an inner smile, and I probably do the same.

I mean, fuck me, the idiocy of these people. What was Nugent's role, really? He probably thought he was the king of implementation, but he wasn't, not really. He was the fall guy. The guy all set up to get the life sentence when, eventually, inevitably, this whole thing unravelled. He'll have plenty of time to reflect on the wisdom of his decision-making in the time to come.

'This man, Jones. You met him?'

'Yes.'

'Once, or on multiple occasions?'

'Five or six times, perhaps.'

'So you would be able to make a visual identification?'

'Yes.'

'For sure?'

'Yes.'

Burnett's yellowish grin expands. Wolfish. He glances behind him at the mirrored wall, where Watkins will even now be taking up position. Watching, enjoying, hoping.

Burnett steps back. Nugent sees, for the first time, the big wad of pictures in my hand.

'Photo time,' says Burnett. 'It's photo time.'

49

Endings.

Endings or, rather, moments that end one thing and start another, new hares leaping off in new directions, starting new lives, bounding away across the frosty turf into a sunlight that's made new every day.

We don't have our convictions yet, but we will. We've handed our case over to the Crown Prosecution Service now. There's still to-ing and fro-ing over points of detail, but the ship is steaming from our waters to theirs. Won't require us again, not in essence, till Burnett and I are called upon to stand in court and give witness to all that we saw and said and did.

Nugent lived up to his promise.

He gave us his everything, no ifs, buts or exceptions.

Much of his story came to nothing at all. 'John Jones' – as I expected, as Watkins too half-expected – proved to have been exceptionally thorough in his camouflage. He seldom met Nugent, and then mostly in the first years of the operation. According to Nugent, the two men hadn't met once in the last four years. When they did meet – in neutral locations in and around London – Jones seems to have arrived by taxi or public transport. Certainly used no vehicle that we've been able to trace. The locations chosen were well away from any CCTV and, given the density of cameras in London, we have to assume the meeting spots were carefully screened beforehand. Most of the business conducted by the two men was handled by phone. Always from Jones to Nugent, never the other way round. Jones's calls came via mobile phones, unregistered pay-as-you-go cheapies that changed repeatedly. The calls were made from random locations across South Wales, London, and England south of Manchester.

If we had nothing else to go on, we'd have to admit that Jones had got away with it. Left no trace. Vanished.

But, from the moment we identified Alina Mishchenko, I felt the prick of gathering excitement. The excitement of a hunter coming upon the signs of fresh spoor.

Broken grasses and new dung gleaming in the dimness.

In this case, the spoor I wanted was anything that suggested that the Mishchenko case might – just *might* – be part and parcel of our own beloved Operation April.

Clues so dim to start with, but gathering in intensity the further we proceeded.

The first clue was Alina Mischenko herself. The April gang is interested only in money, and lots of it. A corpse in a churchyard – that in itself didn't shout 'April' at all. But a *millionairess* dead in a churchyard? A millionairess fifteen hundred miles, and a whole world of experience, removed from the place she ought to be?

That strangely out-of-place corpse murmured that money was somehow caught up in whatever dark roads led her to that place. And if money was present, then some connection to April couldn't quite be ruled out.

At that stage, that one winking lamp couldn't be trusted enough for us to be sure of anything. Not enough for us even to voice the hypothesis.

But the further we went, the more those little lamps lit up.

How many criminal gangs have the financial sophistication

to read complex business accounts? Almost none, but we know for a fact that the men behind Operation April do have sophistication on that scale.

How many criminal gangs can set up those Cayman Islands bank accounts and all the rest of it? Set them up so well that no trace of those kidnap payments ever so much as raised a murmur with our money-laundering guys? Those things might sound easy, but it takes top-dollar expertise to do them well. Expertise that, again, we know the April people to have in abundance.

Even so, April was a long shot. If this kidnap ring had its bosses in London, then there'd be any number of gangs with the required expertise. If, on the other hand, the ring had its base in Wales, a place where sophisticated organised crime is all but unknown, the odds would improve dramatically in our favour.

If, if, if.

Speculation without evidence.

A guess running far ahead of any proof.

But both Watkins and I saw the same few lamps lighting up one by one. Hoped against hope that the odds would shake out in our favour. Twice, Watkins almost breathed her suspicions to me, holding back only because she didn't want to re-light the flames of my obsession.

But we both knew what we wanted and – as I laid out my photos, under Burnett's gun-slit eyes and the steel of Watkins's gaze behind that mirrored wall – we both knew what we hoped to achieve.

Hope against hope.

An evidential coin-flip.

First, I laid out a succession of prints taken from Dyfed-Powys's own database of crooks. A database that, give or take a bit of rural Welshness, looks like any other crooks' gallery in the land.

Impatiently, Nugent said, 'No, no,' brushing them aside, with a gesture of annoyance.

He wanted to describe the individual. Give us an e-fit. But with Watkins silently watching behind the mirrored glass, with the video camera still winking red in the corner, I stick to the plan we agreed beforehand.

Next I spread out some Cardiff crooks. The narrow-eyed, strong-jawed, shaven-headed twenty- and thirty-somethings that our courts and prisons are full of.

'No, no. Not these. None of these.'

Again, he wants to start describing the man. Again, I stop him.

This time, though, I lay out a bunch of different photographs. White-collar types. Professional. Suit and tie, or the sort of casual clothes that mutter money.

The photos are different in another way too. The first couple of sets were mostly mugshots. The kind of things that are taken when someone is taken into custody. Blank wall behind. The glare of a too-bright flash. The unnatural faces of people who are being told what to do and how to do it by a bevy of custody officers.

The photos I'm laying out now are more ordinary. Not quite family snaps, perhaps – no dogs on beaches, no kids with ice cream – but informal. Journalistic. Men on street corners. Guys making phone calls outside coffee shops.

Nugent goes carefully now. Slower.

His dismissals are still confident. 'No. No. Not him.' But he takes his time. Sits forward as he sifts the pictures.

And, one by one, I slip the photos of our Operation April targets into the flow.

Brendan Rattigan: no.

Galton Evans: no.

Owain Owen: no.

Nick Davison: no.

David Marr-Phillips: no.

But then I lay another picture on the table. Ben Rossiter. Part of our B-list. Attached to the gang, we think, but maybe second string only.

The shot was taken by one of our surveillance guys. Rossiter stepping into a silver Aston Martin. It's raining slightly, and Rossiter is slipping off a waxed jacket even as he swivels for the car seat. There's nothing much to read on his face. Just a successful, wealthy man, slightly irritated by the rain.

'That's him. That's Jones. The man I worked with.'

'You're sure?'

'Positive. One hundred per cent.'

'Do you want to see more photos?'

'No.'

I show them anyway. More photos of random white-collar types. More photos of Rossiter. Taken on different dates, at different times of day, with the subject in different poses, wearing different clothes.

Nugent picks the right guy out every time.

'Look, it's him. I *know* the man, OK?'

That's hardly true. Nugent knew nothing about the guy, not even his name. But the visual match is, for now, sufficient. I push Nugent to look at five hundred photos in all. Of those, just six are of Rossiter. He picks out the six with confidence on each occasion.

When we've gone through my stack, I ask Nugent to hold the photos of Rossiter, one by one, for the video camera. He does so, saying, 'This is the man I knew as John Jones. He ran the show. It was his idea, everything. And *fuck* him. Fuck him. Fuck him.'

That last part said with a mixture of anger and tears. Actual tears a-tremble in his eyes.

Fuck him? Rossiter-Jones? Actually, Michael Nugent, mate, your buddy Rossiter-Jones has fucked you up pretty well. Gave you a nice life for ten years, then dropped you in the shit so royally deep, so stinkily thick, that you'll be staring at a prison wall for thirty years, minimum, and your only opportunity to taste freedom again will depend on a judge's clemency and the dice-throw of your own genetic longevity.

And despite what Nugent seems to think, he's given us nothing that would allow us to secure a conviction on Rossiter. Nothing. A case of my-word-against-his. A case hopelessly short of even circumstantial proofs.

But we don't care. We don't care. We don't care. We don't care.

We pass the video straight from that Carmarthen interview room to Markus Hauke and Moritz Windfeder at the BKA. You needed evidence, buddies? You asked for actual tangible hard evidence that a person we suspect of being a bad guy is an A-grade, 24-carat, 140-degree proof Bad Guy? A murdering, kidnapping arsehole who destroys lives for cash?

Okey-doke. Fair enough. Reasonable request. So here's your evidence. Not courtroom quality, but it doesn't need to be. Just a wholly credible accusation from an utterly credible source.

We sent the video over to Hauke and Windfeder, together with the background material they needed to make sense of it. Within the day got back a note from Windfeder. 'OK. Looks really great. We'll talk to Legal.'

Two days more, just two, and Windfeder gives us the thumbs-up. A big, friendly *Alles in Ordnung* from our partners across the sea.

Our favourite maybe-conspirators don't have any trips to Germany booked in the near future, but that's fine. They'll make their next trip soon enough and when they do, the very next time they get together in Aachen, or Dortmund, or Whereverthell, we will ask the Bundeskriminalamt to secure the necessary interception warrants. Audio, video, the lot.

Hotel rooms. Restaurant. Meeting rooms. Cars. Everything.

With luck and a following wind, our principal targets will gather by some quiet German lakeside. Will be attentively served by some softly murmuring Bavarian waitress. Will discuss their lethally criminal business over Kaffee and Torte and Apfelstrudel and Schlagsahne, as damselflies flit and and pond skaters skim the waters beyond.

And all the time, unseen recorders will gather their conversation. They'll be recorded in their restaurants and hotels. Quiet electronics will gather every word they say in their cars and on their phones. They will enjoy their weekend – pleasant, peaceful, productive – and fly back home so royally fucked that they won't even know the scale of the shitstorm that is heading their way.

Operation April isn't formally reopened, but it doesn't have to be. Jackson and Brattenbury will do what needs to be done. And Watkins and I have that savage jubilation. A *maybe we'll get those bastards* one. And if that sounds more like a beginning than a place to end – well, those loping hares aren't tidy about such things.

But those things lie in my future.

Today is mid-February. Valentine's Day.

Snowdrops and crocuses burst through the wet grass of Bute Park. Soft-nosed bombs of colour that rise through the damp earth and detonate softly under a new sun.

Kay tells me she's done up at Neil Williams's place and invites me up there to take a look.

I arrive to find a farm reborn. Stand outside in the softly moving air trying to work out what's changed. Realise that a hedge, overgrown and shaggy with elder, has been cut back hard. It has the pale gleam of sawn wood, the fierce precision of a military buzz-cut. A broken piece of farm machinery has been towed away. A dung heap moved somewhere out of sight.

And, in their place, light and air. A long view down the valley. The little humped bridge where the streams join. You can't see the monastery from here but you can see the stubby tower of the village church shining in the half-sun.

As I stand, the front door opens. Kay and Neil Williams step outside.

Kay has already somewhat abandoned the super-professional look she first brought up here, her clicky heels surrendering to the reality of this farmyard. But there's still a new maturity in her. An assurance in her own competence and professionalism.

That assurance is entirely deserved. 'Incredibly safe and boring' might have been the brief and, yes, I can see Kay has avoided anything that might unduly challenge either Neil Williams or his as-yet-only-theoretical daughter. But the place has class. Into this middle-of-the-road palette of golds and creams and safe beiges, Kay has smuggled a little dazzle. A clear Perspex lamp base on what looks like a block of polished granite. Some jet-black curtain tie-backs that shouldn't work, but really do.

The same thing in the bathroom and Bethan's bedroom, rooms that weren't on the original brief but which Kay wanted to do and to whose overhaul Neil Williams quickly assented.

'We might get going in the kitchen as well,' says Williams, standing proudly next to his design guru. 'We've had chats about it and if the budget is all OK, then . . .'

Williams has changed too. He's had a haircut. He's shaved more carefully than he used to. No peeping curls of long, unshaven hair guarding the hollows under his jaw. His clothes are still emphatically rural. Tweed jacket worn over a dark-olive jumper, a check shirt and a somewhat notional tie. But the jacket looks new and the jumper looks freshly washed at the very least.

I try to figure out if Kay has had a hand in those transformations too. Her face gives nothing away and I

436

can't work it out, but I suspect not. I think Neil Williams has located the change in himself. And it was surely him not Kay that arranged for the hedge to be cut, the dung to be moved.

I think, *What would Bethan see if she returned home today?* What would she think if she came back and saw this? Saw this house and met this man.

And she'd approve. I think she'd approve. I hope she'd have the wisdom to find some kind of meeting point between her father's way of life and her own, more urban, ways. To forgive that old anger of his. To find a new beginning.

Kay wants praise from me and I give it. I do check that she hasn't spent too much money – Williams hardly has the earth to spend – but she reassures me. 'I got everything I could at trade prices. A lot of the pieces came from eBay.'

She did, I know, get a lot of help from Dad. Not directly, but the workmen Kay used were Dad's guys up from Cardiff, who would never have dared be late, do a poor job, or overcharge. If Kay does this thing for a living sometime, she'll need to work with trickier tradespeople, and less-obliging clients. But as a start? As a first toe into the waters of that whole adult world of earning money, getting on? She's done one hell of a job and I tell her so.

This day, however, belongs not to Kay but to Neil Williams and me.

I say, 'Mr Williams, I think we're ready.'

He pats his pockets, finds a car key, checks the kitchen, looks anxious.

'You're fine, Mr Williams, you're just fine.'

We get into his car, a Toyota pick-up. He puts the key into the ignition, but doesn't turn it.

'No promises, Mr Williams. I can't make any promises at all.'

He nods. Acknowledges the bargain.

He drives us as far as Exeter, where we stop for fuel and coffee for him, peppermint tea for me.

'Thing is,' he says. 'When Bethan was small, I was always hard at it. Making my way, you know. Establishing myself. Sometimes, if I came home and I'd been working all day and things weren't like I pictured they ought to be in my head, I'd get snappy. It wasn't anything really, but it probably felt that way to Jo and Bethan. Bethan especially, I think. You know, she's not like me. Not . . .'

He's said all that before and I tell him he's fine. He's doing fine. When we get back to the car, I take the key. Drive on south.

I've already told Williams that Len Roberts, far from raping and killing his daughter, saved and protected her. Kept his silence these eight long years, to defend her and save her from harm.

The day I told him that, he stared at me. Said nothing, except that his eyes were bright and full of matter. Then he strode out of the house and down the hill to Roberts's shack, a determination to do right bulging in his jaw.

I've not seen Roberts since, but I'm sure that wild man will do just fine. He and Judy. The two of them together.

At Newton Abbot, I notice that Williams is starting to get self-conscious about his car. It looks fine to me – country cars are allowed their mud – but I stop off at a car valeting place and we wait as a couple of lads wash the car inside and out, polishing hub caps whose sheen won't last a moment back on the roads of upland Powys. I go into the garage and buy three packets of tulips. Fresh yellow heads, the colour of butter, the colour of sunlight. Rip away the cellophane and elastic bands. Assemble them into a simple bunch.

I hand them to Williams and we climb back into a car that smells like breath mints and loo cleaner.

Newton Abbot to Marldon.

On round Torbay to Brixham.

'Joanne. She's not still living with Sandra, is she?' asks Williams with a hint of gloom. 'She and I never really . . . We never really . . .'

Sandra: that's Joanne's sister, Neil Williams's sister-in-law. The person who gave Joanne refuge when her marriage collapsed.

'No. Joanne's got a place of her own now. It's her we're going to see, not Sandra.'

Joanne: my excuse for this little venture.

I told Williams that now that Parry and the monks were all in custody, it would be safe for Bethan to return. Runaways, especially girls, more often contact mothers than fathers and I told Williams that he needed to repair his relationship with Joanne. Not that I was pushing them back together. Just that the two of them should be able to have a civilised, communicative friendship once again, just in case his little runaway should ever come chirruping at Joanne's door.

He accepted that logic. Never once questioned it.

But it's not Joanne's house where we finally stop.

I pull up at a small terraced house on a hill, with views that peep out to a grey ocean. Houses built of stone below, whitewash and stucco above. Big windows that gather the light. We're parked so we can see directly into a good-sized kitchen. A cluttered, homely mess. No one present. No one visible.

We wait about twenty minutes, then see, walking up the road towards the house, a woman about Neil Williams's age. Short brown hair. A little middle-aged dumpiness. A dark coat and, beneath it, a blue shirt with big white polka dots.

Joanne.

Williams, somehow disappointed, says, 'Oh. I thought she'd look more . . .'

He doesn't say more what.

I don't ask.

Williams is about to get out of the car and approach her, but I restrain him, one hand on his arm. He looks a question at me with his eyes. I say nothing. Just point him back at the house.

Joanne herself lives a few miles round the bay in Paignton, where she works as a hotel receptionist. She was interviewed, just after Christmas, by two of Burnett's burly officers, both male, both in uniform.

I don't know exactly how that interview went, but I do know those two officers returned empty-handed. Back in the second week of January, I went down to see her myself. Unannounced. Not in uniform. Not, strictly speaking, on police business at all.

She didn't tell me anything, not with her words. But she was frightened of me. Agitated. Wanting me to go.

She wanted me to go and I went, but only as far as my car and my binoculars.

I found nothing that first day and had to go back to work, a Monday, the day following. But I came back when I could and, when I couldn't, paid a friend of mine, Brian Penry, to do the watching for me.

A daughter losing all contact with her father – well, that happens. But a daughter and her mother? That's different. Assuming that the mother had always been loving, loyal and supportive, even the angriest teenage runaways tend to get back in touch – and Bethan had never really been angry, only frightened.

So I watched and Penry watched. Long hours in stationary cars. Nonsense playing on the radio. A sea breeze wandering in through the window, itching away at the fast-food wrappers blowing in the foot well.

It took time, yes, but time and waiting have been the theme songs of this case.

Four stone cells and a lifetime of prayer.

Up at the house, Joanne rings a doorbell. Today is a Saturday, Joanne's day off. She didn't come here the first week or two that Penry and I were watching – I think because my visit unsettled her routine – but she seems to have settled back nicely.

Neil Williams watches hypnotically.

The door is answered. We see an interior movement, but nothing further. Joanne enters. The door closes.

Williams, silently, pushes a question at me, but my finger points him back to the window. That big, wide-open kitchen window.

We see nothing at first, then Joanne Williams polka-dotting around by the sink and kettle. She leans up against the sink, bum on the ceramic, talking to someone in the room.

I hear myself say, 'Bethan ran because she was scared and because she didn't want that old Llanglydwen life. That wasn't her. Didn't fit the woman she was becoming. But that didn't mean that her old connections didn't matter. They did and they do. So she came home, sort of. Only halfway so far. She just needs a little encouragement.'

I point again at the window, but I don't need to.

Neil Williams is staring in with an extraordinary, shining intensity. I don't even know if he heard what I just told him.

We watch together, then Joanne Williams pushes away from the sink and, briefly, we see the other person in the room. The back of a head only. Long dark-blonde hair in a pony-tail. Something in the swish of that hair, the movement of the body beneath, says that it's a young person. My age, or a little less.

Neil Williams says, 'Oh!'

The *oh* of a man in the presence of all that is holy, or might be. He stares through the window and grips the Toyota's plasticky dashboard so hard that I hear it creak.

I slip off my seat-belt. Ease my door open. Just releasing the catch, not yet opening it wide.

The girl doesn't turn, then does. A half-profile, glimpsed briefly, then lost again.

'Oh!'

I take the car key and drop it into Williams's pocket.

'Go gently, Mr Williams. It's been a long time.'

He doesn't say anything. Doesn't respond.

But he doesn't have to. This silence – simultaneously sacred and fearful – is his response. He'll do this well, I think. I only hope that Bethan has the wisdom to respond in equal measure. But from what I've seen of her already, I think she will. I think they'll all do fine.

I step out of the car and walk down the hill towards the ocean.

My car is a hundred and seventy miles away in a farmyard in Llanglydwen. I've not given any thought as to how I'm going to get from here to there, but I expect I'll figure something out.

I usually do.

Epilogue

May 2015
And that sounds like an ending, does it not?

I started with two things: a corpse without a crime, and a crime without a corpse.

Poor Carlotta, my crimeless corpse, found a crime that almost perfectly suited our first dark and windy encounter in Ystradfflur. A crime whose investigation finally released four other victims back into the lives they once enjoyed.

And Bethan, it turned out, was no corpse and had suffered no crime. I don't, even now, know what paths led her back from being a teenage runaway in, most likely, London, to an ordinary life spent close to her mother down in Brixham. But I don't need to know. Reunions matter. History doesn't.

But I am not a good person. I am not.

In my defence, I will say this: that I try to be. Most of the time, I do try to be. And when I consider the Seven Deadly Sins, that list of evils which, one by one, I renounced on my night of white-veiled prostration, I think I am not wholly fallen.

Luxuria. I am not generally guilty of lust.

Gula. Gluttony. I am not a glutton. When it comes to the good leaves of the plant *Cannabis indica* – well, perhaps, but then Jesus once turned water into wine. I think he'd forgive a little harmless spliffing.

Avaritia, avarice.

Acedia, sloth.

Invidia, envy. I am not free of them, but few people are. I'm hardly the worst.

It's the two remaining vices that give me pause.

Ira, wrath. *Superbia*, pride.

The two sins whose names that night filled my mouth with an awful silence.

Am I a proud and wrathful person? Was it my pride that led me down that footpath alone? Was it the boiling heat of my wrath that enabled me to do to Anselm what few people ever do to another in their lifetime?

And it is not the first time. I own it. These things fall in patterns and I deny neither the pattern nor its dark consequences. My preference for working alone. The bloodshed which so often results.

Anger and pride.

Also, I want to say: untruthfulness.

I am not a truthful person. I lie and I conceal and I dissemble. I lie to my bosses and to my friends. I make myself appear what I am not. I do those things with aforethought and cunning. Without shame or repentance.

I am not to be trusted.

So here, for the ears of no listening person, I make confession. I have scattered this story with endings, ends which are also beginnings, but I have not told this.

In the third week of January, Aurelia – Miss Ekaterina Zhamanakova – rang me up. Invited me to meet her family. I said yes, yes happily, and we gathered at a country house hotel outside London. Old stone and sweeping terraces. Grey columns and billiard-smooth lawns. A place where kings and duchesses once danced.

There, in that grand drawing room, Aurelia introduced me to her amply bosomed and not underperfumed mother.

Smiled as she watched me crushed in turn by her pinstriped father, her broad-shouldered brothers.

They gave me lunch. A gold watch. A bunch of flowers so big, I near-enough needed a flat-bed truck to get them home.

And thanks. They gave me the thanks that, for all their swank and money, they meant as humbly and sincerely as any family could. I was moved and felt honoured, and I said so, and I meant it.

In the afternoon that followed, Aurelia – I cannot think of her as Ekaterina – walked with me in the gardens. Those wind-blown lawns. Those ancient cedars.

We spoke of many things, but the part I most remember is this.

I asked, 'Do you still pray?'

'On my knee? No.'

'And in your head?'

'All the time, Fiona. Maybe literal every minute.'

She looked sad and troubled as she said it and I had no comfort for her.

But I have still not said the thing. Have not made confession.

Because as I left the hotel that evening, ready for the drive home, Aurelia's father, Yuri, came with me. Leaned against my car. Against the driver's door, blocking admittance.

I already knew that the Zhamanakovs had been prepared to pay the ransom, every jot and tittle of it. Knew that they were one of those who lost their daughter because they chose to make contact with the police. Lost their daughter because we, the law enforcement and intelligence agencies of the United Kingdom, failed to preserve that contact with the sacred secrecy it required.

Despite all that, Yuri said to me, 'I have that money still. The ransom money. I kept it, ready to transfer in one second, because I hoped one day those kidnappers ring up and say, "We still have your daughter. Do you still have the money?"

That never happen, but when you find Ekaterina, the money was still there. All of it. Still waiting.'

I said nothing. My face didn't move. The wind was silent and the cedars held quiet.

'I want you to have it. You save my daughter. Money is yours.'

I told him what every police officer should say. That I was doing my duty. That I was glad to be of service. That police officers are permitted neither to solicit nor receive gifts.

'You don't have to stay in police.'

'But I do.'

'It is a lot of money.'

'Which means it's all the more important I say no.'

'The money is in Switzerland. Very safe. Very private. Very, very private.'

I say nothing.

'Eleven-million dollar.'

He looks at my face and the light changes and the cedars still don't move and he gives a slight shrug and says, 'I send you the details.'

Only then do I move.

I shake my head and say, 'Mr Zhamanakov, I cannot take your money and my "no" really does mean no. But there are some criminals behind this whole thing—' I wave my hand at the big house, the house where Aurelia is a prisoner of nothing more than her own head, her own past. 'Perhaps we will catch those men in conventional ways. In the ways of police officers. Ordinary regular law enforcement. And I hope that's what happens. But sometimes . . . sometimes, we fail. Or rather . . .'

I taper off and Zhamanakov murmurs, 'You might need a little help.'

I echo his phrase. 'Exactly. We might need a little help.'

Yuri gazes at me with those steady eyes and gives, again,

that half-shrug. 'OK. Then when you are ready, you give me call.'

We leave it there. The whole thing arranged as simply as calling a cab, booking a table.

We say goodbye, Yuri and I. A kiss, a hug, a handshake. A deal concluded.

I drive home to Wales with my car stuffed so full with flowers that I look like a mobile florist.

What I've just done – what I've just asked for, what I've just agreed to – would have me flung out of the police so fast and hard that I'd end up in some far distant orbit, able to study the glaciers on Pluto up close and at leisure.

And I confess this.

I am a woman of pride and wrath, and my soul is troubled.

I have asked for peace and peace has not come.

I have sworn at an abbot and rubbed caustic lime in the eyes of a man I almost liked.

I have done these things and I am that woman: prideful, wrathful and without truth.

I am that woman. And I repent of nothing.

Author's note

Caves, kidnap and anchorites.

Caves first. It's true that a broad arc of South Wales is hollow with caves, some of them very extensive indeed. I've been down a few of them including Ogof Daren Cilau, which is best known for having the longest entrance crawl of any British cave: six hundred metres on your belly before you reach a cavern that allows you to stand. The various features that Fiona encounters underground, including the lake in the exit chamber, are all perfectly consistent with what you can discover for yourself if you care to don a wetsuit and crawl into one of those places.

My own years of adventuring underground now lie behind me, but three memories in particular did make it into the book. Fiona's dodgy light, for one thing. I was first introduced to caving by a school teacher whose first passion (like mine) was rock-climbing, but who regarded caves as an acceptable foul-weather alternative. The school didn't own any quality caving kit, so we used to nick stuff rejected by a local 'sub-aqua' club: basically, wetsuits that were falling apart. We drove off to our caves, either in South Wales or the Mendips, equipped with scissors and a fast-drying neoprene cement. We used the scissors to cut the worst bits out of the wetsuits on our laps – the failing seams, the collapsing knees – then fixed new bits of neoprene into the holes we'd made. The smell of drying glue giddily convinced us that, this time, the seams would hold good under stress. They never did, of course, and the wetsuits always commenced their slide into total failure within minutes of our entering the cave.

That part, though, I never really had a problem with. Getting a bit wet and cold was all part of the experience. But for reasons I never understood, I always ended up with the very worst of the, quite bad, torches we possessed. My torch was secured to the battery pack I wore on my waist by a pair of crocodile clips. Mostly those things worked, but whenever we reached an actual tight spot – a squeeze, a boulder choke, a flooded sump – the crocodile clips would go pinging off, my world would go dark, and I'd be left yelling for some so-and-so with a torch to show me where in hell's name the passage was. There's no darkness quite as dark as the black stuff underground, most especially when you have water within an inch or two of your mouth. That's black, that is.

The second memory that guided that part of the book was the flooded cavern, Carlotta's cave. I think I never encountered a cavern as large or as wet as the one Fiona made her exit from, but I do remember walking waist-deep in water through what seemed to me a truly vast chamber, an underground wormhole formed, surely, by a race of giant rock-serpents. That sense – of water, of tunnelled rock, of spaces underground that a single torchbeam can never properly grasp or comprehend – did, I hope, make it into the book intact. It's an eerie feeling.

And then, the final thing. Colour. The sharpest memory I have from all my subterranean excursions arose from the very end of my longest ever trip. We'd been below ground for, I think, twelve or thirteen hours, making a long circuit through one of Wales's most extensive cave systems. We'd had to move relatively fast, because our trip was ambitious and we didn't want to be too late emerging. And in that time, we saw pretty much everything a caver can hope to see: stalactites and stalagmites aplenty, sheets of flowstone, the dull red of styolites, huge caverns, black waters and passages that narrowed to almost nothing. But everything, every single thing we saw, lay within the same narrow colour range. The blues and blacks of stone and water. The reds, ochres and beiges of minerals. Those things viewed by torchlight, and nothing else.

Then – tired, elated, astonished at our own success – we reached the exit. The exit was a grubbly little slot below a small cliff. And through that slot: colour! The whole range of colours visible in a Welsh sunset. Gold and rose and pale green and violet and, in the east, the first dark indigo of night. I remember feasting on those colours as though I was a blind man regaining sight. It felt then like the most beautiful sight of my life. I think Fiona felt something a little bit similar, both on exiting the cave and while smoking with Cesca following her escape from the monastery. You don't know how nice the world looks, until you're close to losing it.

So much for caves. On kidnap, I've stayed as close to the truth as the scanty facts permit. London is indeed the world capital of the super-rich. It is also the world-centre of the kidnap and ransom industry. Because immigrant groups, including the very wealthy, are hesitant about reporting crime to the police, no one actually knows how common domestic kidnap in the UK truly is. That story about the Lithuanian gang who kidnapped a fellow countryman for a ransom demand of just two hundred pounds is perfectly true: you can look it up for yourself. Stories about the very top-end of kidnapping, however, are much harder to come by. No one talks about them and the British law-enforcement agencies may never even hear of them. So I don't really know if there are gangs sweeping the likes of Alina Mishchenko and Ekaterina Zhamanakova off the street – but if not, you sort of feel there ought to be. A sweet little business opportunity, or so you'd think.

And, finally, anchorites.

A friend of mine, a clergyman, referred to this book as my 'anti-clerical novel'. It's not that, or at least I hope it's not. It isn't even, I think, against the whole principle of anchorism (if that's a word.) Back in the Middle Ages, it's not as though there was a whole fistful of opportunities for religiously inclined, but otherwise ordinary, women. If those women – and the vast majority of anchorites were female – chose to have themselves walled into a church, then good for them. It wouldn't have been my choice, but if a girl wants canticles, give the girl canticles. Whatever makes her happy.

Three other observations. First, if my reading is correct, the church authorities do seem to have made a genuine attempt to ensure that any putative anchorites had thought hard and long about their chosen vocation. Certainly, once you'd made your vows, the church was strict about seeing that you adhered to them, but the process of getting to the point of commitment was long and considered. One text of the era warned would-be anchorites that the journey got harder, not easier, as time went by. You'd think that the first year of confinement would be the toughest. Not so, apparently: it was the easiest.

Second, those anchorites were seen as holy, important people, central to the communities that supported them. People came to consult them, bringing their questions, seeking their wisdom via the anchorite's little window to the world. Although my fictional description of the anchorite set-up is perfectly accurate in some ways, it's crucially different in that Fiona, Aurelia and the others were to be shorn of all social contact. By depriving their victims of choice, and by isolating them from the world and all human community, my fictional monks weren't acting as holy men, but as torturers.

And, third, it truly does seem as if anchorites were more numerous in England and Wales than anywhere else in Christendom. Why that is, I have no idea. Yet, to give you some sense of the depth of that tradition, take the area local to where I live now. My wife and I got married in Iffley Church on the edge of Oxford: a building that was, I now know, home to Annora, a famous anchoress. In 1271, one Nicholas de Weston bequeathed money to the anchorites of Oxford and the area immediately surrounding it: three shillings to the anchorite of St Budoc's, two shillings each to those of Crowmarsh and Faringdon, one shilling each to those of Horspath, Hinxey, Seacourt, St Giles's, St Peter's and St John's: places so closely clustered you could drive around them all in a morning, and still have time for coffee and a newspaper.

Oh, and one last thing.

Bier houses – or dead houses – were indeed built by the Victorians as an effort to bring dignity and hygiene to those difficult days between death and burial. Despite government efforts to promote dead houses, they were never built very prolifically and many of those that were built have been allowed to collapse or been converted to other uses.

Yet a few such houses linger on. There's one in the Welsh village where my mother now lives and where I spent all the best months of my childhood. I never knew what the building was: as far as I was concerned, it was just a collapsing shed in the corner of the churchyard. But my mother knew and is currently raising money to restore it. When she's done, the village dead house will be one of the country's finest examples of the genre. It was her passion for that plain, low, undistinctive building which seeded the idea for this book, so thanks, Ma. For that, and everything else.

Harry Bingham

Stay in touch

About once a year, I send out an email alerting readers when I'm about to release a new book. If you would like to get those email alerts – and also, by the way, get free access to a Fiona Griffiths story that is available nowhere else – you can do so by just trotting over to HarryBingham.com and clicking on the 'Free Download' link.

I promise not to clog your inbox with rubbish. I won't sell your details to the good folk who sell Viagra. And if you ever want to unsubscribe from my mailings, it'll be incredibly easy to do so.

I'd be thrilled if you did want to stay informed. Books need readers, and Fiona and I are blessed with an unusually committed and intelligent bunch. We're both mightily grateful.

TALKING TO THE DEAD #1

Fiona Griffiths is the youngest, most junior detective on the South Wales Major Crimes Unit. And when a young mother and her six-year-old daughter are found dead in a squalid Cardiff squat, Fiona is given a minor-seeming task to perform. She performs that task – sometimes following the rules, sometimes not so much – and starts to uncover a much wider and more brutal crime.

That crime is finally solved, in blood, on a remote Pembrokeshire coast. And the reader learns just who this detective is . . . and quite why she's so interested in corpses.

LOVE STORY, WITH MURDERS #2

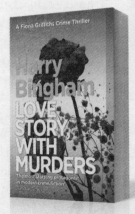

It's end-of-shift. Fiona and a uniformed colleague get called on their way home – illegal rubbish in Cyncoed; how hard can that be? But when they arrive they find, in the stinky bottom of a dead woman's freezer, a woman's leg, complete with high-heeled shoe. The victim is Mary Langton, a pole-dancer who vanished some five years earlier . . . but then new body parts start appearing, and these are dark-skinned, and male, and totally fresh.

Fiona's investigation takes her to some dark places – and some very cold ones – and as she seeks final justice, she realises she's lucky to be still alive.

THE STRANGE DEATH OF FIONA GRIFFITHS #3

A Cardiff superstore has suffered a payroll fraud: phantom employees siphoning cash. It's an assignment that Fiona hates – no corpses – but she's lumbered with it anyway. Then she finds the body of a woman who has starved to death. And it becomes clear that within the first, smaller crime, a vast one looms: the most audacious theft in history. The Serious Organised Crime Agency need a copper who can go undercover, and they ask Fiona to take on the role.

She'll be alone, she'll be lethally vulnerable – and her new 'colleagues' will stop at nothing to get what they want.

THIS THING OF DARKNESS #4

Artwork stolen then mysteriously returned. A security guard dead in a cliff fall. A marine engineer who committed suicide in a locked and inaccessible apartment. These things couldn't be connected, could they? Everyone thinks not, but Fiona – jammed into an Exhibits Officer role she hates – thinks otherwise. As Fiona continues to pursue her enquiries, she comes to realise that she's looking at a crime of breathtaking ambition.

Trouble is, as Fiona closes in, the gang realise they need information and with the police operation in data lockdown, they realise they've got only one place to get it: Fiona herself.

THE DEAD HOUSE #5

It's a howling October night. Midnight in a country churchyard. And lying in an outbuilding is the body of a young woman. There are no signs of violence – but why is she wearing only a thin white summer dress? Why are her legs unshaved? And why is she surrounded by a hundred guttering candles?

Those are the questions that provoke the strangest – and perhaps the darkest – case of Fiona's career. And, in an unforgettable climax, her investigations come to close in on her so very literally that she wonders whether she'll ever see the light of day again.

FIONA WILL RETURN

If you want Harry to let you know when the next Fiona book is due to launch, just sign up to the Fiona Griffiths Readers Club now. You'll get a free, exclusive Fiona story to read, and you'll be the first to know when the next Fiona title is published.

WWW.HARRYBINGHAM.COM/LEV-IN-GLASGOW/